Tear in Reality

SCARLETT HATHAWAY

TEAR IN REALITY

Cover Design by Moonpress | www.moonpress.co

Editing by K. Morton Editing Services L.L.C., @kmortonedits

ISBN 979-8-9879415-2-2 (paperback)

First Edition: September 2023

Second Edition: October 2025

10 9 8 7 6 5 4 3 2

To anyone whose ever felt like they needed permission to be
seen

*ARSINOE
TRIN
RUSADDIR MOUNTAINS
THE ISARA FOREST
SISICA SPRINGS
THE THEMIS COURT
MANTLE
*MANTLE
*CEFTIN
NORDIN
TALEK MOUNTAINS
RIKRE OCEAN
ALEREIS

AURORA FALLS
*BALCOTA
NORTHERN HINA
THE FAE LANDS
WINCHESTER
SAINT DAHLIA
*KINFAIR
THE KOROLHAV SEA
SOUTHERN HINA
*DAVA
N
W
E
S

ALEREIAN INDEX

Nightwalkers (created by the Goddess Aurora)
Witches
Wizards
Guardians
Werewolves
Vampires
Seers

Lien (created by the Goddess Dahlia)
Fae
Mermaids
Nymphs
Elves
Griffins
Sirens

PART ONE | THE MORTAL REALM

CHAPTER ONE
LOLA

Lola repeated the lie over and over.

It didn't matter that she committed the phrase to memory, spending day and night muttering the words to herself as she did her hair, as she dressed and even as she brushed her teeth. The repetition steadied her, grounded her to this new normal. Maybe if she said it enough, the lie would feel real enough that even she would believe it.

Lola paused. Her muttering caught the attention of a mother and child beside her at the crosswalk. When they realized she noticed their staring, they shifted their attention to a very interesting mailbox across the street.

She needed to get a grip. She lied about being human every day, how was this any different? It was simply switching one mask for another. She wasn't just practiced; she was an expert.

Slipping her headphones over her ears, Lola blasted the first song on her playlist. The music vibrated through her skull, the bass so powerful that she felt it in her veins. It hurt, but it felt so good to shut her brain off—to not think about what happened over the summer, or the lie she would tell her friends today, or the blood she had coughed up this morning.

She fell into a steady rhythm as she walked down San Francisco' s cool fall streets, bobbing her head along to the beat as she drowned out the sound of construction and morning traffic.

To say she was distracted was an understatement, three cracks in the sidewalk and a biker nearly killed her on her route, but she kept the volume up high. Spatial awareness be damned.

At this pace, Lola was going to be late, and that was fine by her. Three weeks had passed since the start of the school year. A few more minutes weren't going to kill anyone.

Those first weeks back home were strange. It made her feel like a skinwalker, crawling into a life that resembled her own, but wasn't.

The time was spent up in the confines of her room. Spent coming to terms with the fact that her aunt Kate's home was now her own. It was spent repeating that damn lie.

A hum traveled across Lola's skin, snapping her out of her thoughts and slowing her stride. At first, she thought it was the music. Her body usually had a strong reaction when it was met with a guitar solo, or a beautiful bridge, or a well-timed harmony. She'd get goosebumps all over and sit in utter awe that a person had come up with it. Music made her feel safe. It was a steady rhythm she could rely on unlike everything else in her life. But this was different. This felt wrong.

It was like thin needles were pressing into her skin, alerting her of something—someone. It was like nothing she had ever felt before.

Magick? she wondered.

She hadn't felt the presence of magick in what felt like forever. She didn't remember it feeling like this, she remembered magick feeling good.

She glanced over her shoulder. The streets were overflowing with people going about their daily commute, making it impossible to pick anyone out of the crowd. But what was she looking for anyway? Who would even be following her?

Her eyes landed on a cop car pulling someone over on the other side of the street. She tensed, gripping the strap of her backpack before hurrying down the road.

Maybe she was developing some sort of spidey sense for cops. It made some sense, all things considered. But something still nagged at her, urging her to turn around again.

Lola pushed the thought away. None of this mattered anymore. The feeling could fester for as long as it wanted. She was done practicing.

Besides, it was broad daylight, and the streets were packed with humans, Nightwalkers, and Lien alike. What could possibly happen to her?

Oh, well, someone could come up behind me, stab me, then leave me to die on the sidewalk, Lola thought.

With her luck, the chances of that happening were higher than she liked to admit. And with no interest in testing those odds—or fate—or whatever it was that was ruining her life, she kept moving.

Only when her high school came into view did she allow herself to relax again. If the thought of being murdered wasn't motivating enough, the school resided at the top of a hill. Her legs ached the whole way up and she couldn't wait to sit down.

Her aunt offered to give her a ride this morning, and at the time, walking for thirty minutes sounded preferable to being trapped in a car with Kate. *Idiot.*

When she finally reached the entrance, she took a moment to inspect herself in the glass, fluffing out her black curls and smoothing down her uniform. The dull grays of her skirt and shirt paled against her brown skin. If there was one thing she didn't miss, it was this outfit.

It was lifeless in comparison to her usual clothes. Now more than ever did she need the comfort that came from her floral sun dresses, or the energy that came from wearing her pastel skirts. She couldn't even wear her platforms. She felt so small all of a sudden.

It was silly, primping in front of the window like this, but today was important. She had people to impress and lies to tell.

Entering the building, she was greeted with security and made her way through the school, taking in the familiar space. Lola came across a trophy case and paused, peering inside. *Huh,* she thought. Among the old awards and medals, was something new. A decently sized trophy toppled with a musical note stood out to her. The school's choir won nationals while she was gone.

If Lola had started school on time, she imagined the pale green and white corridors would've been covered in signs and streamers to welcome the rising seniors like herself. Teachers would drape colorful beaded necklaces around them and hand out small baggies of welcome back gifts.

She tried to convince herself that it was okay that she had missed it, but as she continued down the deserted hallway it became harder and harder.

Then the bell rang and the hall flooded with students. *Damn.* She'd officially missed homeroom.

She reached into her bag, pulling out her schedule. Thankfully she hadn't missed anything important, just math. Whose bright idea was it to start her day off with statistics?

On the more interesting note, her next class was music. Before she could allow herself to be excited, her eyes landed on an unfamiliar name. The old music teacher was gone, replaced by someone named Arthur Hanks.

The classroom resided in the basement. Storage cabinets for instruments could be seen in a back corner, but the main room was filled with rows of chairs that arched around the conductor's stand. There were more seats than students, none looking too enthusiastic to be here.

Mr. Hanks was seated at his desk. He was an older man, with scruffy gray hair and stubble. He wore a prim white dress shirt and tan pants.

The bell rang as she descended the stairs into the room. He glanced up at her arrival and announced to the rest of the class, "Please be sure to be in your seats once the bell rings."

Lola prickled at that. She was what? Three feet away from a chair?

She silently took a seat near the back next to a pale blonde girl in a red hoodie.

Mr. Hanks jumped into his lesson, moving at a breakneck pace. Lost didn't even begin to describe how she felt. Besides the snide comment when she came in, he hadn't spared her a glance, much less acknowledge that she'd shown up three weeks into the school year.

She got the attention of the girl beside her. "Does he just like hearing himself talk?" said Lola.

The girl gave her a small smile. "I'm sure he'll get to a point...in an hour or two," she said.

"Be honest," Lola said. "How useless would it be for me to try and even attempt to understand what's going on right now?"

"I don't know, depends on if you value your sanity I guess."

Well, that was perfect, Lola thought. This was meant to be her favorite class, but now it seemed like there was nothing but struggles in her future. *That's just what happens when you miss three weeks of school, I guess.*

"Do you think maybe you can—"

"Does the back row have anything to share with the rest of the class?"

Lola paused, turning to see Mr. Hanks staring right at them. The girl beside her paled, her eyes drifting down into her lap.

"No, not really," Lola said lightly.

"Are you sure?" Mr. Hanks prodded. "Because I wouldn't want to disturb your conversation with my lesson plan." The rest of the class was watching the exchange intently. It must've been the most interesting thing they'd seen this year.

"I was just confused," she tried to explain. "I wasn't—"

"Well yes, that does seem to happen when you miss so much school. I don't think your lack of paying attention is helping you in that department."

Lola fought back her anger. He didn't know her, didn't know what she'd gone through to even end up here today. It was hard to not let her imagination run wild. If she really wanted, she could close his mouth for him. Let her magick run wild and lead a swarm of bees into the classroom, or have a rat run up his pants leg.

God, what was wrong with her? The day had barely begun and magick already corrupted her thoughts.

"Well, if this is how every class of yours goes, I'm not sure I want to attend another one," she said.

Mr. Hanks tilted his head, unimpressed. "Well, let me make it easier for you," he said. "Get out."

Lola huffed, gathering her things and rushing to the door.

"And since being in class is such an inconvenience for you, we can resume this conversation after class, in detention tomorrow," he said. "You and Ms. Watson."

She paused, whipping her head back at him. "What?" she exclaimed. "She didn't do anything."

"I believe it takes two people to have a conversation."

"But I was the one who—"

"Out of the room," Mr. Hanks ordered again. "Now."

Lola cast a look at the girl, who promptly looked away. Great, now no one in this class would want anything to do with her.

She left the room, letting the door shut loudly behind her.

❦ ❦

Lola wandered the halls for the duration of the class, coming back just in time for Mr. Hanks to hand her a detention slip. She wasn't sure why she believed things would be different this year. Missing her first class entirely and getting detention in her next was just par for the course in her life.

Her anger over the situation was quickly replaced with nerves as she approached the cafeteria. She was lucky enough to miss them first period, but she would surely see her friends at lunch.

She repeated the lie in her head a few more times just to be sure.

Upon entering, she spotted them almost immediately, smiling as she realized the group sat at the same table they shared sophomore year. Everything around her was changing, but those guys stayed solid. How lucky was she to have such predictable friends?

She approached from behind Ken, who was fidgeting with the strings of the black hoodie he wore over his uniform. Ken Fell was fair skinned. His hair, which Lola remembered to be wild and unruly around his ears, was cut, the brown curls were longer on top and shorter on the sides. The haircut did wonders for him, it left his face on display, highlighting the edge of his jawline, the dimples in his cheeks.

Lola wrapped him in a hug. He jerked in surprise, his brown eyes looking up at her. "Hi," she said.

Erica glanced up from the homework she'd been doing and jumped out of her seat. Leaving Ken still utterly speechless, Lola rushed to meet her with a hug.

At six feet, Erica towered over her, just as she had their entire lives. She was Filipino with olive skin and long hair that was more orange than red. Her body was lean and toned in a way that made people believe she was an athlete, but Erica had no interest in exercise, much less sports.

"Why are you here?" Erica asked plainly as she pulled away.

"Hello to you too."

Ken, awkward as ever, was still searching for words. His eyes scanned her body, taking in the uniform and most likely coming to the conclusion that no, this wasn't a visit. "I'm very confused."

"Excellent." Lola took a seat next to him. "Hey Troy."

Beside Erica was Troy Dalloway, a dark-skinned boy whose uniform was pressed and straightened with not a wrinkle in sight. But for all it was worth, his face was riddled with frown lines. His short black hair was currently cut in a fade. To her surprise, Troy responded with more than a smile and nod. "Well, aren't you a Houdini act," he said.

"Yeah well, a magician never reveals her secrets." She shrugged. The irony of Troy implying she could do magick was not at all lost on her. Surely Ken and Erica were having an internal chuckle as well. They were both Nightwalkers like her. Ken a werewolf, Erica a seer.

But Troy didn't push the subject; frankly he didn't seem interested in her answer at all. His attention was split between her and the book in his lap.

First and foremost, Troy was Ken's friend, and he made that abundantly clear in more ways than one.

"Screw your secrets," Erica said. "Where did you come from?"

"Maine," Lola said, flashing her a cheeky smile. Erica looked like she wanted to throttle her. "Alright! Alright! So funny story, my dad got a new job, which meant a lot more moving, so he sent me to stay with my aunt for the rest of the year." Was that how she practiced it? Did it sound as sloppy and rehearsed as it felt?

"So, you're just staying here?" Ken asked in disbelief. She nodded.

Erica wasn't as easily pleased. "Why didn't you tell anyone?" she asked. "We were just talking yesterday. How long have you been in the city?"

"Well see, if she told us that, she couldn't be as dramatic as possible now, could she?" Ken said snidely.

"Really feeling the love right now," said Lola. The truth was that nothing felt real until she stepped foot into the school. After months of limbo, never knowing where she would end up, seeing her friends again—realizing that things really would go back to normal—was hard to believe. "Can't a girl just surprise her friends?"

"If only I liked surprises," Erica grumbled, but Lola could still see the underlying excitement she had about her appearance.

"So, what's your dad doing?" Ken asked, causing a sudden ache in her chest.

"Visiting family in New York," Lola said offhandedly. "Then I think he's headed overseas."

Ken's expression turned somber as he asked, "Do you know when you'll see him again?"

She shrugged, hoping that appearing nonchalant would soothe his curiosity. *Please ask something else,* she thought.

Erica took it upon herself to answer her prayers. "How was Maine?" she asked. It was strangely vague for Erica, but she took the bone anyway.

"It was ok. Not much to say except I was almost buried alive in snow."

"I mean, you're what? Two feet off the ground?" Ken said. "Doesn't seem like it would be that hard."

"I'll have you know, I grew an entire inch." She now stood proudly at five foot three.

"I'll alert the media," said Ken. "What about gifts? Did you bring us gifts?"

"I didn't go vacationing, Ken."

He leaned back in his chair, looking at her with unimpressed eyes. "Doesn't matter."

"Well, I'm sorry I broke the ancient laws of traveling etiquette," Lola said, putting her hands up in defense. "If you believe you are entitled to some sort of financial compensation, please feel free to bill me."

Erica, who'd been twirling a pen between her fingers, regarded her carefully. "But how was school over there?"

Lola picked at the lose thread on her skirt, already disliking where this conversation was going. "It was definitely school like."

"Meet any new people?" She was nonchalant in her questioning, but Lola could feel her moving in for the kill.

Lola didn't think her friend had any suspicions, at least not yet, but normal Erica curiosity was just as dangerous. She wanted to know everything about everything. It'd been this way since they were children.

Lola met a lot of people in Maine, but none she wanted to mention and definitely none she considered friends, which is what Erica really wanted to ask.

Talking between them had gotten sparse last year. School had taken up the majority of Erica's time. From community service, to internships, to staying on principal's honor roll, she was mildly busy to say the least.

She shook her head. "No, not really."

Troy made a low, "Hm," sound, eyes still on his book.

Before Lola could question whether that was directed at her, something in the corner of her eye caught her attention. The pale girl from music was staring in her direction.

Ken followed her line of sight, which caused the girl to look away. "Who's that?" Lola asked.

Erica looked over. "Oh, she's in AP Lit with me," she said. "Her names Brooke, why?"

Lola shook her head. "It's nothing, we just have music together."

Within one interaction, Lola had gotten the girl in detention, it wouldn't be a surprise if she hated her guts now.

The thought of spending an entire afternoon with her left Lola with unimaginable guilt.

"Wait, you've been here all day?" Erica said. "How come we didn't see you this morning?"

"I was late...by like an hour," she said. They were all looking at her now.

"You missed a whole period?" Troy said.

She nodded and reached into her bag, pulling out the detention slip. "And then, when I got to second period, I got this." She slid the paper to Ken and watched his face fall as he read it over.

"How?

It seemed she'd rendered him back into only one-word responses. "I expressed an opinion," she said.

"Since when has that ever worked in your favor?" Well, he did have a point there.

Erica shook her head. "How did you get detention already?"

Lola put her hands up in defense. "It wasn't my fault." Which was something they'd all heard a thousand times before, even though it was almost always true. "The guy is a complete *tool*."

She tensed suddenly, feeling the release as a coolness washed over her. That couldn't be right, that only happened when she—

Her eyes widened as the object formed in her hand.

All Witches, like herself, possessed a gift. Lola could call for things— like the screwdriver in her hand now. The thin shaft of the tool nearly stabbed her wrist as she rushed to hide it beneath her thigh.

Had anyone noticed?

Troy was back in his book and Erica didn't seem to have picked up anything.

She felt a nudge on her arm and found Ken watching her. He raised an eyebrow at her, as if to ask if she was ok.

Lola hadn't accidentally used her gift since she was a child. She remembered begging her dad for new toys or dresses, only for them to appear at her feet on their own. But there was no intention behind her words now, no image in her head. Needless to say, she wasn't ok.

She shook off the strangeness of the situation, flashing Ken a coy smile. "Just an eventful day," she murmured.

"I had Hanks last year," he said. "He is the worst." Was he just saying that for her sake? It was hard to tell.

An ear-piercing whistle came from a teacher at the center of the room, signaling that lunch was over. Lola cringed. They still didn't have a bell for that?

"Well, the days still young," Lola said in a chipper tone as the group gathered up their things. She quickly slipped the screwdriver into the bag at her feet. "I still have time to get kicked out of two classes."

"Don't joke about that." Erica was looking at her seriously. "You just got here. Don't make things more difficult than they need to be."

Lola put her hands up in mock surrender. Erica's concern wasn't misplaced. As far as she knew, this kind of behavior was the reason Lola moved away a year ago. It wasn't her friend's fault for believing the lie, Lola had been the one to feed it to her.

All things considered, the concern was good. It meant Erica cared, and if she was too busy caring, she wouldn't be looking.

On the way to her next class, Lola stopped, wincing as a sharp pain seared her throat. She coughed, nearly collapsing into the lockers beside her. When she regained her balance, she covered her mouth, darting to the nearest bathroom in sight. Once the door to the closest stall was locked, she stared down at her hand coated in silver blood.

Now, if only she could get this damn curse under control.

CHAPTER TWO
LOLA

FOR AS LONG AS Lola could remember the curse was there. It wasn't a looming, dark, presence hovering over her head. The curse was as familiar as the back of her hand. She'd grown used to the unnaturalness of herself, to the misfortune and catastrophe that came with being her.

But it had never been this bad before.

At least not physically. She was used to being in the wrong place at the wrong time, to being blamed for the smallest of things. This pain, however, was entirely new. It wasn't constant, which was probably the worst part. Randomly, she would be hit with waves of sickness that would drain her of all energy. A burning would start in her chest then travel its way up her throat until she coughed up blood.

The first time it happened, Lola wrote it off as a one-time event, but the morning proved otherwise, and this afternoon solidified that this was just another thing she needed to endure.

If this was the price she needed to pay, so be it.

She was feeling fine again by the time school was over. Her, Erica, and Ken, rode the bus together, traveling to another part of town. They arrived at a lavish townhouse. It was one of the older Victorian homes in the city. The entrance was barred by black iron gates, leading up to the staircase. The front porch was framed by two marble white columns and above it rested a roof with intricate ornamental ridges.

Lola positioned herself in front of the heavy wooden door, both knuckles at the ready.

"She's gonna yell at you," Erica pointed out.

"No way, I'm her favorite." Ken stifled a laugh. She rapped on the door like a drum until Paris' blonde head peaked out the door, and though she was covered in shadow, the scowl was clear on her face. "What do you—" she started to say, but paused as her blue eyes landed on Lola.

"Rise and shine!" Lola exclaimed, wasting no time in throwing her arms around her. Paris was a vampire, who in her words, was someone the group regularly liked to annoy. Like all vampires, she was nocturnal and if the silk robe and slippers were any indication, this visit had woken her up.

Still in shock, Paris slowly hugged her back. "What are you doing here?"

"I live here again," Lola said. She explained the situation with her dad as Paris ushered the group into the house. Lola squinted as her eyes adjusted to the darkness. Every window was covered by thick crimson curtains, meticulously pinned up to block all light. But the lack of illumination wasn't a problem, the rest of the group could see as well in the dark as Paris could.

While Paris had lived here for nearly four years, Lola never felt like the house was finished. It was sparsely decorated, but the decor she did have were vintage pieces, ranging in different shades of brown, red, and black. It felt like something you would see in a showroom or a catalog.

For a home drenched in so many warm colors, it always felt cold here.

"So, you're staying with your aunt then?" Paris asked, suppressing a yawn. Lola felt a tinge of guilt. Ken had suggested waiting till sunset to visit, but her excitement outweighed her patience.

"Aunts," Lola corrected as they all gathered in the living room. "My aunt Andi's living there now, remember?"

When Andi lost her job in the beginning of the year, her aunt Kate allowed her to move in until she got settled somewhere new. Now seven months later and still jobless, Andi did whatever tedious errands that was asked of her to compensate.

Erica gestured to the cardboard boxes that piled up in the corner of the room by the fireplace. "What's with all the boxes?" she asked.

Paris cast a distasteful look in the direction of the boxes before lounging on the couch. Lola followed after her, draping her legs across her lap. "I cleaned out the bedrooms upstairs," she said.

"What for?" Ken asked.

She took a long pause as if contemplating whether or not she should answer. "My family is coming to visit soon."

Erica sat upright. "What? When were you going to tell us?" she exclaimed.

"I told you just now."

"Well, you sound super excited about it," Ken said dryly. Being the only Nightwalker that was made and not born, vampire families were a rarity. Paris' frustration seemed odd. Most people would consider her lucky. But then again, Lola knew little about her friend's family. As far as she was concerned, Paris spawned into existence two years ago when Ken introduced them.

"Oh, I could write an entire sonnet about how thrilled I am about this."

"But if you don't want to see them, why are they coming?" Erica asked

"Well, if life always worked out the way we wanted, I would've been married to Oscar Isaac by now." Paris shrugged.

"I mean, you never talk about them, and we've never seen them, so why the visit now?" Erica went on, seemingly oblivious to the growing annoyance on Paris' face. She was pushing her luck in all honesty. Lola was surprised Paris even shared as much as she had. "When's the last time you even saw them?"

Paris folded her arms across her chest, but thought for a moment. "I don't know, about three decades?"

"About?" Ken said, eyes wide.

"Hm," said Lola. "I guess you're overdue for a few Thanksgiving dinners huh?"

"It isn't as bad as it sounds, believe me," Paris said with a wave of her hand.

"Paris, you haven't talked to your family in thirty years," Erica said, reiterating it as if Paris didn't fully grasp the statement.

"Hopefully they cancel and I can shoot for forty," she said, grinning.

Paris was in her five hundreds. It was something they all were aware of, but also something Lola knew she'd never fully grasp—at least not now. While her own lifespan was long, five hundred years was something she'd never experience. Even then she'd grow older over time. Painstakingly slowly, sure, but she would grow old. She tried to picture herself as

Paris, immortal, waiting thirty years to see her dad. Her chest tightened at the sheer thought.

"But why not—" Erica started, but Paris cut her off.

"Can we not talk about me right now?"

Erica opened her mouth again.

"Please?" Paris said. It wasn't a request but a command. Erica quickly shut it.

"Fine," said Ken. "But can you put some clothes on first?"

After a lot of begging, Paris agreed to drive them all home. Somehow Lola had missed all the signals from Ken and Erica that this was a terrible idea. Paris drove like an absolute maniac. To her, the speed limit was a suggestion, not the law. Lola's knuckles were left white from gripping the seatbelt too hard. But she could see how someone unafraid to die would drive like this.

What was meant to be a drop off, quickly turned into a visit as her friends followed her inside. Kate Hallows lived in a three-story home that was traditionally styled in lifeless neutral colors. Lola could feel the dread creep up on her as they entered.

"Shoes off," she instructed at the door, and her friends followed her lead. They found Kate in the kitchen, brewing a potion on the stove top. Lola was getting used to the array of herbs and ingredients spread throughout the space. Her aunt was the head of her coven and she was always practicing, always perfecting her craft. When she was working, Kate never used a grimoire, instead opting to experiment until she got what she wanted. Lola was still trying to figure out what that was exactly, so far it just seemed like Kate needed to keep her hands busy.

"There you are," Kate said. Her brown hair was in a braid that fell down her back, her dark eyes focused on the task in front of her.

"I went to see Paris," Lola said.

"I see that," she said, even though she hadn't looked up yet.

Paris took it upon herself to straddle the bar stool in front of the island. "Hello to you too, Kate," she said sweetly. Lola closed the blinds to the kitchen windows so Paris could take off her sunglasses. Not only were vampires vulnerable to the sun, but their eyes were incredibly sensitive. To combat both problems, the shades were enchanted, encasing the vampire in a protective film so they could walk during the day.

Kate quickly glanced up from the pot, her face stoic. "Paris," she acknowledged, before ignoring her again.

"That's it?" Paris said, crossing one leg over the other. "That's all I get?"

"I'm sorry did you want a parade?" Kate said dryly.

"No, I want attention," Paris said. "I feel like I make that very clear."

"Says the woman who never leaves her house," Ken interjected. And he was right, Paris was the definition of a hermit, only ever showing her face when one of them knocked at her door. On the rare occasion she was outside, it was like witnessing an entirely different person.

Paris held a finger up to silence him. "I'll clarify," she said to Kate. "I would like your attention."

Kate begrudgingly set down the spoon she was holding and locked eyes with Paris for an uncomfortable amount of time. And then in Spanish, she asked, "Are you pleased?" The irritation clear as day.

Paris placed her hand on her heart, replying back fluently and with mock sincerity, "You've made my day."

If Lola didn't know any better, she'd think that the two had known each other for years, but no, her friends were about as familiar with her aunt as they were her father. Which was to say not at all. Paris just liked to tease and flirt with anything that moved, so bothering Kate was just a regular part of her routine. Unfortunately for Lola, she actually had to deal with Kate's sourness once Paris was gone.

Kate hadn't always been a presence in her life. When Lola was ten, she wanted nothing more than to get to know her mother's side of the family. Eventually, her dad gave into her pleas and moved them from New York to San Francisco. And while Kate had been around, she kept her distance, only coming when called and never overstaying her welcome.

But something changed once Lola entered high school. Kate opened up her house to her, even allowing her to stay the night whenever her dad worked late. But even that was short lived, as her life had been uprooted junior year.

While things with her family hadn't gone as well as she might have hoped, the move wasn't a waste by any means. It was here that she met her friends after all.

"Lola," Kate said, snapping her out of her thoughts. "Hand me the wild indigo from the cabinet." Panic shot through her. Now? Right here? In front of her friends? While it may have come off as a simple request, Lola could see right through her aunt. Over the past few weeks Kate would randomly ask her questions regarding the craft. They seemed innocent enough, but Lola knew she was being assessed.

Coven leaders were the foundation of Witch society. The honor—more like burden—only fell to first borns as they were naturally stronger. As Kate had no children of her own, Lola was her direct successor.

A jinx as coven head was laughable, but Kate would hear none of it. As soon as she had gotten her hands on her, nearly every interaction turned into a lesson. Lola had managed to avoid them thus far but she couldn't now, not with her friends here.

She went to the herb cabinet, scanning the small jars that ranged from everyday spices to sickly and poisonous. *Indigo root, indigo root...*

At least the name gave her a hint. She narrowed down all the indigo-colored roots and reached for one at random.

"Wild *Indigo*," Kate said, and based on the way she said it, Lola apparently didn't know what shade of purple indigo was.

The sound of keys rattling and the front door opening rang throughout the house. Andi must have been home.

"Ok, they didn't have the brand of steak you like, so don't say I forg—" Andi's words cut off and suddenly the TV in the living room became loud enough to be heard from inside the kitchen. "Kate, look at this," she exclaimed.

Oh, thank God, Lola thought.

Sighing, Kate trotted into the living room with Lola and her friends following after. Standing side by side, Kate had a few inches on Andi, and besides their dark brown hair and sandy complexion, the two didn't look much alike. Where Andi had a full round face, Kate's features were sharp with a toned body to match.

Her mother's side of the family was Salvadorian, and while her understanding of Spanish was proficient enough, her speaking, according to Kate, sounded like a cat being mangled in a garbage disposal. Under her breath, Kate said to Andi, "Lola's friends are here."

Andi casted her a quick look and then gestured to the TV with the remote, the grocery bags piled at her feet.

The news was on, showcasing a reporter in front of an old white house. The area was familiar. If Lola had to place it, she guessed it was only a couple minutes away from her aunt's house.

"This afternoon in the Pacific Heights neighborhood, thirty-six-year-old Lauren Carter was found dead in her home by her friend and neighbor, Erin Liao," the reporter said. "Carter suffered from serious injuries including a broken rib cage and missing heart."

"Yeah, I'm sure that would kill anyone," Paris said. Ken shot her a distasteful look.

"While the actual cause of death has not yet been determined, police believe this could possibly be an animal attack," the reporter said. "We'll keep you updated as this investigation continues."

An uncomfortable silence settled in the room. *An animal attack?* Lola thought. There weren't many animals that could go undetected in San Francisco, and she certainly didn't believe there was a raccoon with enough strength to rip someone's heart out.

How close the attack was unsettled her the most. What if one day she came home to find her aunt's torn to bits? Lola quickly disregarded the thought. Her aunts were Witches, and Nightwalkers weren't fragile. They could handle themselves.

Erica turned to her, looking troubled, and Lola certainly couldn't blame her. "We should probably get going," she said.

Nodding, Lola walked them to the door and watched as they slipped their shoes back on.

"What are you up to tonight?" Ken asked.

"Finally finish unpacking," Lola said. She'd been here for nearly a month and only bothered to start unpacking the other day.

"Well, If you need any help, call Ken," Paris said. He glared at her.

Lola rolled her eyes, waving her off. "Yeah, yeah. I'll leave you to brood in your dark depressing house."

"Much appreciated." She smiled as the group descended the stairs.

"Wait!" Lola exclaimed, following after them. "Hugs."

As if she'd ever let them get away so easily?

"You've hugged us about fifty times since we've seen each other," Ken pointed out.

"Too bad, I want more," she said, drawing them in for a reluctant group hug.

Lola could feel the excitement of the day draining from her as she reentered the house, and with that, all her worries came back to the surface. She checked her backpack when she reached her room. There in the left pocket was the screwdriver she called for at lunch. Tapping her finger to the point, Lola pondered over the tool and its sudden appearance. She'd have to be more careful from now on.

CHAPTER THREE
ERICA

ERICA HAD BEEN TALKING with her mom when the premonition hit her. After Paris dropped her off at home, she and mom went through the usual after school talk. How was school? Do you have any homework? Is anyone bothering you?

She swallowed down the gasp that came as her eyes were forced shut. A sharp pain formed in her head as reality was pushed out of her mind. Her senses went numb, and all that remained was darkness. Then like always, the picture came into focus.

A man with dark hair and dark eyes sits in a bar. He searches the crowd and finds a woman smiling at him. He smiles back.

As the two leave, he drapes his leather jacket over her shoulders. The woman giggles as she leads him into her home.

When he kills her, he does it slowly. Dragging the knife up her thighs as he holds her down and lets her bleed out.

He brings the knife up her abdomen, carving into her as if she were a slab of meat. The woman screams the entire time.

He makes sure to take back his leather jacket before he leaves.

"Erica," her mom called. Erica slowly opened her eyes, blinking rapidly as they adjusted to the light. "Migraine?"

A couple years ago, Erica convinced her parents she had chronic migraines to cover up her premonitions. It was one of many lies she told since learning that while her parents were human, she was not.

Erica wasn't sure how it happened. When she was a child, when the visions first started, she'd been perceptive enough to keep it a secret.

It wasn't until Lola did her life change forever.

Lola and her father moved to the area when Erica was in the fourth grade. It wasn't long before the two became friends, before Erica felt she could trust her with her secret.

She remembered the look on Lola's face. The sheer excitement she felt about finally having a friend who was a Nightwalker like her was obvious.

That was until Erica revealed that she didn't know what a Nightwalker even was.

Apparently, there were Nightwalker and Lien doctors who ensured that the different groups of children were separated and sent with the right families, but somehow, Erica slipped through the cracks. And while all the lying and hiding was difficult, Erica couldn't say she wasn't grateful for the mistake. She wouldn't trade her human parents for anything.

Her mother, Lily Thompson was a thin Korean woman, with thick curly hair she only wore out while at home. She was a criminal defense attorney. This was something Erica only brought up when she told people her father was a baker. Oliver Thompson, a chubby white man with blond hair, ran his own business out of the house. When her parents met, her mother had visited his old bakery while out with a few other paralegals. It was a disgustingly cute and normal story, but then again, so was everything about her parents. Not a day went by where Erica didn't think of the differences between them all.

She didn't have her mother's confidence or her father's passion. She certainly didn't share their cultures. She wasn't even the same species.

"Erica, you're shaking," her mother said. She was, and it took everything in her not to scream.

"I just need to go lie down." But she was already turning away, rushing up the stairs before her mother could see the tears welling in her eyes.

She sat on her bed, counting down from ten until she could steady her breathing. When she managed to swallow the panic down, a wave of sickness came over her next, bile rising in her throat.

What the hell was that?

Erica got up and wiggled the doorknob, just to make sure it was locked.

She remembered the time before she knew Lola, when she would cry to her mother about the things she saw. It didn't help that she had OCD. But it made it easy to explain away her visions for sure.

To her mother it probably sounded like it did when Erica tried to explain to her that she needed a fort of pillows surrounding her bed to keep her safe at night.

But to Erica, learning that it was all real made it more confusing than anything. What was obsession and what was intuition?

Her friends didn't know how violent her premonitions got. When she would have a vision in front of them, she kept the details to herself and her friends didn't pry. She liked it this way, she didn't need to be coddled about things that were out of her control.

This premonition was worse than anything she'd ever seen before, and Erica had seen awful things. Car accidents, fires, earthquakes. And yet every second of this was so detailed and graphic that it almost felt like every horrible act was being inflicted on Erica herself.

She took a moment to mourn the woman in her premonition and laid back on her bed. As her eyes closed, the images came back full force.

What to do, what to do...

Was there anything to do?

She had only seen the interior of the apartment, which wouldn't be helpful. Maybe she didn't focus on the place, but the people. The man was slow and methodical in his killing, which told Erica he'd done this before. His face was already memorized, not out of her own volition, but because everything Erica saw was committed to memory.

There had to be someone looking for him.

She reached under her bed and pulled out the Alereian history book Lola gifted her years ago. Erica had read the book cover to cover, but she always came back to it at times like these.

There were two Realms, the Mortal and the Magick one. The Magick Realm's name was Alereis.

At nine years old, learning that not only were there supernatural creatures called Nightwalkers and Lien walking around, but that they came from another dimension entirely was a whirlwind.

The history book caught her up on what was Lien: Fae, Mermaid, Nymph, Elf, Griffin, and Siren. And on what was Nightwalker: Witch, Werewolf, Vampire, Wizard, Guardian, and Seer.

Seer, Erica thought bitterly. Or whatever was left of them.

She turned to their section in the book, glaring at the near emptiness of it. To her luck, she belonged to a dying race, and with little to no Seers around, her friends were just as in the dark about her useless premonitions as she was.

She didn't know the location, the time or place, nothing. Nothing to tell her how to stop this. And if she couldn't stop it, what was even the point in seeing it?

Erica flipped the book to a page she had marked before.

"Guardians," it read, "blessed by the Goddess to be thy protector."

Guardians were the realm's defenders. They possessed special bonds to those they protected, which allowed them to be the perfect bodyguards.

The Guardian page was ripe with information, spanning centuries in content. She read over the listed abilities again.

The Bond, Flashing, Telekinesis...

Erica pursed her lips, fingers tracing the page. She focused on it, lifting her finger, and along with it, the page. It stayed in midair for a moment before Erica flipped it over, the abilities page out of her sight.

A Guardian would be able to save that woman, but no, she was just a useless Seer.

CHAPTER FOUR
LOLA

THE NEXT MORNING, LOLA was unfortunate enough to get to her first class on time. The bright side was Erica shared this period with her, and allegedly Ken did too, however he had yet to make an appearance today. The downside was that she actually had to do math.

Seeing as she was three weeks and one day behind, it wasn't a surprise she had no idea what was going on. When she was finally released from the torture of probability and data, her teacher held her back. "Lola, can we talk for a minute?"

She tried not to panic. Maybe Ms. Marshall hadn't seen her eyes glaze over and drupe closed for a few moments. She really couldn't take another detention right now.

Erica waited for her at the door, but she quickly waved her off to go on ahead. "Yes?" she asked once the door shut.

Ms. Marshall tilted her head, ushering her to come over. She seemed to be in her twenties, though the darkness under her eyes aged her. Her dark hair was pulled back into a neat bun, but overgrown bangs spilled over the rims of her glasses. "How are you?" she asked.

Well, that was the last thing Lola expected her to ask. "Um, I'm ok," she said with a shrug. She could handle small talk.

"That's good. I know you said you were transferring back, but I know bouncing from school to school can be a lot." She truly had no idea. "There are other things I want to talk about, but I took a peek into your file and noticed some...somewhat concerning notes."

Lola swallowed hard, preparing for the on slot of judgment that was sure to come. Ms. Marshall slid a colorful document into view. Of course, there wasn't a day in her life that that file wasn't following her around. She gave it a quick look over. She expected it to be longer, but maybe it was single spaced.

"Wow," Lola said. "Is that list color coded?"

Ms. Marshall nodded, pulling the rainbow-colored document back to her before Lola could get a better look at it. "By level of severity."

"Seems efficient."

Ms. Marshall regarded her with a look that Lola couldn't tell if it was pure horror or curiosity. "Did you really push a girl into a well?" her teacher asked.

In the seventh grade, Lola's class had taken a trip to a garden. They were meant to be picking out different plants and insects for a biology assignment. Her and another kid were messing around while none of the teachers were watching. She wasn't sure if it was a rock or a loose cobblestone, but she tripped and backed straight into poor Marcy.

Thankfully for everyone involved, the well was shallow, shallow enough that Marcy only left in the ambulance with a broken ankle. But Lola had been suspended even though Marcy told everyone it was an accident.

It wasn't a concept Lola was unfamiliar with though. Accidents didn't happen around her. She was the accident.

Cringing at the memory, Lola quickly interjected. "I didn't push anyone, that was a complete misunderstanding, I swear." It also wasn't even the most concerning thing on that list.

Ms. Marshall gave her an apprehensive look that prodded her to continue. "Ms. Marshall, I know there's a lot you've heard, but you have nothing to worry about from me this year, I promise."

Her teacher studied her for a long moment, assessing her earnestness before taking her file and setting it aside. "Good to hear," she said. "What I really want to talk to you about is catching you up on all the work you've missed so far."

Lola stared at her in surprise. Surely that wasn't the end of it? Surely Ms. Marshall had more concerns? "Oh right, of course," she replied.

"Wednesdays after school, how about you meet me here so we can review?"

If she wasn't still in shock she probably would've groaned. There had to be some other type of tactic at work here. It seemed more likely that Ms. Marshall just wanted to keep a close eye on her. No one disregarded her past like that, you couldn't. "Alright," she agreed skeptically.

"Just until you're caught up." Ms. Marshall promised.

After school, Lola begrudgingly made her way down to the basement to serve her sentence. She told herself it was just for an hour, and that she had nothing better to do, but it was getting hard to rationalize coming here for something so stupid.

The detention room was small, cramped and smelled like dry erase markers and bleach. Her nose wrinkled. The room was narrow but there was just enough space to shove a couple of desks in a row.

Inside there were only about five or six students, one of them being Mateo, who she'd been friends with since sophomore year. He smiled when he saw her.

"Lola!" he exclaimed. "When did you get back?"

"Yesterday," she said, taking a seat at the front of the room. Everyone had the same idea and took all the seats in the back.

"And in here already?" He laughed. Mr. Hanks entered the room. She didn't think he'd be overseeing detention. If she did, she wouldn't have shown up. The last time Lola was in this room, Dean Cain was in charge, and after two years of seeing each other regularly, Lola had managed to get him to warm up with her. But Hanks wasn't Cain. He'd probably make her do actual work here. She slouched down in her chair as Mr. Hanks took his at the front of the room.

Right behind him, the girl from yesterday—Brooke—entered the room, taking the seat behind Lola.

If Lola could slip any further down her seat, she would have.

As the door shut, Mr. Hanks cleared his throat. "Alright, everyone take out a sheet of paper and write about what you did to end up here and what you can do to fix it, I expect at least two pages."

Two pages on learning to shut her yap? Even Lola didn't think she could drag something out that much. Sighing, she searched her bag for a sheet of paper, only to come up empty-handed.

She looked around as students began to write. The closest person to her was Brooke, but Lola wasn't sure asking for a piece of paper was a good idea. Actually, she wasn't sure talking to her ever again was a good idea.

And even if she did, she was sure Mr. Hanks would have something to say about it. She could hear his grainy voice now, "still talking Ms. Hallows?"

Ugh.

Drumming her fingers along the desk, Lola eyes drifted back to her empty backpack. She could call for a sheet of paper. In the grand scheme of things, it was minuscule magick. It didn't really count. She had already gone weeks now without magick. One calling wouldn't have that large of a drawback.

She looked around the room again. No one would notice. She just had to be quiet.

If there was one thing she wished she could change about her gift, it was this. The need to say what she wanted out loud was always risky, and as Ken once told her, she couldn't whisper if her life depended on it.

Before she thought too hard about what she was doing, she knocked her bag off the table and as it hit the ground with a thud, she said, "Paper."

A short burst of relief shot through her veins at the act. Some people glanced up at the sound of the bag falling before quickly returning to their assignments. She hastily opened up her bag, the excitement of creating, of magick, making her impatient.

What she found was a complete mess. The paper appeared to be melting. The lines faded and dripped down the page like rain drops. *What the hell?*

She crumbled it up and shoved it back in her bag.

There it was again. First the tool in the lunchroom, and now this. Was she really so out of practice that she couldn't even call for a piece of paper? The curse liked to bulldoze its way through all types of magick, but her gift had always been untouched. It was the only type of magick her father permitted her to use in moderation.

At the thought of her father, a wave of disgust and shame washed over her. What was wrong with her? How could she have fallen to temptation that easily? *You want to be out of practice,* Lola reminded herself. *Practicing is what got you here.*

As the room around her grew hot, Lola loosened her sweater around her shoulders and looked around. Was she really going to sit here for the entire hour?

For the sake of not getting a second detention, she swallowed her pride, leaning back in her chair to face Brooke.

"Hey," she said softly. "Do you have a piece of paper?"

The girl looked up from her work, which Lola realized was just a bunch of incoherent scribbles. At least someone else thought this assignment was pointless. If Brooke was also affected by the sudden heat she didn't show it. "No, sorry," she said, shaking her head, then returned to her doodles without another word.

While Lola highly doubted that Brooke came here with a single sheet of paper, she didn't push the issue. Dejected, she returned to her own table, fanning herself with her hand.

It was then that she noticed her veins.

The silver blood coursing through her body was strikingly apparent. The trail of silver and black clawed its way up her arms and to her neck. Lola's eyes widened in horror. She pulled her hair forward to cover her neck and yanked her sleeves over her hands.

Nightwalkers were identifiable by their silver blood. Under certain conditions, like stress, you could coax out a Nightwalkers true self like an allergic reaction.

But Lola wasn't stressed, she wasn't angry. She shouldn't have been showing like this.

The heat got to her again, this time a fit of nausea accompanied it. She took in a breath, but the air was thick and heavy, not the soothing rush of relief she hoped for. The heat was no longer hot, but sluggish, sticky humidity.

Her eyelids began to grow heavy, and as she fought to keep herself awake, something grabbed her attention.

In the trash can by the door, a golden object was caught by the light. Lola strained her neck to get a better look inside. At the end of a golden chain was a clear crystal, sitting in the can as if it was nothing but garbage, but Lola knew better. This was a talisman, one that could only belong to a Warlock.

She froze in her chair, too afraid to move.

Magick itself wasn't good or evil, it simply was. Witches, Wizards, and Fae were its users and while they all possessed the same ability, they all practiced in different ways. Witches used spells and potions, Wizards used sigils, and Fae used dust.

Warlocks, on the other hand, used sacrificial magick.

Each Warlock had once been a core magick user, but had been fundamentally changed in the making. Big magick required big sacrifice, and the ones Warlocks chose made Lola sick.

The process of becoming a Warlock involved killing and consuming your own kind. From there, death, no matter how big or small would suffice for magick use.

Lola fidgeted in her seat, reeling with the fact that she shared a room with someone who'd done just that.

She fought to stay awake. The talisman's goal was to expose and weaken her. The talisman was at fault for her drowsiness, for her veins.

It was making her easy prey to catch and kill. But Lola had no intention of becoming a Warlock's next sacrifice. She shot out of her chair and headed to the door.

"Going somewhere Ms. Hallows?" Mr. Hanks asked, putting his paper down. She'd almost forgotten about him.

Her fear told her to not even bother with a response, to get out of the room as fast as possible. But if the Warlock was here, she couldn't let them know she was on to them, she needed an excuse. "I have to go to the bathroom," she settled on.

She reached for the door handle, finding it stuck in place. "Did you lock this?" she asked, appalled at the sheer notion. Lola turned, only to find Mr. Hanks directly behind her. She jumped so hard that she barreled into the door. "Christ!"

"You'll be able to leave in an hour, Ms. Hallows." His voice was static and mechanical.

"Don't you think this is a bit excessive?" she exclaimed.

"Nonsense." And then he smiled, at least, it started off that way. The curve of his grin stretched upward, past his cheeks and up to his eyes. He had more mouth than face. A maw of teeth stared at her.

Lola screamed, backing into the door and scrambling with the handle. "Take a seat, Ms. Hallows." The thing that had been Mr. Hanks, didn't move its lips.

Lola's eyes darted around the room, searching for an escape, only to notice that all the students were staring at her. Staring at her with empty eye sockets.

Without warning, they pounced.

What felt like hundreds of hands grabbed her. She was lifted into the air, being pulled in all directions. They were going to rip her limp from limp. Lola screamed and kicked but it was no use. She could feel her arms and legs dislodge from their joints as they stretched her apart, the pain far too great.

Just when she could feel herself breaking, a hand shot from under her, into her back and through her chest.

She expected to die.

Instead, she woke up in a cold sweat.

"Oh, Lola, you're awake," Mr. Hanks noted. The sound of thunder raged outside and lightning shone through the cracks in the blinds. She was still in the detention room, still at her desk. Bringing a hand up to her cheek, it came back wet with tears. Had it all been a dream?

"I-I fell asleep?" she said, head still spinning. It was like she was drunk.

"About twenty minutes after detention started actually," he said in a matter-of-fact way. It was hard to look at him directly. All she could see was the smiling face.

Slowly, she sat up, taking in her surroundings. Besides Hanks and herself, the room was empty.

"Everyone left," he said, echoing her thoughts. An entire hour passed in a blur. She leaned over to peer into the trash can, only to find the talisman gone. Had it even been there in the first place? How much of the afternoon did she even remember?

Reaching into her bag, she found the distorted piece of paper she tried to call for earlier. Lola couldn't wrap her mind around what was happening. Had the talisman caused the dream or had it been a part of the dream all along? Reality was a blurry line and Lola struggled to walk along it.

Eying Mr. Hanks warily, she stood and began to gather her things. She couldn't stand to be here another minute.

"Lola," Mr. Hanks said expectantly. "Your assignment?"

Right, she still needed to do that. She gave him a strained smile and then pulled a text book from her bag. Tearing out the two blank pages in the front and back of the book, she began to write in big bold letters.

I GOT IN TROUBLE BECAUSE I TALK A LOT.

She switched to the other paper.

I'LL TRY MY BEST TO NOT DO THAT ANYMORE. :)

Two pages. Easy peasy.

She gathered her things and handed her work to Hanks. Before he could look at it properly, she bolted out of the room.

After calling her aunt Andi for a ride, Lola waited at the front of the school, watching the rain pour from the inside. She distracted herself by spectating a race between two rain drops, but once the drop she was rooting for lost, she resorted to pacing instead. And when that didn't work, without thinking, her phone was in her hand and Ken's number was dialed.

He picked up after the second ring. "Hey."

"Hey," she said. "You weren't at school today."

"You noticed, I'm touched."

She rolled her eyes and made a tsk sound. "Off playing hooky without me? For shame."

Ken let out a low chuckle and Lola could almost feel his breath over the phone. "I'm not playing hooky, I had a dentist appointment."

"Ugh, lame."

"What about you?" he asked. "Was detention riveting enough for you?"

She paused. The entire evening was unsettling, but as hard as she tried, where the dream began and ended was still a mystery. If there truly was a talisman there and a Warlock was close, she'd be dead by now, wouldn't she? "It was whatever," she settled on. "I just called because…" God, why did she call him? "Are you still free to help me unpack? Everything's a mess."

There was a beat of silence from Ken before he answered. "Yeah, I should be able to come over later."

"Great," she said, flooding with relief. She wouldn't be left alone with her thoughts; Ken would keep them company. "I don't pay by the hour by the way."

"Oh, I was aware I was being exploited."

The honk of a car horn suddenly made her jump. Looking up, she found Andi's gray Sedan waiting for her. She said goodbye to Ken, threw her hood over her head, and ran into the rain. Despite her best efforts, her curls were drenched beyond repair by the time she reached the parking lot.

Andi pulled off the curb as soon as Lola's door shut and asked, "How'd the detention go?"

"It was alright," she lied. Everything was fine. She was fine. If there was a talisman—and that was a big if—then there were organizations in place that took care of them. Lola racked her brain for the name.

Inlanders.

The Inlander division was a part of the Alereian government that monitored Warlock activity. Members had their identities kept secret to protect them from becoming the targets of sacrifices. Lola figured they were pretty prolific at their jobs seeing as she never witnessed a Warlock attack before. Then again, all the knowledge she had on Warlocks was from vague warnings and scary stories from family members. She didn't know the specifics of how they operated, much less how Inlanders did.

"Is that Kate's jacket?" Lola asked, changing the subject. It looked far too expensive to come out of Andi's closet.

Andi bit her lip and tugged on the hem of the navy-blue blazer. Her hair was pulled back into a ponytail, making her look younger than she already did. Which was impressive since her aunt was only twenty-eight. "Maybe," she said. "I had a job interview this morning, remember?"

"Oh yeah, how'd that go?" Lola asked excitedly. Andi solemnly shook her head. "Oh."

"Eh, it's fine," her aunt said. "It's not like I wanted to work there anyway."

"Then why go?"

"To get Kate off my back," she groaned.

"How's that working out for you?" Lola teased.

"I'm grateful, I swear I am, but she's just so...insistent," said Andi at the same time Lola said, "Insufferable."

Her aunt shot her a quick look in warning. "Hey, that's my sister," she said. "Only I'm allowed to call her insufferable."

Lola huffed and rested her head on the window. "You didn't tell her where I was, did you?"

Andi kept her eyes on the road. "It doesn't exactly take a rocket scientist to figure it out," she said.

Lovely. Now if only there was some natural disaster she could look forward to next, then today would truly be perfect.

CHAPTER FIVE
LOLA

KATE WAS IN THE kitchen when they made it back home. Against her better judgment, Lola decided to see what her aunt was doing instead of heading straight to her room. At the island, Kate swirled a cup of tea in her hand. "You're home," she said. "And here I thought school ended at three."

"Well, you know me, had to stay a couple extra hours to soak up all that learning."

Kate didn't acknowledge her terrible attempt at lightening the mood, instead she pulled out the chair beside her and patted the seat. All of Lola's lies died in her throat. She swallowed and sat down.

"It was nothing bad I swear," she explained. "I mean, I was just in there for talking, if anything it was thrown way out of proportion. I don't even know how—"

"Lola," Kate said. Her voice was leveled but there was enough power behind it to make Lola stop instantly. "I haven't said anything yet."

"Oh."

Kate sighed. "I promised you a fresh start when you got here."

"And it is!" she said. "At least it will be...starting tomorrow, then it'll be even fresher."

Kate didn't look amused. She didn't want to know what her aunt was thinking. They were barely a month into this arrangement, and she probably regretted taking her in. When things got bad in Maine and Lola was being auctioned off to different family members, she remembered Kate being warned about her. Warned about how difficult she was, about how much trouble she would be. It was like having your offenses listed off in a court hearing. There wasn't anything she could do except sit there and take it.

The worst part of it all was that she deserved it. Only a handful of people in her family knew about her curse, Kate being one of them, and she was prepared to handle it. But what she wasn't prepared for was Lola herself. Because what happened in Maine hadn't been the curse, at least not all of it. Lola hadn't been sent to live with Kate because of some magical force out of her control. She was sent here because she fucked everything up. Kate took a chance on her, a risk, and on her first day back, she had already landed back where she started. "I swear," Lola added, hoping Kate saw how serious she was about this.

"If you're gonna cause a commotion, be a commotion. Let me know what I'm dealing with here," her aunt said. "Don't tease me with petty squabbles with teachers and tardiness. I don't like wishy washy, you're either trying or you're not."

"I'm trying," Lola said instantly. Not that it really mattered, she would screw something up again, but if it put her aunt's mind at ease it was worth it to say.

"Good."

Kate took the tea saucer and inverted the cup on top of it. After a long moment she began to rotate it. Lola watched her carefully. "What are you doing?" she asked.

"Reading my tea leaves," Kate said. Lola leaned closer, transfixed with her aunt's work with the cup. Staying out of trouble also meant staying away from magick, but that was nearly impossible in a house full of Witches, especially with one being a coven leader.

Her self-imposed ban on magick hadn't gone as expected. Lola knew her body needed magick to survive, but she didn't realize how much of a toll not using it would have on her. For years she got by using her gift sparingly, staying away from spells and charms when she could. Her dad ensured that she could go on without actively practicing the craft. A calling here and there, that was all she needed. But Lola hadn't realized how painful taking that away would be.

It was like there was a void in her chest where the magick used to be, and every day she refused to practice, it'd grow wider and wider until it devoured her whole.

After the incidents with the paper and the screwdriver, it felt like her magick was fighting back, clawing its way out of her.

Kate flipped the cup upright and stared into it. Lola peered over her shoulder, only able to see a brown blob. "What does it mean?" she asked.

Kate looked up at her. Her face didn't betray what the result of the reading was. "Oh? Is that interest?" she said. "Well, I can certainly include leaf reading in the lessons you've been avoiding."

"Avoiding? Never," Lola said. If Kate found out what she was doing to herself, there was no telling what would happen. She wouldn't understand why she needed to do this, why she couldn't let herself hurt anyone else. At twenty-seven, Kate had been named the youngest Witch in her generation to be the head of a coven. The fact that Lola was even expected to follow after her was insane. While Kate had been blessed in magick, Lola had drowned in it. "But Ken should be here soon so I should go clean up."

Kate raised an eyebrow, but didn't stop her from standing and making her way out of the kitchen. As she left, she cast a look over her shoulder and found her aunt staring longingly into the cup, finger circling the rim.

Ken was there within the hour like he said he would be. Lola led him upstairs to the barren guest room that was now hers. Like the rest of the house, it was very Kate. Beige, plain, and dull. Lola thought of her old room back at home with her dad. Her walls were pink, covered in photocards and fairy lights. Her shelves were filled with clutter, mostly from callings, but there were figurines and stuffed animals she'd collected over the years from thrift stores and carnivals.

Ken sat at the edge of her bed, which didn't even have a comforter on it yet. When he saw the state of her room and the piles of unopened boxes littered about, he didn't comment on the fact that after weeks it was expected for at least one box to be unpacked. No, he simply sat down and got to work.

And of course, Lola didn't expect him to tackle this entire room for her, but his presence made everything easier. She didn't have the will to do much of anything after the summer ended, but the task was less daunting with Ken there. It wasn't a room full of baggage and reminders. It was just one box after another.

"So, I was thinking," she said as she cut open another box. "You, me, Erica, Paris at Sage this weekend."

"Sage?"

"Yeah, it'll be fun." Sage was the name of a lounge the group would frequent back before Lola left for Maine. The night before the move, her friends took her there as a going away party. She didn't remember the last time she'd laughed so hard.

"And you expect Paris to go?"

"She will for little ole me," Lola said sweetly. Paris for all her grumbling would leave her hovel for them. She'd complain the entire time but she'd be there.

"Ok, but do you think your aunt will let you go after your detention?" he asked.

"Ken, I am an adult, I don't need her blessing to leave the house," she said. Ken raised an eyebrow at her. "But I also plan to squeeze in a bunch of begging and pleading throughout the week."

"What was that about anyway?" said Ken. "Yesterday in the kitchen."

She pretended not to immediately know what he was talking about for a moment, before snapping her fingers together in fake realization. "Oh, you mean with the wild fuchsia root?"

"Indigo," he corrected.

"Right, that." She let out a huff of breath. "Hey, look at you. You'd make a great Witch with that memory."

He said nothing, just waited patiently for her to answer his question. Ken was almost impossible to distract. Trying might as well have been wasted effort on her part. She sighed in defeat, the silence too loud and too awkward for her to fill it. "It's coven leader stuff," she explained. "Ever since I got here, every interaction has turned into some type of test. It's exhausting."

Ken knew how she felt about being coven leader. Even without the curse, Lola found the entire thing pointless. The transfer of the title would only be bestowed to her through surpassing Kate in power or in her aunt's death. And since the latter wouldn't happen for hundreds of years and the former wouldn't happen in her wildest dreams, Lola knew this practice was a waste of everyone's time.

"Have you actually sat down and told your aunt you don't want to be coven leader?" Ken asked.

"Uh, no?" Lola said. "I enjoy living, thank you very much."

"It's not exactly something they can force you to do."

"Well at the moment there aren't a lot of options so..."

"So, your plan is to what? Avoid her for the next ten, twenty years?" he said.

"Damn straight."

"You know I really admire your big picture thinking, very inspirational."

Lola rolled her eyes. She never worried about the future, never had a reason to. Right now, all she had to worry about was unpacking one box at a time.

She grabbed the one closest to her, tore it open, and dumped the contents out. If everything was on the floor, she was all but forced to put it away somewhere. Ken joined her on the ground, taking in the random hangers, sweatshirts, and pictures.

One in particular caught her eye. It was a photo of her and her dad at Old Orchard Pier. It was taken the week after they arrived in Maine, when the fights were minimal and hope was still in sight. Her father, James Rae, was a tall Black man and in this photo, he hovered over Lola, smiling brightly in a colorful floral shirt as if they were on some kind of vacation.

After the stress of moving across the country, his beard was neatly trimmed and his hair freshly cut. Lola beamed next to him even though all she could think about were her friends and the life she left behind in San Francisco.

Ken's eyes drifted over the photo and to the leather-bound journal sitting beside it. Sensing his intentions, she snatched it up before he could. "Let me see just one song!" he pleaded.

Lola clutched the book to her chest, shaking her head. "Absolutely not."

She didn't feel the need to inform Ken that there was nothing to see. That she hadn't written anything, at least anything good, in months. His disappointment was clear, but he quickly found a new target to lock on to. The forgotten bass in the corner.

How did he manage to notice everything she didn't want him to see?

Lola intentionally put it there, tucked between her desk and behind boxes. She thought hiding it out of her sight would help, but the guitar's presence was larger than life. It was like a looming darkness creeping behind her, pushing down on her shoulders and bringing her to her knees.

"Can I see it?" Ken asked.

All she could do was nod.

He stepped forward and took the guitar out of its protective case. It was a navy bass with black strings, and written on the back with sharpie it said: *Shoot for the stars, with love, Daddy*

He frowned at the inscription as if sensing the sadness behind it.

"It's nice," he said, turning it over in his hands. "Really nice."

"I know."

His phone buzzed in his pocket and he set the guitar at his feet. Lola went back to unpacking as he retrieved it. Just when

Lola was considering filling up the silence again, Ken's phone suddenly blasted music at the highest volume. She jumped at the noise, whirling on him. "The hell?"

Ken grimaced, pushing every button imaginable to try and turn it off. "Sorry," he said. "My phone is very broken."

After pressing the off button twenty times, it finally obeyed.

"You want me to call you a new one?" He gave her a blank expression in response and she smiled. "Get it? Call?"

"Yeah, I got it, it just wasn't funny." She narrowed her eyes at him. "And I'll pass on that, thanks."

She put her hands up in surrender. "Alrighty." She knew Ken would never accept the offer. He didn't like receiving things from others, much less things made with her gift. But despite her ban on magick and Ken's resistance, she would get him whatever he needed. All he had to do was ask.

"So, who was that?" Lola asked.

It took Ken a minute to realize she meant the text. "My sister, which means you only have me for another hour," he said.

How sad that would be if it were true, Lola thought.

CHAPTER SIX
LOLA

"Lola, are you listening to me?" Lola glanced up to find Ms. Marshall staring down at her. It was the first week of their tutoring sessions. *The first of many,* Lola thought sourly. She was in the front row of Ms. Marshall's classroom, a place she would never be willingly. The front row was where the easy targets sat, and Lola had spent her entire life trying to avoid teacher attention. But it wasn't like she had much of a choice. The room was empty aside from the two of them.

"Uh...yes?" she said sheepishly.

"What did I just say?"

"You said, 'Lola, are you listening to me.'"

Ms. Marshall gave her an exasperated look and held her hand out. "Alright, let me see."

Reluctantly, Lola slid the half-finished worksheet to her. She watched her teachers eyes scan the document, her face pleasantly changing. "This is good," she said, taking a seat in the desk next to her. "There's a lot of improvement here."

"Really?" Lola was surprised. After struggling through yesterday's class, it was a miracle her name wasn't the only thing on the worksheet.

Ms. Marshall nodded. "Now if we could get you to finish the assignment," she said, causing Lola to wince. She intended to finish it, the time had gotten away from her. "Do you write poetry?"

"Huh?"

"The writing in the corner."

Lola froze, resisting the urge to hide behind her hands. She had been too caught up in the act of writing that she'd forgotten Ms. Marshall would actually see the lyrics on the page. She'd been humming the tune since music class. While Mr. Hanks wasn't good for much of anything, the melody he had played today was like an ear-worm. After the nightmare she had in detention, it was hard to admit there was something about him she didn't find entirely repulsive. After annoying everyone around her with her humming for half of the day, the lyrics had slowly began to form in her head. "Oh that's nothing," she said quickly, reaching out for the worksheet, but Ms. Marshall kept hold of it.

"Really? I think it sounds good."

Lola looked up, surprised. "Really?"

Ms. Marshall nodded. "Is this where your head is always at? Writing stuff like this?"

"I guess," she admitted, her nails drumming along the desk. When was the last time she'd been this embarrassed? "They're lyrics."

"Oh, you're a musician." She didn't say it like a question, more like a revelation that made complete sense. Lola didn't have the heart to correct her, musicians made music, and Lola hadn't made anything in what felt like forever. "Is there any reason you're letting this out in here and not Mr. Hanks' class?"

Lola snorted. As if Mr. Hanks could see any of this. "His class is more talking about music than actually making it."

"Ah I see," said Ms. Marshall. "What about when you're at home? Do you have any instruments you play?"

"I have a bass," Lola said. "But I don't really play it."

"That's a shame," Ms. Marshall said. "If you ever feel like getting back to it, I'd love to hear it some time"

This woman was strange, Lola decided. Was this some kind of reverse psychology? Pamper her with compliments instead of scolding her for getting distracted? Lola couldn't say it wasn't working, for a moment, she let herself believe that Ms. Marshall actually wanted to get to know her.

"So let's get back to where you got derailed." She pointed to a problem Lola had started and left unfinished. "What happened here?"

Lola didn't meet her eyes. "I didn't know how to solve it, so I moved on to something else." And she went through that process for nearly every problem until a little over half of them were left unfinished.

"And that's fine," Ms. Marshall said. "But what stopped you from asking me for help here?" Lola frowned. She honestly hadn't even considered it. "You do know that's why I'm here right? To help you?"

Lola shifted in her seat, suddenly uncomfortable for reasons she couldn't describe. Ms. Marshall hadn't even said anything that substantial, she was just doing her job. But Lola couldn't help but be stunned. This was genuine, she could feel it. Slowly, Lola nodded and Ms. Marshall gave her a warm smile, completely unaware that she was the first teacher to ever do so.

CHAPTER SEVEN
KEN

KEN NEVER LIKED SAGE. It was the same thing every time. Since the lounge opened four years ago, all kids seemed to do here was dance terribly and sneak in drugs. His friends followed a similar type of pattern when they were here too. Dance, talk at the bar, then dance some more. When Lola suggested the idea to him, he deluded himself into thinking that this time would be different. But no, while life around them had changed within the last year, Sage stayed exactly the same.

That night, Ken sat at the bar with Troy as Erica, Lola, and Paris danced in the crowd.

Well, Erica wasn't really dancing, just swaying side to side next to the two raving girls beside her. Usually, she would sit at the bar with him and Troy and be on her phone the entire time. But tonight, Paris literally dragged her by her ponytail onto the dance floor before she got the chance. She stood out like a sore thumb, not just from her height, but from how casual she was dressed compared to everyone else here who seemed to think they were in an actual club. Ken couldn't really judge her, here he was in his black jeans and hoodie praying that no one would try and talk to him.

Paris was being strange. She was a lot more enthusiastic to be here than Ken anticipated. To anyone that didn't know her, she appeared like any other dancer, lost in the beat, eyes shut and hair thrown back. But there was something wild about it. Ken had seen Paris dance before. There was undeniable elegance in the way her and the music became one, the way she could glide across the dance floor like it was nothing. This was different. Paris looked like she was fighting the music, daring it to keep up with her.

And then there was Lola, who was shamelessly doing the robot.

That was a reasonable enough explanation to condone his staring, wasn't it?

She wore a crimson halter top and black skirt that hugged the curves of her hips. Her curly hair in two long braids rested over her shoulders. From her black nails to the platform shoes she wore to appear taller, everything about her melded together into a cohesive unit. The illusion of that cohesiveness was always broken, whether it was from a robot dance, an offbeat two step, or the electric slide.

"—and then after your mom, I started hooking up with your little sister," Troy had been saying.

Ken's head whirled toward him. "Whoa, what?"

"Oh, so I finally have your attention?" he said dryly.

Ken's hand went to the back of his neck. He was glad the lounge was so low lit. He didn't need Troy to see how embarrassed he was. "My bad, alright?"

"No, don't apologize," Troy said. "I should know better by now than to interrupt your creepy staring."

"I wasn't staring," Ken said.

"Yeah, you were," Erica chimed in, taking the stool between the two boys. He couldn't exactly retort since he'd been too busy staring to notice her approach.

"Shouldn't you be out there?" he argued, pointing to the dance floor. He did not feel like having this conversation again.

Erica's eyes followed, and she grimaced at the lounge like it was something sickly and diseased. "I've paid my dues," she said. She pulled out her phone, holding on to it like it held all the answers to what was good and right with the world. Ken wished he could join her but it was a miracle if he could receive a text, let alone access the Internet.

Paris strode over to them, practically radiating annoyance. It seemed whatever trance she'd been under on the dance floor was broken by Erica's absence. She plucked the phone right out of the girl's hands.

"Hey!" Erica protested.

"Now, what is so interesting here that you left in the middle..." Paris trailed off as she looked at the screen with wide eyes. She gasped. "Erica, is this porn on your phone?"

She covered her mouth with her hand for extra dramatic effect.

"No, it's not!" Erica reached for her phone, but Paris moved just out of her grasp. "It's not porn."

The sheer fact that Erica felt the need to explain herself made him laugh. Then again, they weren't alone at the bar. Some patrons gave them curious glances.

Lola, who was suddenly all alone, pushed through the crowd to join them. "Whoa, who's looking at porn?" she asked.

"Erica," Ken said, a smile on his face. Erica narrowed her eyes at him.

Paris angled the phone towards Lola as if there was something on the screen to show off. Lola played right along, bringing a hand to her mouth in shock. "Girl, you can't read about knotting in public like that!"

A girl at the other end of the bar snorted loudly.

Erica blushed. "Please, shut up, I will literally pay you to shut up."

Paris held out Erica's phone, which she quickly snatched back. Ken caught a peek of what she was actually looking at, which seemed to be some sort of art tutorial. She mentioned wanting to get back into art this year, it was good that she was pursuing it. Before Ken's phone had broken, he considered getting into photography. But now the whole idea seemed ridiculous.

Paris tossed her hair back and leaned against the bar, disinterested. This is what Ken had been expecting from her.

Lola turned to him, pointing to the purse behind him. "Can you hand me my glasses?"

"Why?" he asked, digging around in her things. Lip gloss, candy, and a songbook? Ken took note of its presence, but left it alone. Finally his hands clasped around her glasses.

"I may have lost a contact lens out there," she said, taking the rectangular, black rimmed glasses and plopping them on her face. Ken wondered why she didn't wear her glasses more often. She looked ridiculously adorable in them.

"I think that's a clear sign you need to take a break," he said.

Lola scoffed, "No way, I'm just getting started." She shot judgmental looks at the other girls. "Though it would be nice if someone would join me."

Suddenly, Paris looked up and the look of utter annoyance in her eyes was now replaced with a mischievous one. "Ken will dance with you," she said.

What the fuck? He side-eyed Paris then looked back at Lola, unsure of what to say. Erica and Paris already had their fun teasing him about helping Lola move in, he really didn't need them meddling now.

The most annoying part of it all was that Ken hadn't even told them about his feelings, they had figured it out for themselves. But if he was that obvious, it was only a matter of time before Lola herself figured it out, and he couldn't have that.

She'd been back in his life for less than a week. She had her father's absence and Kate's expectations to deal with. He couldn't bombard her with his stupid feelings.

Especially feelings that couldn't really go anywhere.

"He doesn't have to," Lola said.

"If I had to dance, so does he," Erica said, suddenly interested in something other than her phone. Ken had to bite his tongue to keep from pointing out to her that shuffling your feet didn't count as dancing.

"Then it's settled," Paris said, and before he could object, she pushed him off the stool and onto his feet. He looked to Troy for support, but he seemed to be more invested with eyeing Paris. Lola took him by the wrist and gently pulled him out into the sweaty mass of bodies that was otherwise known as the dance floor.

"It seems you've been chosen as the sacrifice for tonight," she said.

"I demand a recount."

"Nope," she said, "Now loosen up."

He moved stiffly beside her, shuffling side to side. "You know I can't dance," he said. Perhaps he criticized Erica too harshly.

"Oh yeah, and I'm the reincarnation of Michael Jackson," she joked. At least Lola knew how absurd she looked. For someone that was a musician, Ken didn't understand how she could dance so offbeat. But there was something oddly freeing about it that he admired. She had an infectious confidence about her that made Ken feel a little less ridiculous dancing beside her.

Lola tripped over her own feet and stumbled back into a couple, who were in the middle of grinding right next to them. The two, a girl with green hair and a blond boy, shot icy looks in their direction.

"My bad," she called out, but the couple was already stomping away to the other side of the lounge.

Ken shook his head. "Why must you repel people wherever we go?"

"It's a special skill," she said, throwing her hands up. "So, are you having a good time?"

His eyes drifted away from her face. He honestly wished he was back in his corner with a glass of diet coke. "Yeah, it's fine," he said.

She tilted her head. "Have I ever told you, you're a terrible liar?"

She had, so Ken wasn't sure why he kept trying. It would've been a lot easier if he didn't have to see her face. He lied to her over the phone no problem. "Either I've evolved or this place got really boring," she said.

Ken looked at her surprised. "You're the one who wanted to come here," he pointed out. This was her homecoming after all.

"I know." She paused, then quirked her mouth the way she did when she was thinking. "I just wanted to do something...familiar, you know? Like we used to."

He nodded. San Francisco had been his home for as long as he could remember. He couldn't imagine packing up your life and moving not once, but three times across the country. Being expected to adjust each time seemed exhausting. "Hm, if that's the case, if you still have that Sims game file, we could play it sometime."

Her eyes lit up. "Are you kidding? I would never delete our little family!" She suddenly stopped herself, her eyes wide as if she was hit with a memory. Ken had never seen such a guilty look.

"What?" he asked.

"Well, Jackson may have had an accident...with a stove fire."

"You murdered Jackson?"

"He murdered himself!"

CHAPTER EIGHT
ERICA

ERICA GLANCED UP FROM her phone to check up on Lola and Ken "dancing" in the crowd. She smiled to herself. This was progress. She asked Paris to tell her what the two were saying, but the idea was quickly dismissed with her declaring the place too loud to pick out their voices. While Erica couldn't hear what was going on, it seemed like it was going well.

She looked back at her phone. She was going to learn how to use water color this year if it killed her. And based on the service in this place, it seemed likely. Her phone loaded at a speed so slow that an actual turtle would've been frustrated with the pace.

"Ugh, what is the WiFi password?" she exclaimed. A hoard of eyes turned in her direction. Erica looked around, her face flushing with embarrassment. Suddenly wanting to shy away from everything, she turned her stool to face Paris, who looked far too amused.

How long would it be until Lola got bored with this place and she could leave?

"So, Paris," said Troy. "How's your night been?"

"Painfully dull," she lamented. "I've been contemplating stabbing myself in the neck with that fork for the past fifteen minutes."

Troy let out a nervous laugh, leading Paris to raise an eyebrow. "I wasn't joking. I think it's the perfect way to liven things up in here."

Troy didn't attempt to talk with her much after that.

Erica shook her head. It was like she was trying to be as off putting as possible. Paris and Troy didn't have much of a relationship. Since Paris didn't go to school with them, there were few occasions where the two even saw each other. Years ago, the group fed him a lie about her being home schooled by her older siblings. But Erica knew the real reason they never connected was because Troy was human.

Having known Paris for almost three years, she noticed how avoidant her friend was to human contact. Perhaps Paris would admit it if she asked, but for someone with human parents, Erica didn't know how she'd to react if it turned out to be true.

Paris leaned towards her. "Ok, you have me for another twenty minutes

"It's not like you have anywhere to be," said Erica. It came out a lot snappier than she intended.

Paris raised an eyebrow. "For your information, I do have a life. I actually got invited to a party tonight."

"Oh?" The thought of five more hours of this sounded awful.

The displeasure seemed to be obvious on her face because Paris continued by saying, "No one's forcing you to go." She lowered her voice. "Either way, it's an Alereian party, won't start till midnight."

Now that caught Erica's interest. Midnight was a special time for Nightwalkers in particular. Myths and legends told her that midnight was the hour Nightwalkers were said to be created by the Goddess Aurora. It was meant to be the reason they were at their most powerful at that time.

For a brief moment the rush of power felt like being on a high. At a party where everyone felt on top of the world and invincible it was sure to be chaos.

But besides all that, for Erica, no matter what the circumstances, being around so many Alereian's was a dream. Since knowing Lola, she only visited the Magick Realm once. And while she loved her friends, it would be a lie to say she didn't crave to meet more of her people.

As Troy struggled to recapture Paris' attention, there was a tap on Erica's shoulder. A chill racked up her spine at the touch. She quickly turned, finding nothing there but a folded piece of paper on top of the bar.

Rubbing her bare arms, she looked around the lounge. The entire room was cast in white and blue light. Sitting on the sofas in the back were a group of guys, one Erica recognized as Lola's friend, Mateo, passing around a bottle of beer in an apple juice jug.

By the exit, a green haired girl was passed out in a boy's arms. The music teacher, Mr. Hanks, appeared in the doorway, berating the boy holding her. *Weird,* Erica thought. *What is he doing here?*

She eyed the note again, hesitating before reaching for it. Her fingers barely grazed the paper before the all too familiar pounding in her head started. Her eyes snapped shut and a forceful alien hand ripped the present out of her reach, replacing it with the vision.

The woman's screams echoed throughout the house. Three figures surrounded her, two men, one woman. They wore hungry expressions as they carefully watched her make her next move. But what was there to do? She was trapped and they all knew it.

They didn't move, didn't attack. Simply watched to see what she would do. They were predators, toying with her and soaking up the amusement that came with making this woman believe that there was any hope for her.

She took her chance, darting to the exit. Cheshire grins stretched across her assailants face as they chased after her.

The woman never reached the door. A strong hand grabbed her by the collar and knocked her down. As she struggled to get up, someone grabbed her by the legs, dragging her back into the living room. She struggled, and kicked, and clawed against the hardwood floors but she wasn't strong enough.

The roar of laughter was the last thing to be heard as skin was torn, a heart was ripped out and blood was splattered throughout the house.

Erica choked out a sob and quickly covered her mouth to keep it inside. Hot tears ran down her face as the sick images burned into her mind, immortalizing themselves. The back of her throat tasted like bile. She couldn't think, didn't want to. All that made sense was to run. So she did.

She barreled into the crowd, pushing and shoving people out of her way. And when they didn't budge, she moved them aside with a wave of her hand.

The bathroom was empty when she reached it. The once white walls were now so chipped and old they matched the molding floor tiles. Erica ignored the colorful graffiti written on the stalls and headed straight to the sink, stepping into the growing pool of water coming from underneath.

She turned on the faucet, splashing the cool water on her face. When it did nothing, she did it again and again. Her chest felt heavy, rising and falling rapidly with each breath. It was like the air was poison and yet she couldn't get enough of it.

Erica didn't need to be told that this was the past. She recognized this face. This was Lauren Carter, the victim on the news.

But the worst part of it all, the part that caused her blood to boil and made her sick to her stomach, was that this hadn't been done by an animal.

These were people.

And as she died, Lauren didn't bleed red like a human, but silver like a Nightwalker. Whoever these people were, they were strong enough to kill one of them.

Lola and Paris burst through the bathroom door before Erica could finish her thought. She could see Ken briefly on the other side of the threshold before the door shut in his face.

"What happened? I'm talking to you one minute and the next you're gone," Paris said.

Lola grabbed paper towels from the dispenser and gave them to Erica to wipe her face. "What's wrong?" she asked.

"I— I can't—" Erica wasn't sure what she was about to say but she swallowed the words down. What was she supposed to do? Lola and Paris led her out of the bathroom and to a secluded hallway. She couldn't lie about this, she didn't think she had the strength to even try. The grim details of the vision poured out of her like water and she watched her friends' faces become bleak.

The air of tension in the hall was almost as suffocating as the vision itself when she finished.

It was clear none of them knew how to respond and Erica wasn't quite sure what she wanted to hear.

"I don't understand," Lola said. "You just touched this note and it triggered it?"

"What did it say?" Ken asked.

Erica shook her head. "I didn't even get to read it," she explained. "I left it on the bar."

Paris didn't say a word. There was cold determination on her face as she turned on her heel and marched back into the lounge. The rest of the group quickly followed after.

"What happened?" Troy asked, he seemed only partially interested. Erica put her head down to hide her puffy red eyes.

"It's nothing," Ken said. "Don't worry about it." His voice wasn't convincing but Erica didn't believe he was trying to be. Ken wore an expression that said not to press the issue. Troy looked to Erica then back at Ken, ultimately deciding not to pry.

She wondered what he thought of all of this. To him it probably looked like she had a sudden mental breakdown.

Paris had the note in her hands, twirling it between her fingers. Both sides were blank. "Is this it?" she asked.

Erica nodded reluctantly. There was nothing on it. What were they meant to get from this? Erica's visions had no pattern or rhythm to them. They happened randomly enough that it was completely possible that the note had nothing to do with it. But she couldn't shake the feeling that something was different. This vision didn't gradually reveal itself to her. It invaded her mind, made her feel violated.

The bartender set their drinks on the bar. Two diet cokes and a water. The sodas were probably for Troy and Ken. And since getting Lola to drink water went a lot like getting a cat to take a bath, Erica assumed it was for Paris.

"Can I see?" Lola asked. Paris passed the note over and as it made contact, Lola tensed.

"What? What's wrong?" Ken asked in a whisper.

Lola rolled her shoulder, like she was trying to shake the feeling off her. "Shocked myself," she said offhandedly, setting the note on the bar as if she couldn't stand to hold it.

Paris lifted herself onto a barstool, grabbing her drink and circling the straw around the glass with her finger. She cast a look back at Troy. She wanted to say more but couldn't with him around. "Should we move on for now then?"

Lola frowned. "I actually think we should wrap up here," she said. Erica felt a pang. She couldn't help but feel like she had ruined the evening.

Paris raised her glass. "Here here." She took a drink, barely swallowing before her eyes went wide. The glass fell from her hand, shattering onto the floor as she stumbled off the barstool. Paris pounded a hand on her chest, coughing up the water—trying to get as much out of her system as possible. Erica watched her face turn an unnatural shade of red, watched the droplets of water singe her friend's skin.

She was paralyzed in her shock. That was the only explanation for why she didn't reach out when Paris collapsed.

CHAPTER NINE
PARIS

IN THE FILTHY BACK alley of Sage, Paris hurled beside a dumpster. It was mostly blood that was coming out now, some hers, some not. The pavement was painted in silver and red.

Her friends ushered her out of the lounge, giving Troy some half-assed excuse on the way out. Paris didn't particularly care. Her lungs were on fire, her body heaved with repulsion.

She had swallowed it. Swallowed the Juniper and allowed it into her body. How could she have been so careless? It was barely a gulp, but it caught her off guard regardless. She could feel the poison making its way through her, weakening her with each drop. A vampire that couldn't identify Juniper was a dead one. But Paris was quite familiar, from the smell to the first sip, the plant should have been found right away. She hadn't been thinking, at least not about herself. She'd been too busy thinking about Erica to notice.

It didn't help that she started the night off tipsy. Bad decision on top of bad decision.

Paris looked down at her hands. Her veins were showing, so at the very least her eyes were red as well. After she was done hacking like a rapid animal, she breathed in deeply, taking in the stench of rotting garbage.

"Are you ok?" Lola asked. Paris lifted her head to shoot her an irritable look. "Right, stupid question."

Paris slowly stood, her knees wobbled and buckled so she held her arms out to steady herself. Her friends watched her with troubled expressions. It was humiliating. "Either this was some bastard's idea of a joke, or Sage is suddenly anti-Vampire and I didn't get the memo," she said, wiping her mouth with the back of her hand.

"Or someone was trying to kill you," Erica said grimly.

"It's probably that one," Paris said lightly but the horrified expressions on their faces only grew. She quickly backpedaled. "I'm fine. We should just get out of here."

She took a step forward, her knees buckling under the weight. She would've fallen over if Ken hadn't rushed to catch her, slipping an arm around her waist to hold her upright. "Yeah, you're super fine," he said.

Paris' idea of 'fine' was alive but perhaps not everyone shared her sentiment.

"Who could've done something like this?" Lola said to no one in particular. Her voice was wispy.

Paris had more than a few ideas on who or what was responsible. If it was anyone she had ever crossed in the past, it was most likely a Nightwalker. But the attack didn't line up. Nightwalkers didn't fight underhanded like this; it was seen as cowardly. That only left one option.

"I am fine, I swear." She clutched her head. "Things are just a bit dizzy." Paris knew the effects of Juniper well. The initial shock of it entering her body had hurt the most, but now that the pain was gone, all that was left was the pit of emptiness in her stomach. All of her energy was back behind that dumpster and the pang of hunger was settling in.

"Is there anything we can do?" Lola asked.

Paris let out a dry laugh. Her throat still hoarse and raw. "Well, no, you can't," she said. "But if you don't mind getting me out of here and maybe pointing me in the direction of some blood on the way."

"Of course."

"Aren't there people here you could feed from?" Ken asked.

Before Paris could protest, Erica spoke up. "I don't think we should assume only Paris' drink was spiked. All the drinks from the bar could've been."

Paris nodded in agreement. It was a lot easier to cast a wide net than zero in on a single target.

Ken sighed. "We'll figure something out," he said. "Give me your keys, you're definitely not driving."

"They're in my purse," she said. Most of their things were back in the lounge where they left them.

"Is it even safe to go back in there?" Erica asked.

"Not like we have much of a choice," said Ken, looking around. The back alley of Sage led to a dead-end.

"And we should grab that note you had," Lola added. Erica looked like she was regretting every decision that had brought her there that night but reluctantly nodded.

Together, the group headed back inside. The lights of the lounge assaulted Paris' eyes. Everything was too sensitive and too dull all at once. Every voice blended together in a collective wave of noise washing over her. The smell of trash from outside mingled with the slick sweat of the dancers on the floor. She lingered too long, caught the swallow of a throat in the middle of a drink. Her eyes stayed there, picking out the pulsing vein. Too loud, too much, not enough.

Ken's arm was still around her, guiding her to the bar. The spot where she'd dropped the glass was cleaned up. Troy was still there, concern written all over his face.

"Paris, are you ok?" he asked, noticing the way she leaned on Ken. "Did someone spike your drink or something? You know my dad's a cop—"

"No, I'm fine," Paris insisted. She stood up a little straighter to make a point. "It's just a stomach bug thing, I'll survive."

"We're gonna take her home," Ken explained. Lola grabbed both of their purses from the bar, then searched for where she left the note. The spot on the counter was bare. Lola looked back at them shrugging. *Wonderful,* Paris thought. Something else to worry about.

Troy sent his well wishes as the four of them left Sage and piled into Paris' car. "The paper was gone," Paris said. "Do you think someone took it?"

"It's a blank piece of paper," Lola pointed out. "Who would want it?"

Ken buckled into the driver's seat and started the car. "Someone could've just thrown it away," he said. It was a very reasonable explanation, but Paris didn't believe in reasonable explanations, not anymore, not for a long time. Ken looked back at her. "Where are we headed? Your house?"

What if right now, out in the night, there was someone watching? The person who'd done this to her. What if they were watching their moves, taking down her plates, memorizing the color of her car? Were they waiting to be led straight to her home, to all of their homes?

"There's somewhere closer you can drop me off at," Paris said. She told him the address.

"Is that that party you told me about?" Erica asked. "You're still going?"

"What party?" Lola asked.

"Please, as if I'm going so I can have my socks knocked off," she said, resting her head against the window, it was becoming too heavy to hold it up. She wasn't exactly in a partying mood anymore. Perhaps this is what she deserved for leaving her house today. "It's close and there's blood there."

She let Erica explain to the rest of the group that this was an Alereian party. The absolute bare minimum in hosting an event like this was having a feeding station for vampires.

"Fine, but we're not dropping you off," Lola insisted. "We're going in to make sure you're okay."

Paris started to shake her head, but it made the world spin. "That won't be necessary," she said.

Ken put the car in drive. "Like hell," he said. "You can barely walk."

If she had the strength, she would have argued harder. Two nights ago, some Elf at a bar invited her to this party. But she didn't know him, and she wouldn't know a single person there. Things were different when she was alone. She could walk into shady bars at 3:00 a.m, she could head to parties at midnight and dance with random strangers all night. But now, through the pain and the nausea, all Paris could think was, is this party safe? Was this a place for her friends?

When they reached the address listed on the invitation, they were met with a glass apartment building. The inside resembled that of a lush modern apartment. There was a receptionist behind a mahogany desk that greeted them and asked where they were headed. After giving her the apartment number, she directed them to the elevator.

Classy place so far, Paris thought. But it didn't stop her worry. More often than not, the nicest of places hid the worst debauchery.

They found the apartment door and knocked a couple of times before a man in a flannel with choppy black hair opened the door. "Can I help you?" he asked. The sound of music blared behind him. The scent of sage was strong. There was some kind of spellwork on this apartment, keeping all the noise contained inside.

Paris searched for the message on her phone with the invitation but her eyes were unfocused and her hands were shaking. Lola gently pulled it from her grasp and showed it to the man herself. All Paris could feel was embarrassment.

He quickly looked over the invitation and stepped aside to allow them in. "Alright, enjoy yourselves."

Lola and Erica stepped inside, while Ken waited with Paris, still holding her up. "I'm gonna need a little more than that," Paris said, tapping her foot against the invisible barrier that only kept her out.

"Oh, come in, come in," he said, giving her a clearer invitation.

The two entered and now that Paris was a bit closer, the man, who she assumed was the host, gave her a worried look. She stared right back at him and suddenly he didn't appear that interested anymore.

She broke away from Ken's grasp and leaned against a wall. "Will you be okay from here?" Ken asked.

Paris nodded, now more focused than ever. "Don't go far," she mumbled.

Lola rolled her eyes. "Yes mom."

Letting herself be led by the smell of blood, Paris wandered into the back room of the apartment. The inside was plagued by vampires, blood bags and red solo cups in hand. In the corner was a deep freezer and she quickly approached it, throwing the lid open and grabbing a bag for herself. She ripped it open with her teeth and drank, letting the contents of the bag slip down her throat, rejuvenating her body and warming her up. When that one was done, she reached for another, and chugged that one too.

A male Vampire slithered up to her then, but Paris was too busy drinking to groan. "Whoa, save some for the rest of the party, yeah?" he said. She lowered the bag from her lips, crushing it in her hand. He was handsome, she supposed. Dirty blond hair that fell across light eyes and a strong jaw line.

"What? Are you gonna report me to the blood brigade?" she said, meeting his eyes. His face changed as he got a better look at her.

"Are you ok?" he asked. She frowned. "You look a little—"

"Nice meeting you, party patrol," Paris said quickly and walked away, tossing the blood bags in the trash on the way out.

She searched for the bathroom. After a moment of aimless walking, she found three girls crowded around a door in the back hall. She joined the circle and waited beside them. As soon as the door opened, she shoved past the girl in front of her, into the bathroom. "It's an emergency," she said as the girl shot her a dirty look.

It was indeed an emergency, Paris thought as she looked in the mirror. *I look like death.*

She could see the blood working, filling the hollowness of her cheeks and dullness of her eyes. But her makeup was ruined, practically melting off her face from the hacking and sweating. Why hadn't anyone told her she looked this deranged?

Paris damped a paper towel and did her best to wipe the residue of foundation off. When she was as bare faced as the day she was born, she stared at her soft and delicate features in the mirror. There was something here. Something about the way she looked, the way she carried herself, that attracted these things to her. Dark, sick things that liked to ruin you from the inside out. And Paris had been thoroughly ruined. But that was a long time ago. She had thought—had hoped that these things would stay in the past. It was only now, in the isolation of the bathroom, did Paris allow herself to remember.

The first time Paris encountered a hunter, Tori and she had been feeding that night. The streets of Venice were unforgiving at this hour and among the thieves and thugs were hungry Vampires, ready to make it their playground. It was in the early days of Paris' immortal life. Nearly five hundred years ago, but one of the few nights she could recount in detail.

Tori had chosen Paris to accompany her that evening. Her siblings were back at home with the rest of the clan. While her family adjusted to the others quickly, Paris still found herself attached to Tori's hip. The others took note of this even though she had deluded herself to think otherwise. Maybe Tori noticed too. Maybe that's why they were alone that night.

"Do you hear it, Pavlina?" Tori asked.

Paris closed her eyes and steadied her breath. She just barely had the hang of her new senses. It was overwhelming at times—the sounds and smells. But other times it was beautiful. Like that night. Paris could smell pastries and the dew of incoming rain. The lovely sound of beating hearts met her ears next. It took some concentration for her to pick out the one Tori wanted her to find. A single heart in the crowd, beating faster than all the others.

Paris inclined her head to a nervous looking ginger man. "That one," she said.

"Very good." Tori's praise meant so much to her. A few more nights like this and she would see how quickly Paris was becoming a proper Vampire like her.

As the hunt had begun, the two followed the man through the market and out onto an empty road. It was secluded, yes, but too exposed. Where would they hide his body? Paris thought. Would they be able to lure him back to the city? These questions were left unanswered as a carriage rode into view. Tori grabbed her arm, holding her back.

A man was seated on the mule carrying the cargo while two other men flanked him on horseback. They stopped for the ginger man, but Paris and her brand-new eyes could see they were apprehensive about it.

She didn't understand the conversation that took place, her Italian subpar at best, but the ginger man flailed his arms wildly, urging the men with pleading motions. Paris figured he was drunk and lost, requesting the men for a ride.

A stirring came from the back of the carriage, loud enough that even the drunk snapped out of his begging to take note of it. Paris swallowed, realization dawning on her. These men were not carrying cargo, they were carrying people.

The ginger backed away from the carriage, shouting at the three men as he retreated. Without missing a beat, one of the men on horseback descended his stead and grabbed the man. His hands found his sword and his sword found its way into the man's heart. Just like that, her kill became someone else's.

The man's body slumped to the ground and his assailant mounted his steed. The group continued their ride, venturing down to the beaches.

Slowly, Paris and Tori followed behind.

The men slowed to a stop, disembarking and lifting the tarp from the cart. Piled on top of one another were three prisoners, bound and gagged. They were all Nightwalkers.

Paris could see their silver coloring and multicolored eyes. Nothing was hidden and the men holding them showed no inkling of surprise. Tori's hand flew to her wrist, pulling her back. Paris looked away from the men leading the prisoners out to the dunes and to her friend.

Tori's face was encompassed in fear. Paris didn't quite understand it. The site before her was horrifying of course, but these men were still mortal, still vulnerable. What did they have to be afraid of?

"Nightwalker hunters," she whispered as if that was all the explanation that was needed. She was still only a few months old. Still high on the rush of power she had. Still ignorant to the fact she wasn't invincible. The men stopped, having found the spot they were looking for and beat the prisoners to the ground. If Paris had still been human, the sound of crashing waves would've flooded her ears, masking the grunts and moans of pain. But she heard everything, even the phrases of Italian being hurled at them.

"Filthy beasts."

"Disgusting devils!"

"If those are Nightwalkers, should we not help them?" Paris asked, voice frantic. One of the women, about Paris' size, was brought to her knees. Tears soaked her face.

Tori shook her head, her expression dark. "Do you see her binds?" Paris did. The woman's wrists were red and burning. She saw the redness around her mouth as well. Whatever was special about the binds affected the gag in her mouth too. "They are coated in Juniper. The hunters use it to poison and weaken us."

Paris knew they had weaknesses, of course. But sunlight had been the main one Tori stressed to them. It didn't matter that she hadn't been a Vampire for long, it was unsettling for humans to have this knowledge before she did. She would later learn that there were all types of Nightwalker weakness. Juniper, Wolfsbane, Warlock talismans. "I can't watch them die," Paris said, her voice was barely a whisper.

Tori gave her a pitying look. "Then don't watch."

The hunters lined up their victim's side by side. The man who had killed the ginger passed out torches. Once a spark ignited to flame, each hunter lifted their torch and brought it down upon the Nightwalkers. Paris had never seen fire catch so fast. In only seconds, they went up in flames, screams drowned out by the gags. Paris' eyes were filled with burning flesh and melting faces and muffled cries. She couldn't move.

There was no provoking or taunting or even glee from any of these men. She could tell that their job was to kill and they did it as efficiently as possible. It was the casualness of it all that frightened her the most. To them, killing was like getting dressed for the day. Just another part of the routine.

Tori grabbed her wrist again, this time more forcefully. Together they ran, the smoke and despair in the air following after them. When they returned home to the clan, Paris remembered arguing with Tori. Begging for answers as to why nothing could be done—why they couldn't have helped them.

"And be killed alongside them?" Tori had said. "Pavlina, there are a lot of things in this world that want to see our destruction. You will not survive in it by saving those the Goddess has deemed unworthy of saving." It was times like these when Tori was no longer her friend. She was her caregiver, her mentor, her sire. "Your survival is of the utmost importance. Do not let yourself become a victim of their evil."

Tori made her recognize the smell of Juniper the next night, so that she would never be caught off guard.

But Paris had failed her, time and time again.

Paris gripped her hands on the side of the sink as it all came back to her. The sound of her own screams, the feeling of strange hands inside her chest—

No! she thought. Not here, not now. *My name is Paris Scott. No one is out to get me. No harm will come to me. I am safe.*

Over and over again, she repeated the mantra to herself.

Paris locked eyes with her own reflection in the mirror. She let her face change. Her silver veins traveled up her neck, her blue eyes darkened to red. Opening her mouth, she examined her fangs in the mirror, running her tongue over sharpened incisors and canines.

Sometimes she needed a reminder of what she was—who she was.

You are safe. No harm will come to you.

CHAPTER TEN
ERICA

WITH PARIS GONE, ERICA sat with Lola and Ken in the living room. If she hadn't been so entranced by what she was seeing, Erica would've considered this worse than Sage.

Throughout the apartment, people leaked out of every crevice and corner. It was suffocating but these were Nightwalkers, these were her people. She was overwhelmed in all the right ways.

Everyone appeared too human at the moment, but flashes of eyes and acts of magick caught her attention every so often. Erica hadn't realized how stifled she felt until now. She looked to Lola and Ken, who didn't have the same wonder in their eyes. For them this was casual, mundane even.

But that was to be expected. When they went home, they could shed their human-like skin and bathe themselves in their culture and history. You couldn't appreciate something that surrounded you every day. Her friends didn't need to fear rejection like she did. They had nothing to hide from the people they loved.

She spotted Paris making her way back to them, newfound color in her face. A rush of relief washed over her. Erica had only read about Juniper in books. Seeing the effects firsthand had shaken her. By all accounts Paris should have been in even worse condition. They were incredibly lucky that the dosage of Juniper appeared to be small. "Why are you three losers just sitting here? It's a party," she said.

The three of them sat on a surprisingly untouched white love seat. "Well, someone's feeling better," Lola said.

"Much." She took a seat next to her on the couch, draping her arm along the back of it.

"And I thought this was just a pit stop," Ken said.

Paris shrugged. "It is," she said. "For another hour or two."

Her attitude had certainly changed, Erica thought. Almost an hour ago it seemed she didn't want them here at all and now they were staying to party?

"And that's another dead," a voice said. Erica perked her head up and looked towards the source. To her left, two men sat at a fold up table playing a game of cards.

"That's the third one in the last month," the other man said.

Third? Erica thought. Could they be talking about the murders she'd seen? Her power only revealed two to her. Had another happened today?

"Erica?" Lola said, noticing her absence from the conversation.

Erica instinctively shushed her, holding a finger up. "Listen."

"Yeah, and each one has been bloodier than the last. Has the Council said anything about this yet?"

"Not a damn thing."

The Council was composed of six Nightwalkers that all Alereians answered to. Why would they need to get involved? she wondered. Was it because a Nightwalker had been killed?

While her friends still looked confused, Erica didn't sit around to explain. She left the couch and walked over to the card table. There was shuffling behind her as her friends followed.

"Ere, maybe don't," Paris said in a hushed voice.

"Um, excuse me," Erica started. She wasn't exactly sure what she was doing but it was too late to back out now. "Are you talking about the recent murders going around?"

The two men glanced up from their game. Erica was struck with surprise when she realized that one of them was Fae. Lien didn't blend as easily as Nightwalkers did, Fae least of all. The man before her was inhumanly beautiful in a way Erica had never seen before. His hair curled around his pointed ears, so blond it was nearly white. His skin was pale and flawless and glowing. When she met his eyes, one was a green like jade while the other was blue.

Erica didn't have to look back to feel the apprehension in the air. It wasn't often Lien mingled with Nightwalkers, especially in the Mortal world. But a Fae? Erica couldn't believe that a Fae would be caught dead in a place like this.

"Murders?" Lola said to her. "I thought it was just the one."

The Fae gave the group a careful look over before deciding to indulge them. "No," he said. "The third took place a few days ago."

"Why would the Council get involved in this?" Paris asked.

The other man with dark skin and dreadlocks tied back into a ponytail answered her. "All these murders have all been Alereians."

It was like all the air had been sucked out of the room. Erica went rigid all over. She knew about Lauren Carter, had seen it for herself. But three Alereians? Three dead?

Lola looked at her dismayed, probably wondering how much she knew, but Erica avoided her gaze. "How do you know?" she asked the men at the table. This couldn't have been widely known information, otherwise Paris or Lola's aunts would know.

"I have a buddy who works on the force. The scenes have been locked down hard cause of the blood," he explained. "I'm pretty sure the one who made the news was a Witch."

Instinctively, Erica looked to Lola whose eyes were wide in stunned silence. She couldn't imagine what her friend was feeling. While a lot of Nightwalkers were wildly individualistic, Witches were not one of them. They lived and breathed community and connection. A death like this probably felt like a death in her own family. But Erica's mind was already racing with new possibilities. If Alereians were being targeted, what did that mean for tonight? Had someone truly attempted to kill Paris as she feared?

"Do you or your buddy have any ideas on what could be doing this?" Paris asked.

"A Warlock," Lola said instantly.

"You would think, but it's not only magick users being killed," said the blond fae. "I hear one of them is a Guardian."

"What? How is that even possible?" Erica exclaimed, and if she hadn't already been concerned, now she was. Guardians were protectors, their entire existence hinged on the fact that they could withstand nearly anything. If something managed to kill one of the Realm's warriors, and the Council hadn't taken notice, what exactly did that mean for the rest of them?

"Could be an untamed or hunters," the blond theorized. For the first time, Erica noticed how his eyes would shift between different shades of green and blue as he spoke.

Untamed. That was a word she wasn't familiar with, and Erica hadn't encountered a new Alereian term in years.

"Maybe even a hybrid," the other man said. Erica fought to disguise the jolt that went through her at the word.

The Fae one shook his head. "No hybrid in their right mind would make themselves known like that."

"Well, isn't that the whole point?" the one with dreadlocks argued. "They aren't in the right mind in the first place."

Hybrids were the mix of two different Alereians. Having children outside of ones species was strictly forbidden. The punishment for breaking such a law was the execution of the parents and the child. Needless to say, Erica didn't believe there was a hybrid out there that would risk discovery like this.

Ken tensed at her side. "I don't think someone untamed would go after random people," he said. She was thankful someone else spoke before she said something she'd regret.

"And hunters kill a lot more discreetly than that," said Paris. Erica read about Nightwalker hunters in history books. They had been groups of humans who bonded over their shared hatred of the supernatural. Together they would roam the night, hunting for any creature they could get their hands on. As human superstition grew, these groups died out over time.

But Paris worried her. She spoke of the hunters like they weren't a thing of the past, like they were still active today. Could that be the case?

"Well, who's to say that these attacks are random?" one of the men said.

"Or that whoever's doing this wants to be discreet," said the other.

CHAPTER ELEVEN
PARIS

PARIS SAT SILENTLY IN the backseat of her car. The group hadn't stayed at the party long. All that talk of death and destruction had thoroughly killed the mood and while Paris assured everyone that she was okay, none of them believed her. The blood healed her but she could tell she wasn't at full strength. So, she sat in the backseat of her own car as Ken drove her home.

On the surface, Paris could recognize her friends fear. For them, tonight had been the closest they'd ever been to death. 'How's' and 'what ifs' probably raced through their minds. She couldn't fault them for that.

But something deep within her hated how they looked at her. Their fear was infectious. It was all too familiar. Years of being worried and fussed over came rushing back. She breathed in and out, letting the memories fade away.

"Par?" Lola nudged her shoulder. "Are you listening?"

"No," Paris said simply.

Ken looked at them from the rear-view mirror. "Still dizzy?" he asked.

She groaned. "No. For the millionth time, I am perfectly fine." Ken quirked his brows in doubt but didn't say anything further. Ken and his loud silence always found a way to annoy her.

"You do understand we're just worried about you, right?" Lola said. "I mean especially after what we've heard tonight."

Paris rested her head against the window. She was actually trying very hard to not think about anything that happened tonight. "People die every day," she said. "It's nothing new."

Erica turned from the backseat. "People don't get ripped apart every day," she stated. *That you know of*, Paris thought. "I don't understand what's wrong with at least considering what those guys said."

"You think you're going to get trustworthy news from Faeries?" Paris let out a harsh laugh.

Erica's shoulders slumped in frustration. "Why not? I thought they couldn't lie?" she asked.

"Doesn't stop them from playing tricks," Paris said. "Who's to say him and his Lien buddy didn't want to spook a couple Nightwalkers tonight?"

Erica pressed back in her seat, shaking her head as if her brain simply wouldn't accept the idea. Paris didn't truly believe what she was saying but she had to say something to derail the conversation. When her friends were scared, she was scared.

"These things are pretty complicated, Ere," Lola said.

"Then explain them to me," Erica said. Paris didn't think they had the time to spare to explain centuries of conflict. "Like untamed, what is that?"

Paris dug her nails into her palms. "A Nightwalker nutcase," she said bitterly. Lola launched into a more polite description. It was the rehearsed tale most Nightwalker children were given when they were little. The untamed was like an urban legend among them. A warning that was given when you didn't eat all your vegetables or didn't brush your teeth.

"The untamed will greet you at midnight and tempt you into becoming a monster."

But in reality, the untamed was much more than that. It was where humans got their horror stories about them from, when pain and suffering and despair met at a single point. Where it broke you down bit by bit only to rebuild you in its image. A part of yourself that you didn't know existed awoke and destroyed your life right in front of your eyes.

As the car turned a corner and neared her house, Paris heard the sound of a truck backing up. She sat up straight, suddenly alert.

Shuffling footsteps, doors open and close, and then a voice.

"Set those upstairs." Rose.

Would this night ever have an end?

"Dear God," Paris murmured. She didn't realize she'd spoken out loud until Lola turned to her.

"What?" she asked. They turned the corner and drove down the street. Her house was now in view for her friends to see. "Who's that in your driveway?" She leaned forward between the seats to get a better look.

Paris drew in a breath. "My family." They were meant to arrive tomorrow night. Why hadn't Hunter told her they'd be here early? She watched her friend's reactions. Immediate interest from Erica, as expected, while Lola seemed surprised. Ken, on the other hand, looked as apprehensive as Paris felt. This wasn't surprising. He always seemed able to pick up on the slightest changes in her mood, annoyingly enough.

The moving truck in the driveway was a lot larger than Paris anticipated. She had to instruct Ken to park across the street.

Paris was the first out of the car. Rose's tall, slender figure stepped down from the back of the truck. She wore a polka dot red and white sundress that hugged her hips. *Pretty inconvenient for traveling*, Paris thought. But three movers worked around Rose, hauling a never-ending line of boxes to the porch for her. How long did they think they'd be staying with her?

"Is that your sister?" Lola asked.

Paris nodded, her eyes still trained on her sister. "Rose." She couldn't help the hint of joy that came with saying it. It had been forever since she heard her sister's name.

Rose noticed her approaching and hesitantly waved. "Pavlina!" she called. Pavlina. The sound of her given name sent a jolt through her.

"Pavlina?" Erica said. Paris fought back a grimace. Her sister quickly realized her error, hand dropping to her side. "Hi," Rose said, when Paris reached her. Her mouth was in a thin line. She seemed to be internally hitting herself for the slip up.

"Hey," Paris said. Her sister stepped forward as if going in for a hug, but stopped herself abruptly. Paris decided to put her uncertainty at ease and wrapped her arms around her. She would at least try to follow Hunter's advice. There was no need to open up old wounds unless they sliced her open first.

The pair stood in silence for a moment. Over the past few weeks, whenever Paris thought about her siblings finally arriving, she always envisioned the discomfort that would come from conversation. How they would rehash old arguments or even worse, ask her about her life. She didn't think they'd have nothing to say at all.

"Well this is nice...I think," Lola commented. The two sisters turned their attention to Paris' friends, who stood awkwardly behind her.

"Oh right," said Paris. She had nearly forgotten they were with her. "Rose, this is Lola, Ken, and Erica."

They greeted each other quickly and Rose turned back to her.

"It really is good to see you," Rose said, resting her hands on her shoulders. *Laying it on a little thick, aren't you?* Is what Paris wanted to say, but even she could hear the honesty in her sister's voice.

"Likewise." She didn't know if she meant it or not. Peering into the truck, Paris compared what she saw there to what was on the front porch. Not even a quarter of the truck was unloaded yet. "Don't you think you've over-packed?"

"What do you mean?"

Where everyone else saw junk, Rose saw priceless trinkets and memories. Paris wouldn't have had a problem with it if those 'memories' didn't consist of stuff like that pen she used to write a check fifty years ago. But even for her, this was ridiculous. "I mean, it's only going to be a couple of weeks," she said. "It looks like you're moving in."

Rose blinked. "I'm not?"

Oh no.

"No," Paris said firmly. "What gave you the indication that you were?"

Rose placed her hands on her hips, looking peeved with her tone. But Paris ignored it. "Hunter," her sister said.

The early arrival, the radio silence. He wanted to spring this on her, to make it as difficult as possible to say no. What had he been thinking? Paris should have known better than to trust him— to think there wouldn't be some sort of trick up his sleeve. "Hunter told you that you were moving in?" Paris asked. Rose nodded, her mouth tight. Paris felt the sudden urge to strangle something, specifically her brother. "He's a dead man."

Rose let out a choked laugh that was void of any humor. "Wow. I suppose I should have known it was a lie when Hunt said that you suddenly wanted to host and make up for lost time."

There was truth in that statement, but this was far beyond what Paris agreed to. "God, that doesn't even sound like me," she scoffed.

Rose clenched her jaw. "You're right it doesn't." The bite in her voice was clear. "You never change, do you, Paris?"

"Where's the need when you've already reached your peak," she said dryly, a wry smile on her lips.

Rose took the bait like clockwork. "If that's what you want to call it, fine," she scoffed.

"Is he here?" Paris asked.

"Of course, we came together."

Paris walked away before she even finished speaking.

"You're not even gonna help me with my stuff?" Rose called after her. Paris looked over her shoulder to see her sister standing there expectantly.

"Ask Ian," Paris said. "I'm sure he'll be able to help you figure that out." Rose's face dropped and Paris took pleasure in the sight. It was like she couldn't help herself. The situation had changed and now antagonizing Rose felt as natural as breathing.

"Are you serious?" Paris turned back to catch her sister with her hands on her hips, her gaze piercing. As far as Paris could tell, Rose was probably remembering why exactly the two hadn't seen each other in thirty years. The essence of regret was projecting right off her. Rose gave her a disappointing shake of the head that said, "This is why your all alone," before retreating back to the truck.

Little did she know that Paris liked it that way.

"Are you okay?" Ken asked. His voice shook her out of her daze. She forgotten they were with her again. The sound of their footsteps tailing her managed to calm down her irritation. She needed to remind herself who she was with. She couldn't let them see her like this.

"Of course, why wouldn't I be?" she said, unnatural levity in her voice. The sound of rattling glass coming from inside distracted her before she even made it to the door. Someone was in her house and whoever it was wasn't too concerned with keeping quiet.

"Because that didn't look okay?" Lola said.

"Trust me," she said. "It was all perfectly fine."

"Then why do you look like you're plotting a murder?"

Because she was.

Reaching for the doorknob, Paris realized she was shaking and quickly glanced over her shoulder to see if her friends noticed. Nothing appeared out of the ordinary except they were probably taken off guard by her spat with Rose. She met no resistance when she turned the doorknob and stepped inside, her friends following. "You know, I've safely made it home now," she said. "I think I can manage getting to my room all on my own." It came out more condescending than she intended.

Ken in particular seemed the most embarrassed. "Oh, if you're sure—"

The rattling of bottles continued, this time her friends were in range to hear it. Paris strode swiftly to the dining room, her heart pounding hard in her chest. What if it wasn't Hunter, but Ian? After all these years, was this the way they were going to reunite?

Surely Rose would've warned her about this, wouldn't she?

A rush of relief washed over her when she finally saw the cause of the noise. There, on his knees, rummaging through her alcohol cabinet, was her brother, Hunter. His hair was a dirty blond that was closer to brown, his eyes a similar color. Hunter looked relaxed, wearing gray sweats that greatly contrasted the prim sundress Rose had on. Paris wasn't sure how long her family had been here but it was clear Hunter was already making himself at home.

He looked up as she approached and quickly stood. "Don't be—"

"How dare you?" she growled.

He winced at the sight of her. "Paris, listen—"

"About how you lied to me?" she spat. *Breathe,* she reminded herself. She couldn't lose it, not in front of them. "Did you really think this would work?"

"It kinda did work," he said. She narrowed her eyes. "Just a little."

Paris took a threatening step forward as Hunter retreated back into the table. "The things I will do to you when there are no witnesses will be painful."

He gulped then gave her friends a shy wave. "Hello, witnesses."

They nervously waved back.

She picked up her sister's voice from outside. At first, she thought Rose was talking to one of the movers, but a second, hauntingly familiar voice came almost out of nowhere. It was his voice.

Her body turned to ice.

The sudden change in her behavior must have been obvious because her brother and her friends were studying her carefully. "Paris?" Lola asked.

She stayed silent, barely able to hear her through the sound of her own heartbeat pounding in her ears.

Before anyone could say another word, Paris was gone, back at the front door in the blink of an eye. In the time it took her friends and brother to come out of the dining room, she was already peering out the door.

The presence of her brother sent a jolt so strong through her she forgot to breathe. Ian stood next to Rose, laughing absently at something she had said. Paris, while entirely capable of hearing the conversation, made no effort to pay attention to it. She studied him carefully.

His style hadn't changed at all, black pants and denim were what he practically lived in. His black hair was pushed off to the side.

She let out a ragged breath and he turned toward her. While her eyes were a stark cobalt, Ian's eyes were bluish green, like murky sea water. For what felt like ages, they stared at one another. His gaze piercing and all consuming. When Paris couldn't take the flood of memories coming back or the ache in her chest at the mere sight of him, she quickly closed the door shut.

She dug her nails into her palms, breaking skin easily. Bloody silver moons were engraved in her hands.

She felt Hunter directly behind her, her friends a few feet away. It was all too much. Paris tried to convince herself that today was the problem, that if her family had just arrived any other day things would be fine. But there was no way of knowing now. Now she was drowning in the space between the past and the present. The smell of burning flesh, the sounds of her family screaming, the sting of Juniper in her lungs. It was all bleeding together.

She was back in London chocking on smoke, and then she was back in her house, gripping the door handle.

It jiggled from the other side. Ian was trying to get in.

This was a mistake. She wasn't ready, wasn't even close.

"Paris," Hunter said. "Open the door." His voice wasn't forceful. It was quite the opposite, the words coming out as a plea rather than a command. She turned to look at him, catching the softness in his eyes.

"As soon as he gets in here, I'm gonna—" she whispered but Hunter cut her off.

"You're going to be fine."

She looked past him. Her friends were huddled together, watching the scene unfold. Each of their faces was a mix of confusion and concern. There was something about it that grounded her. Their presence brought her back to reality. She was in the present and things were different now.

She released her hold on the doorknob and stepped back. Lola's hand rushed to hers. She tested the waters, wrapping her pinky around Paris', and when she was receptive, Lola slowly interlocked their fingers.

The front door opened and Ian walked inside. "Hey," he said. It came out like a sigh. There was no denying that he heard everything.

"Hey."

He noticed her friends at her side. "Are you busy?"

She opened her mouth to answer, but it was Ken who responded, "We were just leaving."

Too many things were happening at once for her to keep track of. With her friends out of the way, she'd have one less thing to worry about. She gave Ken a grateful nod. He tried to return her car keys but she pressed them back into his hands. "I'll pick it up tomorrow." The last thing she needed was to worry about them getting home this late at night.

As Ken ushered the group outside, Rose entered the house. The door closed behind them, and all Paris was left with was her family.

CHAPTER TWELVE
PARIS

"Ok, so what do you want?" Paris asked once the door shut.

"I mean, nothing particular at the moment but—" Ian started, but she cut him off.

"Great, I'm going to head to my room." She turned to leave but he reached for her. Paris looked down at where he held her wrist and then back up at him, eyebrow raised. He released her almost instantly.

"We should talk," he said.

She sighed. "It has been a very long night." Even though she had fed, she was exhausted and it wouldn't be for several more hours till she could rest. Paris had never been more grateful that she healed fast. She imagined what her family would've done if they'd seen her only a few hours earlier with burns on her mouth and sullen eyes.

"Please," he said, looking remorseful even though he hadn't done anything. Not yet anyway.

"Fine, you want to talk?" Paris said, crossing her arms. "Let's talk about how Hunter lied to everyone."

She shot her brother an expectant look, which he immediately pretended to miss.

"What is she talking about?" Ian asked.

"I never offered you a place to stay," Paris answered for him. "I was told this was going to be a visit, a brief one at that."

Ian took in their brother, shaking his head. "What were you trying to do?" But that was rhetorical question at best. It was clear that her brother believed that trapping them under one roof would somehow resolve all their issues.

Hunter shrugged. "She'll change her mind," he said.

"No, *she* won't," Paris argued. Being angry was easy, it prevented her from remembering the reason they separated in the first place.

"As if we want to stay with you and your poor attitude," Rose said.

"Aggravating her isn't the best way to make her change her mind, Ro." Hunter glared at her, as if his master plan was already falling apart.

"Oh, be pissy with me all you want," Paris said, throwing her hands up. "But I'm not out of line. This is my house."

Ian took a step toward her and she watched him cautiously. "Look, I know this is a lot for you to handle but maybe—"

"Yes, and as we all know, you are the expert in deciding what's good for me," she warned.

Hunter threw his hands up in frustration. "Okay, that was uncalled for," he said

Ian's face fell and Paris could clearly see the shift in his eyes. "No, it's fine," he said and looked to Paris. "I'm sure you've been waiting ages to get that one out."

"Oh, I'm sorry, should I be groveling at your feet," she said. She looked around the room, making eye contact with each of them, her face indifferent and cold. "I seem to have forgotten just how much of a gift your presence is."

Rose looked like she was gearing up to berate her again but Ian spoke first which is what she wanted. "It is always about you, isn't it?" he started. "You can't comprehend the grueling task it is to be related to you. You don't think about the absolute hell hole you make every space, or the damages we have to clean up. No, you just care about yourself."

Paris let every word sink in. It wasn't hard, all these thoughts had been her own for decades. But now she had to embody them, now she had to prove Ian right.

"I told you this was a mistake," Rose mumbled, but of course everyone heard. Underneath the apathy on the surface, Paris wanted to scream. She didn't stifle the anger, no she let it fester, build. There was no need to look at her hands, Paris knew the silver coloring of her veins itched its way up her body. She could feel her canines and incisors poking the inside of her mouth. Leave it to Rose to push her over the edge.

Of course, she thought this was a mistake. Of course she had no faith in her.

Ian frowned, his eyes never leaving Paris'. "I just don't know what you want from me."

Paris rushed forward, not at Rose, but Ian. The two slammed into a nearby wall, shaking the picture frames hanging on the wall. "Well let me make you understand," she said. Her hand rushed to his throat. Ian reached for her wrist with one hand, but Paris had the other one pinned to the wall.

"Paris!" Hunter scolded, but it just made her grip tighten. Her brother rushed forward, grabbing her by the shoulders and throwing her off. She let him do it. Even though she was the youngest, Hunter wasn't stronger than her, never had been.

Ian fell to his knees, clutching his throat and coughing. Paris looked to Rose, whose face was deathly pale, then to Hunter, who didn't hide his disappointment as he helped Ian to his feet.

"What? I thought this was what you wanted?" Paris said sourly. "Just like old times, right?"

Hunter just shook his head.

"You'll stay the two weeks I agreed to, then I want you gone."

That had to do it.

Paris turned and stumbled from the hallway and into the dining room, dizzy from the rush of violence. Half manufactured, half real. She went through her alcohol cabinet until her hands landed on a bottle of scotch, pouring herself a drink and finishing it in one gulp. She heard her family shuffle out of the hallway and outside. They wouldn't talk about her in earshot, but a talk would be had.

Good, Paris thought. *Scold me, fear me, hate me.*

She poured herself another drink. She hated that Rose was right, hated that she needed to confirm it for her. But they couldn't stay here.

The further away they were from her, the safer.

CHAPTER THIRTEEN
LOLA

LOLA SHUT THE DOOR as quietly as possible. She scoped out the house. To her right, in the living room her aunt Kate was on the couch, a never-ending display of infomercials playing on the TV. *Shit,* Lola thought.

She couldn't tell if Kate was asleep or awake from this angle. Could she make a break for the stairs? She took a cautious step forward, the wood creaking beneath her feet.

"Lola?" Kate said suddenly. *So close,* Lola's thoughts whimpered. Kate pushed herself off the couch and met her at the stairway.

"Oh hey auntie," Lola said innocently.

Kate examined her head to toe. "Are you just getting home?"

"No, I just really like the outfit I wore tonight." It was one in the morning, way past the curfew she had when she lived with her dad. Kate gave her a look of disbelief and Lola waited to be berated.

Instead, her aunt opted to disregard the entire thing instead. Kate rarely, if ever, indulged her nonsense. "You got a call while you were gone," she said. "It was about your dad."

Lola froze. "Oh," she said, anxiety swelling in her chest. "Is something—"

"It was just a check in," Kate said quickly. "Nothing serious, I'm sure you can call for yourself tomorrow."

"No, that's—that's fine." The last thing she needed to hear about was her dad.

Kate gave her an understanding nod. There was a beat of silence where Kate simply looked at her expectantly. She hadn't disregarded Lola's late arrival, simply postponed it.

Lola found the events of the night spilling out of her. With each word, Kate's face grew more and more dire. It was odd seeing her aunt, who was usually so unreadable, look so concerned. The look she wore perfectly encapsulated how Lola felt. The stain of tears on Erica's face and the sound of Paris choking on Juniper appeared in her mind and she was hit with the fear all over again.

"You should have called me as soon as this happened." Kate's voice was deadly serious.

"So much was going on," Lola tried to explain. "We just wanted to make sure Paris was ok."

Even now she was still processing the night's events. One moment she was dancing with Ken and the next she was holding Paris' hair as she puked in an alley.

Kate sighed. "Well at least you left when you did. Who knows what kind of psychos were looking for Nightwalkers in that lounge."

Her aunt seemed to think the same as Erica, that someone tried to kill Paris. But Nightwalker hunters hadn't been spotted in ages. "What do you mean?" she asked, prodding for whatever else her aunt knew.

"That woman, who was killed, was a Witch," Kate explained. Lola's heart dropped to her stomach.

"How do you know?" she asked slowly.

"The head of her coven reached out to me today. He's been keeping things under wraps due to the police investigation," she said. Lola frowned. If Kate knew, that meant the men at the party were right. Someone was attacking Alereians and no one knew what. "I want you to come with me to the burning."

Lola looked at her in surprise. "You're going?" she asked.

"Of course," Kate said. "As another coven head, it's only appropriate for me to go and pay my respects."

A burning was held whenever a Witch died. The coven would gather together to burn the body and perform a ceremony to release the spirit of the deceased. Lola had never been to one before.

"And you're sure you want me to go with you?" she asked. It was a deeply personal ritual, usually only the family was invited. Kate nodded. "Are you sure it's safe?"

"Safe?" Kate didn't know this wasn't a one-off attack, that it was becoming a pattern.

"You said that it was probably some psychos after Nightwalkers. I didn't think hunters were still around," Lola said. "I just thought…" She trailed off, afraid to voice what she thought was happening, but Kate already knew.

"You thought it was you."

She slowly nodded. Her suspicions started when Erica got the note. How could one little piece of paper cause so much damage? Then Paris was poisoned and it all just made sense. If there were still hunters around, how could Paris be the only one affected? It all seemed like an unfortunate coincidence. But Lola had been taught that coincidences didn't exist. All that made sense was that her curse, her bad luck, had seeped out and targeted her friends. The guilt had been eating at her all night. She'd been the one to invite her friends out tonight, and she had been the one to ruin it. On the drive home she agonized over what she was going to do to make it up to them. Seeds of an idea were being planted but what could fully encapsulate, "Sorry you almost died."?

"Well, that doesn't make much sense," Kate said. "Especially if you're still not practicing magick." Lola's face fell, her eyes leaving her aunts. "That is the reason you're not practicing right? You're trying to contain the curse?"

Shame came over Lola, heat rushed to her cheeks. "How long have you known?" she asked quietly.

"Since you started torturing yourself," Kate said easily. "It's like a rot radiating off you." Lola let out a deep sigh. She was an idiot. Of course she would notice. Kate, the prodigy, could pick out a minor disturbance in a room full of people.

"You don't understand."

"Don't understand? Lola, I assure you I understand better than you even do," Kate said. "What you're doing isn't safe. This magick doesn't disappear just because you stop using it, it just builds and builds until one day..."

She let the implication hang in the air. Lola scoffed and turned to walk up the stairs. She couldn't let Kate scare her out of this. She was running out of options. Just a few more months without magick and one way or another a tolerance would build. It had to. "I feel fine," Lola protested.

"You're sick," said Kate. "I can make your elixirs, I have the recipe." The same elixirs that gave her horrible nightmares the first time she tried them? The ones her dad called a bottle of toxins? Those elixirs?

"Why? So I can take them and come out worse the second I'm off them?" Lola rebutted.

"Lola, none of this is 100 percent effective, but this is the best option," Kate said. "Certainly, a better option than whatever the hell you think you're doing."

Lola steeled herself. Not listening to her dad is what landed her here in the first place. She couldn't make that mistake again.

When Kate realized Lola wouldn't change her mind, she continued. "You can't live like this," her aunt said. "How do you expect to—"

"Take over as head of the coven?" Lola finished for her. She stopped in her tracks, looking down at Kate over her shoulder. "I don't."

Kate face quickly changed from concerned to livid. "Excuse me?"

"We both know that's never going to happen, and it's not like you can make me," she argued. Lola didn't have the time, skill, or desire to be coven head. Why even pretend she had a chance?

Lola didn't think of the future often, but if she did end up having children, they would share the same fate as her, the curse following the bloodline. But her aunt was going to live for a long time, just like any other Nightwalker and by the time Kate did pass on, Andi or her uncle Will would settle down with someone. There were options. The coven wouldn't implode within the next decade while they decided on one.

As if the coven would want someone with cursed blood as head Witch anyway.

"So you're not even going to try?" Kate asked.

Her silence was all the answer that was needed.

CHAPTER FOURTEEN
KEN

KEN WAS WRAPPING UP his shift at the Lantern, a small family-owned diner. The restaurant had a retro fifties theme decked in a forest green and white color scheme. It was tiny enough for a few booths and a bar to sit at the front while the kitchen took up the entire back half. Weekdays like this were nice, unlike his usual shift where the diner got busy enough that a weekend brunch rush would leave the place so crowded that he could barely move.

While the day went by at a sluggish pace and the tips were downright laughable, Ken didn't have much room to complain. He picked up this shift after all. Friday would've been the ideal day to skip school, but too many of those in a row and his manager would get suspicious. Unfortunately for Ken, the state of California had a little thing called labor laws for people under the age of eighteen.

Even if that person really needed the money.

Ken was wrapping up his last table when a commotion a few tables over caught his attention. Donald, one of his older coworkers, was being berated by a bearded man in a jean jacket.

"Excuse me for one second," said Ken to his table. He was sure they needed more time to argue over whether they'd pay together or split the check six ways.

"I said no tomatoes, I didn't see you write it down even though I told you to and now my fucking sandwich is soggy," the customer said like he was lecturing a child. Ken fought to roll his eyes. He couldn't comprehend what it was like to have so little problems that a tomato on a sandwich could ruin his entire day.

Donald, the poor guy, looked like he was on the verge of a breakdown. He was only here to get some extra money while in retirement. He least of all deserved the verbal lashing.

"Sir I apologize, really, I—"

"Hey, is everything okay over here?" Ken interjected.

The bearded man rolled his eyes. "No, everything is not ok," he grumbled.

"Well, what appears to be the problem?" Ken asked. "I'll see if I can take care of it." He shot Donald a look that said he should get out of here as fast as humanly possible. The man didn't need any convincing, he was out of sight in an instant.

Ken listened as the customer went through his tomato spiel again. Or at least, he pretended to listen. People liked a hero, someone who swooped in and solved all their problems.

It made them feel special, like they were important enough to warrant this much attention and not just incredibly annoying.

"No, that sounds frustrating," said Ken after the man was done cursing up a storm. "I'm so sorry about that." He reached for the turkey club on the table. "How about I take this away and get you a new sandwich, no tomato, on the house?"

People also really liked the word free.

"That sounds perfect. Thank you so much!" And just like that the man was pacified.

"Mhm," Ken said, resisting the urge to claw his own face off. Sometimes Ken envied his friends' powers. If Paris were here, she'd be able to compel herself out of the interaction completely. But even then, for werewolves like him, shifting, and all the other abilities that came with it, were dormant until eighteen. Of course, he possessed the standard Nightwalker gifts, like night vision and enhanced endurance, yet it got frustrating at times to basically be human in comparison. But Ken waited this long and he only had a few months until his eighteenth birthday. Maybe then he'd get what all the fuss was about.

He made his way to the kitchen and found Donald waiting for him. "Thank you, Ken."

"Yeah, no problem," he said, dumping the sandwich and ordering a new one in the system. What a waste. "I don't know what attracts so many assholes to you."

"I don't know how you always manage to calm em' down," said Donald. "I was sure that guy was about to start throwing things."

"You just can't let them get to you man." The back door to the kitchen opened; Mateo stepped in, drenched head to toe from the storm outside. Ken grimaced. The forecast said nothing about rain today, and he suddenly wasn't looking forward to walking home.

Mateo made eye contact with him and put his hands up apologetically. "Sorry I'm late." Ken passed him a cloth so he could at least wipe his face. "Thanks."

Ken shrugged and checked his phone. His shift was over five minutes ago, which meant he should've left to meet Megan five minutes ago too. He wrapped up his table, collected his tips, and was on his way.

Ken hadn't thought to bring a jacket. With nothing but a hoodie to protect him from the storm, he was quickly doused in a freezing rain that would've given him a cold if he was human.

Entering the rundown shack, or what some people would call an apartment building, Ken winced at the sight of the cracked glass on the front door that definitely hadn't been there yesterday.

Inside his apartment, he heard the sound of someone rummaging through the kitchen. "Mom?" he called out. His heart skipped a beat in anticipation.

"Nope," his younger sister replied. A mix of relief and disappointment washed over him. It was a feeling he became used to over time.

Megan, still in her softball uniform, was making herself a grilled cheese sandwich on the stove. *Good,* Ken thought. That would hold her over until dinner. "You're home late," she noted. She looked so much like Isabel, that it was starting to catch him off guard the older she got. They had the same sharp features and hazel eyes. The only difference was Megan's hair was black whereas Isabel's was brown.

"Mateo was late, again."

"When are you gonna talk to that guy?" she asked, taking her charcoal shaped sandwich off the stove and onto a plate. Ken shook his head and took their dinner out of the plastic bag, grateful, now more than ever for the free meal he got for working at the diner. "Oh, we're out of hot water," Megan added offhandedly.

Ken held back a sigh. He paid the water bill, so at the very least that wasn't an issue. "Out like, 'I took a long ass shower' or out like, 'the boiler is broken and you need to call

Jeremy, Ken'," he said. Jeremy was their landlord who did not appreciate them and their late rent every month. After the quickest move of Ken's life, the three of them landed in this one-bedroom apartment. The situation was less than ideal, with his mother and Megan sharing the bedroom while he took the couch. It didn't bother Ken much, seeing as he never had a room of his own before, but he knew Megan felt differently. Not a day went by where she didn't complain about the lack of privacy.

But Ken's real issue was that the entire building seemed to be held together by Elmer's glue and duct tape. What they were paying for and what they actually got was infuriating.

Megan bit her lip. "I think it's the boiler."

"Great." Another item on the ever-growing to-do list he had.

"There was a letter from dad and Izzy in the mail too."

The two made eye contact. Even though they received letters from their dad and sister every month, it still felt like a surprise each time. "Did you open it?"

She shook her head.

Izzy. Mom. Dad. Three names that took up so much space in their little apartment. Three people he rarely saw these days.

CHAPTER FIFTEEN
LOLA

"WHY ARE YOU SMILING so hard?" Paris asked.

"Uh, because I'm happy to see my friends?" Lola said, smiling wider. Her, Paris, and Erica stood at the threshold of her aunt's house.

"Stop that, it's unsettling."

A few weeks passed since the incident at Sage and Lola had been eager to make up for it. This weekend was her opportunity to give her friends the night they deserved. What started as a group hangout between the four of them quickly dropped to three. Ken was always busy, always had somewhere to be and very rarely had interest in sharing those things with Lola. But despite the loss of his company, tonight would still work. Her home was neutral ground, no outside forces would be able to deliver mysterious notes or poisonous drinks here.

"So, you invited me over to sit around and watch you two sleep? Am I getting that right?" Paris said. Lola knew she'd need more than one evening to accomplish everything she wanted. What started out as a hangout, quickly turned into a sleepover.

"Have you never been to one of these?" Lola asked. "Sleeping is rarely involved."

"I haven't actually," Paris said matter of factly. Lola looked back at her startled. *Oh, that just won't do*, she decided.

Within the hour, the three girls changed into their pajamas and were settled comfortably in the living room. Lola brought down a large fluffy blanket and pillows and sprawled them across the floor.

"Can we please watch something else?" Paris groaned. Twilight had been on for nearly twenty minutes now and Paris was still fighting for Lola to pick another movie.

"No, we need to watch the baseball scene and heal," she said, her face intently focused on the TV.

"But that still leaves the rest of the movie," Paris whined. Lola didn't understand Paris' contempt, any Witch movies she watched were thoroughly entertaining.

Lola's phone went off and she hastily checked the screen. "Pizza's here," she said. Since Vampires couldn't eat, the large pizza was just for her and Erica. "Par, can you get it please?"

Paris got to her feet. "Yes, I will retrieve the pizza I can't eat and return to the movie I don't like, at the sleepover I can't sleep at," she said mockingly as she headed to the door. Lola waved her off with a roll of her eyes.

"We're gonna do other stuff!" she called after her as the door closed. Pausing the movie, she scooted towards Erica. "Hey."

"Hey," Erica replied, drawing her knees to her chest.

"You've been quiet...something on your mind?" While Paris seemed to be moving past the events at Sage, she could see on Erica's face that the night replayed itself in her head.

Erica let out a bitter laugh. "What isn't on my mind?"

Lola considered her words for a moment and then said softly, "I'm sorry you had to see that."

Erica frowned. She didn't need to ask what Lola meant. "I mean, I wasn't the one who died, so..."

"You knew there were multiple deaths before you talked to those guys at the party, didn't you?"

She nodded but didn't look at her.

"Do you...see things like that often?" she asked. Another nod. Lola was at a loss for words, feeling as if she'd been struck. She never asked about Erica's premonitions, always assuming they were too unimportant to mention in the first place. But knowing Erica saw visions like that regularly was nothing short of horrifying. "Why haven't you ever said anything?"

Erica finally met her eyes. "What would be the point?" she said, her voice flat. "It's not like it'll change anything, I can't control what I see. Those people are still dead."

Lola gave her friend a once over, suddenly serious. "You don't blame yourself for that right?" Erica didn't respond. "Ere, there was nothing you could've done."

"There's always something that could've been done," Erica said with a heavy sigh. "And it's all I can think about. It's always fresh. It's always like I'm seeing it for the first time."

Lola held her breath, her heart sinking to her stomach. She couldn't imagine seeing those kinds of horrors and being unable to forget them. Her mind naturally drew her back to the night of her father's accident, the end result the same but the events leading up to it blurry. The how and why had begun to fade but the emotion was still raw and suffocating. Lola knew about Erica's perfect memory, she'd known about her visions, so why hadn't the pieces come together? Why had she never come to this conclusion on her own? Why had she never asked?

"I know what you're trying to do, and it's sweet," Erica said. "But you can't fix this."

Before Lola could say more the front door opened. "Ugh, why did you pause that," Paris groaned, pizza in hand. She shut the door with the heel of her foot. "I was hoping to at least miss some of it."

Erica turned away from Lola, staring back at the screen. The conversation was over.

"What took you so long anyway?" Lola asked, forcing casualness in her voice. Erica's confession still reeled within her. All she could think about was how much she missed, how much she was still missing. She took in Paris' sunny demeanor now, how different it was to the night at Sage, to the night her family returned. Was this an act? Was Paris hiding things too?

"The pizza girl was a flirt." Paris said, making her way over.

"Really?" Lola said in disbelief. "*She* was the flirt?"

"Believe what you want, just know I got you a free soda out of it."

⇥⇥ ⇤⇤

Sunday afternoon, Lola flipped through channels with disinterest as her and Erica looked for something to watch. Paris slept soundly on the couch behind them.

When nothing on the screen caught her eye, she turned the TV off and propped herself up on her elbow. "Wanna play a game?" she asked.

Erica cast a weary look at Paris and shook her head. "Too loud."

Lola scoffed. "The only time it gets loud is when you start to lose," she said.

Erica raised an eyebrow. "And when do I lose?" she asked, already taking things far too seriously. Lola was thankful for it. It'd taken all night but at least Erica was speaking now.

"I'm gonna lose my mind from sleep deprivation," Paris mumbled, her eyes still closed.

"We weren't even that loud," Lola huffed.

Paris tapped a finger to her ear. "Vamp hearing," she said.

"That sounds like a personal problem." That response was greeted with a pillow to the face that knocked her on her back. Erica laughed, the sound pleasant to Lola's ears.

She sat up and threw her own pillow even though she knew it was pointless. Paris caught it with one hand while her eyes remained closed. When they opened, they glared directly at her.

"Ok, I'm awake." The blonde shot up from her spot on the floor, pillow in hand. Lola got to her feet as quickly as she could and sprinted into the hallway. "I'm sorry! I'm sorry!" Lola exclaimed, half laughing.

As she reached the end of the hall, Paris tackled her to the ground. The blonde girl flipped her on her back and began to mercilessly beat her with the pillow. "Oh, but I thought we were doing sleepover things?" Paris said. Behind Lola was an end table that held some family pictures and a fake potted plant. She scurried underneath it, successfully shielding herself from Paris' wrath, but as she sat up, her head banged against the edge of the table.

The table shook, knocking some of the picture frames over and the potted plant on its side. The plant rolled over the edge, falling to the floor, and smashing to pieces.

"Shit," Lola groaned, crawling out from under the table.

"What was that?" Erica called from the living room.

"The sound of Lola getting yelled at," Paris replied.

"Hush," Lola said, waving her off. She got to her feet as Erica came into the hallway to survey the scene. "Great, this is just what I needed."

Erica looked at her curiously. "Why don't you just call for a new one?" she asked. The dirt was easy enough to sweep up, and the smashed pot was white and wrapped in painted flowers. The design was easy enough to replicate, which was important when it came to calling. There were times when she had been in situations like this and one misplaced detail would land her in trouble with her father.

In the eyes of her friends, there was no reason not to use her gift to fix this. And it would be so easy, the idea nearly intoxicating. Her magick nipped at her skin, begging to be used.

Saving her from having to answer, Paris said, "What's that?"

She reached into the remains of the plant and pulled a gold key out of the dirt. Lola's eyebrows furrowed at the object and Erica leaned forward to get a better look. "The hell is a key doing here?" Erica said.

"Lola's aunts are terrible at hiding things?" Paris suggested with a shrug.

"What do you think it goes to?"

"A jewelry box maybe?" Lola tried. Did her aunts own anything valuable? Wishful thinking made her wonder if they had a secret vault around here somewhere. Kate was well off and successful, but not swimming in gold coins like a cartoon duck successful.

Erica shook her head. "It looks too big for that. Maybe a padlock or a door?"

Paris turned to Lola. "Are there any locked doors around here?" she asked.

Lola thought for a moment, before turning to face the door to their right. The basement had been under renovations for as long as she could remember. She would occasionally catch glimpses of Kate disappearing downstairs, but had never seen it for herself. And when she would ask, Kate would inform her that it was none of her business. Eventually, Lola started to believe that even in the short time they spent together, her aunt needed space to escape from her. She hadn't pushed to go downstairs since. "The basement," she said.

Paris stepped up to the door and pressed the key into the lock. It fit perfectly. She turned the knob and the door opened with a creak, leading to pitch blackness. It took a moment for Lola's eyes to adjust, and she made out the wooden staircase leading down.

"So, who's going first?" Lola asked. "'Cause I vote for the immortal."

Paris placed a hand on her hip, but stepped forward anyway. Keeping close to her, the girls walked down the stairs. When they reached the bottom, Lola's hand found the light switch and turned it on. While she knew none of them needed it, the light certainly made things less creepy.

The basement was larger than she expected, almost twice the size of the living room with another door leading to a separate room to the left of them. A large mahogany table was in the center, books and loose papers spread about. Up against the cool gray brick stood a desk with a computer that was in a similar state.

"It's just an office," Lola stated. "Why was it locked?"

"Kate probably hides from you and Andi down here," Paris said. She meant it as a joke but it rang true for Lola deep down.

"Can you stop being snippy for two seconds?" she said.

"We'll see."

The three split up to explore the room. Lola headed to the desk while Paris and Erica looked through the table in the middle of the room.

"How does she find anything in this mess?" Erica asked, flipping through papers.

Lola searched her own pile, quickly coming across a tan spiral notebook. As she read through it, she noticed the book was written in entries, dating back to the end of August. She skimmed it until she found something that held her attention. "Subject has been put down effectively with small antacide injections," she read aloud. Her friends look up from their piles and crowded around her. "Subject refuses to speak. Antacide injections along with electrical shocks cause small damage. No new information on the recent incidents has been discovered."

Electrical shocks?

The three girls stared at the notebook. Erica was the first to speak. "What do you think she means by incident?"

"No idea," Paris said.

"Antacide?" The unfamiliar word rolled off the Witch's tongue nervously. "What the hell is that?" Lola wasn't sure she wanted to understand what Kate was doing with it. Erica pulled out her phone and took a picture of the page. "Whoa, what are you doing?" She pulled the notebook out of view.

"To read over later," Erica said simply. Lola side eyed her, wondering why Erica thought they would need to revisit these. Her friend left her side to search the rest of the room with newfound interest.

"What's that smell?" Paris asked suddenly.

Lola sniffed the air. "Sage," she replied. Being so used to the smell, she didn't really notice it anymore. Smelling sage in a Witch household was about as common as finding a frying pan in a kitchen.

"What is it used for?"

Lola paused, racking her brain. "Lots of things. Protection spells, purification spells, privacy spells. Lots of P's," she said.

"I see," Paris mused. Lola had a feeling of uncertainty settle in her chest. Erica and Paris shared looks and glances she wasn't clued in on. There seemed to be something new she was in the dark about.

"Oh my God," Erica exclaimed. Lola and Paris rushed to her side. She stood in front of a black case, inside were dozens and dozens of vials filled to the brim with an icky black substance. "Ew, what is that?"

"Potions?" Paris tried and looked to Lola for confirmation.

Lola was puzzled at the sight before her. "I've never seen potions that look like that." She bent down and reached into the case, pulling out a vial. Half expecting her fingers to come in contact with cool glass, she was surprised to find heat coming from it. "It's warm."

"Gross," Erica whined. She took a photo of the chest.

Paris' eyes were suddenly wide and alert. "Your aunt's car just pulled into the driveway."

Lola was struck with panic. The room suddenly screamed at her that she didn't belong. What would happen if Kate saw them down here?

Moving faster than she thought possible, the girls put everything back as they found it. She flicked the light off and followed the group up the stairs.

Lola cursed under her breath at the sight of the mess she made on the floor. But Paris was already gone from her side, returning with a broom and dust pan within a second.

The mess was accounted for but the pot remained broken. There was no way around it, she would need to use magick for this. While Paris swept up the remains of the broken pot, Lola focused on the image of the pot in her mind. "*Flower pot*," she called and felt a rush of relief flow through her.

A white plant pot materialized into existence, taking the spot of the old one on the end table. Paris finished sweeping and locked the basement door. She handed the key off to Lola and left to dump the dirt and broken ceramic in the nearest trashcan.

Erica headed into the living room and peered out the curtains. "They're coming up the steps!" she said.

Lola took a brief moment to thank San Francisco for its long ass stairs.

She grabbed the still intact plant off the floor, dropping the key inside the pot before bringing the two together. She let out a sigh of relief as the two fit perfectly. She then made her way to the kitchen to join Paris at the sound of keys turning within the lock.

Kate's voice was the first she heard. "Lola! Help bring these bags inside."

She did as she was told, with help from Paris and Erica. The two left shortly after the fact, but Lola's thoughts remained on the basement. From the things she'd seen, to her friends' faces, there was nothing she could do to wrap her head around it all. But if this weekend had shown her anything, it was that things were more confusing than ever. Erica and her visions, and now Kate and her basement. Perhaps her friends weren't the only ones hiding things.

CHAPTER SIXTEEN
LOLA

"LOLA," MS. MARSHALL CALLED. Lola blinked and looked up at her. "Are you feeling ok?"

Her weekly sessions with Ms. Marshall had been over for a while now, but the tricky part about catching up was ensuring you didn't get left behind on the current. She understood statistics well enough in class, but as soon as she got home her mind went blank. Lola found herself coming in after school for homework help often.

"Sorry, I was thinking," she said. All she could think about was the basement. She didn't understand what they found or what any of it meant, but the whole thing left an uncomfortable pit in her stomach.

"Is it about home stuff again? Because you know you're free to talk about it here," Ms. Marshall said. "And there's always the counselor."

She hadn't meant to let Ms. Marshall in. To Lola's surprise, she hadn't been sent to detention since her first week back. After her spat with Kate, Lola returned to school disinterested and upset. Ms. Marshall pulled her aside, demanding an explanation for her change in attitude.

Many of the details were left out but the feelings remained the same. Ever since, Ms. Marshall had taken an interest in her home life and Lola still wasn't sure if she appreciated it or not. At the very least she wasn't going to talk to a counselor, that was for sure.

"No, nothing like that," she said. "I'm just distracted."

Her phone buzzed at her side. Glancing down she saw a text from Erica asking if she was done. She wasn't, she had about five questions left, but it was clear Erica was getting impatient. It was the third message within ten minutes. "I'm gonna head home," she said, packing up her things.

"Lola, I'm serious."

"I know, I know," she said, waving her off. "I'll come talk to you, I promise."

Ms. Marshall gave her a pensive look but let her leave.

Lola sat outside of a local café with Erica, Paris, and Ken. Now that Paris' family was in the process of moving out, her house was off the table if they wanted to talk privately. It was a pretty small place. Ken had been the one to mention it when the girls told him they needed to talk. According to him, it wasn't usually busy and Lola could see why.

It was an ugly place with lime green walls and bright orange décor. And from what Lola could tell, their interior decorating wasn't the only problem. Their drinks were too. Her herbal tea was awful.

"So, does anyone want to tell me what's going on now?" Ken asked. Erica went into explaining before Lola could even think of what to say. Around midnight, after the girls left, Erica texted nonstop about the basement. Once her brain latched on to something she didn't understand, she didn't stop until she figured it out.

Any other time, Lola loved that about Erica, but now all she wanted was to forget the entire thing had happened.

When Erica finished, Ken's face was in disbelief. "I'm very confused," he said.

"Well, maybe you'd be less confused if you had been there." Lola said, turning away from him.

Ken sighed. "I already told you I was sorry."

She wasn't sure why Ken's absence bothered her so much, but the way his face fell just slightly, made her backtrack, shifting the comment into a joke. "No, no, it's fine, the sting of rejection has since passed." She held up a hand as if to block his apology from reaching her.

"I've been busy," he explained.

"My ego will never recover from this," Lola went on. "I'll wallow in this pain for the rest of my life."

Ken rolled his eyes. "Fine, wallow away."

Paris shook her head at him in disapproval. "Damn, now he just doesn't care." She gave Lola a sympathetic pat on the shoulder, which riled up Ken even more.

Lola left out a fake sniffle. "First he starts skipping plans, next he'll start missing birthdays." She dabbed at her eyes even though they were dry.

"He better not," Erica threatened. Her eighteenth birthday was quickly approaching. The group had been separated during Lola's birthday back in August. She wouldn't allow her friend to celebrate alone like she had.

Ken tilted his head, giving Erica a smile that was slightly strained. Now that Lola was looking closer, she noticed the bags under his eyes and the unruliness of his hair. Whatever he was doing in his spare time, it was clearly taking a toll on him. Ken noticed her watching him, and before she could ask any questions, he redirected his attention to Erica. "Anything else about this secret basement I should know?" he asked.

Erica pulled her phone out of her pocket and brought up the pictures she'd taken. Ken took the phone and scrolled through each photo, but his eyes grew wide at one in particular. "What is that?" He showed them the picture of the vials of black liquid.

"No idea," said Paris. Ken returned the phone to Erica.

He turned to Lola. "How have you never questioned why the basement was locked?"

"Dude, it's my aunt. She could have told me that room was a coat closet and I would've believed her," she explained and it was true. What reason did she have to question her aunt's word? "But since you're so curious, why don't we just go back down there right now?"

Paris was the first to object. "No, thank you," she said, holding her hands up. "What goes down in that house is none of my business. It could be a meth lab for all we know."

"Don't you think you're exaggerating?" Ken said.

Paris shrugged and leaned back in her chair. "Hidden key, secret creepy basement, unknown substance, questionable report on the effects of said substance..."

Lola shook her head. "I showed you one episode of Breaking Bad." She stood from her seat, causing Paris to let out an exasperated huff. "Come on boys and girls."

"Aren't your aunt's home?" Ken asked.

"Yeah, but Kate's taking Andi to a job interview later. We've got plenty of time."

"Are we not going to address how sketchy this all is?" Erica asked as they made their way to the car.

"We'll deal with it when we get there," she said, trying to dilute the edge in her voice. Despite her joking, Lola felt a tinge of irritation at her friend's concerns. This was her aunt after all. What had Kate really done to rouse such suspicion? While her own curiosity about the basement was strong, she knew Kate. A few locked doors weren't about to scare her away.

Paris drove at her usual breakneck speed. The group arrived in front of the house in mere minutes. Lola wished she had more time to prepare or think, but she and her friends were out of the car and up the stairs.

A cry came from inside. Her hand froze as it reached for the handle. More noise from the inside, this time a loud crash. She threw the door open so hard that it slammed into the wall behind it.

The first thing she saw was her aunt Andi's body crashing into an end table. Paris took a protective stance in front of the group, briefly blocking her view of the scene. Lola whipped her head around and saw her aunt quickly get to her feet. Her eyes went wide when she noticed the four friends huddled together by the door.

"Andi—" Lola started but her aunt quickly brought a finger to her lips, signaling her to be silent. Andi motioned with her hand for the four to back themselves into the corner as her eyes flickered between them and the living room she had just been flung out of. Lola's mind had been so occupied between fear and confusion that she hadn't had time to consider what flung her aunt into that table.

The sound of heavy footsteps was quickly approaching. There was someone else in the house.

A man in a black leather jacket stumbled into the hallway and locked his sights on Andi. Lola stepped forward but a strong grip pulled her back. It was Paris' hand around her. Before Lola could argue, her eyes were drawn back to her aunt.

Andi's demeanor changed. A look of desperation transformed into one of resolve. The man charged, but she side-stepped out of the way, grabbing his arm and swinging him into the wall. He recovered fast, spinning around and knocking her to the ground. Lola was finally able to catch a glimpse of his face. The attacker's eyes were pure black, even the whites of the eyes were absent. Along each side of his cheeks were three lines gaping open and closed like the gills of a fish. She'd never seen anything like it before. Who was this? Where was Kate? And what was happening?

The man in the black jacket grabbed Andi by her hair, yanking her forward into the wall. His hand went to her neck, hoisting her up in the air. Andi struggled to push him back, hitting and kicking but the man didn't so much as flinch at the impact. He was unmovable, like solid stone.

"Put her down!" Lola screamed, her voice cracking. She didn't care if Andi wanted her out of the way. She wasn't just about to watch this. She struggled against Paris, whose grip tightened around her arm, keeping her in place. The man—thing—whatever it was, turned its head in her direction.

Andi cast a panicked look at Lola as she strained against him. She used the distraction to her advantage, grabbing his head and using her gift to send a current of electricity straight to his brain.

The man in the black jacket screamed, the sudden shock of pain caused him release Andi as he clutched his head.

And just as he did, an airborne knife found its way into his back.

Lola looked in horror as a black liquid poured out of his mouth. He fell forward into her aunt's body and crumbled to her feet. Andi let out a shaky breath, then stepped over the body as if it was nothing more than trash on the sidewalk. She stared at the four as Kate entered from the other room. There was a gash on her temple. A trail of silver dripped down the side of her face.

"Are you ok?" Kate asked her sister. When she got no response, she followed Andi's line of sight and noticed the group huddled together in the corner.

With her guard down, Lola finally managed to push past Paris and run to Andi, wrapping her in a hug. Her aunt rubbed her back in soothing circles as she struggled to find the words. "Are you alright? What the hell happened? Who was that?" Lola said quickly.

"I'm fine, I'm ok," Andi reassured her, patting her head.

Lola looked to her aunt Kate, whose usual braid was undone and loose in messy waves down her back. Her eyes kept flicking between Lola and her friends by the door. Before Lola could say anything to her, Kate turned on her heel and walked into the kitchen. "Gods above," she swore.

"Kate!" Andi rushed after her.

Lola looked back at her friends, who gave her weary looks in return. She glanced at the body and immediately regretted it. He was slumped face down against the wall, knife protruding out of his back, black ooze seeping into his jacket and out of his mouth. She turned away, quickly heading into the kitchen, hearing her friends follow after her.

"What the hell is going on?" Paris asked. She didn't sound angry, just confused.

Andi exchanged a nervous look with her sister, but Kate straightened herself up, regaining her composure. "It's nothing to be concerned about," she said.

Lola's eyes nearly bulged out of her head. "What? Kate, that man almost killed Andi."

"And you killed him," Ken pointed out. *Dear God, there's a dead man in the hallway,* Lola reminded herself. What was supposed to happen now? What did they do with him? The sudden image of them burying a body shot into her mind, making her sick.

"God, what do we do? Should we call the police?" She couldn't even believe what she was saying. She hated cops, but what other choice did they have?

"I've seen him before," Erica said quietly to herself. Lola nearly missed it.

"What did you just say?" Kate said. Her aunt's focus zeroed in on her friend.

"I had a premonition about him," Erica said carefully. She shifted on her feet, uncomfortable with the sudden attention. "He murdered some woman a couple weeks ago."

"What?" Lola said. This must have been the other Alereian death Erica had seen. Her aunts had been one second away from being next on that list. She thought back to her first day of school, the day she learned about the murders. Hadn't she had this exact fear? But her aunts were alive, they were standing right in front of her. So then why didn't she feel relieved?

"So that was the guy that killed Lauren Carter?" Andi asked Erica.

She shook her head. "No, that was someone else."

Kate gave Andi a knowing look.

Something didn't feel right. The way Andi moved, the knife flying into his back. The confrontation ended as fast as it started. How?

She immediately felt guilty when she should have felt grateful.

Her friends began to set off a string of questions at the sisters.

"What are you gonna do with the body?"

"What was wrong with his face?"

"How'd he even get in here?"

That was it, Lola realized. The front door had been locked. That meant this man had to have been inside before she'd gotten home. Her eyes drifted out of the kitchen and into the hallway. Just as she suspected, the basement door was wide open. "Was he in the basement?" she asked. Her voice no louder than a whisper but it brought the room to a screeching halt.

Her friends followed her gaze. Andi looked practically startled, while Kate's face stayed composed.

"Why would you ask that?" Andi started but Paris cut her off.

"Answer the question," she said.

Lola hadn't even noticed that her friends had stepped back, until Ken took her hand, pulling her back with them. "It's not like that," Andi said, suddenly flustered.

"Then what is it like?" Lola said, her heart pounding in her chest. The adrenaline from the fight hadn't faded. It only intensified what she felt now. Was it fear? "I'm asking if you kept a man in the basement and you won't give me a straight answer." What was happening? Just a second ago she was relieved her aunts were alive, now she was accusing them of something? Accusing them of what exactly? Trapping a murderer in their basement?

"That's because we can't answer," Kate said. Andi looked at her wearily.

"What?" Lola said.

"We *can't* answer you, alright?" she said again.

The room became silent as Kate's words began to sink in. Lola racked her brain for what her aunt meant. Can't, not won't. Were they being threatened? Or maybe they were under oath. Oaths in Alereis were taken seriously. An unbreakable spell was used to ensure that the people under it kept their promises no matter what the circumstances. Were Andi and Kate actually silenced? Had someone made them do this?

Andi moved closer to Kate behind the island. "Maybe we're overreacting? Maybe they don't even know what happened," she said.

At her words, the air above them rippled. There was a light shimmer like something was trying to fade itself into existence. Within the next moment an envelope appeared from the air and fell on to the island. Kate glared at her sister as if she called for this to happen. Andi quickly avoided her gaze, reaching for the envelope. The packaging was a metallic gold, shining under the kitchen lights. The front addressed the postage to the Hallows residence.

Andi flipped it over to open it and Paris gasped. "Is that…?"

The package was enclosed with a red wax seal; a raven resting on inside of a crescent moon. It was the official seal of the Alereian Council.

Andi pulled two documents from the envelope and quickly read them over, her face changing from confusion to fear and everything in between. "What is it?" Kate asked.

Andi swallowed. "We've been invited to the Remembrance Ball."

"We?" said Kate, gesturing to Lola and her friends. "As in all of us?" Andi nodded. "And what else?" There was an edge in her voice.

Andi bit her lip and slowly slid the second document over to Kate.

"We've been summoned to a private meeting with the Realm's Council."

"A summons?" Paris exclaimed, her eyes wide. The gravity of the situation was quickly sinking in. No one was summoned to meet the Realm's rulers for no reason. What had her aunts done to make the Council take note of them?

"We have to go to that too?" Lola asked.

Andi gave another grim nod. Lola tried to swallow down her dread, but she knew it was clear on her face. She peered down at the letter and sure enough every person in the room was mentioned by name. Why was this happening? How did the Council even know her friends were here? How did the Council even know her aunts?

Kate rubbed her temples. "When do we need to be there?"

"1:00 a.m. their time, so 1:00 p.m. here," Andi explained. Most continents in Alereis followed a night schedule. Its capital, Mantle, was no different.

"And they want us to stay until the ball?"

The Remembrance Ball was held every year, the day before Halloween. This meant they would be spending almost two weeks in the Alereis. That was longer than Lola had ever stayed.

"Why do we have to go?" Ken asked. "What did we do?"

"You didn't do anything," Andi reassured him, wearing a regretful look on her face.

Paris crossed her arms. "You're right. *You* did something," she said. "What could you have possibly done, that was so bad it got us all a Council summons?"

Kate gave her a level look. "It's complicated," she said. Paris scoffed which Lola agreed with. Complicated felt like an understatement.

"Do we meet you here tomorrow then?" Ken asked.

Kate shook her head. "We can't let you leave."

"Excuse me?"

"If you need to go home and pack, one of us will go with you, but we can't let you out of our line of sight," she explained. "You have to stay here tonight."

"You just said we didn't do anything," Lola said, her agitation growing. "Now you need to watch us?"

"Yeah and we can't just be gone for two weeks," Erica explained. "At least I can't, I have school and my parents to worry about."

"And my mom is out of town right now," Ken said quickly. "I can't just leave my sister home alone."

"Look, we'll figure it out, alright?" Kate said, her voice firm and ripe with irritation. Lola wasn't sure she deserved to be irritated considering her problem had now become her friend's.

Everyone began to make arrangements. Kate agreed to drive Paris, Ken, and Erica home so they could pack for the trip ahead. Andi would stay behind with Lola.

They left the kitchen, passing back through the hallway, where the four stopped abruptly. The body was gone. Pools of black and the knife on the floor were the only indication that something had happened here at all.

"What happened to him?" Erica asked warily. She glanced back as if checking to see if he would pop up behind her.

"I thought he was dead, where'd he go?" said Ken.

Kate huffed. "Trust me, he's dead."

"Then where's the body?" Paris asked.

Nothing but silence came from the two. It was unlikely any of their questions would be answered any time soon.

Paris exited the house with a scowl on her face as Erica, Ken, and Kate followed closely behind. The front door slammed shut.

When they were gone, Lola took the chance to examine the hallway. The black ooze, which she now assumed was blood, splattered across the wall with no body to show for it. The knife on the ground wasn't the kitchen utensil she initially thought it was.

This was a dagger. A weapon. A different kind of black substance Lola didn't recognize covered the blade. It was matte, almost as if it was airbrushed on.

Andi bent down to pick up the dagger, making eye contact with Lola as she did. Her aunt's expression told her nothing and everything at the same time. She bit her lip and turned away, heading back into the kitchen.

Lola sighed.

This was going to be a long night.

PART TWO | THE MAGICK REALM

CHAPTER SEVENTEEN
LOLA

AFTER ONE OF THE most sleepless nights of her life, Lola sat in the back of Kate's jeep, rubbing her eyes. After her friends and aunt returned to the house, Kate seemed adamant on staying silent and heading straight to bed. So, the four huddled together in the living room as Andi watched over in a nearby armchair.

Watched over.

Lola wanted to scoff at just the memory of it. To know her aunts didn't trust her not to take off running was insulting, to say the least.

She looked around the backseat. Ken and Erica stared silently ahead, while Paris slept on her shoulder. Lola couldn't imagine any of her friends leaving either. The perfect time to abandon her would've been when Andi was attacked. And while Lola was initially angry with Paris for holding her back, she knew her friend just wanted to protect her.

When the group came back last night, she learned how they got around their current obligations. Ken apparently had to beg one of Megan's friends to let her stay over last minute, and Erica reluctantly agreed to let Paris compel her parents, who now believed she was on a senior trip. Compulsion was an old Vampire power that allowed them to convince people of almost anything. It gave Lola the creeps, but she supposed it came in handy in times like these.

The car slowed to a stop and she looked out onto the old cemetery. A sea of headstones stared back at her. All you could see for acres was white on grass that was too green. She wondered whose sick idea was it to put the entrance to Alereis in a graveyard.

She nudged Paris, who groaned loudly. Lola figured her friend had more than enough reason to be extra miserable. The whole trip would throw off her sleep schedule and it would probably be hours before any of them would see a real bed.

She quickly grabbed her bag from the back and followed the rest of the group through the gates of the cemetery. As they walked, she felt a fit of nausea in the pit of her stomach at the mere thought of being surrounded by graves. Both marked and unmarked. *Relax*, she thought. *Just imagine you're in a garden...full of dead people.*

A blur crossed her line of sight, and Lola looked out of the corner of her eye to see a pale figure wandering the headstones. She watched its blank expression search for something, somehow still exuding immense sorrow through its gaze. It stopped in its tracks suddenly and then looked straight at her. Faster than lightning, Lola glanced away as casually as she could.

She'd been taught to ignore ghosts for as long as she could remember. As soon as a spirit noticed that someone could see them, they'd latch on to the Witch in hopes they would help the spirit cross over. Because that's all ghosts were after all, trapped spirits with unfinished business. But only a Head Witch could truly converse with the dead, so it was agreed, at least within her coven, that ghosts were more trouble than they were worth. Lola waited a few moments before glancing back to find the ghost had resumed its endless state of wandering once again.

The group reached the center of the graveyard, where the mausoleum stood. It was a small marble structure, no bigger than a garage, with twin columns and a dome roof.

Kate approached first, pulling the door open and gesturing for the rest to pass through. There was little concern of mourners noticing them trudge luggage through a graveyard. By the time anyone came to confront them, they'd be long gone.

The inside was a cramped dimly lit space where cobwebs and dust collected everywhere. The group walked to the very back of the structure, then down to the burial chamber where a single casket sat. It was empty, only there for show just in case a human found their way downstairs. But the casket wasn't important. It was the gray brick wall behind it. Mounted on it was a single unlit candle in a gold holder. Kate placed her hand against the space next to it and in only a few moments did the opening appear, growing in size until it revealed a corridor.

A light on the other side led the way as the group walked through, leaving the Mortal Realm behind.

The corridor ended in a large building so white that one couldn't tell where the floors began and the walls ended. Paris squinted upon entry, the room so bright she needed to slip on her shades. It was filled to the brim with people. At the beginning of the dozens of lines, stretching throughout the building, were small toll booths, each filled with an Alereian official, allowing and denying access across.

They had reached the border of Alereis.

The group waited in the most uncomfortable silence Lola had ever experienced as they stood in line for half an hour. At the front sending travelers through was a stern-looking woman, wearing the same gray double-breasted suit as the other officials. When they did reach the front, the woman harshly grabbed Kate's hand and pulled it toward a metal machine that pricked her finger. Lola winced at the sight but saw no reaction on Kate's face, almost like she was used to the feeling. The woman at the booth rubbed her aunt's finger on a glass plate, leaving a streak of silver blood.

Once the woman saw there was Nightwalker blood on the glass, she hastily let her through the gates. Rules in Alereis were strict. The blood test was there to make sure only Alereians got past the border. Nightwalker blood, silver and Lien blood, gold. The rest of the group made it across with ease.

Past the gates and chaos of the border, they were met with one exit leading outside and another leading to the transit system. Her aunts took her by surprise by disregarding the exit entirely. The transit system was an incredibly expensive mode of transportation. Kate was an accountant while Andi was painfully jobless. How did they expect to afford this?

Stepping on to the platform, they approached a man shouting into a microphone, "Now boarding for Mantle!"

He extended his hand toward their group, waiting to receive their tickets but her aunts simply reached into their pockets and flashed their IDs at him.

Lola exchanged a glance with her friends, who were just as taken back as she was. The IDs were issued by the Alereis government and gave those within it access to almost anything. First the Council summons, now government-issued IDs? Lola filed both of these things in the back of her mind to think over later. The man studied the identification carefully before stepping aside and ushering the group inside the closest car.

The transit system was set up in a way that reminded Lola of a train. The car, or the large metal room, had a handful of people inside. There were no seats, just poles that connected the floor to the ceiling. She'd never ridden the transit before, but she had a decent idea of how it worked. Put together by magick in an attempt to replicate a Guardian's flashing ability, the transit was only used for long distance travel. The only reason it was so expensive was because of all the magick it took to make such a thing possible.

A voice boomed throughout the car, announcing that they'd be departing. Lola braced herself against the pole. She would've felt more comfortable with this teleportation thing if they were going down the street, not going to a different continent. The only bright side was that there weren't any oceans between Trin and Mantle.

The doors to the cars snapped shut and the room began to grow warm. A low hum erupted below her feet. Suddenly hit with a wave of dizziness, Lola's grip on the pole tightened. A weightlessness came over her body. In a panic, she looked down to see her hands dissipate into nothing. She shut her eyes but found herself suddenly falling forward. Paris grabbed her by the collar of her shirt, pulling her upright. Lola could see that the pole she was holding on to was now a few inches away.

Less than a second passed and it was already over.

If her stomach hadn't been flipped inside out, she would go complain to someone about the faulty design of this new car.

Looking around, it seemed she wasn't the only one disoriented. People all around her struggled to regain their composure. When the doors opened, the crowd exited with an urgency that even Lola felt.

"Are you okay?" Ken asked.

"Could we never get on that again?" she said, placing her hands on her knees as she inhaled large breaths. When her throat stopped feeling so tight, she stood carefully. Apparently feeling terribly sick was just part of the journey of getting to Mantle.

"It wasn't that bad," Erica said, who looked a lot better than Lola felt.

"Are you kidding?" Paris said stretching. "It felt like my whole body was being rearranged."

Erica's face looked troubled, but before Lola could complain some more, Kate called them from across the platform. Her and Andi were waiting by the exit.

The walk through the capital was just as Lola imagined it. Rows of plain brick townhouses stretched along the coastline. Monuments and military bases were large and prominent here. Lola heard this was the norm as no one even batted an eye when a hoard of Guardians ran drills throughout the streets. Mantle resided in the south, making the change from fall to spring jarring for her. The night air was humid and miserable. The time change was odd too. Even from someone who grew up in New York's nightlife, seeing this many people active so late felt almost wrong.

They finally arrived at a classy inn that—unsurprisingly at this point—the Council also arranged for them. They had three rooms. The pairs being, Lola and Erica, Paris and Ken, and Kate and Andi. Lola thought that if the Council was footing the bill, they could've at least given them private rooms, but she didn't bother to voice her complaints.

Once settled and unpacked, Ken and Paris made their way into her and Erica's room. It was the first time the group had been alone since yesterday afternoon. Paris lay across Erica's bed, debating on if she should sleep. While it was night time here, she still hadn't slept since they transitioned from mortal time.

"When do they want to see us again?" Paris asked.

"One," Lola answered. At that, Paris shut her eyes.

"Why do they need to see us anyway?" said Erica, pacing around the room. She always paced when she was nervous.

"We saw something we weren't supposed to and now they're doing damage control," Ken said simply. He sat in the chair in the corner, arms crossed.

"How did they even know that we were there?"

"They're under oath," Lola said. She was finally able to tell them all she had been thinking about the past day. Or did the new time zone mean it had been multiple days? She decided to stop thinking about it the moment her brain started hurting. "It must have been broken the minute we came in."

"But it's not like we know what they're under oath for," Ken pointed out.

"Yeah, but you saw those IDs," Lola said. "They work in the government. They're hiding something important and I think it has something to do with those murders."

As the idea turned over in her friends' minds, Paris said, "Those guys at the party said the Council hadn't made any statement about the deaths, maybe that was for a reason."

"No wonder they're in so much trouble," Ken said.

"No wonder *we're* in so much trouble," Erica pointed out. She fidgeted with the ends of her hair, running her fingers through the strands and tugging at them.

"Erica, relax. They're not gonna lock us up." He seemed to rethink this statement the moment he said it. "At least I think."

"Oh my God."

"Ken, stop talking," Paris mumbled into the pillow.

"Why would they arrest us? We didn't do anything wrong," Lola argued. "We were just there."

Paris sat up. "Everyone, relax. No one is getting arrested," she said, but even she didn't look too sure.

"Oh yeah, they'll just have us sign a magick NDA."

Paris pressed her lips together and rolled on to her back, staring at the ceiling. Over the next few hours, they let their thoughts run wild until Kate and Andi knocked on the door. It was time to see the Council.

The Themis Court was huge. Lola had never seen it up close. It was practically a palace. The towering building comprised of stone, brick, and marble was split into two wings that stretched for acres. Through the black gates, there was a large driveway, wrapping around a fountain that might as well have been a pond. The Council lived and worked here with hundreds of staff, government workers, and members of the Guard. It was the heart of Alereis.

Kate and Andi seemed confident in where they were going. They took several doors and turns with ease. No one stopped them or offered their assistance. Lola wondered how many times they had been here.

The group ended up at a door in a lone hallway and Kate knocked. Could you just knock at the Council's door? Lola wondered.

Kate carried the black case the girls had seen in the basement. The one with the black vials. Opening the door was not the Council, but a man with dark skin dressed in a pinstripe suit. He looked her aunts up and down. "I hear you got summoned," the man said. He seemed amused with the idea.

Kate raised an eyebrow. "From who?" she asked.

The man shrugged. "Around," he said. "So, what, are they calling you in to receive a medal or something?"

"We didn't come here to chat, Marcel," said Kate, utterly unimpressed with him. She held up the case. "We're just here to turn this in."

He rolled his eyes and snatched it away, bringing it into the office as they followed. Marcel sat the case on the desk and threw it open. The vials filled with black ooze were put neatly on display. He regarded each vial intently before looking back up at the aunts. "Wow, you went over the quota for the month and you're early. I must say that's dedication."

"Can you just mark us off so we can go?" Andi said.

"Will do," he said with the fakest smile Lola had ever seen on anyone. Kate was already turning away when he straightened up, closing the case. The smile dropped instantly with a conflicted look taking its place. He sighed. "Do you need any help?"

"No," Kate said without missing a beat. "I can handle it." She ushered the rest of the group out of the room and slammed the door shut behind them.

"Maybe we should let him help," Andi said as they continued down the hall. Kate shook her head without looking at her.

"No, the less people involved the better."

"What was that about?" Lola asked. She hadn't spoken to Kate since last night. "And what was in those vials?"

"Nothing you should be worrying about right now," Kate said. "We need to focus on making sure this meeting goes as smoothly as possible."

"And how do we do that?" Erica asked anxiously.

"By letting me do all the talking." She shot a look at Andi, who tensed. Two large double doors stood before them and Kate hesitantly placed her hands against them. With a sigh, she pushed forward and led them into the grand hall.

It was a dark room with rows of velvet seating and large crystal chandeliers above. The Council was the first thing in sight. At the end of the room, all six members were perched behind an elevated desk that resembled a judge's bench. Were they on trial? Lola wondered.

For the past three hundred years, after the dismantle of the Nightwalker monarchies, a Council member represented each of the races. Witches, Guardians, Vampires, Werewolves, Wizards, and Seers. Lola struggled to swallow down her unease as they walked down the aisle, slowly approaching the bench. The Council stared down at them, large and imposing like eagles gazing down on prey.

The Vampire seat holder, Alexandria Bale, addressed them. "Kate, Andrea." Alexandria had pale skin and silky black hair that was pushed neatly behind her ears. She wore a plum dress that was otherwise simple beside the black string that laced up the bodice. Her focus was zeroed on Kate and Andi. Her blue eyes piercing and disapproving.

"Councilor," they greeted her. Andi avoided eye contact while Kate's composure stayed as sharp as Alexandria's.

"I wish we were meeting under better circumstances," Alexandria said. "I assume you know why you're here?"

Andi opened her mouth, but Kate went on before she could get a word out. "We don't actually," she said firmly. This was a tactic Lola was familiar with. Never confess to something you haven't been accused of yet. Alexandria raised an eyebrow and exchanged a look with the other Council members. "Would you be willing to explain?"

Liam Reed, the Wizard seat holder, slipped on his glasses and looked down at the document before him. The Council member was tan-skinned and dark-haired. "Does breaking your oath hold any significance to you?" he said, motioning to the four. He gave them a seething glare that made him look like a rat.

"I don't see how," Kate argued. "We haven't told anyone anything. This meeting alone has done more harm than either of us have."

Lola wondered if this would work. It was true that without the Council's message she wouldn't have guessed the severity of the situation her aunts were in. But she would still have questions. If it weren't for the Council, would her aunts have figured out a way to cover up what she had seen? Would she have believed them?

Brier Elliot slammed her hand down on the desk. Her brown hair was braided into a crown around her head and she was decorated in jewels. Lola might've considered her pretty if it didn't look like she wanted to eat them. "You held your own investigation and captured and interrogated a subject without our knowledge. That is not your job," the werewolf seat holder said.

Lola thought of the notepad down in the basement. It mentioned a subject. Had that been the man that attacked them? Had they documented his torture?

"With all due respect, I'm required to report my findings to my superior, which I have," Kate said. "It's not my fault they haven't reached you yet."

"Oh really?" Brier said. "And who have you been reporting to?"

"Marcel Gould," said Kate. Andi looked at her sister appalled. Lola stared silently, unsure how to feel herself. She hadn't expected that when Kate had refused Marcel's help it was so she could throw him under the bus.

"Andrea, is this true?" Liam asked.

Andi visibility swallowed like she had to force the words out. "Yes, councilor."

"We were simply gathering evidence to prove that these attacks in the Mortal Realm are worth your attention," Kate said.

Alexandria sighed, looking particularly bored as she rested her head in her hands. "Three murders, Kate. Three." She emphasized the number as if it was too insignificant to matter.

"It's not the quantity, it's the frequency, the brutality—"

The Vampire rolled her eyes. "Please, you saw worse within your first year here."

It was hard to say what unsettled Lola more. How disinterested Alexandria seemed to be in these deaths or how familiar she seemed to be with Kate.

"That's not the point," Kate said firmly. "I'm trying to do my job and you keep roadblocking me." Kate had to be insane. It was the only thing that made sense. Lola was certain you couldn't talk to a Council member like that. She prepared herself for the worst but the councilor simply cocked her head, amused.

"You're right, Kate, this isn't the point," said Alexandria. Kate clenched her jaw, her eyes hard. "While taking things into your own hands, the subject escaped and attacked you while your niece and her friends were present. Unintentional or not, that is absolutely unacceptable." It was clear Kate had lost them now.

"Agreed," said Liam, his voice brittle. "Let's move on with this. While this was a Council, as far as Lola could tell, the other members were only there to agree with Alexandria.

The Vampire continued, flipping aimlessly through the papers on her desk as she spoke. "Since this is your first offense, how about a one month suspension?" she said. While it was posed as a question, Lola knew it wasn't. "As for this lot, I propose that they be immediately drafted into the Inlander division."

Lola believed she must have heard the Councilor incorrectly. Did she expect them to not only enlist in the military but to join the Realm's personal Guard? She suspected her aunts did some government work for Alereis, but the Inlander division? Did that mean these were Warlock attacks after all?

For a moment, Kate's cool composure dropped, replaced with utter horror. If Alexandria's words didn't scare Lola, this certainly did. "Excuse me?" Kate said.

Her question was ignored as Brier addressed Alexandria, clenching her jaw. "Why go through all the trouble when we have so many other alternatives to deal with them?" she said.

"Agreed," Liam said.

Whatever these alternatives were, Lola was sure that she didn't want to find out. Was there anyone in this Council that she could appeal too? It seemed even the members that disagreed with Alexandria didn't have the groups best interest. There were three other members who hadn't spoken yet. Christina Blanchard, a Guardian, Zaria Herring, a Witch, and Tempest Swanson, a Seer. If anything, their silence as the meeting unfolded was louder than any objection.

Kate shook her head. "I don't understand," she said. Alexandria gave her a look that Lola could only describe as pity.

"We have a secrecy to uphold, Kate, we can't just have civilians walking around with what they know."

"Know? Know what? We don't understand half of what we saw," Paris said. The entire room turned its attention to her.

Kate looked like she wanted to strangle her but the Council didn't appear too concerned with her outburst.

Liam spoke up, "Doesn't matter, even the smallest bit of information can prove to be dangerous for us all. No exceptions."

Lola could see in her aunt's eyes that she was looking for anything she could argue with, but it was clear that nothing was going to stop this from happening. "There has to be something else you can do," Kate said.

"This isn't up to you, Kate," Alexandria said. She gestured to Lola and her friends. "This decision will be up to them."

Before Lola could ask about the decision they were making, Alexandria continued, "Honestly, Kate, I figured you'd be more grateful for such a small punishment, especially considering we haven't even gotten to your other offense." The councilor suddenly grew serious.

Kate took a step forward. "What other offense?" she said carefully.

"Bringing a hybrid across the border."

Confusion swept the room. The accusation was ridiculous, there were no hybrids with them. And as far as Lola was aware, none of them knew any hybrids. She was beginning to think that summons was some kind of setup. If they couldn't punish her aunts for accidentally breaking their oaths, they would punish them for crimes they hadn't even committed.

Kate scoffed, almost looking amused with the allegation. "What?"

"Don't play dumb," Brier sneered. "We have the blood sample on hand."

Kate still didn't look convinced. "Then you must've had a mix up."

Everything happened so fast. The letter opener left Alexandria's hand before Lola had even seen her reach for it. The object moved at frightening speed, heading straight for Erica's chest.

Erica let out a scream, squeezing her eyes shut and throwing her hands up.

Lola felt her body go cold. The letter opener stopped in midair. *No*, Lola thought as the dread crept throughout her entire being. This couldn't have been right.

Erica hesitantly opened her eyes. Realizing what she had done and that everyone was staring at her, she quickly dropped her hands, the letter opener dropping with them.

"No," Alexandria said, a smug look on her face. "I don't think there has been." She gazed down at a piece of paper in front of her. "Hm, Guardian and Seer blood. Interesting combination."

Guardian blood?

"You could've killed her!" Lola exclaimed, heart pounding in her chest. Her shock was mixed with utter horror. She felt violated on Erica's behalf. The blood test was meant to prove that Nightwalkers were passing the border. Who gave them the right to test her DNA like this?

Alexandria seemed to finally take note of her. Her eyes softened, almost like she had sympathy for her. "She shouldn't exist in the first place," she said. Lola stared at her in shock.

"And if you had been wrong?" Lola asked through gritted teeth, her surprise transforming into rage.

Alexandria gave her a half smile. "My dear, I am never wrong."

Alexandria had hurled a knife at her best friend's chest and had the nerve to pity her. Lola didn't care who this woman was. She didn't care that she was a councilor, didn't care that she was the face of the entire realm. None of that mattered, not anymore. One day, Lola would make sure that Alexandria Bale would regret having ever met her.

"Councilor, I swear—" Kate started.

"No need for an explanation, Kate, your punishment has already been made, we're quite through here. We expect an answer within the next week."

"We still need to speak with Miss..." Christina Blanchard, put in. Even though she was sitting down, Lola could tell that the councilor was a slender, tall woman. Her hair was an icy blonde, and her eyes were nearly black. She had been silent this entire time. Was there a sudden interest now that she believed Erica had Guardian blood?

"Erica," Erica whispered. "Erica Thompson."

"Why do you need to speak with her?" Andi asked, her voice low.

"To discuss her trial."

"Trial?" Lola exclaimed, the outrage pouring out of her.

"You all know the law," Alexandria explained. "Hybrids are strictly forbidden to exist. We need to deal with the situation accordingly."

There were no circumstances where Lola wanted Alexandria to deal with Erica. She looked over to her friend, only to find her shaking. Lola hated that the Council could see how much they were getting to her.

"I do know the law," Kate retorted, taking a step forward. "Meaning I know you can't put a minor on trial without parental consent."

Lola figured that would be the end of it. Humans were just as forbidden from crossing the border as hybrids. There was no chance the Council would consider getting in contact with Erica's parents. But Liam didn't look like he was through with them. He waved her aunt off and said, "An Alereis citizen is of legal age at sixteen."

"She's not an Alereis citizen," Kate said firmly. "She was born in the Mortal Realm and follows mortal law."

Liam started to argue, but Alexandria held up a hand to silence him. "She's right, she's a child," Alexandria said.

"A child who shouldn't exist," Liam urged. Lola wanted to smack him.

Alexandria directed her attention to Erica, eyes filled with curiosity. "How old are you dear?"

"Seventeen," Erica managed to say.

"And your date of birth?"

Oh no, Lola thought. *No, no, no, no…*

Erica hesitated.

"If you lie, we'll know," Alexandria said, her voice cold.

With a swallow, Erica's voice shook as she said, "October 20th."

And just like that, what seemed to be Erica's last chance, was ripped from underneath them. Alexandria smiled at Kate. "Now if I know my mortal law, this means we'll just have to wait a few days then, right?" she said. Her aunt stayed silent. "And since you're keen on being argumentative, Kate, you'll be in charge of her defense."

"Security! Separate them!" Tempest Swanson, the Seer seat holder said. As the Council descended from their benches, the room was flooded with six Guards. Three surrounded Erica while the others moved to escort the rest of the group—aside from Kate—out of the room. One of the guards grabbed Erica, shoving her forward.

Lola had enough. "Don't touch her!" she yelled, moving forward to push the guard away. Before she made contact, another guard intercepted her. He threw her over his shoulder like a sack of potatoes. She kicked and pounded her fists at him, but it was no use.

"Put her down," Ken said, reaching for her waist to try and pull her off. And when another guard came after him, Paris threw herself into the mix, jumping on to his back.

"Guys, stop!" Andi said.

All of the security made them a priority, quickly overpowering the group. As they were thrown out of the hearing room, Erica cast back a look of panic before the doors closed them off from each other.

CHAPTER EIGHTEEN
KATE

KATE KNEW SHE WASN'T as concerned as she should have been. The hearing was a complete shit show. Everything that could have gone wrong, did. Her niece and her friends were now on schedule to become Inlanders—with one of them on schedule for execution if this trial went south. But even then Kate was unfazed. It all had to do with the fact she was assigned to be Erica's defense. If the Council's goal really was to kill this girl—which Kate didn't believe it was—they had made a terrible mistake.

Kate and Erica were escorted through the back door of the hearing room by the building's security. Through the back hallway and to the side was a small room with a desk, a bed, and a toilet in the corner.

This was the holding room, which was one step above a jail cell.

When she placed a hand on Erica's shoulder, the girl jumped at the contact. Once the last guard left, she guided her to the bed and took a seat beside her. "It's going to be ok," Kate said.

Erica put her head in her hands. "How can you say that?" she said, her voice breaking. Tears leaked through her fingers and on to the floor. "I didn't know this would happen—"

Kate shushed her. "I'm going to get you all out of here," she promised. She didn't believe the sentiment comforted the girl, but that didn't matter. Kate had already sworn to herself that she would keep her word. It was her fault they were in this position after all.

"How?" Erica asked.

None of them had known Erica was a hybrid, not even Erica herself. While that may have explained them bringing her across the border, it didn't explain why she deserved to live. Kate had worked under the Council for the majority of her life. She knew how they thought. Moving them with emotion wouldn't work, they wanted practical reasons to keep her around. All that was left for Kate to do was think of some.

She left Erica to her own devices, hearing sobs as soon as she shut the door.

Kate knew she was being too hopeful, because not a moment later she ran into Aria Hart.

"Hallows," Aria greeted her. The woman had a pale complexion and short pale hair to match. Aria wasn't particularly tall or imposing, but she was muscular. A lot of Nightwalkers were naturally strong, but Aria made it a point to show off her strength. Today she wore a sleeveless silk dress shirt that left her arms on display for all to see. Between that and her broad shoulders, the woman took up more space than she was worth.

"General Hart, what are you doing here?" she asked. Whenever Kate saw Aria, it was sure to be a horrible day.

This was proved true when Aria said, "I have orders to start scheduling an interrogation with some hybrid abomination that's made its way over here."

"They sent you?" Kate said. "Surely the general has more pressing things to attend to than some girl."

Aria smiled cooly, her pale green eyes twinkling in amusement. "I do, but you can imagine my curiosity once I heard your name attached."

Of course she did. Kate didn't know when it had happened or what she had done, but for as long as she could remember, Aria hated her. At first it had flattered Kate that someone with so much power was threatened by her. Even before becoming General of the Alereian military, the Harts were already a prestigious family. They came from a long line of Huntresses, with Aria also going to become the head of their division in the Guard. Huntresses were assassins, though Kate supposed their official term was special operatives. Either way, all of those women were elite killers, blessed with strength and skill from the Goddess to carry out her mission in the name of the Realm.

At least, that's what they wanted everyone to think.

After getting to know Aria over the years however, she had become a lot less threatening and more of a nuisance than anything.

"Honestly, Kate, I figured even the likes of you would keep better company."

"She's just a child, Aria," Kate said, but appealing to the general's good nature required her to have one first.

"Yes, and I'll make sure to make that child squirm," she said. "Just for you."

The General walked away, leaving Kate fuming. The summons had ended only moments ago and there were plenty of officials qualified to handle the interrogation. Everything had already been set in motion before they had even arrived. And Aria Hart had been hand selected just to make Kate's job a nightmare.

She marched her way to Alexandria's private office. She found her way easily and no one stopped her from coming in, they all knew who she was.

The office reflected Alexandria perfectly. It was a dark space composed of browns, blacks, and deep reds. Everything was neatly in its place, not a speck of dust or disarray in sight.

"Are you doing this because of me?" Kate asked.

"Hm?" Alexandria looked up from her desk, eyebrow raised.

"Are you doing this because I rejected the position you offered?"

Alexandria let out a small laugh. "Do you think I'm that petty?" Kate did. It wasn't unusual in the slightest. The Councilor didn't express their displeasure with words but with action. Kate had years of experience under in the warm light of her support as well as the cold scrutiny of her disappointment. "You reject every position I offer you."

Not only had none of those positions interested her, but it was clear to Kate that no matter where Alexandria put her, she would be doing more work as an Inlander than anywhere else. Of course, that made her an oddity to the rest of the Guard. She was probably the only person to have ever volunteered to be demoted, but no one needed to understand Kate's reasoning but her.

"Councilor, I'm serious," Kate said.

"Alex," she insisted.

"Alexandria," Kate said instead.

The Council member sighed. "No Hallows, this isn't about you," she said. "You know the law as well as I do. You'll have to answer for what you've done just like everyone else."

"I know that, but these children—"

"Will learn early that these are the cards that are dealt within the Guard. They will either thrive like you did, or crumble through their own merit," Alexandria said. "I look forward to seeing how you convince me to spare this girl's life."

Kate looked forward to it too.

CHAPTER NINETEEN
LOLA

"YOU'RE LUCKY THEY DIDN'T add 'assault of Council security' to the list of charges," Andi said.

"Well at least I didn't just stand there while they took Erica," Lola sneered. She saw a look of hurt flash across Andi's face. After being thrown out of the hearing room, her aunt had ushered the group into Marcel's office. Lola couldn't wrap her head around everything that had just happened. Erica was a hybrid. Half Guardian, half Seer. It didn't make sense. Or maybe she didn't want it to make sense. Lola had always thought Erica had an athletic figure, it seemed to have more to do with genetics than she thought. She seemed to have no reaction to the transit system either. Was it because flashing was natural to her? Even her height, which Guardians were infamously known for, was suddenly a dead giveaway.

Lola thought of Erica, abandoned on the side of the road as a baby. Her parents knew the consequences and now Erica would pay for them years later. Her leg bounced in place. She couldn't just sit here, not while they had Erica. "I don't understand," she said. "We've brought Erica across the border before with no problems."

"We didn't have a Council summons then. They take security very seriously for visitors." Andi drew in a heavy breath. "I'm gonna go check on them," she said, turning to Marcel and then motioning to the three of them. "Watch them please?" He nodded.

Once again they were being monitored.

Marcel's office was a decent size. His L-shaped, walnut desk was pushed in the corner and square leather seating was against the wall. Plaques lined the walls, all awarded to Marcel for being the top performer in his department. When Andi was gone, Lola asked, "So, how long have you worked with my aunts?"

"I wasn't aware watching would also involve talking," Marcel said.

"Well, now you're aware," Paris said. She left her seat and stood over him

Marcel's eyes stayed on his desk, refusing to be intimidated by Paris or to even make eye contact with any of them. "Not my place," he said.

"It's not like you're not already involved," Ken said suddenly. Marcel gave him a side glance.

"What's that supposed to mean?"

Ken shrugged, letting the implication hang in the air. Lola was surprised, this was so unlike him. There were many words she'd used to describe Ken, but manipulative was not one of them. Marcel made a disapproving sound with his teeth but answered. "Andrea has only been here for about six years," he said uncertainly. "But I've known Kate since we were in college."

Lola nearly shot from her seat. Kate had spent decades in this world, spent decades lying to her family. It made sense considering all she had seen today, but the confirmation was staggering. It only gave her more questions. "Oh my God," she said.

"I feel like you should be having this conversation with them," he said warily.

"And I feel like if they really wanted me to know they would've," she said "So, she's been an Inlander for years then?"

Her aunts being Inlanders was the only thing that made sense to her. There was no other position in the Guard that they could hold. But so many things still didn't add up. The man who attacked them definitely wasn't a Warlock, and that's who Inlanders dealt with, wasn't it?

"I didn't say that," Marcel said firmly. Maybe it was for the sake of his own oath. "Gods, if that were true, maybe she'd be a little better at taking direction."

"What's that supposed to mean?" Lola asked. Even after everything that had happened, for some reason she still felt the need to defend her aunts. Considering Kate's response during the summons and the plaques on Marcel's wall, he was clearly her superior in some way.

"Kate's done a couple of different things. She was head of public affairs for a time, Alexandria's assistant for another. She's not used to being down here with us little people."

"Assistant?" Lola exclaimed. She knew she hadn't imagined it. Kate and Alexandria knew each other. The familiarity even more disturbing now that she knew the context behind it. Her aunt didn't just work in the government, she worked under the most powerful woman in the Realm. The contempt in Marcel's voice now made sense. He believed Kate thought she was too good to work under him. "When was this?"

Marcel shook his head. "Aht aht, I've said enough," he said. "Now, tell me how I'm involved in whatever it is your aunties have dragged you into."

Staying true to his word, Ken relayed the events of the meeting to Marcel, whose reaction was exactly what Lola was expecting. "That backstabbing viper," he cursed. As if on cue Andi entered the room with Kate in tow. Lola got to her feet. "Where's Erica?" Lola asked.

"She's in a holding room," said Kate, her voice flat.

"Holding room?" Ken repeated in disgust. Lola imagined Erica in a dusty cell, devoid of light and any other living thing. She'd go crazy in there.

Kate cast a quick glance at Marcel. "Let's not talk about this here," she said.

"Holding room for what?" Paris asked, her voice firm. Marcel leaned forward, propping himself up on his desk. Was he enjoying this?

Kate sighed. "To keep her until her birthday."

"So, we're just going to leave her?" Ken said.

"We don't have a choice."

"Bullshit," Lola said.

Kate raised an eyebrow at her, almost daring her to continue. "Excuse me?"

"Use your connections, pull some strings, do something!" Lola said.

"And who exactly told you I had connections?" Kate asked, an edge to her voice that could cut ice. She looked at Marcel again, who shrugged.

"Please," she begged. "You can't leave her there alone."

"It's just for two days, and as soon as they're over, I will do everything within my power to get her home," Kate said. She sounded so certain that Lola almost trusted it.

"You better," Paris said, her voice low and eyes level with Kate's.

"Paris," Lola said uneasily, but her friend ignored her, keeping her attention on Kate and Andi.

"I don't know what you two have just dragged us into, but if any harm comes to any of them—"

"It won't," Andi answered quickly. Kate didn't seem interested in rebuttals, in false promises.

"You don't know that," Paris said firmly. "But do you know what I know? I know that we wouldn't be in this situation if you hadn't kept that thing in your basement."

Marcel gasped. "Kate, you didn't." The disapproval was clear in his voice. Kate didn't respond, keeping her eyes locked with Paris.

"If anything happens to Erica, it's going to be your fault," Paris said. Lola winced even though none of this was directed at her. "You do understand that, right?"

"I understand," Kate said. Nothing about her aunt's face betrayed what she was thinking. It managed to make Lola angry. How could she be so calm and composed when Erica's life was on the line?

"Good," Paris said, taking a seat. "Just making sure we're on the same page, because if you don't do something to fix this, I will."

An uncomfortable silence rang through the air as Paris' words cut through. It was times like this where Lola had forgotten that Paris wasn't just her friend. Sure, when they were alone, they could laugh and joke together, but the rest of the world didn't have the luxury of seeing that side of her. Her Paris wasn't here. Right now, all there was was the centuries old Vampire who was not to be trifled with.

Her hand gripped the leather armrest hard. It was like she needed to anchor herself to the chair to keep herself from leaping across the room. Lola didn't know what Paris expected to do, but the coldness on her face told her that she intended to follow through on every word. Nothing was out of the realm of possibility. And it was scary.

Ken was the first to break the silence. "So, what happens now?"

"You decide," Andi said, and somehow an even greater tension rippled through the room.

"Decide? Just like that?"

Paris scoffed. "At this point I don't even know what an Inlander does, and now you want me to decide if I want to be one for the rest of my life?" Neither Kate or Andi questioned or denied their conclusion that the two were Inlanders. Lola supposed this meant the time for secrets was over.

"That's just how it is. We can't tell you anything unless you're drafted," Andi confirmed.

"It's true," Kate explained. "No one ever knows what they're truly getting into. You're either drafted or you're naive enough to volunteer."

Marcel snickered at that, which left Lola confused. It didn't seem like this was something her aunts had signed up for either. There was so much she wanted to ask. Twenty years was a long time; what had Marcel managed to learn about Kate? If her aunt had worked here for so long, then why didn't she ever talk about it? And what had brought Andi to join recently?

Then there was another thing Lola didn't quite get. While the Guard certainly wasn't the low-class position Marcel had made it out to be, Kate was once Alexandria's right hand. What was worth leaving all that power behind?

"And what if we don't want to be drafted?" Ken asked. "What happens then?"

"There's a spell—"

"Very experimental!" Marcel chimed in from his desk. For someone who was cursing her name mere moments ago, Lola noticed the way he looked at Kate with gleeful amusement in his eyes. She wondered if there was something else there. Surely in twenty years he'd be able to pick up that Kate was a lesbian.

"Yes, experimental," said Kate, who shot him a glare. "If it works, you'll have no memory of yesterday."

Lola looked at her aunt in confusion. Memory manipulation was something only Vampires were capable of, it was the reason Erica's parents thought she was on a senior trip right now. How long had the Council been trying to replicate this? "How experimental is this exactly?"

"It's fairly recent," Kate said. "But it has been successful."

"That's our alternative?" Ken shook his head.

"What kind of choice is that?" Paris said, crossing her arms.

"But if it does work," Andi interjected. "You'll be able to go back to your lives like none of this ever happened."

The statement hung in the air. Lola looked down at her hands. Two options. One that would change their lives forever and the other that would set everything back to normal. Two options and one week to make their decision.

CHAPTER TWENTY
LOLA

Erica's absence was felt the hardest on the way back to the inn. If she were here, Lola had no doubt her mind would be at work. Theorizing and bouncing ideas off the rest of them until they could plan their next move. But the journey back was quiet. No one wanted to talk about what had just happened.

Her shared room with Erica was painfully empty. Even though they hadn't stayed in the room for long, Erica was notoriously messy and remnants of her littered the space.

Lola took a seat in the armchair by the window. She needed to breathe. She couldn't think of Erica as if she were already gone. There was still hope, still a chance she could make it back home.

A loud bang from outside made her jump. She peered back the curtains. The Themis Court was only a few minutes away from the inn. It was a destination hot spot in Alereis. The plaza around the capital, including its surrounding areas, were ripe with spots for tourists. While the summons had provided them rooms here for free, Lola couldn't imagine how expensive the inn was to any other visitor.

She scanned the plaza and found the source of the noise. Two carts had collided in the middle of the street. One was flipped over, its handler racing forward, trying to catch the trial of decorations that spilled along the road.

Decorations?

Lola checked the clock on the nightstand. It was 2:00 a.m. and the crowds outside were busier than ever.

Had the meeting truly been over that quickly? Erica was taken from her in less than an hour? She didn't think she'd ever get used to this. The passage of day, the movement of the sun, it made time progress. But night was everlasting, continuous darkness you couldn't find your way out of. There was no point in sleeping but even then Lola doubted she'd be able to.

Instead, she went to Ken and Paris' room.

Ken opened the door for her. He and Paris were still fully dressed, though Paris was laid across her bed, her eyes shut tight. Lola couldn't blame her, it had been nearly twenty-four hours since she last slept.

"Did you hear that crash?" Ken asked her.

"Yeah it was some sort of accident," Lola explained. "Think they're setting up for some kind of party."

"It's for the festival," Paris answered from the bed. It appeared she couldn't sleep either.

"Festival?"

Paris rolled on her side to face them. "They usually hold a festival leading up to Remembrance Day." The whole thing felt odd. The rest of the city was gearing up for a celebration while Erica's life hung in the balance. Ken grimaced, seeming to share her sentiment. "Great, something else to look forward to," she said, and peered into the room. "You guys heading to bed?"

"No, I'm exercising," said Paris, nestling herself into the pillow. Lola turned to Ken.

"I was going to look for something to eat," he said. "Do you want to come?"

A few minutes later, she found herself walking along the plaza with Ken at her side. Paris had already warned them that due to the festival, little Mortal food vendors would be available. Remembrance Day was a time where the Council and city leaders tried to decrease the visibility of anything Mortal related. As they walked, searching for anything that remotely resembled a burger, they passed stalls being built and lights being strung.

"Probably for the best," said Lola as they retreated to a park bench. There wasn't anything remotely human in sight, and she wasn't exactly in the mood to be adventurous. "I think I'm going to be sick."

There was a beat of silence before Ken said, "She's going to be okay."

"I know," Lola said quickly. "I mean, she has to be...I just..." She trailed off, fear and exhaustion mixing together and weighing her words down.

"Has your aunt Kate mentioned a game plan?"

Lola shook her head. "If she has one, it's not like she'd tell me." The bitterness in her voice was more obvious than she would've liked.

Ken nudged her. "We could always stick her in a room with Paris for a couple minutes," he said lightly. "I'm sure she'll come up with something." Ken looked over expectantly, like he was waiting for something, but Lola only stared, uncertain. "What? You think Kate could take Paris?"

"What are you doing?" she asked, hoping her question sounded genuine. Perhaps she'd been awake too long herself, because suddenly nothing made any sense to her.

Ken looked down. "Trying and apparently failing to cheer you up," he said, awkwardly rubbing the back of his neck. "I'm just going to blame that on the lack of burgers."

Lola wasn't sure how to respond. It was unlike Ken to joke at a time like this, and it was very unlike her not to join in. For as long as she could remember, she had always been the one to lighten the mood. It was an easy role to step into, expected even. She was the one who messed around, who started trouble for no good reason. She didn't take things seriously.

She didn't know the last time she had let someone see her so upset. It felt strange.

As her silence continued to fill the air, Ken laid a hand on her arm. But for some reason it wasn't comforting. She was hyper aware of his fingers grazing across her skin, giving her goosebumps. It was all she could think about. It took her a moment to breathe and regain her thoughts. "How could I bring her here?" she said finally.

"You couldn't have known."

"Couldn't I?" she argued. "We've known each other for years. How could I miss this?"

"This isn't your fault," Ken insisted, but Lola had trouble believing it. She had been the one to bring Erica into this world after all. The more she thought, the guiltier she felt.

"Did I ever tell you that she was found on the side of the road?" she said, recalling everything Erica had ever told her about her birth. "I always thought it was strange how she had ended up with human parents, but now..."

Ken caught on, filling in the blanks. "You think it was deliberate," he said slowly. "You think they were hiding her." It made sense, all things considered. Erica's birth parents would never have been able to take care of her, much less be seen with one another. They all knew the law. Different Alereians couldn't be together, that's just how it was. The only option left was to give Erica away, to give her her best chance in the Mortal world.

"And I just served her up to the Council."

Ken stood from the bench. "I'm not gonna sit here and listen to you blame yourself."

"So, you're gonna stand there and listen to me instead?" she wondered. Ken didn't find that funny.

"Do you want to know who's actually to blame?" he started. "The Council."

Lola quickly looked over her shoulder for any onlookers. "Keep your voice down." They were in the capital, there was no telling who was listening in.

Ken rolled his eyes. "It's true," he said, his voice lower this time. "That law...it's cruel."

She nodded in agreement. Her entire life she had been told that Alereian blood didn't mix well together. That it led to horrible outcomes and strange children. But Erica didn't fit the depiction in the slightest. She seemed perfectly fine. "Erica isn't dangerous," she said. "She doesn't deserve this."

"No one deserves to die because of the way they were born," Ken said firmly. Lola knew he wasn't talking about her, but she couldn't help but be affected by his words. For the past few hours, countless thoughts rushed through her head. How had Erica's situation slipped through the cracks? What part did her aunts play in all of this? Would Paris truly follow through on her threat? It was a useless cycle that never ended in any answers.

But with Ken, she realized, she never had to wonder. In a world of unknowns, it frightened her how well she knew him. The way he'd play with the strings of his hoodie when he was nervous, or the flick of his eyes when he was caught in a lie. Or how no matter how annoyed he claimed to be with her, the curve of his lips always gave him away.

Right now his body was rippling with tension, his jaw tight and hands clenched at his sides. She could see the frustration and passion in his eyes. She didn't have to explain her feelings to Ken because she could see them so clearly mirrored in front of her. "I like you better like this," she said suddenly. Ken's eyes widened in confusion and she quickly added, "I mean, I just like seeing you care about stuff."

"I don't usually care about stuff?" he said, taken aback.

"No, it's just...you're usually just a lot more nonchalant about it," she clarified.

Ken seemed uncomfortable, suddenly looking away from her. It was only then did Lola realize she had been staring at him.

"I care," he said, as if it was a definitive thing he needed her to accept. "Just because I don't say it much out loud doesn't mean I don't." He locked eyes with her. Lola's heart was racing but she couldn't find it in her to look away.

They left the park, continuing their walk in silence and coming across a bakery. Inside there were two small tables, already occupied by patrons. Two workers stood near the counter, chatting with one another in what Lola could only assume to be Lereis, the Alereian language. Lola didn't realize people still spoke it. But if there was any place she'd encounter a dead language it would be in Mantle.

"What are we doing in here?" Ken asked as she scanned the baked goods laid out in front of her. "I'm pretty sure you're not allowed sugar after midnight."

She rolled her eyes. "I'm not getting anything for myself," Lola said. Ken was right. It was pointless sitting around blaming herself, especially when there were still things she could do. It wouldn't fix everything, but she had to believe the smaller things still counted for something too.

CHAPTER TWENTY-ONE
ERICA

Erica often had the same dream. She was at a party, glittering dresses and blaring music surrounding her. At the top of the estate's staircase, a man tapped a spoon against a champagne flute, calling for a toast. The words were muffled as were most details in the dream. It was a hazy blur that felt like a memory she couldn't quite recall.

But the one clear thing in the room was always the fire.

There was a shout and the toast was stopped. Partygoers shoved past her, clambering for locked exits. The heat of the flames would be the last thing she felt before she woke up. The dream never changed, always ending at the same point. But there was the inkling of something more right beneath the surface, she just couldn't get to it.

Erica already knew it was Kate at her door that evening. No one else was allowed to visit her. The woman came every morning and night for the past two days. Still not used to the night schedule, Erica had managed to catch each check in. But it wasn't like it mattered whether she adjusted or not, she barely slept these days, and when she did it was plagued by nightmares.

The victims from her visions would haunt her. She would relive their deaths, no longer as a humble observer but an active participant. Erica would assist their murderers, holding the women down as they kicked and screamed. Then the scene would change. Erica would find herself in the victims place, being ripped into and apart. She would wake up wondering if that's what the Council planned to do to her.

On the night of her birthday, Kate brought her a dozen cupcakes, courtesy of Lola. The bakeries in Mantle didn't supply her favorite, red velvet. But even though the flavor was odd, and she was trapped, a world away from her family, knowing that Lola went out of her way to get these made Erica sob.

She was nine when she met Lola. The two were paired together for a project at school and became best friends the way all kids did. Lola declared it one day and Erica had just gone along with it. It took Erica a couple months to decide for herself that she made a good decision. It wasn't like she had many friends before Lola. She enjoyed the company, even found herself getting attached to the girl. But even at nine, Erica knew attachment would do her no good. The little voice in her head had awakened, telling her that she needed to stay away from Lola, that she'd end up hurting her somehow.

The moment she decided to listen is when she got the premonition. She saw Lola and her dad in their car. A speeding red rover came behind them and smashed into the bumper. The premonition cut off before she could see the aftermath. As Erica had gotten older, her premonitions had gone from short flashes to fully played out scenes. She couldn't decide whether one was worse than the other.

After school the next day, Erica begged her friend not to drive home that evening, but Lola refused to listen until she explained herself.

"Sometimes I can see things," Erica had confessed. "I see things happen before they actually do. I saw you get in a car accident."

She waited for Lola to call her crazy, to walk away and get in the car anyway, but instead, she looked at her and said, "You're a Seer?"

"A what?" She had heard the word psychic on TV before, but never Seer.

"A Seer," Lola said again. "You can see the future right?"

Erica's confusion had made Lola hesitant to say more. She demanded proof that Erica was special. Erica knew a quick way to do that was to let Lola get in that car, but she didn't dare.

An idea struck her. She grabbed a rock from the ground and cut her finger with it. Lola looked at her with wild eyes, but didn't stop her. Erica winced as the rock scraped her skin but she didn't care. Her blood—her weird, silver blood would convince Lola.

A single drop pooled at the tip of her finger and her friend stared. But soon that stare turned into a huge grin. "I've never met another Nightwalker my age before," she exclaimed. "This is perfect!"

Another? Erica had thought. She didn't know what a Nightwalker was, but Lola made it sound like they were the same. Like she wasn't alone. "What are you?" Erica asked.

"I'm a Witch," Lola said proudly.

"You're lying," Erica said. With what she could do, it was surprising she was still as skeptical as ever.

"Nuh uh," Lola said, taking the rock from her and cutting her own finger. Silver blood dripped from it. Erica stood in awe.

"Look," Lola said, displaying their bleeding fingers side by side. "You're just like me."

Just like me. The words rang through Erica's head now. She wasn't just like her, not by a long shot.

When Erica had envisioned her eighteenth birthday, her parents had always been a part of the picture. They would wake her up with gifts and serve her arroz caldo like they had every year. But today she was in Alereis, being escorted to her interrogation with nothing but toast for breakfast. Kate didn't say much, but Erica supposed she didn't need to. Last night she went over the preparations for today.

She explained that today would primarily act as a test. Erica had always been a good test taker. She had a borderline photographic memory that had gotten her through school this far. It helped that she was naturally curious, a trait that drew her to wanting to be an engineer—to learn how things worked and why they did. But knowledge wouldn't be her friend here, only incriminate her further. So, when Kate's advice had urged her to play to her ignorance, Erica fought everything within her to go along with it.

Themis Court security flanked them as they reached the interrogation room. Kate stood by, waiting for Erica to enter. She would be on her own from here.

She took a deep breath then stepped into hell.

The interrogation room was empty aside from a long table and three chairs. It was low lit, either for ambiance or because they didn't need much light. A woman, who Kate described as the General, and a man Erica didn't recognize, sat on one side. Having a General oversee her interrogation shot a fear so chilling into Erica that it almost paralyzed her. It was clear the Council already made their minds up about her. Why even do all of this?

Erica didn't realize she still stood by the door until the man ushered for her to sit down.

She complied, her knee hitting the bottom of the table as she bounced it up and down. "Ms. Thompson, I'm Mr. Aaron Mathis and this is General Aria Hart," he said. "We'll be evaluating you today."

"Evaluating?" Erica said. Is that what they were calling this?

"Yes, we'll be evaluating your background and your behavior to ensure you're not a danger to yourself and others."

Erica had heard of this just like all the other Alereian horror stories. Hybrids were forbidden with good reason. She had seen the disfigurement in pictures, seen how wrong things could go. Human DNA didn't matter, the Alereian blood always came out on top. Hybrids were the opposite. It wasn't a harmonious union, but a collision of species, each fighting for dominance over the other. Sometimes that inner fight led to outer violence.

While Erica herself had never experienced this, it was apparent enough for all hybrids to get an immediate death order.

"Let's start with your parentage," Mr. Mathis said.

"What about them?"

"Who are they? Where are they?"

"I don't know," Erica said, immediately knowing who they were talking about. Her human parents may as well have not existed according to the people here. "I don't know anything about my bio parents."

"Never got curious? Never went digging?"

She shook her head. If she was being honest, it was one of the few things she had never been curious about. Erica never understood why people were so surprised when adopted kids had no interest in their biological parents. Her adoptive parents had given her home while her "real" ones had abandoned her on the side of the road.

Of course, now things were more complicated. It looked like her bio parents abandoned her, either for her own safety or for theirs. And could Erica really blame them after what she was going through right now?

"That's a shame," said General Hart. "And what of your adoptive parents?"

"They're human," she explained and watched as the two exchanged a look. "I didn't even know what I was until a few years ago."

More than a few, but Kate did say to play up her ignorance.

"You were raised human?" General Hart asked, a hint of discomfort in her voice. Erica nodded, figuring that her life must sound like the General's worst nightmare. After a few more questions about her life, the General said something that surprised her. "What is your relationship to Kate Hallows?"

"Uh, she's my friend's aunt," Erica said.

"And before this trip, were you fairly familiar with her?"

"I guess."

"And yet she didn't manage to pick up on your nature?" she said.

"No?" Erica wasn't completely sure how to answer. She didn't want to make Kate look bad, none of them had known what she was.

But what did that matter now? Kate explained that they would all be questioned, just being associated with her was a crime in itself, but bringing her across the border? It was an insult to the law. If they couldn't prove their ignorance, they could be executed right along with her.

God, what was wrong with her? How horrible did someone have to be to do this to people she supposedly loved? How could she drag them into this and watch as they were punished for it.

She wondered if Aria and Aaron could tell what she was thinking, if they could feel the anxiety dripping off her.

"I only ask because she's been pretty adamant about you," Aria continued. "She put together a plea deal rather quickly. Has she told you about it?"

Erica shook her head.

"Well, she thinks you're worth a lot more than you are, especially to the Guard," she said. "Are you aware of Mr. Mathias' position?"

"No," Erica said, her mouth dry. The General sighed. Why had Kate told her to play dumb? She could feel their opinion of her depleting by the second.

"I'm the head of the Guardian division," he explained. The Realm had its military, but it also had the Guard, which acted as its special forces. It was broken into three divisions; Inlander, Huntress, and Guardian. "Guardian numbers haven't been as high as I would like, especially this recent year. So many young people are defecting out of their duty, but perhaps you can change that."

"Me?" Erica asked. She thought of the Guardian who had been murdered. Perhaps the numbers were depleting for a good reason.

"Don't be too flattered," General Hart said quickly, her green eyes narrowing.

"Kate suggests you be allowed to live as a Guardian," Mr. Mathias said. "She believes the best way to test you is to see your commitment to the cause."

"Personally, I don't think you have what it takes," the General said.

That was because she didn't. She didn't have what it takes and didn't know why Kate thought differently. Guardians were protectors, warriors—Erica had no fight in her.

"That's yet to be seen. Perhaps Kate's confidence in her shouldn't be taken lightly," Mr. Mathias said to Aria.

The General wore a pinched expression. "Hallows is desperate, that's what she is."

"What are you talking about?" Erica asked.

"Well, she's offered up her own niece to be your charge," Aaron said.

Lola? Her charge? This whole encounter was becoming more confusing by the minute. She had spent the entire meeting showing how ignorant, how incapable she was, and now Kate wanted her to prove her worth as a Guardian? Erica couldn't protect Lola, she couldn't even protect herself.

"But I have no experience," Erica pointed out. "You're just gonna give me a charge?"

"Thompson," Aria addressed her, no formalities attached. "Do you know what a Huntress does? I was put on this very earth to eliminate monstrosities such as yourself. I have no qualms putting an Alereian life in your hands because you would be dead before any harm could befall her."

Erica avoided her eyes, their cold indifference making her heart race and mouth dry. Erica had thought Aria would feel some sort of cruel satisfaction from her death. But the truth, that she wouldn't feel anything at all, was far more frightening. She had a clear image of the general now. In her mind, killing Erica would be the same as squatting a fly. Causal and insignificant. This was all a job to her, and Erica another task to carry out.

"Precisely," Mr. Mathias agreed, which shocked her. What Erica had believed to be kindness was simply common courtesy. Aaron thought she was just as obscene as Aria did. "While it will take some work, I do believe we can shape you into an upstanding citizen, Ms. Thompson."

Kate's goal suddenly became so clear. She wouldn't be allowed to be Erica here. Not the human she pretended to be with her parents, not the Seer she pretended to be with her friends, and not the Hybrid she actually was. All she was allowed to be was an empty vessel for them to shape and mold. Erica didn't know what the rest of her life would entail if she took this deal, if it would even be a life at all. But she didn't need a vision to see herself being broken apart and put back together into something unrecognizable.

Would she like this new person? Would they be better?

"And besides, once your peers are drafted—which we assume they will be—you'll act as an Inlander alongside them," Mr. Mathias explained. "That should give you decent enough experience."

"Should you choose to accept the deal, it will greatly influence the decision at your trial later tonight," General Hart mentioned.

It was a threat disguised as a choice. That's how Erica saw it. Take the deal or meet her end.

Mr. Mathias met her eye. "Whether it was your mother or your father, your existence is evidence of how far they strayed from their mission. A true Guardian does not put their duty on hold to fulfill their own desires," he said. "You see where that got your parents. It will do you well not to make the same mistake."

CHAPTER TWENTY-TWO
LOLA

Lola knew the Council couldn't possibly put together a trial so quickly unless they already had their answer. After her own questioning, she walked with her friends and Andi to the hearing room. The four of them had been split up and interviewed individually, all the questions about Erica.

Lola was questioned by two semi-important people whose names she had already forgotten. They asked how long she and Erica had been friends, if she knew Erica was a hybrid—obvious things she knew the answer to. Andi had informed her that friend's interrogation was carried out by the General herself. All Lola could hope for is that they hadn't harmed her.

Kate and Erica were already inside when they entered the room, along with the General, a man she didn't recognize, and the two who interviewed her. Lola figured the small size was due to them wanting to keep Erica's situation a secret. She nudged Paris. "Who's that?" she whispered.

"Aaron Mathis, head of the Guardian division," Paris explained, her face grim.

Ken looked startled. "Two Inquiry members here?" he said. Andi didn't say anything but she looked just as surprised. The entire Council and two leaders of the Alereian special forces were here. It was them against the most powerful people in the Realm.

She watched Erica as they took their seats. Her eyes were down, fidgeting with her hands in her lap. Even if she could talk to her, Lola wasn't sure there was anything she could say that could calm her nerves. For the past few days, Lola could only imagine what horrors she had experienced on her own. But from the outside, she looked well kept. No marks or bruises coated her skin and she seemed clean and well fed. While it was the bare minimum, it gave Lola some relief. No irreversible damage seemed to be done. If they all made it out of here alive, could they return home and pretend this had all been a bad dream?

The Council entered from the side door and she felt a spike of fear in her own chest. She would soon have her answer.

"Let's get started," Alexandria said once the group reached the podium. "Today we will be determining the fate of Erica Thompson, who will either be released or scheduled for execution immediately."

"General, based on your assessment, are there any other questions you'd like to ask Ms. Thompson before we make our decision?" Liam said.

"Yes actually," she said, walking over to Erica. Lola could see her aunt Kate clench her jaw. "Ms. Thompson, how old were you when you first started developing your powers?"

"Uh, around five?" Erica said. She phrased it with uncertainty, but Lola knew Erica remembered nearly everything.

"And would you say you have a firm grasp on them by now?" the General asked.

Erica tensed. "What do you mean?"

"In practice, do you have a firm grasp of your abilities?"

"I mean, it's not exactly something I can practice," Erica said. "When I get visions, they're usually random—"

"Random?" she repeated, making sure to meet the Council's eyes. "Meaning you have no control over them, yes?"

"That's not—" Erica began, but Kate cut her off.

"It's not exactly like she has many people to learn from General," she said dryly. "I'm sure you're aware that Seers are hard to come by."

"Kate has a point," Brier said, though she seemed disappointed to be agreeing. "Your report did confirm that the girl was raised human on top of that. There's not much to be done there."

The General fought back a scowl. "I'm simply noting the unpredictability present," she said pivoting. "But this does lead me to my next question. I notice, Ms. Thompson, that you only seem to refer to your Seer half, does this mean your gifts on your Guardian half hadn't developed until a few days ago?" Erica went incredibly pale, her silence became the loudest thing in the room. Aria took note of this and continued, "Because I find it very odd that in eighteen years they never manifested, especially considering how early your other ones came in."

Kate quickly interjected, "Didn't you just talk about unpredictability, Aria? Who's to say Hybrids get their powers the way everyone else does?"

"Kate, let the girl speak for herself," the General said, taking a threatening step toward Erica. "Erica Thompson, did you or did you not, know about your nature prior to your hearing with the Council?"

"T-that's a lot more complicated than—" Erica started.

"It's a yes or no question," Aria said sternly.

"Answer the question, Ms. Thompson," said Alexandria.

Erica's leg bounced so hard under the table it was practically vibrating. "Y-yes. Yes, I knew," Erica said. "But that's not—"

"And you came across the border anyway. Which I'm sure you're aware is an act of treason," Aria said, her voice was disappointing, but the victory was clear on her face. "Those are all my questions."

Brier pursed her lips. "We'll be taking the next ten minutes to make our decision."

As the Council dispersed and Aria took her seat, Lola stared straight ahead.

Erica knew. Lola didn't know when or for how long, but she'd known and hadn't said a word.

Erica was her best friend. The only explanation Lola could think of was that she had done something to make her hide these powers. She tried to picture herself in Erica's place—to discover all of this on her own—how scary it all sounded.

Erica wouldn't look at her—wouldn't look at any of them. Even from here, Lola could see the erratic rise and fall of her chest.

Was this the information that would damn them all? There was no telling what would happen after the decision was made. Would they take Erica away? Would they kill her right in front of them? Lola didn't think she could bear it if this was her last memory of Erica. Her head held down—shying away not just from the world, but from them too. What would she do if she never saw her face again?

Paris leaned forward. "Don't you have some sort of counter defense?" she hissed.

Kate shook her head. "No, we're done here."

Her friend's hands clenched into fists at her sides. Lola had a feeling that if they weren't in public, Paris would've jumped over the chair and attacked Kate right then.

"Done?" Ken said, appalled. "You barely tried!"

Kate narrowed her eyes, but turned back around without a word.

That couldn't be it, could it? General Hart had a right to be smug, she had gotten an admission of guilt. Erica's innocence, her survival, it was tied to her deniability. Accidents could be forgiven, but if Erica knew she was breaking the law, she was all but doomed. Lola's mind raced with possibilities.

In one scenario, they fought off the Council then and there. In another, she used her magick to cause some sort of distraction to escape right before the verdict. Then in another, they would wait before the execution to sneak into Erica's holding room and break her out.

But in every instance, the end result remained the same. And if she couldn't get Erica home in her wildest dreams, what chance did she have in reality? So, instead of fighting the helplessness she felt, Lola sat there paralyzed, waiting as the minutes ticked by. Each one more painstakingly slow than the next.

As if on cue, the Council returned to their bench. They had taken ten minutes to decide if Erica should live or die. Ten minutes was what they thought she deserved. "We've reached a decision," Liam said. Erica kept her head down.

Lola's heart was hammering so hard she could feel it in her ears. Her hand seemed to slip into Ken's. His was slick with sweat but she squeezed it tight anyways. Time slowed. The hearing room was so silent that every creak of moment or shuffle of papers echoed throughout the room.

All eyes in the room were trained on Alexandria, waiting with bated breath for her decision, because in truth, Lola knew it all came down to her. "Ms. Hallows," Alexandria addressed her. Kate stood and faced the Council, her eyes locked with Alexandria's. "The terms of your plea deal are fair. We agree to let Ms. Thompson go."

Erica's head snapped up. Lola felt the massive weight in her chest finally give out. "Yes!" she yelled out, not caring about the odd looks she got. Nothing else mattered. Erica was going home.

Aria rolled her eyes and began packing up her things as Kate approached the desk. "Thank you, Councilors," she said. Satisfaction from the victory couldn't be seen on Kate's face, just the same cool expression she always wore.

Alexandria looked at Erica, eyes narrow. "Do not make us regret our decision, Ms. Thompson," she said, her voice had a quiet edge to it. Just as quickly as it came, her expression changed to something more pleasant. "Case dismissed. See you all at the Remembrance Ball."

CHAPTER TWENTY-THREE
PARIS

Paris had never been so upset to shop in her entire life. Earlier in the evening, she, Lola, and Erica were accompanied by Andi to a local boutique to shop for the Remembrance Ball, one of the most high-class events in the Realm. According to Andi, wearing Alereian styles would show as a sign of respect.

Spring in Mantle meant cool, lightweight fabrics. It meant deep shades of color and flowing silhouettes. The dress Paris had picked was a midnight blue that shimmered under light. It was floor length, with lace sleeves and a sweetheart neckline. She hated how good she looked in it. She hated that she had to spend the rest of her night dressed up to put on a performance for The Council.

Paris sat on Lola's bed before the event, braiding the girl's hair. "Keep your head straight," Paris scolded her, directing Lola with her hand.

"Ouch!" Lola said, snapping her head forward. Paris finished off the braid and pulled out some curls from the front to frame Lola's face.

"There," Paris said. "You look gorgeous."

And she really did. Lola picked out a black gown with a corset bodice that hugged her curves all the way down. She wore gold hoop earrings and necklaces that contrasted Paris' own silver jewelry. Getting ready together was almost fun. Paris hadn't been to a ball in decades and Lola had never attended one. For her friend's sake, Paris decided she would treat tonight like the special event it was meant to be. In the past, the most important parts of the evening for her had always been the hours before the ball, where she would get ready with her sister. They would pick out the right accessories, the right makeup and do each other's hair. Sharing this with Lola almost made it easy to forget why they were here.

Paris glanced at the bathroom door again. Erica spent the last twenty minutes, alone, getting dressed inside.

After the hearing, Ken, Lola, and herself had an unspoken agreement to give her space. Not that it needed to be agreed upon, Erica had no trouble avoiding them on her own. It gave Paris plenty of time to think about Erica and the revelation of her hybrid nature. But she quickly realized she wasn't too interested in theorizing the why and the when. Not when Erica was here with all the answers she wanted.

It was tempting to barge into the bathroom now, lock the door behind them, and demand answers. But after the week her friend had, that would only be pouring salt on the wound.

There was a knock at the door. Lola stood to open it and revealed Ken on the other side, wearing an all-black suit.

When he saw her, his jaw went slack and Paris had to hold back a laugh.

"Hey," Lola said.

"Hey," said Ken. It came out like a sigh. "You look beautiful."

Paris bit her lip but said nothing. She could see Lola beaming from across the room. "Thanks."

It was hard not to ruin their moment. It wasn't like the Mortal Realm here. They had to be careful showing that kind of affection in Mantle. Paris had never given much thought to the hybrid law before. Being a vampire left her infertile, meaning it had never truly applied to her in the first place. There wasn't a microscope over who she dated or who she was allowed to be in love with. Paris had never worried about Lola and Ken before. They were both young enough to get away with flirting and casual dating. It was meant to be harmless, at least it was before the summons. Now with the Council's watchful eye on them, things were more dangerous than ever.

Lola's aunts came out of the room across the hall, both wearing simple dresses. Andi in white and Kate in red. Paris gave Kate a look through the door. She had meant every word she said to the woman back in Marcel's office. Though Paris was frustrated with Erica's silence, there was no telling what she would've done to the people in that room if the trial result was different. There was a high chance she'd be the one up for execution next. "Everyone ready?" Andi asked.

Paris was definitely not ready. She was still debating on which lip color went best with her dress.

The bathroom door creaked open as Erica stepped outside. Her hair was pulled back into a ponytail and the gown she wore was a sparkling emerald green. The room went silent at the sight of her, Lola being the first to break it by saying, "You look beautiful."

Erica gave her a small smile. "Thanks."

Lola looked over at Paris, who still had two different lipsticks in hand. "Par, wrap it up!"

Paris rolled her eyes and went with a red lip because a red lip went with everything. "Alright, alright," she said, coming out of the room with her hands up.

"Flashy much?" Ken said to her as they left the inn.

As they fell back, she said, "How come Lola gets called beautiful and I get flashy?"

His eyes widened and looked forward to see if anyone had heard. He quickly composed himself. "If I complimented you, you'd hold it over my head until I died."

She rolled her eyes and said, "Look, if I'm gonna be forced to go somewhere, the least I can do is look good."

He shrugged. "Fair enough."

Outside was a coach. A sign hung on the door displaying Kate and Andi's names. The two cautiously approached it. "Hm," Kate mused, inspecting it. Apparently, they weren't expecting a ride either.

Once the two determined the carriage was safe, the group piled inside. There was no driver, no horses. Paris couldn't see it but somewhere on this coach was a sigil. Sigil magick was invaluable. Depending on the wizard who drew it, its versatility and effectiveness made it perfect for everyday application. The sigil on the carriage held specific instructions and when the last person was seated, it took off down the road, even though its caster was miles away.

Though she had tried several times over the years, Paris could never live in Alereis. Amongst other problems, the world was reliant on public transportation, and Paris loved her car too much to give it up.

She could appreciate the world for what it was though. It was quieter, the sounds of the city she was used to were replaced with the chatter of conversations as they passed. The air smelled cleaner, the sky brighter. The night was peaceful and the cool breeze from the harbor washed over them.

The carriage approached the Themis Court, falling in line behind several others that undoubtedly held high ranking officials within the Guard and military. The group traveled inside with the other party-goers who were draped in silk and diamonds and headed toward the ballroom.

The space was a splash of brown and gold. The lighting dim for the few Vampire guests, offering a warm glow across the marble floors. There was no mingling, everyone seemed to know exactly where they were headed as soon as they stepped inside. Everywhere Paris looked, there was a new elite to take in. Just out of the corner of her eye, she saw General Hart talking with Mantle and Trin's Prime ministers. The lack of presence from other territories wasn't surprising. Paris had always felt that Mantle, with all its parades and balls, was always putting on a performance. Everywhere else in Alereis, Remembrance Day meant nothing more than a day off school. If anyone was expected to acknowledge a massive day of loss, it was the capital.

The group found a table near the buffet area and took a seat. "We should go make the rounds," Kate said to Andi.

"And I need to find the bathroom," Erica said a moment later. Paris was learning just how fast those long legs could carry her because within a moment she disappeared into the crowd, with Kate and Andi following behind.

"I should go with her," Paris said, standing up from her seat.

"Paris," Ken said warily. He knew she was eager to get answers from Erica and probably thought she intended to corner her.

"It's a girl thing, Ken, relax," Paris said. If she was being honest, she was more interested in what Kate and Andi were up to. She caught a glance of them talking with Marcel and Wendy Michaels, a seat holder on the Inquiry. The Inquiry's authority was directly under the Council's. It was composed of the Prime Ministers of each territory, along with the heads of each division of the Guard. Recently, Wendy's Mortal Realm relations position had been added.

Paris thought of the attacks happening back home. Alereis treated Mortal-born citizens like a forgotten stepchild. Under your care and yet not truly yours. It was a lot harder to govern people who lived a Realm away, Paris admitted, but not impossible. One position wasn't going to change years of absentee parenting.

What do you know? Paris thought as she passed them. *And why does it have to involve these kids?*

She found Erica standing near the hallway, looking particularly lost. "Found the bathroom?" Paris said, walking up to her.

Erica crossed her arms. "You're not funny," she said.

"That's subjective," Paris said, then motioned for her to follow. "Come on, I think I remember seeing a restroom on the way in."

Paris didn't expect the girl to follow, but perhaps she actually did need to use the bathroom.

"So, you've probably been to one of these before huh?" Erica asked as they walked the halls back toward the entrance.

"Oh, yes, plenty of balls."

"I've always wanted to go to one, you know? The dances, the pretty dresses, the music—I thought it would be some sort of magical experience," Erica said, an air of sadness in her voice. "I didn't expect it to be like this..."

Paris frowned as the two fell into a steady pace. This she could understand. The last ball she attended came rushing back with unpleasant memories. "When I say balls, I don't usually mean ones here," she explained. "They're not really keen on inviting us Mortal-borns to these types of things anyway."

Mortal-born was the term Alereis natives used to refer to those born in the Mortal Realm, while Realm-born was the term for the exact opposite. Neither was used in good taste, but Paris didn't particularly care who heard her. It was no secret that some born in their homeland had a low opinion of them, not even considering them real Alereians. It was worse for Vampires, who already had a point against them for being born human. Even with Alexandria on the Council, it had done little to change their standing.

"Maybe that's for the best," Erica said. Paris studied her, wanting so desperately to understand what she was thinking. They finally came across the restroom and paused at the door.

"It's our last night here," Paris said, hoping it would bring her some sort of comfort. "We leave first thing tomorrow night and then it's over."

Erica nodded and gave her a pained smile. "Yeah, I know."

As she stepped inside the bathroom, Paris knew it was a lie. Erica was half Guardian and this was her world now. If she didn't learn to settle in it, these people would eat her alive.

Erica paused at the door. "Am I going to die?" she said suddenly.

Paris frowned. "Ere, they're letting you go, they're not going to—"

"No, I mean, am I going to die one day?" she asked again. "Guardians are immortal, Seers aren't, so, which am I?"

Paris pondered the question for a moment, unsure. "I guess you'll just have to find out like everyone else," she said carefully.

"Not you," Erica pointed out.

Paris shook her head. "Everything dies, Erica," she said. "Whatever takes me will just be a surprise."

CHAPTER TWENTY-FOUR
LOLA

AFTER PARIS AND ERICA left, Lola sat alone with Ken at the table. She watched as his eyes drifted over to the buffet table. The spread was ripe with all the meats, sides, and desserts she could imagine. Ken gave her a once over then frowned. "What?" she asked.

"I was checking to see if you had a purse," he said. She didn't, just a small crossbody bag.

"Are you trying to smuggle a plate?"

He shrugged. "I might as well be productive about our time here." She snorted as he stood from his chair. "Do you want anything?"

"Cake," she said, pointing at the piece of chocolate cake on the dessert table.

"Any actual food?" he asked.

"Cake."

"Hm, that sounded a bit like steak that time," Ken said as he began to walk away.

"You know that's not actually steak right?" she pointed out. "It's malhorn or something."

"It's steak shaped."

She pouted. Why even ask her if he was going to deny her dessert for dinner? Lola made sure to look painfully disinterested when Ken returned and put a plate of mystery meat in front of her. "This isn't cake," she said.

"I know." He took the seat next to her. "Eat."

She huffed and grabbed her fork. "Alright, dad." He rolled his eyes.

A hush suddenly came over the ballroom and the two looked up. The Council stood side by side at the top of the spiral staircase, addressing the crowd. Their ability to command the room without a word was almost eerie.

"Good evening," Alexandria started off. She looked the way she had at the hearing, lush and proper. "I would like to thank you all for gathering here to commemorate the 60th anniversary of the Battle of Winchester. A truly dark time in our history, where we were at odds with one another, where trust was fragile after such a devastating betrayal from our brothers and sisters across the sea. But while we may have rekindled our relationship with the Fae, let us never forget the lives that were lost on this day." Nods and murmurs erupted across the room. "If you all will give us sixty seconds of silence to honor those who fought for us."

People around the room began to bow their heads, her and Ken following suit. The Battle of Winchester was the bloodiest war in Alereian history. Of all the things she was ignorant about in the Magick Realm, the war was something everyone knew. Over sixty years ago, the Fae had plotted to overthrow the government. The Fae proved to be difficult enemies. They were immortal magick users after all. That, along with the support of a few other Lien, the war went on for four years.

According to some, the war was the reason there were so few Seers nowadays. In conflict, their gifts were invaluable. Many were said to be killed to keep the opposing side from gathering information, while some Seers went into hiding out of fear.

When the moment of silence was over, Lola and Ken quietly ate their food. "I figured a ball would be a little more interesting," she said, picking at the plate with her fork. The ballroom was engaged in a choreographed dance that almost resembled a waltz. She thought to ask Paris about it, but she hadn't come back since going after Erica.

They had been gone for what felt like ages and Lola couldn't help but imagine what the two were talking about. Had Paris done the impossible and gotten Erica to open up? Lola knew the answer was within her grasp, right past the doors of the ballroom, but she wouldn't move. She stayed in her seat, playing with the food on her plate.

She couldn't understand why she hadn't gone after Erica herself. In her mind, Erica's release had been filled with tears of joy and hugs that lasted for hours. But Erica had barely spoken in days, and Lola hadn't made an attempt to reach out either.

She stood suddenly, the built-up energy flowing through her.

"Where are you going?" Ken asked.

"I don't know." Sitting here suddenly felt unbearable. "To snoop around."

Ken looked confused. "Lo, this is probably the most secure building in the universe," he pointed out, probably thinking that would convince her out of it.

"I'm not planning a heist, I'm just gonna look around. Are you coming or what?" she asked.

His brows knitted together as he thought it over. "I don't know."

"When's the next time we'll get to explore the Themis Court like this?"

After a moment's hesitation, Ken followed her out of the ballroom and into the hallway. Lola decided for herself that for the rest of the night she wouldn't be here against her will. She'd be like any other tourist who visited Mantle. She took in the east wing. The intricate detailing of the ceilings, the rustic murals on the walls, and glittering chandeliers. She appreciated it all for what it was, but in the back of her mind all she could think about was how long Erica had wanted to visit Mantle. She wouldn't find any beauty in this place, not now.

After some time, Lola and Ken found themselves walking into a portrait room. Paintings of war, Queens and Kings, and Goddesses surrounded them.

"Whoa," Lola said, stopping in front of a portrait of the Goddess Aurora. The painting depicted the Goddess with raven hair and pale skin. She was displayed sitting in a meadow, the night sky overcast. At her side was a pack of wolves at attention. Her charcoal eyes seemed like they were staring straight into her soul. Lola broke away from her gaze. She didn't remember the last time she had spoken to the Goddess, but then again, it wasn't like Aurora would answer to someone with cursed blood like her.

"What is it?" Ken asked, noticing her frown.

"It's Remembrance Day and there's barely any Dahlia art out." She had noticed the lack of the other Goddess on the way in. Ken took a glance around the room. There were only two portraits of the Goddess on display. Dahlia, Goddess of Day and Mother of Lien was the sister to Aurora, Goddess of Night and Mother of Nightwalkers. One of the paintings mirrored Aurora's, with the Goddess in a field of flowers, her bronze skin bathed in sunlight.

While the Fae may have started the war, Nightwalkers finished it. Ultimately, they were no match for Alereian military power. That toppled with the fact that fighting Nightwalkers in the dark was next to impossible. The losses experienced on both sides were devastating. It was called Remembrance Day because it was a day of mourning for everyone.

Ken's mouth was a firm line. "That's probably because they're celebrating something else today."

They abandoned the portrait room and wandered through the halls. It wasn't long before the two came across an extension of the building made entirely out of glass. Ken took a cautious step forward, testing the sturdiness of the floor. When he determined it solid enough, the two walked through the passage, Lola's heels clicking the entire time.

Lola gasped as they reached the exit. The glass passage led outside to the Council's rose garden.

A cobblestone pathway trailed its way throughout the garden. One path led to a black gazebo, another into a hedge maze, and one to a grand marble fountain in the very center of it all. The pair took a seat on the small brick wall that enclosed the flower beds behind them.

"This place is...wow," Ken said. She nodded at a loss for words. Red, black, and white roses grew everywhere; vines of flowers even wrapped the lamp posts lining the path. The gleam of moonlight in the fountain's water reflected across the garden, illuminating everything it touched.

Lola pulled out her phone and earbuds out of her bag. "You have service here?" Ken asked.

"No," she said. "But my playlist is offline, and I don't know about you, but me and the Council have very different music tastes." She offered him an earbud and played the first song. Ken jumped at the opening guitar riff. She snickered, turning the volume down and putting in her own earbud.

The familiarity of the song was welcomed. Its lyrics and beat washed over and enraptured her in a story that was not her own. It was nice to disappear for a moment.

"Are you going to join?" Ken asked. And she was back in the garden.

Lola nearly scoffed. "Is that even a question?" she said. Uncertainty was written all over his face. It made her heart stop. "Why? Are you?"

She hadn't considered that one of her friends would want to join. But Ken? The notion itself felt wrong. "I don't know," he said honestly. "There's not really a choice, is there?"

Lola frowned. In her eyes the two choices were clear. One offered all the answers to her problems on a silver platter while the other only opened her up to more questions. What did the Council know that the rest of them didn't? Why were her aunts involved and why had that man ended up in their basement?

"There's a chance the memory spell will work, and you can go back to life as normal," she pointed out. She had been turning the options over in her head day after day. The memory wipe would be a reset. A clean slate. A fresh start.

"I guess that's technically true," he said after a long moment.

Lola looked up at him. "What do you mean?"

"I mean I technically get my life back," Ken said. "But nothing really changes, you know? All of this will still be going on, I just won't know about it."

But was that really so bad? Lola thought. All of the changes and revelations they had been exposed to the past week had been enough to last a lifetime. Nearly every moment since she returned was filled with stress and panic. Maybe this was a gift in disguise.

"Don't they say ignorance is bliss?" she said lightly.

Ken gave her a small smile. "Maybe, it's a lot to think about," he said. "Especially when you think about Erica having to deal with these pricks by herself."

Lola froze, grabbing her phone and pausing the music instantly. "What do you mean?"

He sighed, a defeated look on his face. "Erica's plea deal. The only reason she gets to come home with us is because she agreed to work as a Guardian."

The garden was gone again, suddenly she was in the hearing room, heart racing, palms sweating. Erica's fate unknown. "How long?" she said quietly.

"Forever."

She was going to throw up. "Wait, how do you know all this? Did she tell you?" Lola didn't think she could bear it if Erica was only avoiding her.

"No, I had a couple questions for your aunt Andi after the trial and she let it slip."

There it was again. Someone else was checking on Erica. Someone else was asking about her fate.

Lola felt so far away from her body. It was like she was watching herself through someone else. She saw a docile girl. The girl that Kate, and perhaps even her father, wanted. This girl didn't ask questions, she followed orders and stepped aside when decisions needed to be made. Did Ken see this stranger now? Did he recognize it as her?

"I don't know," Ken continued. "I just know I wouldn't feel right knowing there was something I could do and just not doing it, you know?"

She didn't think she could answer him honestly.

Lola looked at him, really looked at him. This was Ken. Ken who would drop everything to help her if she asked, Ken who considered giving up his life if it meant Erica didn't spend hers alone. Despite everything he still found it within himself to care, to try. She realized she admired that about him the most.

Ken stood, taking her hand in his. "Come on, dance with me," he said suddenly.

"What?" He hated dancing. The suggestion caught her so off guard that her previous thoughts dispersed.

"Dance with me," he repeated. Ken unplugged her earphones, letting the music play on full volume. There was no one else around, just the two of them. Uninterested in questioning him further, Lola stood, letting the music grab her attention again. She shook out the stiffness of her body and bobbed her head up and down. If her hair wasn't braided back like this, she'd probably slap Ken in the face with it.

The song ended, abruptly changing into a slow ballad. It sounded like the instrumental to a song she knew but couldn't quite place at the moment. They stopped to look at each other. Lola hurried to change the song. "Wow, shuffle is awful," she said.

"No, keep it," he said. She looked up at him in shock. "Do you think we can pull off the dance they're doing inside?"

He held his hand out to her. She considered it for a moment, then took it carefully. "I highly doubt it," she said. The two stood face to face. Ken had one hand in hers and the other on her waist. They moved in time to what Lola considered a waltz, but couldn't quite be sure. She moved through the steps pretty confidently until she stepped on his foot with her heel. "I'm sorry!" she said.

Ken winced but laughed it off. "It's fine," he said.

"Told you. I'm a certified bad luck charm."

"If that were true, I wouldn't want to stay here with you." The single statement disarmed her completely. Deep down, she wanted to correct him, to argue. But how could she? Ken looked at her and didn't see the curse or how wrong she was. He looked at her like she was something wonderful.

Lola smiled and watched the smile be reflected back at her. He looked over her face intently. She had always thought his eyes were beautiful. Some people were enamored with blue or green eyes, but brown eyes, especially Ken's, had depth, had warmth. Ken's eyes made her feel at home.

They got back into the rhythm of the music. A soft steady violin guided the rest of the orchestra. She let Ken lead, still so lost in his gaze that she was taken by surprise when he said, "I'm going to spin you."

Reacting far too late, Ken spun her outward and then pulled her back in. Lola was in a fit of laughter the entire time. It slowly died out as she realized the position she was in. She was pressed against Ken's chest, his arms wrapped around her. She held her breath as his fingers trailed down her waist.

They weren't following any steps now, just swaying in time to their own rhythm. The strings built on top of one another, a steady incline to its climax. The two locked eyes and for a moment time seemed to stop. Ken leaned in slowly and she found herself turning, pushing up on the tips of her toes to reach him. Her lips barely brushed against his when she felt the burning in her throat.

She pushed him back, falling into a coughing fit. The violins faded underneath it.

"Are you ok?" he asked, moving toward her, but she held an arm out to stop him. She turned away, coughing into her hand. Droplets of silver coated her palm. *Shit,* she thought. *Why now?*

When her coughing subsided, she balled her hand into a fist and cleared her throat. "Yeah, I'm fine."

Was she really going to kiss him? Here of all places? What was wrong with her? It was like she wanted them to be back up for execution.

Ken looked over her with concern. "Are you sure 'cause—"

The sound of a commotion coming from the front of the building caught their attention.

"What the hell was that?" Lola said, pulling away. Ken stood up straight and she caught a glimpse of an expression she could only assume was disappointment. She wanted to stay in the moment with him and talk about what they had almost done, but the blood on her hands had her moving away faster than ever. Whatever was happening at the front of the building was the distraction she needed. A blessing in disguise.

Instead of heading back inside, Lola and Ken cut through the garden to the courtyard. Her heart stopped as they reached the entrance. An angry crowd had formed around the gates. If they were loud enough to be heard from the garden, Lola was sure someone inside had noticed the commotion too. It took her a moment to realize this was a protest. People in the crowd held signs that read, "FAE MURDERS" and "NO PEACE FOR LIEN."

Over and over, they chanted, "We deserve a seat!" She could only assume this meant a Council seat. But that didn't make sense, there had never been Lien on the Council. And after the Battle of Winchester, she wasn't sure there would ever be.

But as quickly as the gathering started, it was interrupted by General Hart and the Themis Court security team.

"This is your one warning to remove yourselves from government property!" Aria yelled into the crowd. But the protesters continued their chant.

She motioned to the security guards to move forward and converge on the crowd. Forming a line, the guards pushed the crowd away from the gates and off the steps of the building. Lola watched as General Hart drew a sigil in the air with her finger. It was the shape of two triangles intersecting one another.

When she finished it off, a bright light flashed into the crowd, blinding them. Lola and Ken jumped back, shielding their faces from the light. When they looked back, people ran screaming in all directions, falling over themselves and each other as they struggled to see.

Lola looked to the General who stood on the sidelines, visibly pleased with her work.

Back in Maine, she believed it was the most homesick she would ever be. Tonight, had proven just how wrong she had been.

CHAPTER TWENTY-FIVE
KEN

THE DAY AFTER RETURNING to the Mortal Realm, it was straight back to work for Ken.

There was one hour left of his shift but Ken didn't mind. Anything to distract him from his time in Alereis.

It wasn't like it was hard. It was Sunday and the brunch rush always left the diner so crowded he could barely move. Ken was wiping down a table and preparing it for the next round of customers when he caught sight of the rain outside.

Again?

He didn't think he could stand to walk home another day in a storm. It was beginning to feel personal. Like the world had some sort of vendetta against him for just trying to get through the week.

Ken's mind began to drift without meaning too. He was back in Alereis. Back at the inn after Erica's trial.

Things had gone too easy and Ken didn't take good things for granted. It usually meant there were strings attached.

He was hoping for Kate, but he found Andi in their room.

"I know that you can't tell me much," he said. "But I need some type of reason as to why you would willingly commit yourself to this?"

"It's hard to see it right now," Andi said. "But we do a lot of good, I promise you."

Ken reminded himself of the man they had killed. That there were probably more like him roaming the city.

His sister was staying with one of her human friends until their mother got back. *If their mother got back*, Ken thought bitterly. He remembered the man's strength and the fight the sisters put up against him. If another being like that came for Megan, it would tear the human family apart and then her along with it.

"And then if you aren't exactly the moral crusade type," Andi said. "We're well compensated."

Compensated?

Ken had nearly forgotten that this wasn't as much of a prison sentence as it was a job. "But Lola said you've been looking for work. Why do that if you already have one?" he asked.

Andi seemed a bit embarrassed at the call out. "Well unfortunately I gotta live in the Mortal Realm where the conversion rate to US dollars is decent at best and I need this thing called insurance," she said. "But it's better than nothing."

Ken hated that he was tempted, hated that he was even considering it. But he had little options. Someone had to take care of him and Megan, and he couldn't do it at the diner for the rest of his life, and he certainly couldn't afford to leave and learn how to do something else.

When life was utterly hopeless like this, you took what you were given and you made it work.

That's when Andi let Erica's plea deal slip, and suddenly the choice became abundantly clear.

"Fell!" Mateo called, snapping him out of his thoughts. "I need you to cover table five for me." And then he rushed off before Ken could respond. He sighed, making his way to the table and thinking of Lola the entire time.

The look of horror on her face when he told her he was considering joining the Guard. The way she pushed him away during their dance.

Had he really misread things so poorly?

Maybe this was for the best. It wasn't like he could ever have an actual relationship with her. It was easier if she didn't feel the same way, it just saved him a lot of disappointment.

Shouts suddenly erupted from the kitchen. Curious, Ken headed off to the back of the restaurant, spotting Chef Andrews arguing with one of the bussers near the stove. He quickly intervened. "Hey!" He stepped in between them.

On the floor in front of them, a pile of broken glass coated the floor. "What the hell happened here?"

"This idiot just dropped two plates," Chef Andrews said. "We're behind on orders because of him."

Ken frowned. So that explained the growing line in front of the host stand.

"Only because you keep breathing down my neck," said the buser Ken didn't recognize. In a small place like this, everyone knew everyone. He must have been new. "I can't focus!"

Suddenly questioning why he came over here in the first place, Ken rolled his eyes and said, "Look, Gary, can you just give him some space? It's been a long day." A long day into a long week, into a long month.

Ken reached down to grab one of the larger pieces of glass. As he struggled to have a firm grip around the smooth porcelain, his hand slipped, slicing his finger. "Shit!" he hissed.

"You alright?" Gary asked. Ken quickly balled his bleeding finger into his fist. "Maybe try the broom and dust pan, yeah?"

Ken didn't know what was wrong with him, reaching for broken glass barehanded. He was too wrapped up with Alereis, Inlanders, and Lola, to think straight. He winced, the sting from the cut shooting pain through his hand. He rushed to the bathroom, hoping no one had caught a glimpse of the dripping silver. Someone else would just have to sweep up the mess outside.

When Ken got home, he set Megan's dinner on the counter. With it was a slice of cheesecake. It was his peace offering for leaving her for almost two weeks. He'd have to wait until softball practice was over to find out if his apology was accepted. His hours were still warped from the trip, so in the meantime, Ken decided a nap was in order.

His pull-out bed took up too much space during the day. And even though he was alone, Ken had heard too many complaints to risk taking it out now. He fell into the couch face first, eyes barely shut when the jingle of keys came from the front door. His heart stopped.

His mom walked in, her hair in a messy bun, bags under her eyes. "Hi, honey." She walked straight past him. There was no indication that the two hadn't seen each other in two weeks.

"Hi," he said.

"Pizzas in the fridge," she said, even though he hadn't asked. He could see her through the bedroom door, shrugging off her outside clothes and climbing into bed. When his mom still had her job, Ken saw no problem with this. But now of course he knew she was coming home to sleep off a hangover. To sleep off whatever damage she had done the previous night.

He waited just for a moment. Perhaps something in him still had a shred of hope that his mom was still there. That she would ask him a question, any question. If there was any inkling that she cared about him. His hope was met with silence.

Ken shut his eyes and drifted to sleep.

CHAPTER TWENTY-SIX
LOLA

THERE WAS A DULL grayness to the night sky when Lola and Kate made their way to the burning site. Lola suspected that it was a bad omen. If it wasn't already agreed upon, she would've found herself anywhere else in the world tonight.

The head of Lauren Carter's coven, Remi Black, lived in a large house off the coast. The Black coven obviously had money, the Sea Cliff neighborhood was notorious for its large houses and its expansive and manicured backyards. The crash of waves against the cliffside was loud enough to cover the chanting and the private nature of the neighborhood meant no one would bother them. It was the perfect place to hold the burning.

She stood outside with Kate, who she had barely spoken to since they returned home. Her aunt knocked and a second later, Remi opened the door, greeting them both. "Kate, you made it," he said, ushering them inside. Remi was a South Asian man decked in white ceremonial robes.

"Of course I made it," she said. "This is my niece, Lola."

"Nice to meet you, Lola," he said, extending his hand. She shook it carefully. "Is this your first burning?"

She nodded. Nightwalkers had extended lifetimes. She wasn't expecting to ever attend one, at least not for a long time.

Remi's expression was grim. "Well, hopefully it's your last one for a while," he said echoing her thoughts.

"We're so sorry for your loss," Kate said as they followed him past the foyer. Two spiral staircases stood on either side, and to the living room that was plastered in whites and golds. Surrounding them was a balcony that looked down onto the plush loveseat and open hearth. There they were greeted with what Lola assumed was the Black coven. Everyone was in their best outfit. Lola wore a deep plum dress and black platform dress shoes that Kate disapproved of. Her aunt had chosen a simple navy dress, her hair back in its usual braid. There was a table display of food to the side. People stood around it, filling their plates and whispering amongst themselves. They were probably all wondering the same thing she was; how could this have happened? "Did you get the flowers I sent?"

Kate had all the answers, but all she would offer Remi was her sympathies. Lola clenched her jaw. She should have fought harder against coming tonight. With all she had learned over the past few weeks, how was she meant to sit with this coven and pretend she knew nothing?

Lola didn't have the stomach to eat anything, so she waited alone as her aunt made her way around the room. Kate made frequent stops and each person seemed to recognize her somehow. Lola didn't understand how she could remember so many faces. If it was all an act, Kate deserved an award for it.

After a few minutes of talking, Lola watched as a woman threw her arms around Kate, sobbing into her chest and startling them both. What was she to Lauren? Lola wondered. A sister? A mother? A friend? Nightwalker ages were notoriously confusing.

Lola waited for Kate to pry the woman off her. She hated being touched. But the moment never came. Her aunt stood there, patting the poor woman's back, letting her cry into her shoulder for as long as she needed.

Was this the expectation of coven heads? Burning bodies and being cried on?

Well, not everyone was crying. The vast majority were chatting easily, even laughing with one another, leaving her confused. "Are you sure you don't want to eat anything? Only a couple minutes till we start." Remi appeared next to her.

"No, I'm fine," she said, tearing her eyes away from Kate and the crying woman. "Are you sure it's okay for me to participate in this? It doesn't really feel appropriate."

She didn't know Lauren, didn't know a single Witch in this coven. Was it right for her to be here as if she mourned the way they mourned? When she heard what happened on the news, her first thought was of relief that it wasn't her aunts.

Remi noticed her watching the group laughing together in the corner. "We've already had the funeral," he explained. "We've had a few months to mourn and everyone's already gotten their tears out. A burning is about celebrating a Witch's life and helping them move on."

Lola drummed her fingers on her thigh. If she was this uncomfortable now, maybe she should've been grateful she hadn't been invited to the funeral. Though she'd never voice it aloud, large groups of Witches made her nervous. A voice deep down told her that somehow, they'd be able to tell she was cursed. That they could sense how wrong her magick was. It was rare when her own coven joined together. Being shamed out of a stranger's coven hadn't been on her list of worries until now and suddenly the fear felt all too real. "I know, it just still feels odd to me."

"Well, you know covens, we usually only gather like this for birthings or burnings. This is the first time a lot of us are seeing each other in months."

Remi looked at the clock on the wall. It was time. "It is now five minutes to three," he announced to the room. "If you'd all follow me outside."

Lola could feel the air in the room shifting. Would they see the body?

Kate rejoined her and the two followed the rest of the coven to the backyard.

Three in the morning was the prime time for a burning, along with midnight. Both marked the veil between the living and the dead being at its lowest. The fire pit was set up in the center and a white fold up table lined with different herbs stood beside it. Right next to the pit was a black duffel bag. The closer she approached, the stronger the stench emanating from it became.

All that was left of Lauren Carter was inside that bag.

The flames licked the crackling wood, devouring it bit by bit. Lola felt no heat coming from it, just the cold dullness that was always there. She didn't even notice she was drifting toward the pit until Kate took her arm and quickly steered her away.

Remi stood in front of the fire pit as the rest of the coven circled around it. "Good evening, everyone. As you all know, tonight we come together to celebrate and release the spirit of Lauren Carter, child of night," he said and then gestured to the bag sadly. "This is all we could recover of her."

Against her will, Lola wondered what exactly had been recovered. It was clearly enough to complete the ritual, but it had been months since Lauren's death. What poor soul had gone through the process of collecting all the pieces?

"But nevertheless, we will continue the rite as planned and free Lauren from this plane so that she may join the rest of our coven in the afterlife," Remi continued. Witches shared the notion that even in death your soul was still tethered to your body. Unless a burning was performed, that Witch's soul would be trapped in a void like purgatory for eternity, unable to join their collective ancestors on the other side.

The collective were the ones that bestowed gifts. When Witches were born, their ancestors handpicked the ability that would best suit that individual in life. Coven heads acted as the bridge, they were the only ones capable of carrying out the blessing on the physical plane.

Lola had learned on the way here that Lauren had been a lost Witch taken in by the Black coven. After this ritual was done, her soul would join Remi's ancestors in the afterlife, not her own.

Remi instructed everyone to join hands as he lit the fire. Lola found herself holding hands with her aunt and the crying woman she recognized from earlier. There was still a sorrowful look on her face, but it was clear she had steadied herself for this moment. Remi grabbed the bag that contained Lauren and tossed it into the flames.

Next came the part Lola had been dreading. Remi opened up the floor for offerings. Any Witch with anything worth giving would be able to offer it to the ancestors in an attempt to sway them into letting Lauren cross over. Several people stepped up with different plants, valuables and possessions. Lola had nothing to give, nothing but her blood.

Blood was sacred. There was so little that could top a blood offering. Especially coming from a neighboring coven. It would be a show of solidarity, an act joining her bloodline to theirs.

But Lola didn't move, didn't make an attempt to.

She could feel Kate's eyes burning into her, before her aunt stepped forward, ready to do the very thing Lola was thinking. Remi handed her the knife and Kate swiftly sliced her finger, letting just a few drops of blood drip into the fire.

The flames roared with life. The ancestors seemed to be pleased. Lola wondered what would happen if it was her blood in there.

As the flames grew higher, and burned through the bag, Remi led the coven in a chant. Lola knew the air should've been heavy with magick, but all she could feel was a prickle of it brushing against her skin. She said a silent prayer for Lauren. An apology for standing there and doing nothing when her soul was at stake.

She wondered if the spirit would forgive her. That somehow, Lauren would understand that it was better this way. That somehow—even from the other side—she could feel Lola's magick, restless and desperate beneath the surface, and know everything bad and wrong that came with it.

Lola stayed silent throughout the ritual. She let the shame wash over her. The Black coven had opened up their home to her, offered their food to her, and bared their grief in front of her, and now she would give them nothing in return.

CHAPTER TWENTY-SEVEN
LOLA

LOLA MADE HER WAY down the hallway and outside the school. There were only three days left until she had to decide whether to join the Guard or not. But she logged that decision and all it entailed in the back of her mind for now.

When she found Ken, she resisted the urge to sit next to him on the front steps. "Hey."

"Hey."

The two hadn't spoken much since exploring the Themis Court grounds. Lola thought of the two of them, dancing along the cobblestone. They were so close—close enough to hear the other's heartbeat. And then she had a hacking fit in his face. She cringed at the thought of it. She needed to act normal, like the entire thing hadn't happened at all. While the implication of what they had almost done terrified her, she was far more concerned about if Ken had seen the blood on her hands. If he did, he hadn't made it known to her.

She convinced herself that forgetting about the entire evening, about Ken's soft hands and gentle eyes, was in everyone's best interest. She had gotten caught up in the moment. That's all it was. "How are you feeling?" he asked. *Well, that's a loaded question*, Lola thought. She wasn't even sure what exactly he was referring to.

"I'm fine," she said.

"Fine?" He gave her a once over. "Just fine?"

She nodded. "Yep, let's get this over with."

He gave her a look filled with disbelief before shaking his head. Like she had picked the wrong topic. "Is she even coming?"

"Said she would." She had convinced Erica to ride home with them today, omitting the fact that Paris would be picking them up.

"Why does it feel like we're setting a trap?" Ken sighed.

"It's not a trap," Lola said, dismissing him with a wave of her hand. "We're just keeping her in the car until she answers our questions."

"I'm beginning to see flaws with this plan." He scratched at a bandage wrapped around his palm.

"What's with the bandage?"

He picked at the edges of the adhesive. "Cut myself at work," he said.

"And it hasn't healed yet?"

He shook his head. "Must've been deeper than I thought."

Erica's form approached them and Lola quickly got to her feet. "Oh, here she comes." She wrapped her arm around Erica's waist when she reached them. "Hello, beautiful."

"Hey," Erica said uneasily. With Ken at their side, Lola directed them to the parking lot where Paris' car pulled in. Erica shot her a look, her jaw set tight. Paris was only up during the day when asked. This was already tipping her off, Lola could tell.

Paris parked near the back of the lot and the group greeted her as they climbed inside. "What are you doing here?" Erica asked.

Paris locked the doors and turned the car off. "We wanted to talk to you," she said. *Okay*, Lola thought. Maybe Ken was right, this did seem like a trap.

"About what?" Erica said, crossing her arms.

"What happened at your interrogation?" Ken asked. "Did they do anything to you?"

"You mean besides threatening my life? No, no they didn't," Erica said, voice dripping with aggravation. "They told me what's expected of me now, what dates to come back—they have my whole life figured out."

Lola couldn't see her face from the backseat, but she could hear the pain in her voice. She knew Erica—knew her goals, her dreams, her plan. All of that had been derailed over a few days and someone else's plan took its place. "How long have you known?" Lola asked.

Erica sighed, needing no clarification for what she meant. "A while now."

Silence overtook the vehicle. Hurt wasn't the right word for what she felt. Lola wasn't even sure if she was allowed to be hurt considering what she was hiding. Maybe she didn't hurt for herself, but for Erica. The fear she must have known was something Lola couldn't even comprehend.

"It's complicated," Erica said. "I wasn't completely sure. There's not a lot of info on Seers, I thought maybe I just had some undocumented gifts but..." She trailed off.

"Why didn't you tell us what you were thinking?" Ken asked.

"You know why," she said, waving him off.

"No, I don't," he argued. "Do you really think we care about that stuff? That we would turn you in?"

"I didn't know what to think." She gripped the handle, turning to face Lola. "Your aunts work in the Guard. If they had been anyone else, things could've gone very differently." She was right. Lola knew deep down that the only reason Erica was alive was because of Kate. Kate and her experience. Kate and her connection to the Council. "Can you blame me for keeping this to myself?"

"No," Lola said slowly. "No, I don't blame you."

"But you're mad at me."

"No one's mad," Ken said.

"Paris is," Erica said, casting a glance at her.

Paris, who had been silent this entire time, drummed her fingers along the steering wheel. "I'm mad at you for being stupid," she said finally.

"Paris—" Ken started.

"If you had any indication of what you were, you shouldn't have gone across that border," Paris said. "You shouldn't have put yourself in danger like that."

"I don't think you can just ignore a summons like that," Erica pointed out.

"If you trusted us enough, we could've figured something out."

Erica cast her eyes down into her lap. "I'm sorry," she said.

Paris rolled her eyes. "I don't want your apology, dumbass," she said. "I just would've preferred not seeing those realm-borns turn you into an asshole."

For the first time that week, Erica let out a small laugh. "That's your main concern?"

"I don't know man," Lola said. "I can see how all those fancy balls can suck the soul out of you after a while. One moment you're one of us and then the next you're asking what our net worth is."

"I'm cool with it as long as you bring us back their food," Ken said with a shrug.

"I'll keep all that in mind," Erica said, her smile fading a bit. "But it doesn't matter anyway, I'll probably last a week before they've realized they made a mistake."

Guardians had always been a mystery. They were detached from the rest of Alereian society and it was unclear if that was by choice or not. There was something about Guardians, whether it was their stature or their fierceness, that made them nearly unapproachable. Erica had that same reserved nature now that Lola thought about it, but she didn't have the same coldness. "Don't say that," Lola said. "I'm sure you'll do great." There was a fighter within Erica, she wasn't like Lola, she didn't give up.

"Not like I have much of a choice, it's part of the deal," Erica said. "How am I supposed to be responsible for someone else's life?"

"Erica, you will be fine. We will all be fine," Paris said firmly. "Guardians are trained their entire lives, it'll probably be years before you have to do anything serious. It's not like they've already given you a charge."

Erica tensed, hope draining out of her face. "I do have a charge," she admitted. All eyes in the car turned to her in shock.

"What? Who?" Lola asked.

"You."

She blinked. "Me? Why me?" She leaned forward and stuck her head between the driver and passenger seat.

"It was Kate's idea, a show of good faith maybe?" said Erica. "Her trusting you with me was enough to convince the Council, I guess."

"Does this mean you two will have to be bonded?" Ken asked. Lola honestly didn't know what being bonded entailed. She knew it was a special connection only Guardians and their charges shared, but what did that mean exactly? What was so special about it?

Erica looked to Lola. "I mean, only if you want to," she said. "All I know is that they're using this whole thing as a test, just to see if I'm worth it or not."

What was Kate's goal here? Guardians were typically reserved for those the Council proclaimed were important enough. If that was true, why agree to give Lola one? Why hadn't Kate told her about this beforehand?

Lola sighed. "Of course I'll be bonded to you," she said. "Whatever it takes to keep you out of that hearing room."

Erica held her gaze for a moment, eyes filling with gratitude. She smiled.

Paris put the key back in the ignition. "Are we ready to go?" she asked, starting the car.

Lola opened her mouth to respond when she remembered that she hadn't told Ms. Marshall they wouldn't be meeting today.

"Gimme one sec," she said. Paris unlocked the doors and Lola sprinted back into the building and up to Ms. Marshall's classroom.

Her footsteps echoed throughout the near empty halls. It was a Wednesday and most clubs and sports teams wouldn't be meeting until the end of the week. She entered the stairwell, running straight into Mr. Hanks. She rushed to conceal her face but it was too late. "Ms. Hallows," he said, he seemed just as excited to see her as she did. "Shouldn't you be getting home to work on my assignment?"

She gritted her teeth, counting down the weeks until she never had to sit in his class again. "I'll be heading out soon," Lola said.

"Very good. The last thing you need is to be loitering in the halls." He went on his way, pushing past Lola when she wouldn't move out of his path. She let out a groan once he was out of earshot and hurried up the stairs.

The whole encounter had soured her entire mood. The fact that Mr. Hanks couldn't even comprehend that she could be here for an important reason was not lost on her.

She made her way to Ms. Marshall's classroom, trying her hardest to forget about unnatural smiles and empty eye sockets. It was easier in class, when she could tune out Mr. Hanks, but she didn't think she ever wanted to be alone with him again. It's what kept her out of detention for so long. That and Ms. Marshall.

Lola approached the classroom, reaching for the door handle, only to find it ajar.

She knocked, then pushed the door open. At first she thought Ms. Marshall had left. The lights were off and the chairs were stacked on top of the tables. The blinds were shut too. Only small cracks of sunlight escaped in between them. But Lola could see Ms. Marshall at her desk. Her teacher's chair was turned away from her, a video playing loudly on her laptop. "Hey, Ms. Marshall," she said. Lola stepped into the room and approached the desk, trying to get her attention. Sometimes her teacher would play music during their tutoring sessions, but it was usually mellow and calming. What was playing on the laptop now was utter garbage in Lola's opinion. No message, no rhythm, just noise. "Ms. Marshall!"

There was no response.

The song was loud but Lola was practically at her side. There was no way she couldn't hear her. A horrible feeling set in Lola's chest as she reached out, grabbing the back of the chair, and twirling it around.

There was a hole in her chest. Lola could see the fracture of ribs poking out through her blouse. Her body was set up like a doll. Her eyes stared straight ahead, completely glazed over like glass, and her back was straight with her hands clasped together in her lap. Ms. Marshall sat prettily in a pool of her own blood.

Silver blood.

Nightwalker blood.

Lola screamed.

CHAPTER TWENTY-EIGHT
LOLA

LOLA HELD ANDI'S HAND as the sound of sirens surrounded them. After finding Ms. Marshall, she called her aunts, unsure of what else to do.

While she waited, she locked herself in the room and sat on the floor. No one could see the blood, no one could see her here. Lola's eyes never strayed from Ms. Marshall's mangled form.

"I don't understand," Erica said. Her aunt and her friends stood outside the school as law enforcement closed off the scene and escorted lingering students out of the building. Kate walked outside and made her way to them.

"The scene was cleaned up before anyone could see anything," she explained; just as Lola had thought, Kate had contacts with Alereians who worked in law enforcement. They had stopped anyone from seeing the body, but there were still students and teachers who had seen Lola leave the room.

She gripped her aunt's hand tighter.

Ms. Marshall was dead.

Lola hadn't known her for long, she hadn't even known much about her, but what Lola did know was that Ms. Marshall was perfectly kind, perfectly considerate, perfectly decent. What had she done to deserve to die like this?

Lola struggled to keep herself from shaking. Flashes of the hole in her teacher's chest roamed through her mind. "Who did this?" she asked.

"Police are searching the area," Kate said. "Though whoever did this is definitely gone by now—"

"No," Lola said. "Who did this? I know you know."

Andi looked to Kate. "Lola, you know we can't—"

"Can't tell us, right, got it," she said bitterly. "Well, are you gonna find out who killed her?"

Another tense silence from the two.

"I don't know," Kate said. Lola gave her a baffled look.

"I know the Council told you to stop investigating," Paris said, giving them an accusatory glare. "But are you honestly going to listen to them? Someone was killed in their school."

The statement hung in the air.

Ms. Marshall had been brutally killed in the middle of the day, in a public building, and no one had noticed. Whoever did this had been in their school, had known what room was hers. The laptop had been on full volume to drown out her struggle. Everything had been planned.

"Even if we wanted to continue, we're suspended," Kate said, and when the group gave her more outraged looks, she explained further. "We'd be monitored if we acted."

"So there's nothing," Ken said, his voice flat.

"No, not nothing," Kate said, leaving Andi surprised. Lola understood what her aunt meant. Even if her memory was successfully erased, these deaths would continue just like Ken said. With the Council's disinterest and her aunts out of commission, there was no one else. Could she let herself forget the outrage she felt for Ms. Marshall? For Erica? For any of the people she cared about? The answer was simple.

"Sign me up," Lola said.

"What?" Andi said.

"I want to be drafted," she said. "Let's get this over with."

CHAPTER TWENTY-NINE
PARIS

"Hunt, open the door!" Paris knocked for the third time. She knew she was used to being up in daylight more than other Vampires, but this was ridiculous. They couldn't be that deep asleep.

After the fourth knock, Paris heard movement from the other side of the door. Hunter peaked his head out a second later. "Can I help you?" he said with a yawn.

"How are you?" she asked.

"Uh, tired?" he said. "What are you doing here?"

"I just came to check on you," she said. Paris hadn't seen any of her siblings since she kicked them out last month. While the group searched for a house, they had been staying in this apartment complex. It wasn't as nice as what Paris assumed they were used to, but then again, she hadn't given them much time to look.

He gave her a long stare. "You wanted to check in?" he said. Paris narrowed her eyes, he was definitely making it hard for her not to turn around and go home.

"Yes."

"Oh," said Hunter, letting out another yawn. "Did you have to do it so early though?"

She groaned. "You're really making this difficult, you know that?"

"Making what difficult?" he asked. He seemed to be on the verge of laughing. "Caring about me?"

Of course she cared about him, she cared about all of them, that was the only reason she was here. Paris hadn't known her friend's teacher, but her death hadn't scared her any less. The woman had been killed only minutes after her friends had left the building. Paris thought of Lola, straddling her knees in front of the door of the classroom. There was a hollowness in her eyes. Paris knew that look well. It was one none of them deserved to bear.

Kate and Andi worked to get the group's drafting request approved. Until then, they were left wandering blind.

While Paris didn't know who this enemy was or what they wanted, what she did know was that they were targeting Alereians, and on that list was everyone she cared about.

"I want you to move back in with me," she said. Her family didn't know there was a threat in the city, at least under her roof she could look out for all of them.

Hunter blinked. "You do? Why?"

"I changed my mind." She shrugged. "You were right, I didn't give this a fair shot."

Her brother looked over her carefully. Paris concentrated on keeping her breathing steady and erasing the uncertainty from her face. She could do this. If she was meant to protect them, she had to. "I don't know, Ian's still pissed with you for attacking him," he said.

"Tell him to get over it."

Hunter rolled his eyes. "I'm sure that'll go over well," he snorted. "What's the real reason you're doing this, Paris?"

"Does it matter?" she said. "You're getting what you wanted."

He frowned. "What I want is to make sure you're okay."

Paris didn't need to tell him how pointless a pursuit that was. If he hadn't given up on her already, there wasn't a chance he would ever. Whether she deserved it or not was still something she didn't know.

CHAPTER THIRTY
LOLA

LOLA LOVED MUSIC. AT an early age, her dad had instilled it in her with vocal and piano lessons. But her true love was the bass. She remembered the first time she held one. The weight of it in her hands and the feeling of the amp vibrating through her chest was exhilarating. She thought of the bass in her room. After years of begging, it had been an eighteenth birthday present that she couldn't even stand to look at now.

She sat in music class with a keyboard and stand in front of her. Days had passed since she found Ms. Marshall. The school had shut down for the rest of the week and reopened the following Monday. Kate and Andi asked her to stay home this morning, but getting out of the house was what she wanted more than anything. It wasn't her aunt's fault, but just being around them served as constant reminders of everything she didn't know. She looked at them and wrestled with the fact that no one was investigating Ms. Marshall's death, no one cared but them.

Seeing the substitute at her desk that morning hurt, but hurt was something she knew how to deal with. Helplessness was a completely different beast.

She still reeled from her declaration that in a few days she would be drafted. But strangely enough she didn't regret it at all.

The assignment today was to play a few chords to practice hand placement on the keys. Seeing as she was already pretty proficient at the piano, Lola did a reasonable amount of slacking and a horrible amount of thinking. After attempting to play something she'd been working on, Mr. Hanks quickly scolded her.

"Uh, it's Lola right?" a voice said. Lola looked up to find Brooke at her side. "Do you know how to do this?"

Lola assumed "this" meant the assignment, so she nodded.

"Could you help me?" Lola agreed and showed her which keys were which and where to place her hands, demonstrating on her own keyboard. "Thanks, I've been struggling for the past twenty minutes."

"Yeah, no problem," Lola said. Perhaps Brooke had gotten over the detention incident or maybe Brooke hating her was all in her head.

There was a beat of silence as the girl looked like she was considering something. Finally, she said, "You were the one who found Ms. Marshall, right?"

Lola's face fell. Word had traveled fast. Now instead of being the girl with a record, she was the girl who had seen a dead body. Teachers treated her differently all day, all except Hanks of course. Someone was bound to ask her about it eventually. "Yeah, that's me," she said, her voice flat.

"I'm sorry," Brooke suddenly backpedaled. "I shouldn't have even asked—"

"No, it's fine."

"No, that must have been horrible and you probably don't want to be reminded of it," she said. She was right, but the dam Lola had built up was faulty—already there were splits and cracks in its structure. It was only a matter of time before the whole thing came down.

"It was horrible," she said quietly. "She was just doing her job and now she's dead."

Lola fought the urge to cry as a new thought emerged. What if this was her fault? Ms. Marshall had been doing her job that day, she had been waiting for Lola. Waiting for their routine meeting. Would she have gone straight home if not for her?

Brooke gave her a pitying look as if she could see the spiral in her mind. "She was a nice lady," she said.

"You had class with her?"

Brooke nodded. "Last year. Had her for tutoring too. The police were knocking around that apartment building on Sanchez Street and that's how I found out we were neighbors." She let out an empty laugh as if she had told the punchline to a bad joke. She peered over the desk to where Lola's phone lay open. "You listen to her?" she asked, gesturing to the Lana Summers album cover that Lola had as her background. It was a pretty cover, Lana's face was made up with collage art of all different bright colors.

"Yeah, do you?" Lola said with newfound enthusiasm.

"Yeah, actually me and a couple of my friends were heading downtown to look through the vinyl collection at this thrift store," Brooke explained. "Pretty sure I saw a couple Lana records when I was there last time."

"Wait, you're going today?" Lola asked.

Brooke nodded. "You should come." She told her the address and headed back to her own desk to play the keyboard a little less terribly.

Paris offered to pick her, Ken, and Erica up from school, which Lola found odd but didn't question. As they climbed inside the car, she wondered if this was a good time to take advantage of Paris' newfound kindness and ask to get dropped off downtown.

"No," Paris said flatly after she asked.

"Please!"

"That's the exact opposite direction of your aunt's house."

"Come on, Paris," she pleaded from the backseat.

"What do you want a vinyl for anyway?" Paris said. "I didn't even want vinyls when they were all we had. Big stupid disks."

"I want to collect them!" Lola explained. "I'll get in, look for one, and get out."

Paris glared at her from the rearview mirror then groaned, "Fine."

Lola shook a fist in the air. "Woo!"

"How do you know they even have Lana Summer vinyls?" Ken asked.

"Brooke told me about it in second period," she explained.

"Who's that?" Paris asked.

"Just some girl at our school."

"She invited you?" Erica asked. "The girl who allegedly hates you?"

Lola nodded. "Go figure, right?"

"Or the entire thing was just in your head," Ken said, which was definitely correct but Lola couldn't give him the satisfaction. She made a point to ignore him.

Paris eyed her in the rearview mirror, suddenly suspicious. "I thought this was just a pitstop?"

"Oh it is, Par, just for another hour or two," Ken said, quoting her. Paris glared. Ken tensed, turning away and coughing into his elbow. The cough sounded like one of Lola's, raw and ragged. "Are you okay back there?" Paris asked. Ken gave her a thumbs up, head still buried in the crook of his arm.

Lola rested a hand on his knee as the hacking subsided, worry coursing through her. "I'm okay," he said softly, placing his own hand on top of hers. After a moment, he flushed at the realization, or maybe it was because he had nearly coughed up his lung. Either way he pulled his hand away, Lola doing the same, embarrassment flowing through her.

The four of them drove to the thrift shop in silence. When they did reach it, Paris circled the block twice with no parking spot to show for it. They were left with the option of parking a couple streets over.

As the group piled out of the car, Lola asked, "Have you seen anything?"

Erica shook her head. Lola frowned, she had hoped Ms. Marshall's death would be like all the others, that Erica would at least catch a glimpse of the killer. But there didn't seem to be much luck in that pursuit either.

Erica saw the clear disappointment on her face and said, "I'm sorry, if I could control it, maybe we would've figured something out by now."

Lola was hit with a pang of guilt. "No, Ere, it's not your fault," she said quickly. "I'm glad you don't have to deal with seeing something like that."

If Ms. Marshall's death was their idea of discrete, Lola couldn't begin to imagine what those visions had shown Erica. She felt horrible for even asking. Her friend had experienced two deaths and now Lola wanted to know if she saw another?

Erica gave her a pained smile and lagged behind the rest of the group.

"I just don't understand," Paris said to Ken.

"That's because you're bitter and old," Ken replied.

"What's with the rush to become a grandma? You have the rest of your life for that." It seemed Paris was still grappling with the fact that vintage was popular.

Lola met their pace as the group crossed over an alley.

"It's trending, Par, you're not supposed to get it," she said.

Paris huffed. "I just think it's stupid—"

Ken collapsed to the ground. It was so sudden that Lola hadn't even comprehended what was happening. But Paris was ready, she caught him in her arms in the time it took Lola to blink. "Ken?" she said. There was no response.

Paris dragged him back and propped him against a building beside them. She took hold of his face, lifting it up to get a better look at him. His eyes were shut, his breathing shallow. Lola was shaken with alarm. Had he hit his head earlier and not told anyone? Did this have something to do with his cough? Paris looked just as shaken but she suddenly paused, her head whipping behind them. Lola followed her gaze.

Erica was gone.

A loud crash came from within the alley. Lola looked from Ken to Paris, a silent struggle passing between them. Another clang. They left Ken and raced into the alley.

There were three of them. These three completely average-looking men surrounded Erica. One, who was wiry and brunette, had his hand around her mouth, smothering her screams as they dragged her down the other end of the alley. The other two, one blond and the other dark haired, were dodging the assault of trash cans.

That had been the sound. Erica used her power to move the garbage cans in their direction with as much accuracy as she could. The brunette holding Erica released her mouth to push her hands behind her back instead.

Paris rushed forward with lightning speed, heading straight for the one that held Erica, tackling them both down.

Lola looked back at Ken, only able to glimpse the length of his legs. But he hadn't been moved, he was still there. Still safe.

Her eyes were on his for two long because not a second later a hand reached out, knocking her into the brick wall. She winced but steadied herself just in time to see her attacker pull a knife from his waistband. He lunged and Lola darted out of the way, feeling the slash of the blade swipe against her arm.

She gritted her teeth as the man reached for her again, throwing her to the ground. The gravel of the alley was rough on her skin. It hurt, way more than Lola knew it should. Her body was weak, far too weak.

Lola caught a glimpse of Erica scrambling to the side, arm bleeding, as Paris struggled with the brunette. She wrestled her way on top of him and struck his face so hard that black blood drew out of his mouth. He took the full force of Paris' assault, his face becoming bloodied and bruised. His hand lowered to his side, swiftly pulling out a knife, and slashing Paris across the face. She flinched, giving him the opportunity to throw her off.

Lola turned her attention to her own attacker. He stumbled on top of her and she thought quickly.

"*Bat*," she called. A metal bat formed in her hands. Before the man could process what had just happened, Lola swung it with every ounce of strength she had. As it connected, she caught a glimpse of his eyes. They were pitch black.

He dropped to the ground and her hands trembled so hard she thought they would fall off. Up close she saw how young his face was. She looked around to find that what she thought were men, actually appeared to be boys her own age. But she didn't let the thought settle, looks could be deceiving. Paris looked like a teenager too.

Lola looked up just in time to find the blond boy charging at her. She lifted her bat. Before she could strike, an object flew into the side of the boy's head, knocking him to the ground. Lola looked to Erica, whose hand was outstretched.

She could see Paris still fighting with the brunette. With a wave of her hand, Erica took hold of what Lola could now see was a brick, and sent it into the back of his head, causing him to stumble forward. Paris took the opportunity to smash a crate to pieces and skewered him with the jagged pieces of wood.

Lola jumped back as if she had been impaled herself, choking back a gasp at the sight. As the man fell to his knees in agony, Paris ripped the wood from his gut and stabbed him over and over again. Erica ran to her side. "Paris! Paris, stop!" She grabbed her arm.

Paris glared, droplets of black blood coating her face. There was a seething rage behind her eyes that made Erica let go. Paris looked around them, anger fading from her face and transforming into worry. Lola followed her gaze and found, to her horror, that the boys around them began to heal.

Paris grabbed Erica's hand and took off running; Lola followed after.

Ken was still in his spot in front of the alleys entrance, and before Lola could even worry about what they were going to do with him, Paris scooped him up and carried him in her arms like it was nothing.

They sprinted out of the alley, pushing past pedestrians and getting strange looks in the process as they got to the car. Paris slammed on the gas, and for once, Lola was grateful for it. When they got a far enough distance from the alley, Lola's nerves didn't calm. Her breaths were too quick, too heavy, and her heart pounded so hard in her chest, she feared it might jump out.

When they reached her aunt's house, Lola pounded on the door, too shaken to remember she had her own keys until Kate opened up.

Her aunt took in their disheveled states and the cuts on their body. "What happened?" she asked, ushering them inside.

"They tried to take Erica," Lola said. Erica had her arms wrapped around her. Perhaps she was trying to steady herself but anyone that gave her a good look could see how much she was shaking. Lola touched her arm and she jumped at the contact. Ken was hung across Paris shoulders; she moved him toward the couch and rested him across it.

Andi exited the bathroom and took in the horror that was the four of them. "What happened to him?" she asked.

"I don't know," Lola said, voice shaking. "He just collapsed."

Her aunts rushed to look over Ken, examining his body for any injuries. "How badly was he hit?" Kate asked. "I don't see any blood."

"This was before they attacked us, not after," Paris said.

"Well, was he acting strange today?"

Paris pursed her lips, displeased. "He was coughing during the car ride."

"Yeah like he was sick," Erica added. *But that was impossible*, Lola thought. They didn't get sick. Then she remembered the cut.

"Check his hand," she instructed.

Andi pulled back the bandage, revealing a fresh cut that leaked thick yellow pus out of it. Lola held back a gag. "Yeah, that's Wolfsbane," Andi said. Lola was shocked that Andi could recognize it immediately. It was easy to forget that her aunt Kate wasn't the only seasoned Witch in the room. "Looks like it got into his bloodstream, infected the cut."

Lola's mind flashed back to Sage. First Juniper, now Wolfsbane? "Are you sure?" she asked. "Wouldn't he able to tell once it cut him?" When Paris drank the Juniper, she reacted immediately. The plant burned her throat, singed her skin.

"Wolfsbane is slow acting," Paris explained. "It's not like Juniper, it doesn't hurt to the touch. You have to ingest it to let the poison work."

Lola looked over Ken. The poison was working alright. He was laid out on the sofa, eyes fluttering as he drifted in and out of consciousness. His breathing so shallow that she could barely see the rise and fall of his chest. Her thoughts were shouting at her. *Not again, not again, not again.*

"We can do something right?" Lola asked, her voice frail. "To cure it?"

"Doesn't seem like he got a large dose. His body should be able to heal itself in time," Kate said, considering his stiff body. "I should be able to make something to speed up the process though."

Lola had never been more thankful for her aunt's love of potions. She waited in agony for what felt like hours as Kate got to work. When she was done, she returned with two vials in hand.

Kate held up the vial in her right hand. "This is to clean the cut." A watery liquid a shade of blue-green swished around in the tube. She raised her left hand. A murky brown liquid that resembled sewer water filled the vial. "And this is for him to drink."

Erica grimaced while Lola made a nauseated noise. "Are we sure you aren't the one going around poisoning people?" Lola said.

Her aunt gave her a deadpan look and stuffed the two vials in her hand. A buzzing came from her back pocket. Kate reached for the phone instantly. "Just make him take it," she said, before walking away to take the call in another room.

Erica held Ken's palm open as Lola poured the potion onto a clean cloth. Her hands trembled. "Hey," Lola said. "How are you doing?"

"In one piece," she said, looking down at the gash on her own arm.

Lola lifted her sleeve, showing off her own wound. Searing pain shot through her. With aching bones, and throbbing skin, Lola didn't let on to the agony she was in. She looked at Erica who treated the slice like it was no more than a paper cut, then at Paris, whose wound had already healed over. One calling couldn't compensate for weeks of no magick. Her body was at its limit. "Look, we'll have matching battle scars," Lola said. She forced herself to smile and saw Erica's nerves ease away.

Ken stirred beneath her. "W-What's going on?" His words were slurred.

Lola gently shushed him and lifted the vial to his lip. "Drink this," she instructed but Ken jerked away in disgust.

"What is it?"

"Something that'll make you feel better." Ken still looked apprehensive. "You don't have a lot of room to complain Mr. Would-hide-a-zombie-bite-in-an-apocalypse."

"Zombies aren't real," said Ken. He downed the potion in one gulp, cringing in repulsion.

Kate reentered the room, now with four envelops. "Good timing," she said. "Your papers just came in."

CHAPTER THIRTY-ONE
LOLA

Lola stared down at the document in her hands. Her aunts ran through the agreement with the group. They had gone over benefits, terms of service, and compensation. But then came the one line that made them all pause.

"You didn't say we couldn't leave," Erica said.

In signing these documents and drafting into the Guard, they would agree to be stationed as Inlanders in San Francisco. Unable to leave unless directed otherwise. Lola thought of the family she had back in New York, would she never be able to visit them?

During the summer, when it was decided that she'd live with Kate, she remembered things being arranged mostly over the phone and video chat. She even had to take the plane to California by herself. Had this been the reason why?

"It's not that bad," Andi said, though her face betrayed her.

"How am I supposed to go to Carnegie if I can't leave the city?" Erica said, but it was clear she was mostly speaking to herself. Everyone knew the answer to her question. None of them would be leaving, not any time soon.

Lola had thought of college, but probably not as much as Erica or Ken. Majoring in music had once been the obvious choice, but the older she got, the less realistic it seemed. But what else was she good at? What else was she interested in?

With Erica as her Guardian, her friend would be at the mercy of where she chose to live. Lola would move to Pennsylvania in a heartbeat if it meant Erica got to attend her dream college.

It seemed this choice didn't matter too much now.

"Why is there no date listed for the years of service?" Paris asked, looking at Kate critically.

Kate met her gaze. "You know why."

Not only did the Council control where they lived, but they could release them from service on a whim. Or not at all.

"They really expect us to join something we don't understand in the slightest, don't they?" Paris said.

"Par," Lola said. "You don't have to do this, you know?"

Lola thought back to the attack. Paris, face coated in blood, stabbing the attacker over and over. It scared her more than she would've liked to admit. Paris had always been like a big sister to her. Always offering advice, always looking out for all of them whenever she could. Seeing her so violent was jarring. It was the same feeling she had months ago after Paris's family arrived. The Paris she knew was never shaken up like that. What if being an Inlander brought that out again?

Apparently, Paris felt differently, because she looked at Lola like she was crazy. "Of course I'm doing this," she said. "I'm not going to let you guys have all the fun near-death experiences behind my back."

Lola wanted to smile, but for some reason couldn't muster it. She looked back at the agreement.

One little signature in exchange for all the information they desired.

"If it helps, I feel like it's worth it, for the protection alone," Andi said.

"You were attacked in your own home," Ken pointed out, an unimpressed look on his face.

"But we're alive," Kate pointed out. "Can't say the same for a lot of people the last couple of months."

"Kate!" Andi scolded her, clearly appalled.

"I'm being honest," she said. "They got lucky today. You know it and I know it. The longer we delay this, the less we'll be able to help." She turned to the group. Her aunt always had a firmness to her, but Lola could see something deeper in her eyes now. A silent plea that was just for her. "So sign, don't sign, as long as it's a decision."

One little signature.

Lola took a pen in her left hand, its weight suddenly multiplying as she stared down at the document. They were all the same except Erica's, which stated that she would only be acting as an Inlander until she was initiated as a Guardian.

After a moment's hesitation, the rest of her friends followed her lead. One by one they signed.

When they finished, they looked at the two sisters with anticipation. "Now what?" Lola asked, and just as she did, the documents crumbled into dust in their hands.

"Now we talk," said Kate. She stood from her chair and motioned for the group to follow her down to the basement.

Venturing down the stairs, Andi said, "Where to even start?"

"How about you finally tell us who the hell tried to kill us today?" Paris suggested, a tinge of annoyance in her voice.

"Those were the same guys behind the murders, right?" Lola said. "And the ones who attacked you?"

"Yes," Andi replied.

"So, who were they?" Ken asked, stumbling as he walked, the wolfbane still affecting him. The group crowded around the round table in the basement. "What are they?"

"That's kind of complicated to explain," she said. "First you have to understand—"

"They were demons," Kate said abruptly.

"Excuse me?" Paris said.

"Or we could just come right out with it," Andi murmured.

Kate shook her head and grabbed a piece of paper and pen from off the table. "Honestly, Andi, no need to overcomplicate this."

"What do you mean demons?" Lola asked.

"Exactly what I said," Kate said. "You were attacked by demons."

Without warning the world seemed to come to a halt. *Demons?* Her only experience with the term was the human definition. Beings with unexplainable powers with ties to the darkness. The definition that more often than not referred to her own people.

"I don't understand," Lola said. There were Nightwalkers, there were Lien, and there were Humans. There wasn't anything else. At least nothing she had been taught about.

Kate drew four circles on the piece of paper, all interconnecting like a Venn diagram. The group leaned closer to get a better look. Kate pointed to the very middle where all the other circles connected. "This here is the Mortal Realm," she said, labeling it. She then pointed to the circle above it. "And this one is the Magick Realm."

"But there are three other spaces," Erica said, her eyes widening. "Are you saying there are other realms?"

Kate nodded. She took her pen and wrote inside the circle directly under the Mortal Realm, labeling it, "The Demon Realm."

"There's been other Realms out there this entire time and the Guard has just been keeping it a secret. Why?" Erica asked.

"And why in over five hundred years have I never come across one of these demons?" Paris asked.

"The Council has their reason for keeping this a secret," Kate said. "For one, it'd be a lot harder for us to do our job."

The pit in Lola's stomach grew five sizes. One for each realm she saw on the page. Five realms, not two. She was raised as a Witch her entire life, always taught that keeping the secret of their existence was more important than anything. But there was another secret, one larger than the one she had kept all these years.

It was too much. Is this what it felt like for the humans that knew about them? To have their reality shattered, to learn they weren't as significant as they thought they were?

"And what is an Inlanders job exactly? To kill them?"

"Not just kill them, erase them. We make sure the general public never finds a trace of them."

"But why?" Lola asked. They were at a clear disadvantage. Ms. Marshall and Lauren Carter hadn't even known something was after them. Hadn't even realized there was a need to be cautious.

"The truth of the matter is we're not experts," Kate said. "Demons know far more about us than we do about them. We can't enter their Realm, we can barely capture them. The only certain thing is that they can be killed. If the public finds out how truly ignorant we are to this threat, how do you think they'd react?"

Lola's own panic gave her all the insight she needed. After only a few weeks in Mantle she knew that Nightwalkers took pride in their strength more than anything. Undermine that with the prospect of something greater and the entire system would come crumpling down.

"What exactly are these things anyway?" Ken asked. "Why are they killing us?"

Kate paused for a moment, thinking of the best way to explain. "I want you to think of a demon as like a parasite. One that looks like a person and talks like a person, but isn't. Underneath it's skin is a monster that feeds on energy," she said. "A soul is the purest form of energy there is. A demon will kill you, steal your soul and increase its own strength tenfold."

"The stronger the being, the stronger the soul," Andi put in. "They'll take whatever they can get but they prefer a Nightwalker one."

Steal your soul. The words echoed in Lola's head. She had always known that when she died, her soul would join her ancestors in the afterlife. But if a demon absorbed your soul—your essence—what happened to you? What happened to Lauren Carter? Was she just gone forever? Had their ritual been for nothing?

"So how do you stop them? The ones we fought in the alley just healed right back up," Paris said.

Kate traveled to the back of the room and retrieved the black case they saw her give Marcel back in Mantle. Setting it carefully on the table, the group gathered close as she opened it. There were fewer vials filled this time. Only a handful contained the oozing black substance from before.

"What is that stuff?" Lola asked, scrunching her nose.

"That is demon blood," Kate said nonchalantly.

"Oh my God. Why do you even have that?"

"That's the job," Andi said.

"To collect demon blood?" Paris asked.

"Well, there's more than that. We monitor and record the demon activity in the area, patrol the neighborhood..."

"So, a lot of fucking work?" Paris ran her fingers through her hair. This was more than just killing them. They barely escaped a fight with some demons and now they were supposed to get close enough to drain them of their blood?

"But what's the blood for?" Erica asked.

"The only thing strong enough to kill a demon is a demon," Kate paused, letting the statement sink in for them. "We have tried everything. Burning, beheading, stabbing. The things just won't die, not by our hands. What does work? Using their own strength against them. We take their blood and make a weapon out of it. We call it antacide."

Lola remembered the reports she had read in this very room. Her aunts had been using antacide injections to interrogate the demon. If she was correct, it must have been like receiving mini doses of poison. She thought of what they had done to Ken, to Paris. *Good*, she thought. Let them have a taste of their own medicine.

Kate twisted the vial between her fingers. "Lace some of this on a weapon of choice and you can kill almost any demon."

"Almost?" said Lola.

"Yes, almost."

A chill traveled down Lola's spine. Kate set the vial back in the case, then rolled up her sleeve, holding out her bicep for them all to see. "Once you're initiated, you get one of these," she said. The Inlander insignia was branded into her arm. It was a crossbow surrounded by leaf laurels. Lola had seen her aunt's bare arms before, there was no way she could miss a brand like that.

"They brand you? That's metal," Lola said. When she was suddenly hit with the prospect of one day being branded herself, the idea became a lot less cool. "I mean in a really messed up kinda way."

"You also get one of these."

A short sword unraveled itself in Kate's hand. It was a shining piece of steel with a black hilt. "How did you do that?" Lola was stunned. As far as she knew, summoning was something unique to her.

"It's the brand," Kate explained. "It's infused with magick. When you're paired, you'll be matched with a weapon you can summon on command."

"So let me make sure I'm getting all of this," said Paris. "You track a demon down, bring it back here, take its blood, then kill it?" Something clicked in Lola's mind. She looked over the locked door across from them, remembering the smell of sage that day. A sound proof spell?

"The demon that attacked you," Lola said. "You did bring it down here."

Her aunts studied her carefully. Andi gently nudged Kate, who rolled her eyes. "Yeah," she said. "We brought it down here to question it and it escaped."

"Does that happen often?" Lola asked.. "You just have demons chilling in the house while I'm asleep?"

Lola didn't know what she felt. Shock? Betrayal? All the time she had spent worrying about some danger coming for her aunts and they had invited the threat into the house. This operation was happening right beneath her feet. The look on her face must have concerned them because Andi rapidly shook her head. "No, no, that was the first time we've done something like that," she said, looking regretful.

"That's fine and all," said Erica clearly preoccupied with other thoughts. Her eyes were still on the Venn diagram on the table. "But there are still two other spaces. What else is out there?"

Kate sighed. "We don't know," she admitted.

"Well then how—" Ken started, but Kate cut him off.

"The diagram is a little misleading," she explained. "Think of the Mortal Realm as neutral ground, and the four other Realms have access points to it, not to each other. The Alereis border for example, only we can get in and out. Same goes for all the other Realms." She pointed to the two empty circles. "If whatever's behind these two Realms never wants to come out, we may never know what's there."

"So, I assume the Demon Realm—" Paris began.

"Has its borders wide open," Andi finished for her.

"Is something wrong?" Ken asked. "I mean, if demons have always been around, why the sudden urgency? Why were you questioning one?"

"Around September, a huge increase in demon activity came up out of nowhere. It started getting colder, the weather started acting weird..."

Lola remembered the weeks of freezing rain and storms they had gotten back-to-back.

"A lot of demons showing up in one place at the same time isn't a good look," Kate explained.

"So, you started investigating?" Lola said.

"And the Council won't take us seriously," Andi said bitterly.

Kate nodded. "I don't believe in coincidences. Murders this frequent and this brutal aren't random," she said. "And I don't believe your attack was either."

Like all Nightwalkers, there were several legends about Guardians that Lola had heard over the years. One that stuck out to her in particular was of their origin. It was said that the first Guardians were cast out of the Goddesses circle, exiled to Alereis, doing all they could to work off their karmic debt in hopes of one day regaining Aurora's favor. Ever since, Guardians only had one mission: guide and protect Alereis with their lives. Now Lola finally had an idea of who they were protecting them from.

She walked the halls of the Themis Court with her aunts and Erica as they followed a Guardian to the ceremony room. His skin was tan and he and Erica matched each other in height. He wore a white uniform jacket with black shoulder lapels. On the left breast pocket was the Guardian insignia, black leaf laurels surrounding a shield. Guardian colors were white and black, while Inlanders seemed to be black and gold. Based on what the General wore at the trial, Lola figured Huntress's colors must be brown and black then. "So, what exactly do I have to do?" Erica asked him.

"Nothing really," he explained, not looking back. It was the first time he had spoken. "We'll get you into the ceremony room and wrap the bond around you. You'll say the oath and then you'll be bonded as Guardian and charge."

It sounded easy enough, but it meant so much more. Guardians were only reserved for the most important there was. Lola still wanted to know how Kate convinced the Council she was valuable enough to need one.

"We usually only do that after you've been trained and initiated. However, I've been informed that we're here under special circumstances today?" He said it like a question, waiting for confirmation on what those special circumstances were, but Erica stayed quiet.

When they reached the ceremony room, the Guardian held a hand up. "Wait right here." His body dissipated into a flash of gray light and within a second, he was gone.

"Rude," Kate grumbled.

"This is weird, right?" Erica asked Lola. "It's not just me?"

"Never thought I'd be in the Themis Court once, let alone three times," Lola said. "So no, not just you."

The Guardian peeked his head through the doors. "We're ready for you." The group approached, causing him to shake his head. "Just the two."

After a quick look at her aunts, who both nodded, her and Erica stepped inside. The room was stark marble white, almost blindingly so, and at the end of it a man in white and gold robes stood behind a podium.

Lola nudged Erica as they walked down the aisle. "Dude, are we getting married or what?"

She joked but the reality was all too similar. The two of them would be bonded for life today. Where she went, Erica followed. They would know each other more intimately than they had through nearly ten years of friendship. Was she ready for Erica to know her so deeply?

Erica stopped and stared ahead at the podium, her mouth in a thin line. "Still sure you wanna do this?"

She nodded instinctively. Being brave for Erica was as easy as breathing. If this is what she needed to do to keep her alive, it was as good as done. Lola held out her hand, offering it up for her to take. "Let's get hitched."

Upon reaching the podium, the man in white robes opened a brown case in front of him and took out what Lola assumed was the bond. It was a golden rope that held a faint glow. Without a word, the man took one end of the bond and wrapped it around Lola's arm and did the same to Erica's, tethering them together. Lola was quickly learning that Guardians as a species probably weren't known for polite conversation.

"Repeat after me." His voice was deep and commanding. "As above, as so below, let my fall from grace be atoned. As I walk these lands, I swear to watch over, guide, and shelter this soul as if it were my own. And as Aurora has made it so, I will stand for Alereis and all its inhabitants until my fight is over. Blessed by the Goddess to be thy protector."

Lola could practically see the beads of sweat forming on Erica's forehead at the mere thought of that oath. She gave her friend a reassuring smile. "Hey, it's just me." She wasn't sure if this promise being between them rather than a complete stranger was better or worse in Erica's eyes. Lola couldn't remove the crushing weight of responsibility she now carried but she could do her part to lighten the load. *Note to self,* she thought. *Try not to die.*

Erica locked eyes with her, taking a shaking breath and slowly repeated the oath. With each line, Erica struggled. She pushed through the lines with such effort that Lola couldn't be sure her friend didn't feel the weight of each individual word.

"Blessed by the Goddess to be thy protector," said the Guardian.

"Blessed by the Goddess to be thy protector." Erica repeated. The bond suddenly gave off a warmth that traveled throughout Lola's entire body, and then something in her core snapped into place. It felt solid and permanent and ancient. She wondered if Erica felt the same. Did that mean it was done? Did she have no say in if the oath went through or not?

After a tense moment of waiting, the warm energy began to fade and the Guardian removed the bond from their arms. "We're done here. You're free to go," he said, packing up. The allure and authority gone from his voice. Now he just sounded tired.

"Wait, that's it?" Lola said.

"We usually make a bigger event out of it for initiates who've earned it," he explained offhandedly. Erica winced. "But at its core, this is all it is."

He took the case and headed toward the back room, leaving the two alone. Kate and Andi stood from the bench outside, when the two returned. "How are you feeling?" Andi asked.

"Underwhelmed," Lola said. "Maybe a bit tingly."

She imagined what an actual bonding ceremony was like. Erica would be among her peers, celebrated and revered like all Guardians were. But here she was, bonded to her in a half-baked, closed-door ritual with only one witness to bear it.

CHAPTER THIRTY-TWO
KATE

KATE WALKED ALONGSIDE HER sister in the park. It was around 3:00 a.m. and the two were on patrol. They were dressed in all-black leggings and T-shirts. The official Inlander uniform, black and silver gear made of material as strong as Kevlar and as light as cotton, was mostly for formalities. It didn't seem practical or discreet to be wearing matching military garb in a park.

Patrols were often uneventful. Walk around the neighborhood, make sure the idiots who were walking alone this time of night weren't killed, take the blood when you could. It was pretty simple.

Kate surveyed the area. They hadn't spotted any corpses yet, which was always a good sign. Her hopes of getting a few hours of sleep tonight were crushed as they entered a clearing near the edge of the park and were met with an unpleasant sight.

Three figures, one female, two males, blocked off the path. Keeping a jogger from passing through.

Jogging? At 3:00 a.m? Really? Kate thought. Sometimes Kate thought these people wanted to get murdered.

"Mugging?" Andi tried. Hopefully, this was just some human altercation. Something they could resolve easily. While Kate believed human affairs were none of their business, Andi would not take that as an answer.

"Guess we'll find out," said Kate as they advanced on the group. "Hey! Is everything alright over here?"

The young woman examined her with a glare. She had dark blonde hair and pale skin. "Yeah, we're all good here, thanks," she said, dismissing them. But the jogger looked over at them with wide eyes. He was shaking.

"Yeah, he's fine, lady. Why don't you mind your own business?" one of the men said.

The jogger took his opportunity. It seemed these jogs were doing him well, because he quickly disappeared into the park, leaving Kate and Andi alone with the group. One of the men groaned in frustration.

"Don't worry about him," the young woman said, her eyes clouded to black and her face lit up. "Ooh, two Nightwalkers are a much better trade."

Demon eyes could see right through a person. It was how they could pick out souls. How they knew who was a Nightwalker.

Without giving Kate so much as a glance, Andi took it upon herself to send courses of electricity through their bodies. They fell to their knees wincing, trying to shake off the sensation. The young woman was the first to be able to fight through it.

This one had to have been the leader, the one who had consumed more souls than the rest.

As she advanced, Kate reached for her magick, and when she finally had a grasp on it, she unleashed a wave of pain on the demon.

The young woman screamed, withering and convulsing on the ground. Kate was manipulating her muscles, pulling and tearing at certain tendons she deemed fit. The Inlander brand began to tingle on her forearm as Kate summoned her weapon. The sword unraveled itself within the palm of her hand. Kate had made sure to lace it with antacide before they left.

She would have to kill this one quickly. If she had broken out of Andi's hold so quickly, attempting to subdue her again for the blood would only cause them problems.

The girl raised her head, teeth bared and glaring. As Kate raised her arm to strike, a powerful force slammed into her. One of the male demons had tackled her down. With her focus broken, the girl got to her feet, the other demon quickly following behind.

The demon Kate struggled with rolled her over, positioning himself on top of her. His hands clutched around her throat, choking the air out of her lungs. Andi rushed over, drawing her dagger, and sinking it into the back of the man on top of Kate. His body stiffened, allowing Kate to kick him squarely in the chest, knocking him off her.

Kate pounded a hand across her chest as she coughed. "Dammit." The two demons were nowhere in sight.

"It's my fault," Andi said, holding up a syringe filled with blood. "I took too long."

Kate waved her off. She didn't need to hear excuses. "Whatever, I just need this bastard to hurry up and turn to dust." She kicked the demon's corpse.

Andi bit her lip and retrieved her dagger from his back. They stood in the park, waiting for the body to disappear in silence.

When the two got home, Kate was ready for a long shower and the chance to throw herself into bed. But as soon as the front door opened, she was confronted with the words, "Where were you?"

Lola stared down at them from the top of the stairs. It was four in the morning, she had school in a few hours.

Kate locked the front door and sighed. "On patrol."

"And you didn't think to tell me?" she said, her voice like ice. In all honesty, Kate hadn't. With Lola's new understanding of what was actually happening, she wondered what her niece thought of their sudden disappearance. How long had she been here waiting?

"Force of habit," Andi explained. "We should've said something."

"I called," Lola said. "You didn't answer."

"A ringer kind of defeats the purpose of stealth." Kate meant to say it lightly, but her niece's frown only grew.

"What do you expect me to do?" Lola said quietly. "You just want me to sit here all night while you're out risking your lives?"

"You're not coming with us on patrol if that's what you're getting at," Kate said firmly. She needed to get ahead of this nonsense before Lola took it any further.

"But why? I've signed the papers—"

"You have signed papers to be drafted but you're not an Inlander, not yet," she said. "You have no training, no magick, and you barely survived your last run in with a demon."

Lola bristled at the mention of no magick and Andi looked at her strangely. Kate had nearly forgotten she hadn't informed her sister of their nieces' recklessness.

"What do you expect me to do if something happens to you?" Lola said, swallowing hard.

"Lola, nothing's going to—" Andi started, and Kate was grateful Lola cut her off before she lied.

"You really just expect me to just sit around and do nothing?"

Kate met her eye. "Yes," she said.

Lola's body visible slumped. She stood from the steps, turning away and making her back to her room. "How can you ask me that when you're all I have left?"

CHAPTER THIRTY-THREE
LOLA

LOLA SAT IN HER room that night on the phone with Ken. The last time she left had been for dinner hours ago. It was midnight, which meant she couldn't sleep, and since she knew Ken was awake too, making the call was easy.

"Does it look like they're leaving out again tonight?" he asked.

"I don't know," she said. "I haven't been out there for a while."

While her aunts were out patrolling, Lola had woken up in the middle of the night, scared out of her mind that something had happened to them. Ken talked her down until they returned.

Perhaps she should've called Paris, someone who'd actually be awake at that hour. But her fingers had a mind of their own and told her to call him. Clearly her first instinct had been correct, because Ken answered on the second ring and stayed awake with her for the next three hours.

From book and TV show predictions to mindless ramblings around 3:00 a.m, Lola just barely distracted herself from the numbing fear that coursed through her.

When Lola saw him at school this morning, she felt bad seeing him so tired, but he assured her that he didn't mind staying up with her. "Thanks again for last night," she said.

"And that is the third time today," Ken said. "Believe it or not, Lo, but on rare occasions your company is enjoyable."

She smiled. "I don't know what came over me," she said. "I thought I was becoming okay with the whole Inlander thing."

"You can be and still worry about your aunts," he said. "But they've been doing this for years, Lo. I'm sure they're much better off than us."

She nodded along, then remembered he couldn't see her. "Yeah, you're right," she said. "Hey, do you wanna stream BvR?" BvR was a sci-fi show the two had never gotten around to watching aside from when Lola first showed it to him back in the tenth grade.

"I've seen it," Ken said.

Her brows furrowed in confusion. "What? Since when?" she said.

"Well not all of it, I watched up to season ten after you kept talking about it," he said. There was a long pause as she was filled up with absolute delight. "Hello?"

"You listened to one of my recommendations?" she said slowly.

"I guess on some, but very minimal occasions, you also have taste." She could feel his smile through the screen.

"Wow. There are seventeen seasons though, we've got a long way to go," she said. "But damn, I can't believe you watched it without me."

"Kenny, why can't you—" A loud slurring voice came from his side of the phone. The sound cut off. Frowning, Lola looked down to see that Ken had put her on hold.

After a few moments, Ken came back. "Hello?" he said.

"Hey, what's up?"

"That was just my mom, sorry," he said. Lola had met his mom, but from what she heard, she barely recognized that as her voice. "What were you—oh yeah, haven't you already seen it?" This time the long pause came from him "Why do you care so much if we watch it together or not?"

The way he said it made her bite the inside of her cheek. There was humor in his voice. Like it was a question that he already had the answer to but asked simply for the hell of it.

She swallowed. "I just like seeing your reactions to stuff, I dunno," she said, words suddenly becoming difficult to muster. "And I usually have to force you to watch stuff so this is a damn miracle."

"I see," Ken said.

He was so annoying.

"You ask a lot of questions, mister."

"And you are an expert at avoiding them."

Lola heard Andi calling her from downstairs. They were leaving for another patrol. She hadn't gotten a feel for how often these patrols took place. Her aunts were experienced at sneaking around. Catching them yesterday was just bad luck. She sighed as she heard the front door close. "They left," she said to him, hoping her voice didn't sound too pathetic.

"I can stay up," he said. It wasn't a question. All she had to do was say the word. God, she wanted him to more than anything. The thought of being here alone made Lola want to curl up into a ball. But instead of begging him to stay, what came out of her mouth was, "No it's fine. Kate was right, I need to learn to adjust."

"That doesn't mean you have to adjust alone."

"Ken, I'm not gonna let you sit on the phone with me all night again," she said firmly.

"Who said anything about being on the phone?" he said, mischief in his voice. Oh, that was never good.

"What are you talking about?"

There was a pause, as if he was letting the anticipation build up. "Can you be ready in thirty minutes?"

CHAPTER THIRTY-FOUR

KEN

SNEAKING OUT WASN'T AS fun when no one else was home to catch you. Ken didn't know what came over him, but once his mom left, he couldn't help himself. If she was going to be out all night, so was he.

Lola was waiting for him outside her house. She wore an emerald green sweater tucked into a black skirt and was adorned with gold jewelry. Clearly, Ken's request for her to slip something on, fell on deaf ears.

Thankfully, his mom's boyfriend had picked her up tonight, leaving Ken free to take the truck. The two piled inside, with giddy laughter. "Okay, where are we going?" Lola asked. An impromptu 1:00 a.m. drive did mean they were limited with their options, but Ken had come up with a few ideas.

They arrived at a park which had an outdoor roller rink. After a moment of hesitation, Lola called skates for both of them and they sat on the outside steps lacing them on. "If I fall and break something, are you liable or the company you called these from?" Ken said.

"Definitely the company," Lola said.

"But are you not technically the manufacturer?" he said.

"I see myself as more of a delivery driver."

Ken narrowed his eyes. "You don't know that for sure," he said. "I still say I have grounds to sue."

She rolled her eyes and they stepped up to the rink. Lola took a few hesitant steps forward and Ken followed behind, keeping a close eye on her. "I thought you knew how to skate?" he said.

She set one foot onto the smooth floor of the rink and gripped the edge. "I do," she said. "I just have to take a second to remember."

He nudged her forward so they could both get into the rink. "Stop!" She swatted his hand away.

"Then go!" he urged.

She got both feet into the rink and he placed a hand on the small of her back. She tensed, looking up at him and then quickly away as he guided her forward. They mostly stayed on the sidelines as Lola shuffled along the rail. After a few moments she finally found her footing and picked up the pace, gilding away from him. "See, I got it."

Ken caught up with her, which prompted Lola to move even faster and farther away. He wasn't sure if this was a race or a chase, but it sure went on for a while. After a couple laps around the rink, he came to a stop while Lola gilded right past him again. "Are you done?" he called out after her.

Lola looked back at him as she circled back around. She didn't move her legs, letting the momentum from the skates carry her back. She grabbed onto Ken's shirt as she rolled straight into him, dragging them both down. Lucky for her, Ken broke her fall.

Lola pushed herself up from on top of his chest. Ken froze, unsure if he was dizzy from how close she was or the concussion he probably had. "I don't know how to stop," she said sheepishly.

"You don't say?"

It took a couple searches for them to find restaurants that were open all night. Finally, they came across a pizza place and 3:00 a.m. pizza sounded better than nothing.

Ken went to grab two takeout menus, but Lola took it upon herself to take a kids' menu and crayons for herself. They agreed on a pepperoni and bacon pizza that they'd eat in the car.

While waiting, Lola opened up her kids' menu and surveyed the drawing. It was a picture of a frog in a pond, sitting on a lily pad. She opened the box of crayons and surveyed the selection. Red, brown, and purple. "Really?" said Lola.

"I know." Ken nodded along. "You'd think you could get a decent box of crayons in here."

"What kind of establishment are they running?" She held up the three crayons. "What color should the pond be? Red, brown or purple?"

"Uh purple," he replied.

She nodded. "I mean between the options of the red sea, shit water, and radioactive sludge, I'd say you picked the best one."

Before they could even start on the word search, their order was ready. As they left, Ken held the pizza in one hand and felt Lola brush against the other. He held his palm out, a silent invitation. Very carefully, she let her hand slip into his. They interlocked, connecting like two puzzle pieces fitting together.

They drove to the beach. Sitting in the back of the pickup as they ate and watched movies on Ken's laptop.

Lola leaned into him. Tension and worries from earlier melting away. Ken didn't think of his mom, drunkenly roaming the streets of the city or waiting for him back at home. He thought of Lola and her touch. Of how even after a year away she was still the grounding force in his life. He couldn't imagine being here with anyone else—holding anyone else like he held her.

Ken knew there was more to Lola than she let on. There was something that ate away at her, the same way it ate away at him. But in that moment, there were no expectations or secrets or shame between them. When they laughed it was full and unfiltered, the air of uncertainty around them gone. No deflecting or distracting. It was like they were in their own little reality, she and him. Like nothing outside of this car mattered.

"Ken. Ken wake up." Lola's voice pulled him out of his slumber. Ken opened his eyes and looked down to find her head resting on his shoulder. He took in the scent of her marshmallow and vanilla conditioner.

"Hm?" he said, still groggy.

"We fell asleep," she said, sitting up and moving a respectful distance away. The loss of contact hit him immediately, the cool air taking the place of her warmth.

Ken looked over his shoulder to catch a view of the beach. Daylight cast over the sand. Everything was golden, including her. Ken had never believed in Gods but if the stories were true, the real Goddess of Day was right in front of him. "It's morning," he said, stretching his arms over his head.

"Yeah it's—" A look of horror came over her. "It's sunrise! You gotta get me home!" She scrambled to her feet. Ken swallowed, quickly following after her. This definitely held grounds for panic.

He drove her home as fast as the speed limit would allow even though the damage was already done. Kate and Andi had to have been home for a while now. Lola instructed him to park a block away when he reached her house. She told him there was no use for them both to get yelled at.

"It was my idea. Are you sure I shouldn't—"

"No, Ken, the worst I'll get is a shoe thrown at me and screamed at," Lola explained. "You? Kate will probably hex you, or strike you with lighting or something,"

"Well, I definitely like being uncharred," he said, then frowned. "But still, I shouldn't have done this. It was a bad idea."

Lola shook her head and looked at him like he was ridiculous. "It was an amazing idea," she assured him, her voice soft. "I had a really nice time."

He had to fight back a grin. "So did I," he admitted.

They sat there for a moment, staring at each other, unsure of what to do next. His eyes drifted from her eyes down to her lips, then back up. All he wanted to do was lean in, to kiss her. But he held himself back and just as that fight within him started to give out, Lola said, "I should probably get in there."

He cleared his throat. "Right, yeah." Why did he keep doing this? At every opportunity, he'd managed to wind up in the same position. Why couldn't he stay away?

"Right, um, bye," Lola said, her hand hovering over the door handle. Before she could leave, Ken reached out without thinking. He grabbed her wrist, holding her there. He could feel Lola freeze up at the contact. She looked down at his hand, then up at him, waiting in anticipation. Her lips parted. But Ken didn't know what he was doing, only that he didn't want her to go. *Say something!* his mind hissed.

He thought quickly, slowly releasing her, and reaching into the backseat to retrieve the kids menu from the pizza place. "You uh, forgot to take your picture," he said.

"Oh," said Lola. He couldn't read her expression. Was she disappointed? Relived? "Thank you." She took the menu from him, offering a small smile before she left the truck. It took everything in him not to bang his head against the steering wheel.

Lola scrambled down the street. As he watched her disappear inside the Hallow's house, Ken sighed. If he never saw her again after tonight, he wouldn't have been surprised.

PART THREE | THE DEMON REALM

CHAPTER THIRTY-FIVE
LOLA

"How could you have been so stupid?" It was the fifth time Lola had heard it that morning.

Kate and Andi had been on the couch surrounded by candles and crystals, as if they planned to conjure her up. When Lola revealed she hadn't been kidnapped, Kate had thrown a shoe at her and proceeded to scold her ever since.

As she got ready for school, utterly exhausted, the two berated her with questions she struggled to ignore. "Did you want to spite us?" Kate said. It had been hours and she was still fuming. "Put us through what we put you through? Is that it?"

"What?" Lola exclaimed. How could she even think that?

"I don't know how long it's going to take you to get this, young lady, but this is our job—"

"God, that's not it, I swear!"

"Then what was it then?" Lola had left Ken's name out of the conversation, claiming that she went out on her own for the night. Of course, that made things seem worse than they were, but she couldn't stand the thought of her aunts hating Ken for this. Especially for something that had made her entire year. Kate would never understand how badly she needed last night to happen. She wasn't sure Ken fully understood himself.

Something clicked within her and it was almost like her entire year away meant nothing. When Ken looked at her, he didn't see the troubled girl from Maine. He didn't see the things she had done or the people she had hurt. He just saw her. Life wasn't the way it used to be, no, but that one moment had been better than anything in the past. And before last night, Lola had lost hope that that was even possible.

Maybe different wasn't so bad after all.

"I don't know, okay?" she said, crossing her arms.

"You don't even bother to learn magick to protect yourself, but you think you're good enough to go out in the middle of the night alone?" Kate said.

"I felt like leaving so I left," Lola sneered. "Anything was better than sitting upstairs alone."

"You don't just leave the house 'cause you feel like it," Kate said firmly. "You don't get to—"

"You're not my mom, Kate!" Lola exclaimed. She regretted the words the moment they left her lips and for just a moment she could see Kate's anger falter. If there was one thing this family didn't do, it was bring up her mother. Her mother who had passed on to Lola nothing but a curse and an empty grave plot.

Andi rushed into the room, having finally heard their argument. "Hey! What the hell is wrong with you?" she said, her eyes were wide. "Don't bring your mother into this and don't *ever* talk to Kate like that," she said.

Kate put a hand up to stop her, not breaking her eyes away from Lola. "I may not be your mother," she said slowly. "But you will respect me if you expect to stay here any longer. If not, the door is right over there."

Lola held her eye with a glare. She threw her bag over her shoulder and rushed to the front door. "I gotta get to school," she said. There was a ringing in her ears, and her entire body was shaking.

"Lola—"

"I'll see you later." She closed the door without another word.

Lola had shown her face at school, keeping up appearances with her friends and pretending everything was fine for most of the day. She was gone before last period. The back door to the gym was never locked or monitored. It had been her escape route for years now.

She was on her way to Sanchez Street, which on the bus was only a couple stops away from the school. Lola recalled her conversation with Brooke. Ms. Marshall lived in the apartment building here and while Lola wasn't sure what she expected to find, at the very least, one person would be investigating her murder.

She reached the building and was lucky enough that the apartment had a digital directory. She scrolled to 'M' and found an 'S. Marshall'. Lola frowned, she hadn't once thought of Ms. Marshall's first name before.

A key card was required to enter. Lola paced outside, waiting for her chance. After some time a family left the building, holding the door open long enough for her to slip inside. Ms. Marshall's apartment was on the second floor. Lola pulled the bobby pin from her hair, prepared to pick the lock on the door when she was met with no resistance from the handle.

Unlocked? Had someone been here before her? Lola entered before she lost her nerve. To her utter shock, Ms. Marshall's things were still here. If she thought she liked Ms. Marshall before, seeing her apartment sealed the deal. It was maximalism to its fullest degree. Burnt oranges and deep greens and blues covered the space. Every shelf and nook had some sort of knickknacks within it. And plants were everywhere, half of them fake and the other half barely alive.

What was going to happen to this place? Did Ms. Marshall have any family that could collect her things? Or were these trinkets one day away from ending up at a dump?

Her phone dinged in her bag. Lola found a text from Erica waiting for her.

Where are you? We're heading to your aunts

Lola quickly thought up a lie. She didn't need anyone worrying over her.

Hanks is holding me back for practice. I'll catch up!

Erica sent her a thumbs down. **Call when you're free!**

She pocketed the phone and walked to the bedroom, passing a wall of classic vinyl's, even noticing a Lana Summers one. It all made her heart ache. Ms. Marshall had a personality, interests, a life. And now it was all gone.

It looked like a tornado had hit her room. The closet doors were wide open, clothes dangled off the hangers and covered the floor. In the corner by the bed was a packed suitcase. She approached it cautiously. This room definitely felt like the aftermath of packing a day before a trip.

Lola searched through the front pockets of the suitcase, finding a large day planner. She flipped to the month Ms. Marshall had been killed. Sure enough, there was a flight scheduled for the very next day. Nearly every detail leading up and for the trip was jotted down in a to do list.

Final sweep of apt

Trash ID

Meet up with M for details before boarding

Meet W at gate C after landing

This was strange. Lola couldn't tell if these names were abbreviated or redacted. And why did her ID need to be trashed? Was it because it expired? But that didn't make any sense. Who got a new ID a day before a flight? There wasn't a feasible way a new one would arrive in time. The more Lola stared at the planner the less it made sense.

Had her teacher been packing for vacation or to disappear? Was it possible that she knew she would be killed?

Lola stuffed the planner into her bag. Everyone needed to see this.

Suddenly feeling like she had overstayed her welcome, she called Erica and headed to the door. "Hey, are you at my aunts?"

"Yeah, we're waiting for you."

"Tell them to start without me, I'm on my way. Just keep me on speaker." After her fight with Kate, she dreaded going back to that house. It truly didn't matter what she did or how much had changed, she would always end up in the same cycle over and over. It would be no surprise to find her bags packed when she got home.

She heard Erica explain the situation and soon Kate began to speak. "We talked to the head of the Inlander division today and think you should be put under some protection," she said. Lola nearly stopped walking. That hadn't been what she was expecting at all.

"Shouldn't we be working together to find the demons that are doing this?" Paris asked. "Hiding away isn't going to help that."

"You don't understand," said Kate. "What's happening to you is highly unusual. That incident at Sage happened months ago. Someone took the time to poison you, weaken you, and then they just left you alone?"

"Well maybe it was because we were in a group, and in public."

"Alright, but then a few months later, this one also gets poisoned and walks away fine as well."

"I don't know if I would call it fine," Ken mumbled.

"You said you thought we were being targeted," said Paris. "Same demon, same shtick."

"But that's the thing, demons don't have a shtick," Kate said. "They find you, they kill you, they take your soul. They don't play the waiting game and they definitely don't use poisons."

"We're not always together and yet they waited till we were to try and take me," Erica said, but it sounded like she was thinking out loud.

"We don't have a lot of knowledge, but we sure as hell know they can't tell what kind of Nightwalker you are just by looking at you." Andi explained. "But somehow they've known just what to use, which means—"

"Which means they've been watching us," Lola said. She was filled with pure dread. Her first week of school came rushing back. The detention, the dream, the Warlock talisman. Someone was messing with them, using their weaknesses against them and she had been the first victim without even knowing it.

A familiar feeling came over her as a chill ranked down her spine. She pulled her sweater tighter around her. With a reluctant sigh, she retold the experience to the entire group. The more she spoke, the clearer it became how close her exposure to the talisman mirrored the tales of her friends. The deafening silence of the other end of the call told her she was wrong to assume the talisman was a hallucination. So, so wrong.

"Why did you keep this to yourself?" Andi said, baffled.

"I thought my gift acting weird was more of me problem, not a Warlock talisman problem," Lola said honestly, hoping that Kate would be able to pick up on her hidden meaning.

Maybe if she hadn't made herself sick in the first place, she would've been able to tell the difference. "And I figured that the whole thing in detention could've been a fever dream. I just didn't want anyone to worry in case it was nothing."

"And how do you think we feel now?" Kate said. Lola was grateful Kate couldn't see the shame on her face.

"So what, now Warlocks are involved?" Ken asked.

"If that were true then they'd only be after Lola, and it's very clear that they want all four of you."

"I don't understand," Andi said. "Demons can't use talismans, they don't have magick. That and the poisons—where exactly are they getting this stuff?"

Lola was a couple blocks away from home. There was the feeling again. This time goosebumps ran across her arms. She looked both ways and behind her. There was nothing out of the ordinary that she could see, but there was a growing pit in her stomach.

"I'm almost home," she announced. Her friends and family knowing she was nearby would give her some semblance of peace. She looked at a nearby street sign. "I'm on the six hundredth block of—"

A pair of strong arms grabbed her from behind. Her phone fell out of her hands, crashing to the pavement. She screamed and could hear a faint, "Lola?" coming from the other line.

Before she could call for help, a hand covered her mouth.

Lola struggled against them to no avail as she was lifted off the ground and carried back. She kicked until her attacker's grip faltered just slightly. But as she pulled away, her head was struck hard.

She tumbled toward the ground and everything went black.

CHAPTER THIRTY-SIX
ERICA

AN HOUR HAD PASSED since Erica felt the sharp pang in her chest. It was an unfamiliar sensation that shot fear through her spine. She knew what had happened before she heard the scream.

The group searched up and down the block. They called, texted, and shouted at the top of their lungs with nothing to show for it. When they accepted that Lola was long gone, they regrouped inside Kate's house.

Far past worrying, Erica felt herself being consumed by dread. If this was how she felt, she couldn't imagine what Lola's aunts were going through. The two were sporadically in and out of the living room, bringing in random objects to set on the coffee table.

Ken stayed quiet, looking more detached than Erica had ever seen him. He faced forward with dead eyes, taking in the chaos that was the two sisters.

"Are you sure you felt her?" Paris asked for the third time. Erica gave her a grim nod. She couldn't quite explain it, but she knew that something was wrong. After the pang in her chest came a sudden weight that lodged itself in the back of her mind, carrying along with it, a silent plea for help. It was an instinctual and foreign feeling, one she hoped to never experience again.

Erica's thoughts couldn't help but return to that day in the alley. The absolute terror she felt as strange hands took hold of her and that horror only rising when her friends came around that corner. She thought they were all crazy for chasing after her. That they were downright fearless. But now Erica was just starting to understand. This wasn't about fear. Even now as she was terrified beyond belief, there was no question on if they would find Lola, only when.

Andi and Kate sat on the floor in front of the coffee table. Kate moved aside a paperweight and spread out a map of the city onto the table.

"What's this?" Ken asked.

"Locator spell," Kate replied. She held out her hands and Andi placed a pointed crystal attached to a thread in one and a vial in the other.

"Do you need any help?" Andi asked tentatively.

Kate shook her head, uncapping the small vial with red powder. She took some in her hand and sprinkled a decent amount onto the map. Holding one of Lola's skirts, Kate shut her eyes and dangled the crystal above. They all watched as it began to move in small circles.

Andi placed a hand on her chest, letting out a sigh of relief. "Oh, thank the Goddess."

"What? What's happening?" Ken asked urgently.

"It's working, which means she's alive."

Relief washed over Erica and her friends leaned forward. The crystal continued to move in broader circles until it covered the entire city. She noticed that whenever it hit a particular area of the map, it seemed to deflect the powder causing it to spread, like an invisible force was pushing it away. After a couple more swings toward that area, the crystal sparked. Kate dropped the thread like it had shocked her.

"Is that supposed to happen?" Erica asked.

Kate uncapped a marker and drew a circle around the area the powder had spread. "She's somewhere here," she said, pointing at the circle.

"That's not very specific," said Paris. It was a broad circle that covered an entire area of the city.

"Well it would've been if something wasn't blocking me."

"What, like another Warlock talisman?" Andi suggested. Kate nodded.

"So, it's probably the same demons who went after Lola in detention, right?" Ken said.

"Maybe," Kate said. "Or there are multiple demons with multiple talismans, which is a different type of hell." She rubbed her temples then looked up at Erica.

"What?" Erica asked.

"You can flash," she said, realization dawning on her. "You can flash to Lola and bring her back here."

Erica gaped. She hadn't even thought of that.

"But we don't even know where she is," Ken pointed out.

"Doesn't matter," Kate shook her head. "Guardians should always be able to go to their charges."

All eyes in the room turned to her. Erica swallowed. "But I don't know how," she said. "I mean, I've never done it before and—"

"Please just try," Kate pleaded. The intensity of her gaze was so much that Erica glanced down in her lap. She took a deep breath and closed her eyes. She thought of her body disappearing, of the weightlessness she felt back on the transit. She opened her eyes and found herself still in the room, the group watching her with disappointing eyes. "I'm sorry," Erica murmured.

"So, what do we do now? Drive around and see if we spot her?" Paris asked.

"No, we have to make sense of this first," Kate grumbled, pointing at the map. "Why are they even keeping her alive?

I mean if they just wanted her soul, they would've taken it already."

"You want to theorize when Lola could be dead any minute now?" Ken said, he sounded like he was holding himself back from snapping.

Erica glanced down at the scar that was left from her own attack and suddenly had an idea. "No, she's right," she said. "What if they're using her as bait? We already know they want all of us. Maybe they think having us out looking for Lola is the best way to draw us out."

"But why are they going through so much trouble?" said Paris.

"Have you pissed off anyone lately?" Kate tried.

"Define lately."

Ken shook his head. "What makes you say that?"

"Lola found that talisman at your school and your teacher was killed there," she said. "It has to be someone with close access to you."

Erica didn't want Kate to be right. A whole new form of paranoia was created at the thought of anyone from a stranger on the streets to someone in their daily lives being a demon. How was she ever going to function knowing that they were everywhere. Andi picked up a notepad and marker. "We're going to go through everything until we have a list of names."

CHAPTER THIRTY-SEVEN

KEN

"No," Ken said. "Absolutely not."

At the end of it, the group had three recurring names pop up. Mr. Hanks, Mateo, and Troy.

Just as he had thought, this was a colossal waste of time. Troy was one of his best friends. There was no way he was capable of something like this. There was no way he was a demon. Everything else made sense he supposed. Through the process of elimination, they realized there was a recurrence between the people around them the past few months. Going off Kate's theory that it was someone at school, they fit the bill. But at the end of the day, it was still a theory, and Lola was still gone.

"I've known Troy for years and I'm sure he's had plenty of opportunities to kill me," he argued.

"We're just exploring every possibility," said Andi.

"Shouldn't we at least consider it?" Erica said. He bit his tongue. Ken expected this from Paris, but even Erica was going along with this? She knew Troy, she went to school with him just like he did. What about him screamed murderer?

Ken's leg shook. He couldn't just sit here, and he didn't understand how any of them could either. "Well, we got what we need for now," Kate said. "You guys can go."

"That's it? You just expect us to go home?" Ken asked.

"For the time being, yes," said Kate, sporting that same stoned faced expression. It was unbelievable.

"But Lola—"

"Will be better helped by us putting this together and presenting it to the Council," Kate said firmly.

"They won't care," he argued.

"I'll make them care," she said with so much confidence it was almost delusional. By the time Kate did wear the Council down, Lola would be dead.

"But—"

"There's nothing else we can do," she said, her voice distant. "Go home."

As the group piled out of the house, Kate motioned for him to stay back. "Can I talk to you for a minute?" She closed the front door, shutting him off from the rest of his friends.

"I know it was you Lola was out with last night." Ken didn't bother to deny it, he simply waited for her to continue. "I already have enough trouble with her, I don't need you encouraging it further."

Did she really think this was the time?

"That wasn't what I was trying to do. You left her here and she wasn't okay," he said, trying to keep his voice even. "And Lola isn't trouble. I mean, I know she can be a lot sometimes, but maybe she'd be better off if you'd stop expecting her to be perfect."

Kate narrowed her eyes. "And what if something happened that night?" she said coldly. "You know what I care about, Kenneth? Her safety. I'm not trying to actively put her life in danger."

"That's not fair," he said. But wasn't it? Ken thought for a moment that maybe he was selfish, that maybe last night had been fueled more by his own family issues than Lola's. That he was looking for an escape in her rather than the other way around.

"We got into a fight this morning, did she tell you that?" she said slowly. Her words didn't betray the hard look on her face. "And now I don't know if what I said will be the last thing I'll ever get to. So for your sake, you better pray I see my niece again."

Ken swallowed and Kate reopened the door, ushering him outside.

Ken was raised in a trailer park within the city. He remembered the excitement he felt when his mom got a new job and they could finally afford an apartment. Their first place was nice. A two bedroom in a decent neighborhood. Him and his sisters shared a room, but Ken didn't mind. Instead of bunk beds, Isabel had a trundle bed. She'd pull it out and she and Megan would sleep side by side in a way that reminded Ken of a motorcycle car.

Life had been good for a few years. Then his parents' marriage failed and it all started crashing down. The divorce had taken his mom by surprise, but Ken saw it coming, they all had. Maybe if he warned her, everything that happened after could've been avoided.

His dad had never been a city guy, so it wasn't a shock when he decided to go wild. Ken wasn't sure what crushed his mom more, him going off the grid, or Isabel going with him. He hated how she begged them to stay—how she cried and pleaded. If they wanted to leave them, that was their choice. But it was also Ken's choice to hate them for it.

The weeks after they left were hard, but not unbearable. However, just as they began to adjust to their new lives, the call came.

His aunt, Olivia, had been killed in a house fire. He didn't know her well, that side of the family lived in Washington and didn't usually have the money to come visit. Ken remembered his mom disappearing into her room after the call. She locked herself inside and stayed there all day and all night. No pleading from him or Megan would make her come out.

The next night was a full moon. Him and Megan waited for her in the living room, counting down the minutes. She had to come out tonight, Ken thought.

And sure enough she did.

He knew instantly that the woman that came out of her room was not his mother. Ken wasn't quite sure how he knew, but he always had a talent for reading people. He noticed people's faces, their body language, and how they spoke, even when they didn't think he did.

His mother came out of her bedroom ten minutes to moonrise. She didn't address Ken and Megan and her face was blank. She headed straight to the kitchen, grabbing the Tubberware of leftovers, a bottle of water, and a bowl.

Ken approached her slowly from behind. "Mom," he said. "You don't have enough time to get to the den, what are you—"

She turned around and when Ken met his mother's eyes they were filled with pure hatred. His mother had never looked at him like that. She had never even raised her voice at him, but this look was so frightening it caused Ken to freeze. She shoved past him and headed back to her room.

He shook off his surprise, following and grabbing her arm before she could disappear through the door. If she turned now she would destroy the apartment. The neighbors would be able to hear everything and maybe even call the police. "You can't shift in here!" he exclaimed. That was his mistake.

His mother snarled at him, throwing the food and water to the ground. Ken remembered the spike of fear that went through him as his mother shifted. The change was instantaneous and his mother's wolf, black and large enough to reach his hips, growled at him.

Megan shot up from the couch, watching carefully as Ken slowly backed away. "Mom?" she said.

"Megan, don't move," Ken said. Their mother's eyes remained trained on him. Everything Ken knew told him that if he ran, she would chase, but what choice did he have?

Ken who couldn't shift. Ken who had no special abilities of his own. He was defenseless.

He looked to his right, eyes landing on the coffee table. Maybe he could use it to herd her back into the bedroom?

While Ken was thinking, his mother went for his arm. He wasn't sure who screamed louder when her jaws bit down, him or Megan.

Ripping her off him hurt more than the bite itself. Her teeth scraped his skin. The pain so intense his vision went white. With what little energy he possessed, Ken kicked her and while she was down, he ran for the coffee table and held it up like a shield. Arm dripping with blood, Ken shoved her back into the bedroom, with Megan shutting the door between them.

Hot tears ran down Ken's face as he cradled his arm, the sound of his mom's howls and destruction ringing throughout the bedroom.

Ken absently pulled at his sleeve as he recalled the memory. It took forever for his arm to heal, and even then, he was still left with a scar.

Just as he predicted, they were kicked out of the apartment and forced to uproot their lives in only thirty days. But what Ken hadn't expected was that his mother would never be the same after that night.

The realization of what was happening struck him too late and he paid for it. But now, Ken felt that same all-consuming fear as someone else he cared about was being taken away from him. He wasn't going to wait this time, he couldn't.

"What was that about?" Paris asked, leaning against the side of her car.

"Nothing," he said quickly, descending the steps of the Hallows house. He walked past the car and down the sidewalk.

"Where are you going?" Erica asked. He stopped and threw his hands up.

"To look for Lola, since no one else wants to," he said.

"But they said—" Erica started, but Ken cut her off.

"I really don't care what they said." His fists clenched against his sides. "Are you really just gonna go home?"

"As opposed to what?" Paris asked.

"The map. The area the locator spell picked up."

"You mean nearly half of the city?"

"It's a start," he said desperately.

"It's a wild goose chase," she said.

"It's something." And that something had to be better than nothing.

"And probably a trap, remember?" Erica pointed out. Ken let out a groan and waved her off, turning back on his heel.

"Ken, don't be stupid!" Paris called after him. He kept walking, eventually hearing the sounds of the car doors closing and the car starting. Ken looked to his left to see Paris driving alongside him. The passenger window rolled down. "Get in the car."

"No, thanks," he said.

"Don't you think we want to find her too?" Erica asked.

He stopped in his tracks and sighed. "Of course, I do." He saw a look cross Paris' face as she considered him.

"Ere, do you remember what that map looked like?" she asked.

"Yeah," Erica said.

"Ken, get in the car and let's go."

CHAPTER THIRTY-EIGHT
LOLA

Lola let out a low groan as she woke. Her body was pressed against hard cement. Every muscle ached and her head was ringing. She firmly pressed her hands to the ground and pushed herself onto her knees. A spot on her temple throbbed the most.

She placed a hand there and found it was still wet with silver blood. She hadn't been here long—wherever here was.

"So, you're a Nightwalker," a male voice said.

Lola jumped to her feet, stumbling slightly, and whipped her head toward the guy leaning against the wall. It was only then did she fully take in her surroundings. They were in a cell, possibly underground. She didn't see any windows in sight and the cell itself was rusty and old.

"And you are?" she coughed out.

He eyed her warily before answering, "Fae." He changed his eyes to blue and gray to demonstrate. Fae eyes were two different colors, some even working like mood rings.

"Witch."

He stood. "I'm Finn," he said and pointed to a child in the corner. The boy looked eleven or twelve at best. "This is my brother Erick."

Finn looked to be her age. He was a tall and lanky guy with jet-black hair and fair skin, his brother being no different, just with a younger face. To Lola, the Fae had always been ancient and all knowing. The sight of two Fae children was staggering.

What were they doing here? Lola's aunts were right, this was strange. Based on all the attacks that occurred over the past few months, none of them involved detailed kidnappings, and none of the victims had been Lien.

Had this been going on in the background? Were there Alereians her aunts missed?

The boys were still staring at her and she realized she still hadn't introduced herself. "I'm Lola."

"Are you okay?" he asked, pointing toward her head.

"I'll be fine." She smoothed down her uniform skirt, which she realized had ridden up a little too far. "How long have you been here?"

"Maybe an hour before you got here?"

"And how long have I been here?" she asked.

"I don't know, thirty minutes?" Finn said. That was good, but it told her nothing about how long it had been since she was actually taken. It couldn't have been more than an hour, could it? "Do you have any idea what these guys want?"

Lola shook her head and moved toward the cell door. "No idea," she lied. Ever since she signed those papers, she followed the same rules her aunts did. She was on her own and they were all going to die here if she didn't think of something fast.

She peered through the bars. To her left was a long row of identical jail cells and to the right was a small corridor that led to a much larger room. There on the wall hung a silver key. There was no guarantee that it was the key to her cell, but it was better than nothing.

"You saw how bright they are, don't start having doubts now," a cold feminine voice said. It sounded familiar.

"But ma'am, what about the job?" a masculine voice asked.

"We haven't seen anything like this in years, we'd be idiots not to act now," the feminine voice said. "The job will still get done, don't worry."

Lola wished she could see what was going on past that corridor.

"Of course, but you should know Sunday is still talking about his offer and some of the younger ones are agreeing with her."

The woman groaned. "Still? Make sure to tell Sunday that until this nest is under new leadership, we will not be making deals with that snake. We have our orders and that's that."

These demons had a leader and yet it seemed they were carrying out orders. But if not from her then who? The voices dispersed down the hall and Lola brought her attention back to the key. She squinted hard. It was going to be nearly impossible to get a clear look at it. The world was a blur with her contacts gone, and the backpack that held her glasses was missing. Lola wasn't sure if she'd be able to take every detail of the key into account, but it was worth a shot.

She turned her back to the bars and held out her hand. She worked to create a clear picture of the key in her mind and imagined its formation inside her palm. "*Key*," she called in a low voice. The particles fought and struggled to take form and what she got was even less than what she was expecting.

A half-melted key with irregular rigging sat in her hand. Lola stared at it in confusion until dropping it to the floor and watching it vanish into dust. "You're kidding me."

"They knew who they were going after." Finn pointed to an object in the corner outside of the cell.

It was a Warlock's talisman.

CHAPTER THIRTY-NINE
ERICA

WITHIN THE CIRCLE THE locator spell created on the map, was the diner where Ken worked. And though nothing could persuade him that Troy had been involved in this, Erica managed to convince him that it wouldn't hurt to look into the other names on the list.

Mr. Hanks may have given Lola the detention in the first place but Mateo had been there as well. He had access to them at school and access to Ken while at work. The position he was in was more than desirable for a demon.

It was odd being at the diner. Erica often forgot he had a job, he so rarely mentioned it. As they entered the restaurant, Ken seemed uncomfortable as if the two parts of his life were finally meeting and was unsure what to do about it.

The place was mildly busy for the middle of the week and the group took a table in the back, surveying the room.

"Are you sure he works today?" Paris asked.

"Yeah, he usually works Wednesdays," Ken said. As if on cue, Mateo emerged from the kitchen, carrying two trays to a nearby table. "That's him."

"Alright so he's here, but how exactly do we figure out if he's in on it or not?"

"We could head out back and talk to him," Ken said. "Worst case scenario is that he's human and you'll just have to compel him to forget afterwards."

"And what if he is the demon? He'll either attack us or play dumb until we're off his trail," said Paris. "We need a sure way to know."

"His blood," Erica said suddenly. "Demon blood is black remember?"

"And how exactly do we get him to bleed?" Ken asked.

"It's a restaurant," Paris said. "Accidents happen."

Ken looked worried. "Accidents that won't cause lasting damage if we're wrong, right?"

Erica fiddled with the menus set out in front of them. They were paper, their corners sharp.

Mateo came to their table to take their order. "Ken, hey," he said and surveyed the group. "Is Lola not with you?"

Ken tensed, clenching the sides of his seat. Erica felt the sudden emptiness at the table. It was odd for Lola not to be with them. She struggled not to think too much about it.

They were going to get Lola back. "No, she's at home," Erica said quickly. Ken looked like he was about to lose it.

"Ah okay," said Mateo. "What can I get for you then?"

The three of them ordered light things. A salad and two sandwiches, none of which would probably be eaten. "Alright, I'll bring that right out."

Erica watched as he began to collect the menus. She honed in all of her focus on one in particular. She imagined it slipping through Mateo's hand, sliding against his palm and into his skin. He reached for the menu and within the same second she flicked her fingers underneath the table. "Ouch!" he exclaimed, jerking back his hand. Paris and Ken look at her in surprise. It was odd openly using her Guardian powers in front of them.

"What happened?" Ken asked Mateo.

He hissed and held up his hand for them to see. "Paper cut."

The blood was red.

CHAPTER FORTY
LOLA

Without any magick, there wasn't anything Lola could think of that would get them out of here. There were no windows, no weak points of any kind in the cell. With no appearance of any demons, she simply sat and waited for whatever horror they were in for to arrive. The pull of the talisman exhausted her and slowed the healing of her wounds. Everything, everywhere hurt.

Lola fought the urge to laugh as she thought of what her dad would think if he knew she was in here.

In trouble again? he would say. There would be humor in his voice as he waited to see what elaborate excuse she would come up with to explain herself. It was like a game. If the excuse was creative enough, he'd reduce a day off her punishment.

But Maine changed all of that, as her run-ins with trouble became more frequent, the light in his eyes died a little more each day she came home.

It started with talking back to teachers, then it was getting into fights, and then it was destruction of property. Lola didn't realize how far things had gone until he picked her up from the police station.

It was all terrifyingly easy. For what felt like her entire life, she was the girl who found trouble. It got tiring at times, to fight against it. To prove her innocence. So, Maine was when she decided to stop fighting. What was the point if everyone already thought the worst of her? Why resist the inevitable when she could revel in it instead? She would no longer be the girl who found trouble, but the girl who was trouble incarnate.

In its own way, it was a form of control. She determined what she did and how she was viewed. But that so-called control was thinly veiled chaos, and it caught up with her a lot faster than she intended.

Lola remembered the night she went through her dad's grimoire. He hid it in a place he thought she'd never check, but Lola had always known it was there. She didn't read from it, didn't touch it, didn't so much as look at it simply because he asked. For seventeen years, she listened to him with no questions asked. But now she was done listening. Now she wanted to do magick.

She no longer remembered the spell she'd been attempting. The events of that night had become blurry. But she would never forget what happened when her father caught her.

"Lola, put the book down!" he exclaimed. Lola nearly jumped out of her skin at the sudden sound of his voice, he sounded terrified.

She held her hands up as if she had been caught holding a loaded gun. "Dad, I wasn't going to do anything dangerous," she said. "I just wanted to see if I—"

"You can't. You know you can't," he said firmly.

"It's one little spell, how much damage could it cause?" she asked even though she already knew the answer. The weeks leading up to that night, she tested the waters with the smallest of spells. After one attempt, she tripped over a crack that hadn't existed a moment before. And after another, a sandwich she bought spoiled before her eyes. These were little consequences to account for the magick she had done. And the best part was that it only affected her.

She planned on telling her father that she could handle the curse. She could take on the risks of doing magick.

The dismayed look on her dad's face told her it wasn't even worth mentioning. "Lola, you have put me through so much here, but now you have crossed a line," he said. "Give me the book."

Lola's grip on the tome tightened. She shook her head. The simple gesture stunned him. His eyes widened and his mouth parted. It took him a few seconds to respond. "Lola, I'm serious."

"So am I," she challenged.

"You're going to get yourself or someone else hurt," he said. The statement made her flinch but she remembered her experiments. She had prepared for this. "I'm only going to ask you one last time, young lady."

She only offered him silence.

Her father then did something she would have never expected. A spell.

He recited it in the old Witch tongue that had long died out. She didn't catch all the words, her ignorance in spell work failing her, but like any Witch she could understand the ancient language well enough to decode the intent of the spell. All she got was one word: sleep.

Her father was trying to put her to sleep.

"No!" she shouted, anger pulsing through her. She shot back without thinking, reaching for one of the few spells she knew. "Escade!" Release.

A powerful force burst across the room. It knocked Lola and her father down and wasted the room around them. She remembered getting to her feet, the world still spinning. She remembered locking eyes with her dad and his still form.

Lola was back in that moment, rushing to his side and trying to wake him up. She checked his pulse, felt him breathing and yet his eyes wouldn't open.

Suddenly, she was alone in an unfamiliar city with no family or friends for miles.

The days after the accident were a nightmare. Both sides of her family tried everything they could to no avail. Then human doctors got involved, but they claimed there was nothing they could do for him either.

Her father was in a coma and there was nothing she could do about it.

If there was one bright side to her current situation, at the very least, if she died now, she'd never have to face her dad if he ever woke up.

With no windows to indicate whether it was night or day, Lola spent the next several hours thinking before succumbing to her exhaustion.

Someone shook her awake. She jerked up, swatting their hand away, only to realize it was Finn. He held his hands up in defense, then pointed outside the bars. Lola heard the sound of footsteps and got to her feet, pressing herself against the back wall. Finn took a protective stance in front of his little brother, who cowered in the corner of the cell.

Two men—demons—approached, gawking at the three of them like animals in a cage. One of them removed a key from their back pocket, unlocked the cell, and placed the key back inside. They entered slowly, eying the three of them like merchandise on display. Lola could barely breathe as their gaze locked on her.

Suddenly she lost their attention. One of them made a move towards Finn, pushing him to the side with ease and yanked Erick by the arm. *No.*

"Hey!" Finn exclaimed, getting back to his feet.

The little boy was screaming, trying his best to escape the demon's grip as tears ran down his face. Finn tried to reach him, but was quickly thrown to the side once again.

Without thinking, Lola charged herself at one of the demons, managing to get her arms around him. The demon quickly shook off his surprise, groaning in annoyance while the other demon pulled Erick out of the cell. He grabbed Lola by the collar of her shirt and tossed her to the side as if she were nothing more than a fly.

He left the cell and it locked behind him, then rejoined the other demon as they dragged the screaming child down the hall.

Lola stood, pain from the impact flaring in her legs. Finn was frantic. "Dammit!" he screamed, kicking the wall.

She walked over, placing a hand on his shoulder. "Hey!" He turned around, eyes blazing black and red. "Calm down, we're gonna get your brother back."

She held up the key she had taken from the demon's back pocket.

⇶ ⬸

Lola's eyesight was shit. Beyond shit. All Nightwalkers were naturally blessed with durability and night vision, so how come 20/20 vision wasn't a package deal? The Witches' eyes were in a constant squint. If she had known she was going to be kidnapped yesterday, she would've placed a fresh set of contacts in her nonexistent pocket.

Once out of the cell, Finn used the sleeve of his shirt to take the Warlock talisman down out of fear of touching it directly. Unsure of what to do with it, she told him to throw it as far as he could down the corridor of cells. They went in the opposite direction.

The two quickened their pace as they traveled through corridors and stumbled upon a stairwell leading up to an exit. They found themselves standing in a hall filled with dozens of rooms. Further ahead was a nonfunctioning ice machine and elevator. They had been underneath some abandoned motel.

She and Finn made it to the deserted lobby where sheets covered the furniture and dust covered the sheets. Straight ahead were the front doors. They missed Erick completely. Had he been in one of the rooms? "He's probably back downstairs," Lola said, turning around. "We should head the other way."

Finn stared at her surprised. "You should go on," he said. "I'll go back."

"I told you I was gonna help you get your brother back and I am." She shrugged. "You can't use your magick anyway, so you'll need my help." Lola learned from Finn that without dust, Fae magick was basically nonexistent.

A look of gratitude crossed his face and the two raced back downstairs. Lola knew this was risky. Every bone in her body screamed at her to run toward the exit, but she kept forward anyway. She claimed her gift gave her an edge over Finn, but what was she supposed to do? Call for a weapon and hope for the best? She didn't know how to fight and the demon in the alley practically froze there and took it when she called for the bat. A knockout spell or a spell to get a message to her aunts seemed way more useful than her gift at the moment. Her neglected lessons with Kate came to mind. The last time she practiced magick had been that night with her father. Could she handle another disaster like that?

Her confidence seemed to shrink to its lowest when they finally found Erick. In an open space through an archway was a room full of cardboard boxes and crates. Lola assumed these were supplies, but did demons even need the same necessities she did?

There were four of them in the room. Erick was tied to a pole and the demons around him paid him little attention. They seemed bored, like they were waiting for something.

The room had two exits. Lola and Finn headed through the one at the rear, diving behind stacks of crates and crawling their way toward Erick.

"This is getting ridiculous," a masculine voice said.

A feminine voice shushed him. "Do you want to be killed?"

"Come on, we're all thinking it," he said. "This isn't what we were hired to do. Why are we wasting our time with this?"

Lola nearly paused. Were these demons as out of the loop as she was? Finn nudged her and gave her an expectant look. Right, she was meant to be saving them now.

"*Knife,*" she called, praying that no demons heard her. It formed flawlessly in her hand. With no talisman around, her gift worked as fine as it ever had.

She held out the blade to a very confused Finn and quickly pointed to the rope that bound Erick to the pole. He nodded and shifted closer to his brother.

Lola stared down the hall of the exit farthest from them. "*Pots. Pans,*" she called. Four metal pots and pans formed mid-air and fell to the ground with a loud clang that echoed throughout the halls.

The demons snapped to attention. "What the hell was that?" one said. Two of them headed out to investigate while the others craned their necks to look. Finn hastily cut his brother's restraints.

The demons who were still in the room peered past the threshold. "*Dumbbells,*" Lola called. Two dumbbells formed above the demons. They were much smaller than Lola imagined, about 15 pounds at least, but they did the trick. The weights crashed down, knocking them to the ground.

Finn grabbed his brother's arm and dashed behind the crates. The group scurried to the back exit.

"Hey!" a demon said, spotting them. He tossed the dumbbell off with ease and got to his feet.

"You couldn't have dropped an anchor on them?" Finn asked as they ran.

Lola huffed. No, she couldn't, actually. Calling for bigger things had never come to her. Even now, calling three times in a row left her winded.

The sound of heavy footsteps echoed behind them. Lola heard the sound of crackling, and she wasn't sure how she knew, but she shouted, "Move!" and pulled Finn and Erick aside as something flew past them.

Whatever it was, it smashed into the spot they had been, leaving a scorch mark. Lola looked behind her and immediately regretted it. They were a lot closer than she initially thought, a lot faster too. She heard the crackling again and saw something form within one demon's hand. He threw it at her.

She ducked just in time, but it caused her to stumble forward as they reached the stairs. She grasped for the metal railing to break her fall.

Something grabbed at her ankle, yanking her down hard. Lola's grip on the railing was lost and her head slammed against the edge of the step. She twisted on to her back, kicking at the demon holding her, but he wouldn't budge.

As the demon pulled her to him, Lola's mind raced. Finn and Erick made it through the doors. She had to think of something or else—

"*Knife!*" she called. Before it finished forming in her hand, she was plunging it into his eye. The demon screamed and released her, hands rushing to his face. Lola rushed up the steps, all too eager to turn away from the sight of black blood squirting from his socket.

She pushed through the exit and found Erick and Finn waiting for her in the lobby. They hadn't left her.

At the sight of her, and the demons that followed, they got moving again. Lola ran until her legs burned and she could hardly breathe. And when she could finally feel the sun on her face, she pushed on even harder.

CHAPTER FORTY-ONE
LOLA

LOLA SLUMPED AGAINST A lamp post, catching her breath. Finn and Erick were beside her clutching their stomachs. They had run six blocks before eventually blending into a busy crowd. She looked around. It was the first time she fully comprehended that anyone could be a demon. The urge to keep them away from any seemingly innocent face was strong.

Next to them was a fairly crowded coffee shop. Lola motioned for the Fae to follow her inside. They drifted toward the back, away from windows, and took a seat, their bodies finally allowed relief. At least, her body. The Fae seemed tired but certainly in better shape than her.

Lola rested her head on the cool table and let out hot, heavy breaths. Her hair was slick against her scalp and puffy near the ends. Finn got up from their table and came back with complimentary cups of water. She grabbed one and gulped it down eagerly. With her adrenaline dying down, she was painfully aware of how much she needed food and water.

She knew they were still in San Francisco the moment they left the motel. But where in the city?

Lola turned to the table closest to them where a Black woman in a pantsuit sat. "Excuse me?" Lola said, the woman looked up. "What time is it?"

The woman looked down at her laptop. "Two thirty."

"Do you mind if we use your phone to make a call?" Finn asked.

The woman nodded, fishing her phone out of her purse. She looked them over with mild concern as she handed it over. Lola was thankful they didn't bruise easily, but then she remembered the cut on her head. God, they probably looked awful.

While Finn and Erick made their call, Lola glanced down at the menu and caught sight of the address printed on the bottom. Her heart swelled with newfound hope. They were in Ken's neighborhood, she realized, maybe only a block or two away.

Once Finn was done, he held out the phone to her. She called Kate, but ended up having to call twice since Kate avoided numbers she didn't recognize. "Hello?" Kate said with a brashness she hadn't expected.

"Kate?" Lola said, her voice cracked. She really didn't want to cry in front of these people.

"Lola? Lola, honey where are you? Are you okay?" Her tone changed instantly to something that was frantic and desperate.

"Kate, I'm sorry—"

"No, no, not right now," Kate hushed her. "Just tell me where you are so we can come get you."

"Come to Ken's house, I'm close," she said.

"I'll see you soon."

"Ok." She hung up, handing the phone back to the woman and thanking her.

"Our dad's on the way," Finn told her.

"That's good."

"Where are you headed?"

"My friend lives around here," she said and rose from her seat. Friend wasn't quite the right word, not anymore, but she didn't bother to correct herself. "I'm gonna stay with him till my aunts show up."

"Hey, thank you for helping me get my brother back," he said earnestly. "Not a lot of people would've stuck around after we got out of that cell."

"Thank you," Erick said softly. It was the first time she heard him speak.

She forced a smile. "Don't worry about it."

Today would stick with the poor boy for the rest of his life and he'd never know why it happened or who was after him.

"Hey, put your hands underneath the table," she instructed. Erick did as she asked, a confused look on his face. "*Toy.*"

Erick looked down at his hands in shock before showing off the toy she called for. It was a superhero action figure. Every kid liked toys, but Lola hoped something heroic looking would bring him some much-needed comfort. "You'll hold on to that for me, won't you?" she said. He nodded enthusiastically. All the bad thoughts already drifting from his mind.

"Seriously, if you ever need anything just let me know, okay?" Finn grabbed a napkin and gestured to the pen on the woman's table. "Do you mind?"

She handed it over. He wrote his number on the napkin and gave it to Lola. She clutched it firmly. "Thanks."

And with that she left the coffee shop, hoping she could leave the last twenty-four hours behind with them.

Lola climbed up the stairs of Ken's apartment building. She took them two at a time and vigorously knocked at his door when she reached it.

The door opened and there stood Ken, taking in the sight of her. He was frozen in place, looking as if he'd seen a ghost. Without a word, he pulled her inside, engulfing her in his arms. She sighed into his chest, savoring the feeling of him around her, the comfort that came with it. They stayed like that for a while and when they did pull apart, Lola felt the wholeness and safety disappear with his embrace.

She explained everything that happened over the leftovers he gave her. A fact she somehow missed was that Ken could cook. He served her the most delicious beef stew she had ever tasted. He let her shower and brush her teeth and she called for a sundress to slip into, throwing away her dirty uniform. Six callings in one day. It was more than she had done in months.

Ken sat on the couch with a first aid kit when she returned. She moved her hair aside to show him the gash on her head.

"They really didn't do anything to you?" He eyed her with concern.

"Other than knock me upside the head and throw me in a cell? No," she said as Ken cleaned her cut.

"Why didn't you tell me about the talisman?" he asked. Her face fell.

"I was stupid," she said easily.

"You're not stupid," he said firmly. He was wrong, but she wasn't about to argue.

"I guess it scared me, so I decided to pretend it wasn't happening." She didn't know if Ken was satisfied with her answer.

He studied her before saying, "I'm just glad you're okay."

She thought back to how it felt to plunge that knife into the demon's eye. She didn't feel okay.

"I lied," she said suddenly.

"What?"

She told him about her detour from school yesterday, which now felt like a lifetime ago. She had put everyone through so much trouble, unsure if any of it was even worth it. If she hadn't gone off on her own in the first place, maybe her time in that cell would've been avoided. But what would've happened to the two Fae boys? "The planner was in my bag." The bag that was currently being held by demons. "All that for nothing."

The urge to cry was building in her throat. Here with Ken was the safest place to cry that there was. But she swallowed it down, still unable to let herself breakdown.

"That might not be true," Ken said. She looked up hopefully. Ken went on to explain the working theory the group had come up with while she was gone.

They believed that the demons planned to use her as bait to draw the rest of the group out. Lola didn't know how she felt about the worst twenty-four hours of her life being reduced to nothing more than bait, but it was a start.

"Well, if that is true, it obviously it didn't work," Lola said.

Ken looked at her seriously. "Lo, of course we went looking for you."

Lola sighed, unsure if she should feel grateful or concerned that they cared enough to search for her. "Ken, you shouldn't have done that."

"I wasn't just gonna leave you," he protested.

"You should have," she said. "I could live with them just having me, but all of you?"

Ken shook his head. "You wouldn't be alive. That's the point."

"Ken—"

"You would've done the same for me." And just like that, he had her.

She looked down at her hands, quickly changing the subject. "You guys really think that Troy could've had something to do with this?" she asked.

"I don't know, it's just a hunch." He shrugged. The disinterest told her all she needed to know.

"Which you don't agree with."

"It could be anyone at school if you think about it."

"Well, that's comforting." Her and Troy had never been close, but even then, it was hard to imagine a world where he'd been responsible for what she had gone through. Lola sighed, looking around. The silence and emptiness of the apartment suddenly became apparent to her. "Where is everyone?"

"Megan has softball practice till five." He closed up the first aid kit.

"Oh, what about your mom?" For a split second, she saw a hint of annoyance cross his face.

"Uh, probably out with her boyfriend," he said slowly. "I don't really know."

"I didn't know your mom started dating." She hadn't heard a lot about his mom since his parents' divorce over the summer. "What's he like?"

"A dick."

Seeing as Ken never mentioned him before, that was pretty much the answer she was expecting. "Damn, I'm sorry," she said.

"Yeah, it's whatever."

"Is she out often?" she pried.

"Lola, we don't need to get into this," he said. "I mean after what you've been through—"

"And I'm fine now," she assured him. "You're always taking the time to listen to me ramble in the middle of the night. Just tell me what's going on."

He took a moment to think over the idea before saying, "I don't even know where my mom is these days."

"What does that mean?"

"When my dad and sister left this summer, my mom took it pretty hard. It got even worse when we couldn't afford our apartment anymore and had to move here. Then she met Justin and he made her happier, at least I thought he was," he said, the words spilling out of him easily. Like all he needed was for someone to simply ask.

"At some point things were just off about her. She started getting irritated at the smallest things, she was tired all the time, and when she wasn't tired, she was with him. Then bills stopped getting paid on time. So when she was fired from her job, and I found out it was because she was drunk at work, it all started to make sense."

She sat in utter disbelief. "Have you told anyone else about this?" she asked.

"My grandparents know, but they live in Washington so there's not much they can do from there except send me some money once in a while."

"How are you guys even affording this place?" she asked, looking around the apartment as if she couldn't comprehend that they were even sitting in it now.

"Sometimes my mom gets money from Justin, but most of the time it's just me."

She blinked. Was she hearing this right? Not only was Ken responsible for himself, but for his sister and the entire house. Lola suddenly felt guilty berating him every night when there were already so many burdens weighing on him. "Ken, that's crazy. Does it look like she's getting a job soon?"

"She told me she was looking." Lola gave him a blank look. "But that was a while ago."

He sighed and shook his head. "Look, it's not like that. My mom—she's going through a lot."

"A lot of people get divorced, Ken, most don't do this," she said, her anger rising. "And your dad should be here until she gets it together." His face scrunched up in frustration as if he was looking for a way to make her understand, but couldn't. He met her gaze with uncertainty.

"If I tell you this, you have to promise me you won't tell anyone, okay?"

"Of course." She placed a hand on top of his, suddenly worried.

He took a deep breath and said, "My mom went untamed."

It was the last thing she expected to hear. While Lola knew for sure going untamed happened, it was different than knowing someone it happened to. It was too taboo and the fact that Ken trusted her enough to tell her made her feel worse than she already did.

"My aunt died right around the time my parents were getting the divorce," Ken explained. "She couldn't handle it and just snapped."

"By snapped, you mean?"

"My mom wasn't my mom," Ken said, voice barely above a whisper. "She was something else and it was scary."

Lola wanted to know what he meant—what his mom had done. But Ken's grim expression made sure she didn't dare ask.

"It's just hard seeing her go through that and now this," he continued.

Lola shook her head. "You still shouldn't be stuck dealing with all this. You deserve better," she said after a moment. Frankly, she didn't care what his mother was going through. You didn't abandon your kid when they needed you the most.

He gave her a small smile and held her hand. "Thanks."

"I mean it," she said. "I wish I could've been there when all this was going on." It had only been a few months since summer ended, all of this was still so recent.

"Lo, you were on the other side of the country, there was no way you could've known. Paris and Erica don't even know," he assured her.

"I know, I just...I don't know." She frowned, the weight of his revelation holding her down. A moment of silence passed as he stroked the back of her hand with his thumb.

"You're amazing, you know that?" he said suddenly. Her heart jumped in her chest.

"What do you mean?" she said, tripping over her words a bit.

"I mean, I was ready to overturn the whole city to look for you, and here you are," he said. "I don't think many people could've gotten out of that on their own."

Lola looked down, the intensity of his gaze suddenly too much. "I was just trying to get out of there like any sane person," she said.

"You saved that kid," he pointed out. "You're brave whether you want to admit it or not. It's one of the things I like about you." Though her face was hot and flushing, she looked up to meet his eyes. There wasn't a hint of uncertainty within them. He really believed those things about her, meant every word. And who was she to disappoint him? To tell him that she was a liar and a fraud. To tell him that the person he was describing didn't exist.

Ken's hand left hers and cupped her face. She winced at the contact. Ken, thinking he'd done something wrong, quickly pulled away. "Sorry, should I not—"

"No, no, it's not you," she reassured him. "I just hit my face...a lot."

"Oh." He frowned. He leaned forward, and ever so gently, left a kiss where his hand had been. Lola held her breath as he then brushed her hair away to leave another on the cut on her forehead.

Ken became eye level and their noses were just barely touching. His hands rested under her chin, tilting her face up toward him. "I'm going to kiss you now."

"Please do," she said, and their lips finally connected.

Lola hadn't realized how much she wanted him until she was kissing him. Every inch and every fiber of her being had been sparking within her, building up until she finally exploded. Ken's mouth was hungry and desperate against hers. They needed this, needed it like pouring rain in a drought. She melted into him, wrapping her arms around him to keep them close. She let Ken lead her until she was giddy and breathless. Unable to contain herself, Lola smiled through the kiss.

Ken pulled away, his brown eyes shining. He had such pretty eyes. It took one look at one another for them to burst into laughter as if the funniest thing just happened.

"Wowza," Lola said once their laughing fit stopped.

"Did you just say wowza?" Ken looked like he was about to laugh again.

She nodded. "I can also say gee whiz, or jeepers, or blimey, or—"

Ken cut her off with a laugh. "Shut up," he said playfully.

"Make me."

Taking her up on her challenge, their lips reconnected. Lola's brain shut off and her stomach did backflips as the two exchanged quick, playful kisses that made her tingle all over. "Hm, I should be annoying more often," she said once they broke apart.

"First off, you're always annoying," he said and looked down at the napkin Finn gave her, plucking it off the coffee table. "And second, while you were running for your lives, this Fae made sure to give you his phone number." His voice was teasing.

She rolled her eyes. "Shut up, it wasn't like that."

"Then what was it like?"

"He told me to call him if I ever needed a favor," she explained.

"Oh, a favor, interesting," he mused.

"Stop," she whined and he smirked in response. A thought tugged at her mind. Ken had revealed something deeply personal, something that could put his mom in danger. Her own secret weighed on her. Maybe he would understand. "Hey, there's something I should tell you—"

His phone rang, cutting her off. Her face fell. "Hello?" he said, Lola took the opportunity to snatch the napkin back. "Your aunts are outside."

And just like that, reality sunk in. She didn't regret her moment with Ken, but she was highly aware that it couldn't happen again. As Ken walked with her out of the apartment, she could see the same sad realization cross his face.

Beyond the glass door outside, she could see Kate's car but before she headed downstairs, she hugged him one last time. "Thanks for letting me get cleaned up here and for telling me..."

"Yeah, don't worry about it," he said sincerely. "Wait, what did you want to talk abou—"

"Nothing important, don't worry about it," she said quickly. She could tell he wanted to ask more but let her go.

As Lola stepped outside, she was met with an embrace from both of her aunts. She took as much comfort as she could as they held onto her like she was the most precious thing in the universe. Faintly, as if it was mostly to herself, she heard Kate say, "Oh, mi Lola, tu eres mi tersoro."

Lola stayed silent for most of it until they were in the safety of the car, driving away from Ken's house. Only then did she let herself fall apart in the backseat.

CHAPTER FORTY-TWO
LOLA

L OLA STARED UP AT the ceiling. Since she got home, she had been up in her room, drifting in and out of sleep. Every time she closed her eyes, she was back in her cell, or stabbing her knife through the demon's eye. His black blood sprayed out of him. It coated her face, her hair, her clothes. Her dream-self screamed right along with him as if she was the one in pain.

So even though she was exhausted, she didn't attempt to sleep again. She counted the cracks in the ceiling, the chips of paint, and drywall.

There was a knock on her door that made her lose count. Without giving her the okay to come in, Kate entered the room with Andi. "How are you feeling?" Andi asked, a cup of tea in her hands. She held it out to her, the warmth felt nice against her palms. Lola didn't understand why her aunt asked. They saw her breakdown in the car. She hated crying, hated the sting of tears and choking over your own spit that came with it.

"I'm better," she said, and it was true. She was much better than the sobbing mess she had been in the car.

"That's good." She took a seat at the edge of the bed.

Lola looked up at Kate, who continued to stand off to the side. "Kate, I'm so sorry—"

"Don't." Kate held up a hand to stop her.

"But I am sorry for what I said," she went on. "You were right, what I did was stupid."

"Just stop, alright," she said. "You are a good kid, okay? You don't need to prove that to me. Detentions, expulsions, I'll understand. All I care about—all I've ever cared about is whether you're safe."

"I'm not going to lie. I want you to be coven leader. But more than anything, I just want you to be able to look out for yourself."

Lola gave her a startled look. It wasn't exactly an apology, but more than she thought she'd ever get from Kate. It wasn't like her aunt had anything to apologize for. She was right. The attack in the alley, her escape with the Fae, even that night at Sage. Everything was a stroke of luck. She knew too little to be any help to the people she cared about.

She was so afraid to try and her reluctance had nothing to show for it. She was still scared, still terrified of practicing again, but if anything was worth the risk, it was this.

"Are you down to do an impromptu lesson then?" Lola asked and Kate smiled.

Lola still didn't like the basement, but she was becoming used to it. She and Kate sat together at the table in the middle of the room. "What's behind that door?" Lola asked, pointing to the other room beside them.

"That's where we interrogated the demon," Kate said, gesturing to the room on the right.

She shuffled through the mess on the table and grabbed the family grimoire. Several pages were bookmarked with colorful sticky tabs and random pieces of paper. "Now, we don't have a lot of time, but I can run through a few things." Having been passed down for generations, the book's pages were stained yellow from its age. The spells and knowledge within were so ancient that it was still written in a Witch language long forgotten. Since Kate was the family head, it rightfully belonged to her.

Her aunt flipped to a tabbed page and pointed to the instructions. "Uh, shouldn't you be showing me the demon trapping spell and not"—Lola squinted at the page—"energetic connection?"

"Baby steps, Lola," Kate said. "Connecting to someone's energy is a little difficult to get a hold of at first, but simple and quick enough for you to do with minimal supplies."

"Okay, but how does this help me in a fight?" Lola asked, scratching her head. "And I thought the only thing strong enough to kill a demon was a demon?"

"Not kill, but they can definitely be hurt," Kate said, and for a moment she became deadly serious. "Lola, we don't have enhanced strength, or can shift into animals or teleport. All we have is our magick. Our magick is our only defense, understand?"

She nodded nervously.

Kate returned her attention to the instructions in the book. "You remember how I described demons as a sort of energy monster?" she said. "Well, magick in its own way is energy too. Once you make that connection, you can tap into people's bodies, minds, and sometimes even their spirit."

Kate began to explain spirit ties and their properties and Lola became very lost, very quickly. Her ignorance was blatantly apparent as her aunt's words reached her but never fully sunk in. The lack of understanding quickly transformed into disinterest. How was this going to help her fight a demon?

Kate shut her eyes for a moment. "You still wanna see the demon trapping spell, don't you?"

"Just really quick," Lola pleaded.

Kate sighed and flipped through the grimoire.

⇝⇝⇝ ⇜⇜⇜

Her friends sat opposite Kate and Andi on the couch. Paris rested her head on Lola's shoulder and said, "Our club meetings are becoming more and more frequent. Is everything alright?" After what happened to Lola, Paris committed herself to picking the group up from school every day. Lola appreciated the gesture but the drain of being up during the day was clear on her friend's face.

"Another summons came from the Council this morning," Andi said. From the exhausted looks from her friends, Lola could tell they were all looking forward to it.

"When do we leave?" Erica asked, the anxiety at the thought of returning was clear on her face.

"That's the thing, only me and Kate have been called."

"I hope this is about our request for protection," Kate said.

"When do you leave?" Lola asked.

"Tonight."

"And when do you come back?"

Kate sighed. "In two days."

Two days? Lola thought. She felt her own anxiety spike. So much could happen in two days. Paris was poisoned in one night, she had been taken in an afternoon. Two days away was two days too long.

Kate must have read her face because the next thing she said was, "And this is where the problem starts."

"You're just gonna leave after what happened?" Ken said in disbelief, and Lola must have imagined it because for a split-second Kate shot him a chilling look. But that couldn't have been right.

"It's not like we want to leave right now," Andi said. "And we don't have travel approval for all four of you."

Kate looked Lola dead in the eye. "But we can bring you."

Lola froze, letting her offer sink in. She could leave and be behind the protection of the Realm's borders, the protection of the entire Alereian military. She'd be safe with her aunts, away from the dangers here. "No," she said, shaking her head.

"No?" Kate looked surprised.

She looked to her friends. "I'm not just gonna leave them here." It was outrageous to even suggest that she go. After what she had been through, she couldn't leave her friends' fates to chance.

"What if something happens to you while we're away?" Kate asked, her face scrunched up with tension.

"Once again, I see your deep concern for the rest of us, Kate," Paris said dryly. Kate shook her head.

"Lola, you should go," Ken said. She looked at him with narrowed eyes. "Your aunt's right, it's not safe for you over here."

"It's not safe for anyone over here," she corrected him. "I'm not just gonna abandon you."

"Lola, you can't stay in this house by yourself," Kate argued. Before Lola could retort, Paris said, "She can stay with me."

Lola eyed her curiously. "I can?" She hadn't really checked in with what was going on between Paris and her family. Had things resolved themselves?

"If you want to," the blonde said.

"Do I want to?"

Paris shrugged.

"Is there anything you forgot to mention that we should include in our report?" Andi asked Lola.

"I think I got it all." She went through the entire ordeal with them, from where the motel was located to the fact that the group of demons appeared to be taking orders from someone.

"Good," said Kate. "We should be able to raid that building soon."

"If they're not already gone," Andi added.

Lola hoped that wasn't the case. That motel was basically a goldmine for them. Comfortable living space above and a cellar below for their victims. Someone was probably taking her place in that cell now. She hoped that in taking away their home, it would take away some of their power.

The evening quickly approached after the meeting was over. Paris drove Ken and Erica home but would return for Lola. She packed her bags as her aunts packed theirs.

Kate handed her a folded piece of paper once they met at the bottom of the stairs. Lola opened it to find a spell written inside. She looked at her aunt curiously. "If anyone even looks at you the wrong way," Kate said slowly. "Send us a message."

She nodded, but a knot formed in her stomach. Her aunt was already overestimating her casting abilities. She looked at the spell again. It was written in the old Witch tongue. How was she even supposed to pronounce this?

Kate looked at Paris expectantly. "Have you ever shot a gun before?" she asked. Lola looked up in surprise. What kind of question was that?

Paris slowly glanced over at Lola then gave Kate a nod.

Kate pulled a small tranquilizer gun out of her bag, along with a vial of antacide. She handed them to Paris, who put it in her purse. "Those darts are filled with antacide, which should knock a demon out," Kate said.

"How come I don't get any weapons?" Lola asked.

"Lola," Kate said slowly, placing her hands on the girl's shoulders. "If you were to die it'd be because a demon sucked out your soul, not because I gave you a gun and you shot yourself."

Fair enough, Lola thought.

Both of her aunts hugged her goodbye with Andi whispering promises in her ear, all about how this was all going to be over when they came home. Just for a moment, Lola let herself believe in them.

CHAPTER FORTY-THREE
LOLA

Hunter and Ian sat in the living room as Lola was guided inside by Paris. "Okay, you both remember Lola," she said. "She's going to stay here for a couple days. Do not speak to her unless directly spoken to."

Lola nudged her. Their first impressions of one another were rough enough as it was.

Paris rolled her eyes. "Suit yourself," she said. "Though I warn you, they aren't good company."

"And you are?" Hunter asked.

"Of course, I'm a delight."

"We must have you confused with a different Paris then," Ian said.

Paris glared at him. It seemed things calmed down significantly since the last time she'd seen them together.

"Where's she staying anyway?" Hunter asked.

"In my room," Paris said, then panic seemed to creep on her face. "Which is very unclean. Stay here."

She turned to walk up the stairs. "Do you need any help?" Lola asked.

"No, no, you stay down here, away from my things that should not be seen by the public eye."

"Ew," Ian said, his face scrunched up as she left.

Lola took a seat on the couch next to Hunter. "So, Lola, how long have you known Paris?" Hunter asked.

"For about three years," she responded. "How long have you and Paris been uh...related?"

Maybe Paris was right and they shouldn't have been talking to each other. But Hunter snorted and said, "You know, since birth."

"Nice."

Paris came back downstairs and motioned for Lola to follow her. "Okay, you can bring up your stuff," she said.

Suddenly eager to leave this interaction, Lola gathered her things and met her friend on the steps. As they walked, Paris said, "Did you really ask—"

"Please don't," Lola said quickly. Paris laughed and out of the corner of Lola's eye, she could see her brothers smile at the sound.

Lola woke up in the middle of the night. The past couple of days were spent sleepless, so she wasn't sure why she thought tonight would be different.

Stretching out her arms, she hit something on the nightstand, knocking it to the floor. Sighing, Lola dangled over the bed and reached around until her hand came in contact with something underneath. It was an empty bottle of wine.

Lola hung herself back over the edge and peered under the bed. There were four more empty bottles of alcohol there, along with dirty clothes and other garbage. Had this been what Paris was hiding?

She got up and put the bottle back where she found it. Lola wasn't sure what she was looking for as she left the bedroom. She wandered the halls a bit, perhaps hoping to run into Paris, but what would she even say to her?

Momentarily forgetting that everyone in this house was nocturnal, Lola was surprised to hear voices coming from the dining room.

"I convinced her to let us stay, didn't I?" Hunter said.

"Well, it doesn't really matter if we never see her, now does it?" said Rose. "Maybe we should call Tori, she was always better at dealing with Paris."

Hunter scoffed, "Tori is part of the reason we're in this mess. You want to piss her off more?"

There was a sigh from Rose. "She scares me sometimes, Hunter."

"I know."

Someone cleared their throat from behind Lola. She jumped, whirling around to find Ian standing there. "Are you looking for Paris?" he asked.

Lola clutched her chest as her heartbeat steadied its pace. "Yeah, where is she?"

"No idea," he said. "She usually goes out around this time."

"And you don't know where?"

Ian shrugged. "She doesn't really tell me," he said. "Is there anything I can help with?"

Lola quickly shook her head. She wasn't even sure if she wanted to discuss this with Paris, let alone her brother. "No, it's fine," she said. "I should probably get back to sleep anyway, I have school in the morning."

Confusion crossed Ian's face. "You're in high school?"

She nodded. "Is there a problem?"

"No, I guess I should be happy she has any friends," he said. Lola wasn't quite sure what his problem was but before she could open her mouth to defend Paris, he continued, "but she seems more at ease around you, it's good for her. Thank you."

He moved past Lola to join Rose and Hunter in the dining room. Lola stood alone in the hallway, finally realizing why Paris didn't talk about her family. Nothing about these people made sense. Initially, Lola thought her confusion stemmed from the fact that she was an only child, but now she truly didn't know whether they loved or hated each other.

As Lola made her way back to bed, she decided that she wouldn't talk to Paris about this. There seemed to be five hundred years of baggage for her to unpack and Lola knew from her own problems that once that bag was opened, it could never be closed again.

CHAPTER FORTY-FOUR
LOLA

Lola met Ken and Erica outside the front office as they waited for Paris. The school hallways emptied themselves. Paris arrived just as the majority of students headed home or to their respective clubs. "There you are," Erica said.

"Excuse me for ever resting my eyes," Paris groaned.

While Lola still didn't quite understand how to use the messaging spell Kate gave her, she wanted to help in any way she could. Her aunts would be presenting their report to the Council any time now, but the summons still put them on a time crunch. There was more to discover here, she just knew it.

The group walked into the main office. It was empty aside from a secretary typing at his computer. Paris walked over to him with a sharp look in her eye. "Leave and take a walk around the school," she compelled. He blinked then slowly got out of his seat, walking past the group as if they were invisible to him. Seeing compulsion at work gave Lola the chills. She was thankful she wasn't human and stood immune to its effects.

Once the room was clear, Erica took a seat behind the desk. "They're still logged in," she said.

"What exactly are we looking for?" Ken asked.

"Personal files, medical records, that kind of stuff."

Since their current hunch was that their attackers were in the school, it only made sense for them to look into the school files. "There's gotta be something suspicious in there," said Lola. "Start with Hanks, he gives me the creeps."

They went through every document with his name on it that they could find. It was exhausting. Arthur Hanks was fifty-five years old, had been teaching for twenty years, and had a daughter who attended their school. But so far, there was nothing that connected him to the demon's attacks besides the fact that he was new to the area. After just twenty minutes of searching, this investigation had already gotten old.

"Lo, I don't think it's him," Ken said.

She pouted. "But creepy mustache, and creepy dream," she argued.

"Are we really just going off what you thought you saw in your high-ass state?" Paris asked. She was inspecting her nails, unconcerned with what was happening on the computer.

Lola thought for a moment. "Uh, I guess."

"I'm just gonna switch over to the student files, and check out Troy's records," Erica said, dismissing her. Lola didn't know why Erica wasted her time on that. They knew Troy long before any of this happened, no way it was him. She leaned against the wall as Erica worked, staring at nothing in particular. When she did return to Erica, something caught her friend's attention.

"What?" Ken asked, noticing the same thing.

Erica wore a concerned expression as she made eye contact with Lola. "Lola, you got kicked out of school?"

Panic shot through her, consuming any other rational thought she had. They were all looking at her. Staring her down. Judging her. Lola kept her eyes level with Erica's, she rushed over to the computer. "You went through my records?" she demanded, standing over her. It was the first time she'd towered over Erica in her entire life.

Erica paled at her harsh tone. "Lo, what is she talking about?" Ken asked.

"I didn't mean to," Erica stuttered. "It was in the student records, I—"

"Close it," she demanded, praying Erica didn't see anything else. "Close it now!"

Erica quickly got a hold of the mouse and exited the tab. "What happened—" Erica started, but Lola cut her off again.

"That's none of your business," she snapped.

"Easy," Paris said.

Stupid. She was so fucking stupid. Why didn't she think her school records would be there too? This was her idea and all it had done was open herself up to questions she wasn't ready to answer. They were supposed to be investigating demons, not her. "Just focus on what we came here for so we can leave," she said to Erica. She hated how angry she sounded. How guilty. She needed to breathe, it wasn't Erica's fault she overlooked this.

Erica's eyes fell back to the screen and the group stood in an uncomfortable silence. Eventually, Erica sighed and shook her head. "Nothing on Troy that we don't already know."

"Do Ms. Marshall," Lola blurted.

"I thought we were searching for the demon," Paris asked.

"I just want to check something." She had a hunch.

Erica did as she asked, pining through the files and then stopping in surprise. "Huh," she said.

"What?" Lola asked.

"She had plans to resign."

Lola looked at Ken. Perhaps that planner had been useful for something after all. She had been right, Ms. Marshall had been running. Lola told the rest of the group about her time in the teacher's apartment.

"You told me you were in Hanks class," Erica said, a look of betrayal on her face.

"I know, I'm sorry."

"Forget that," Paris said, getting to her feet. "How did you find out where this lady lived anyway?"

"Well Brooke had...told me..." Lola trailed off. Why had Brooke told her that? She tried to remember their conversation. Brooke had come to her after Ms. Marshall's death after ignoring her for half of the semester. Lola had thought it was pity, but now she wasn't sure.

"Brooke?" Ken said uncertain.

"Ere do a search on Brooke Watson."

After a few minutes of searching, Paris asked, "Anything incriminating yet?"

"Maybe," Erica said, the rest of the group turned to her expectantly.

"Wait, really?"

"Well, I was going through Brooke's records and couldn't find anything but her middle school, so I just figured she was homeschooled for a bit," Erica explained. "So, I Googled her name and found her in a list of finalists in a track competition."

"And?" Ken said, not following.

"And I found a picture taken at the competition and this isn't Brooke."

The rest of the group walked behind the computer to see for themselves. The girl in the photo smiling brightly and holding a certificate was a skinny girl with dark skin and hair.

"So, that's not her?" Paris asked. *Unless she tans really hard in the summer, no,* Lola thought.

Erica shook her head.

"So, two people with the same name can't go to the same school?" Ken questioned.

"Same first and last name?"

"It's possible," he said, Lola frowned at him. "I'm just being realistic here." His phone went off, making her jump. "Hello? No, I'm still at school, why?"

He put the phone on speaker so they could all hear. Troy's voice came from across the line. "Oh, good, I thought so," he said. "Some girl ran into me while I was leaving, said she was looking for you. Just making sure you're still there."

Time came to a standstill as they stared at one another.

"What girl?" Ken asked.

"Uh, I don't know, white girl, blonde hair," Troy said. "Like half the girls at this place." But it was all they needed to hear. Troy, as nonchalant as ever, continued talking. "Well, I'm just passing the message along, talk to you later."

"Yeah okay," Ken replied and hung up.

"Get to my car," Paris said urgently. "Now."

They made their way out of the building swiftly and came to a halt in the parking lot.

All four of the tires on Paris' car were slashed and flat.

"Dammit!" Paris exclaimed, kicking the rim over and over. Just above them, sunset was quickly approaching.

CHAPTER FORTY-FIVE
LOLA

Lola spent the next few minutes attempting to call for new tires. After the fifth try with no luck it was settled, she just couldn't call for things that large. The guilt hit her again. Maybe if she had practiced more, her gift could've been of more use.

Paris made sure to grab her purse from the car before the group abandoned it all together.

"Should we even wait for the bus?" Ken said. "What if someone's waiting for us there?"

"We could call for a rideshare?" Erica suggested.

"During rush hour?" Paris responded.

Standing around the school waiting for a ride while Brooke knew where they were wasn't an option either. They decided to walk together, heading to Kate's house, which was the closest and safest.

The four took a detour from Lola's regular route in hopes of avoiding any surprise attacks these demons had coming. How many times had Brooke set her up? Lola wondered.

She thought back to her first day at school. Brooke had been there when she accidentally called for that screwdriver. She remembered her eyes locked on her at lunchtime. Then there was that day in detention. Brooke had taken the seat right behind her. Then again on the day Erica was attacked in that alley. Hadn't it been Brooke who told her to head to that part of town? How hadn't she noticed she had been there at every turn?

Daylight was fading and the group quickened their pace. Why did the sun set so early in the winter time? Lola wondered if her friends felt as ridiculous as she did. Nightwalkers afraid of the dark. The whole thing felt like a big joke.

They stayed close to large groups of people as they walked, but the crowd thinned significantly as they cut through a nearby park. By the time they reached its center, Paris said, "We're being followed." Lola felt her body stiffen and looked over at her friends, who came to a halt. "Keep moving!"

They complied and kept their faces forward, never looking back as Paris listened intently. It was only when Lola herself could hear the increasing sounds of footsteps coming in their direction did she begin to panic. "Run," Paris whispered to them.

The group took off in an instant and the demons gave into the chase.

Lola's heart pounded furiously in her chest. They just needed to make it out of the park, she kept telling herself. At her side, Paris reached into her purse and withdrew the tranquilizer that Kate gave her. She stopped running, faced their pursuers and took aim.

Lola, Erica, and Ken looked behind them, stopping in their tracks. "Keep going!" Paris yelled.

After some hesitation they listened. There were six demons behind them coming at full speed. As they came across a playground, which Lola was thankful for having no children, she heard a few groans of agony behind them. There was something else, a faint crackling in the air that was interrupted by Paris meeting them at lightning speed.

"Did you get any?" Erica asked.

"I shot two, but then they started to—"

"Move!" Ken yanked Paris toward him as a bright gray ball—the same ball of power Lola had seen underground—soared past them and hit a slide, leaving a scorch mark. Lola didn't dare look behind her to see if it was the same demon she had stabbed in the eye.

Dodging and weaving as they ran, Lola hated her shorter legs. She felt like the rest of her friends had to pace themselves in order to keep her in sight. If Paris were sane, she would've left them long ago.

Lola could see the clearing of the park in sight. Paris quickly stuffed the tranquilizer back in her purse as they made their way through it. She had never been so glad to see people in her life. There weren't enough strangers on the street for the group to blend in, but she sure hoped nothing would happen to them with witnesses around. But then she remembered the alley. In broad daylight they attempted to take Erica. That brief relief she felt quickly died out.

Even though her legs were sore and her lungs burned, she pushed forward. She directed her friends across the street as a gap between speeding cars became available. The demons staggered back a bit as the opening closed and they were at risk of being hit.

Safely on the other side of the road, the four continued taking turn after turn in hopes of losing them.

Breathless, Lola looked over to Erica. Her friend stopped completely, unable to take it anymore. She bent over, arm clutching her stomach, coughing furiously.

They gathered around her as the demons rounded the corner down the street. Ken placed a hand on her shoulder. "Come on, we gotta go," he urged.

"Wait a minute," said Erica, straightening up. She looked like she was going to pass out. She pulled them behind a parked car and had them crouch down. "I wanna try something. Hold on to me."

They obeyed nervously. When nothing happened and the demons quickly approached, fear shot through Lola's system. "Erica, whatever you're gonna do, do it now!" Lola exclaimed.

Erica shut her eyes, her face twisted in concentration.

At first there was nothing, then Lola felt it. Her body became weightless as it was gently lifted off the ground. A gray light enveloped them and she felt her body disappear.

Almost instantly did the light dissolve around them and they staggered forward. Recovering from sudden dizziness, Lola realized that they were somewhere else. Erica had flashed them here.

"I was aiming for the house," she panted. If she didn't look exhausted before, she definitely did now. Lola looked around. They had traveled across the block.

"It's close enough, let's go," Paris said. Ken wrapped an arm around Erica to hold her up and they were off again.

The house was within reach and they hurried up the street. Hastily, Lola pulled out the keys to the front door and unlocked it, her hands shaking. The four launched themselves through the threshold, slamming the door behind them and locked themselves inside.

"Do you think they know where I live?" Lola asked.

"They've been watching us," Ken said.

"And they know where you go to school," Paris pointed out. "I don't see why they wouldn't."

Lola slid to the floor exhausted, she couldn't do this anymore. There was little time before they got here. She pulled out the messaging spell Kate had given her out of her jacket pocket. It looked like she would need some supplies to make it work. Of course she needed supplies right now.

"What's that?" Ken asked, looking over her shoulder.

"A spell to get a message to my aunts," she explained.

"And how's that going?" He sounded hopeful.

"I'm figuring it out," she said, the tightness in her chest growing. It seemed like she'd have to burn the message to her aunts while thinking of the destination. She could manage this, she had too.

"Guys." Paris pointed at Erica, whose face was expressionless and eyes were shut tight.

Ken sighed. "Here we go."

When she was finally released from the premonition, they watched her anxiously. Her face was grim.

"What now?" Lola asked.

"Brooke is coming here," Erica said. "Tonight."

CHAPTER FORTY-SIX
LOLA

Lola's first instinct was to run. Erica's flashing had only given them a head start. It wouldn't be long until the entire house was surrounded. Memories of her time in the demon nest assaulted her. She was back on the motel steps, every cell in her body screaming that she should save herself. But where was there to go?

Without a car, her aunt's house was the safest place to think of. And who was to say Brooke didn't know where the rest of her friends lived? No, they couldn't put their families at risk like that.

"When?" Paris probed Erica.

"I just know it's tonight."

Paris sighed. "Well, that just means that a demon could be on her way to kill us from now till sunrise."

"Sorry, there wasn't a well-placed clock in my premonition," Erica said. All she had seen was Brooke breaking down the front door. In order to make that as hard as possible, Paris hauled the bookshelf and table from the dining room, barricading the entrance.

But how much strength a demon possessed was still a mystery. Would any of this really do any good? Lola's gaze drifted to the basement as an idea struck her. Once again, she'd have to descend underground if she wanted them all to survive.

⟫⟫⟩ ⟨⟨⟨

Waiting for Brooke to arrive was even more agonizing than running from demons. The ones who had followed them here hadn't broken in yet, hadn't even attempted to. It seemed they were all waiting for the demon leader to arrive.

Lola sat cross-legged on the floor of the basement, Ken at her side. They were in the side room. The symbol her aunts had drawn to trap that demon was thankfully still there. Lola planned to use it again.

Ken rubbed the small of her back, sensing her nerves. "You can do this," he said softly. Could she?

She had barely figured out the messaging spell and now she wanted to attempt this? Something even her aunts had struggled with? Using her gift was one thing. It was a natural part of her. But casting came from a deeper place, a place she hadn't been to in years. "I'm not strong enough to do this by myself," Lola admitted. "I'll have to keep the spell going the entire time, so once she's in the circle you'll have to kill her before I lose hold of it."

She knew they would need to kill Brooke but hearing herself declare it out loud still struck her. A few hours ago, Brooke was just a girl at their school and now they were plotting to murder her before she murdered them.

Ken nodded, a sad look on his face as if he had the same thought. Paris and Erica were upstairs, their job was to wear Brooke down and lure her into the circle. Ken's job was to make sure Lola didn't die in the process.

She clutched the grimoire in her hands, reading over the spell again. The sound of heavy banging came from upstairs and then a loud crash. She shot Ken a panicked look. "Don't focus on that," he said. One of Kate's daggers trembled in his hands. He pointed to the spell on the page. "Focus on this."

She let out a shaky breath. He was right, this entire thing was relying on her.

A struggle was clearly going on upstairs. She could hear the clash of glass and other things being thrown or broken. Lola had to remind herself that Paris had the tranquilizer and that Erica had her powers. They would be fine, everything would be fine.

"Lola!" Erica shouted. She started the spell.

"*Tutores per umbras da mitis vintutem. Tutores per umbras da mitis vintutem,*" Lola recited over and over. She was surprised at how easy the words rolled off her tongue. She didn't understand what they meant, and yet she did all the same. Her magick rose to the surface and released itself into the world.

And it felt amazing.

For months she had suffocated, taking in short gasps of breath every time she used her gift. But now she inhaled deep, filling her lungs—filling her soul until the air lifted her off the ground.

The circle glowed a warm red and the basement door flew open. Lola heard a yelp, then tumbling down the stairs. At the end of it came Erica, next Paris. Lola continued the spell, fighting the urge to run to them.

Paris quickly got to her feet and helped Erica up. Footsteps descended after them. Lola lowered her voice.

Brooke's figure came into view from the doorway.

Without saying a word, her very presence was frightening. She stood with purpose, her eyes focused and face unreadable. It was the seriousness that caught Lola off guard the most. At school, Brooke always seemed out of it—lost in her own little world. This was different. Her silence was no longer an endearing part of her shyness. Now it was something eerie and cold.

Paris fired three shots. Brooke dogged each of them with ease. When Paris went to fire again, she found herself out of darts.

A ghost of a smile crept across the demon's face as she advanced. In response, Paris decided to throw the entire gun at her face. Using her speed, she grabbed Erica's hand and took them into the room where Lola and Ken waited.

Brooke shook off the hit and quickly followed, looking aggravated. From their position in the corner, she and Ken stayed out of her line of sight as Erica and Paris held her attention. Lola felt the crackle of energy before she heard it. A gray ball formed in Brooke's hand. She hurled it at Paris and Erica, who ducked just in time. Scorch marks were left on the wall behind them.

With her attention fully focused on hitting their friends, Ken shot her a glance. He was gonna take the opportunity. He slowly approached, dagger raised. In one swift motion, Ken grabbed Brooke's arm and plunged the blade straight through her hand.

Brooke screamed through her teeth, backhanding Ken with her uninjured hand. He flew across the room, crashing into a plastic chair. Lola felt a pang in her chest. She couldn't help them, couldn't move. She had to continue the spell. While Brooke yanked the blade out of her hand, Paris took the vial of remaining antacide out of her bag. The demon advanced on her, grabbing the wrist holding the acid, and squeezing it until there was a sickening crack. Paris gritted her teeth, dropping the vial. It smashed into pieces on the floor.

Brooke tossed Paris aside and settled her eyes on Erica, who was backed into a wall. "Ere, the acid!" Ken called out to her.

Quicker than lightning, Erica's hand shot out, willing the puddle on the floor into the air and straight into the demon's eyes.

Brooke let out a piercing shriek, hands rushing to her face. While she was temporarily blind, Paris snapped her wrist back into place and rushed her, pushing her into the circle. Brooke stumbled back with a grunt, skin sizzling and smoke pouring through the cracks of her hands.

Lola almost let out a sob when she revealed her face. Where the demon's eyes had been were now empty sockets. The acid burned straight through.

Brooke herself seemed to be over the initial pain. She took a step, attempting to leave the circle as if she could continue like this. It was only when her foot couldn't cross the barrier did she look distressed.

"Interesting," she murmured. "What happens now?"

Lola cast a glance at the rest of the group who looked tired and uncertain. Paris picked up a dagger from the floor.

"I know you can't see me," Paris said. "So let me put it like this, answer our questions and I won't stick this dagger through your heart."

Brooke cocked her head to the side. "Do you really think you're in a position to be making demands? My nest is outside surrounding this entire house. I've instructed them to raid the place if I don't come out in twenty minutes."

There was a beat of silence.

"I can make this quick, painless even," she continued. "Or you can be ripped out of here limb by limb. The choice is yours."

"Painless? Is that what you call what you did to Ms. Marshall? Or all those other people?" Ken asked, lips curling back in disgust.

Brooke shrugged. "Got your attention, didn't it?" she said simply. "Don't take it too personally, I was just doing what I was hired to do."

Lola steeled herself as she continued chanting. She wanted to scream. Ms. Marshall had a hole in her chest and Brooke didn't care, didn't even bat an eye when asked to.

"Hired by who?" said Erica.

Brooke snorted and the sound was so odd that Lola almost stuttered. "It's best if you worry about yourself. If you do make it out of here, with all the attention on you I'm sure someone else will be right behind me."

Ken and Erica exchanged worried looks, but Paris shook it off, heading into the other room to get more antacide. *Good,* Lola thought. She panted between words. The cool rush of air had transformed into something else. Each syllable felt like water pressure on her body, slowly crushing her. Something wet leaked onto her upper lip. She brought her hand to her nose and it came back bloody. They needed to hurry, she couldn't hold it for much longer.

"What? No more questions?" Brooke said. Even with no eyes, there was something in her face that was pitying. When none of them answered, she went on, "Since you've made your choice, let me just say this; what I did to all those other Alereians wasn't personal. What I'll do to you will be."

Faster than Lola could see, Brooke turned and hurled a ball of energy straight at her. Her hand and eyes had healed while she was talking.

Lola screamed as it collided with her shoulder. Her flesh burned and the pain was all she could process. It blurred her vision and slowed down time. The sizzle of her own skin was loud in her ears.

Ken and Erica rushed to her side, but it was too late. The spell was broken and Brooke was free. The demon stepped out of the circle, throwing another energy ball at Lola. She could barely move—barely think to move out of the way. She shut her eyes, waiting for the impact to come. But it never did.

She opened her eyes to find the ball floating in midair. Erica threw her hand back, throwing the orb back in Brooke's direction. Paris charged into the room, dagger coated in black. Brooke moved to evade Erica and Paris at once.

Ken knelt at Lola's side. "Can you move?" he asked, panic in his voice. She clutched her shoulder, tears stinging her eyes, but nodded anyway. He helped her to her feet.

She saw Brooke grab Paris by her hair and slam her head into her knee. Lola winced. Blood leaked down her arm, the pain so bad she could hardly stand, but she needed to do something. Brooke took hold of Erica. Ken left her side, rushing toward them but the demon's fist slammed into Erica and there was a crunch of something breaking.

The words tumbled out of Lola's mouth before she could think them over. "Dumbbells!"

The equipment formed above Brooke and landed on her head, knocking her down with a grunt. But Lola wasn't done yet. "Stick, string." She gripped the objects tight in her hands.

Brooke looked up and got back to her feet. "You're gonna kill me with string and a stick?" she said, an amused smile on her lips.

Lola prayed this spell did what she thought it did. "*What's long lost must be found, let this cord connect and bound.*"

Brooke stopped in her tracks, hand rushing to her heart as if she felt a tug on it. Lola knew this because she felt it too. She had connected to Brooke.

Well, not Brooke, but the energy that resided inside of her. The energy she got from all the souls she consumed. Lola could feel them swirling inside of her, restless and desperate. She took the string and wrapped it around the stick that represented Brooke. The demon grimaced, clutching her arms around her body like her insides were tied up in knots. "What are you doing?" she asked through gritted teeth.

After Lola was done wrapping the cord, she took both ends in her hands and snapped the stick in half. Brooke fell to the group with a yelp. She clawed at her throat, coughing raggedly. Black blood flew from her mouth.

Choke on those souls, bitch, Lola thought.

Paris was up and in the blink of an eye, she was in front of the demon and plunging the dagger in her heart.

A gasp escaped Brooke's lips before she collapsed.

CHAPTER FORTY-SEVEN
LOLA

BROOKE SAID HER DEMONS had the order to raid the house after twenty minutes. Lola had a feeling that time was up when the sounds of footsteps came from upstairs. "There's too many of them," Ken muttered to himself, shaking his head.

Erica clutched her bloody broken nose, looking toward the door. She used her power to shut and lock it, but even that wouldn't hold for long.

The message to her aunts was sent, but there was no telling how fast they would get here. Lola's gaze landed on Brooke, whose crumpled body leaked blood onto the floor. She grimaced at the sight. Her eyes fixated on the symbol on the floor next. "Get in the circle," she said.

"What?" Paris said.

"If it can keep things from getting out, maybe I can make it keep things from getting in," she explained.

"So, we'd be trapped in there?" Erica exclaimed.

"Do you have a better idea?"

As the sound of footsteps descended the stairs, none of them argued further. Her friends jumped into the circle while she grabbed the family grimoire from the corner. Lola stepped inside the circle just as a heavy pounding hit the door.

She began the chant and it weighed on her like an anvil on her back. Her body wasn't used to using all of this magick. The overwhelming sensation made her want to explode.

The door burst open and Erica put up a hand to stop it. Her and the demons on the other side were in a struggle. Erica grimaced as the demon's strength overpowered her, knocking her hand back down to her side.

The door flew off its hinges and the nest flooded into the room. There were about six of them. Lola could see the anger cross over their face as they took in Brooke's pitiful form. They advanced on the group, eyes blazing. Lola kept up her chanting.

One demon reached out in an attempt to grab her, but found his hand unable to pass through the circle.

She swallowed hard as she recognized his face. It was the demon she stabbed in the eye. He looked directly at her, glaring. Stepping back, he let a ball of energy form in his hand and hurled it at them. She shut her eyes but the energy connected and dissolved into the invisible field separating them.

This just made the demons angrier. They clawed at the field, punched it, even threw chairs at. But nothing would penetrate the circle.

The demon she recognized walked up to the circle, his voice low as he said, "You can't stay in there forever. You're going to have to stop chanting at some point."

He was right. Each word hurt to say and Lola could feel the blood drip out of her nose again.

Just when she couldn't take it anymore, more footsteps came from upstairs. *More demons*, she thought. The entire nest was here to drag them out of the house. Limb by limb, just like Brooke said.

She wanted to shut her eyes and hold Ken's hand as it happened, but the grimoire was occupied in her uninjured arm. Lola didn't want these demons to hear her last words to her friends—didn't want them to have that satisfaction. They looked at one another, the silent meaning passing between them with ease. They knew she couldn't hold on either.

She had failed them and they knew it.

The footsteps descended the stairs just as Lola became too breathless to continue the spell. The demon could see it happening and smiled.

Then an arrow flew through his eye.

Lola gasped, jumping back into Paris. The demon fell to the floor dead. The entire room looked at the door. A woman dressed in brown tactical gear stood at the forefront with a crossbow. These weren't demons. These were Huntresses.

Other women moved around her, charging into the room, weapons raised. There were more Huntresses than there were demons. Lola saw two women take on one demon. When the demon got a good hit on one, the other came out behind her, sword drawn, and stabbed it through it's throat.

The carnage was all over the room, the Huntresses were ruthless, cutting through limbs and slitting throats with no care. The group stayed huddled together in the circle, unsure what to do.

"Guys!" Andi called out to them. At the door, Kate and Andi urged the group to follow. Lola had never been so happy to see them in her life. The four raced out of the room as the fight continued behind them.

"Upstairs, now!" Kate said. Lola let herself look behind her, just in time to see a demon thrust its hand through a Huntress' chest. She screamed.

Kate grabbed her by the shoulders and pushed her up the stairs. But she was already losing consciousness before they reached the top.

Lola gritted her teeth as Ken took care of the burn on her arm. She had caught a glimpse of it when she woke up and nearly passed out again. It was blistering and turning from red to black. The cool water stung as Ken cleaned the wound.

"Seven demons, and one of ours dead," one of the Huntresses said once the fight was over. They all watched as the remaining Huntresses carried their dead comrade out of the house. Her body would be burned and her ashes would be scattered back in Alereis. There was so much death in this house that Lola could feel it lurking over her shoulder.

Kate and Andi had successfully managed to get the Council to agree to sending a small strike team to the Mortal Realm. The plan had been to wipe out the nest, but after getting Lola's message, her aunts split the forces between the locations. Half of the Huntresses came to the house while the other went to raid the old motel. Lola wondered if any of them had been killed there too.

The place was a mess. When Brooke arrived, Erica had essentially thrown anything within sight at the demon to slow her down. Broken glass from smashed picture frames and vases scattered the floor.

"Ow." Lola pulled away.

"Hold on," Ken shushed her, gently wrapping her arm in gauze.

"You're really good at this, you know?"

"Well, you've given me a lot of practice," he said.

"Any time, Dr. Fell," she joked even though he could feel her shaking. She looked to Erica, who sat across from them. Andi was at her side, pressing a cold compress to her nose. "How are you doing?"

"My nose is still broken," she said.

"Keep your head up," Andi said. Erica straightened up. "We're gonna have to take you to the emergency room."

"It looks like the swellings going down," Paris pointed out. And sure enough it was. The ugly purple around her nose was fading and Lola could clearly see the fracture on its bridge.

"I guess those Guardian genetics are good for something." She tried to smile and winced. "I'm sorry about your house."

Kate looked behind her at the carnage in the dining room. "You did all of this?"

"She saved my life too," Lola said. The image of the energy ball shooting toward her flashed in her mind. If her arm wasn't fucked and Erica's nose was intact, she would've been strangling her in a hug. Erica looked surprised as if she herself hadn't processed this fact, then flushed.

"Well, what was I supposed to do, just let you get hit?" she said.

"You could've." She wasn't about to let Erica downplay what she had done. When it came down to it, Erica would look out for her no matter how much it scared her.

Her friend went silent and Kate said, "Seems I made a good choice after all." She crossed her arms. "Don't apologize for the house, you could've burned it down if you needed to. I'm just glad everyone's alive."

While that might've been true, the weight didn't lift from Lola in the slightest. She didn't need to be a Seer to know that this brief moment of safety was only temporary.

CHAPTER FORTY-EIGHT
LOLA

IT WAS ONLY A few days after Brooke's death did her aunts call for the group to gather again. Lola wasn't looking forward to it in the slightest. As her friends arrived and headed to the living room, Ken stayed behind, waiting for her as she descended the steps.

"Hey."

"How's the arm?" he asked.

"Still gross."

"And how are you feeling?"

"It hurts like a bitch," she said.

"Not the arm," he said. "You."

She thought for a moment, frowning. Brooke being dead should've brought her comfort but thinking of her crippled body on the basement floor saddened her more than anything. "I don't know," she said honestly. Her friends had survived but there were still so many dead—and that didn't even account for Brooke's final warning.

"When you were at my house," Ken said slowly. "You were about to tell me you got kicked out of school, weren't you?"

She looked away, saying nothing. "Lola, we almost died the other night and if it wasn't for you, we would have," he said. *If it wasn't for my aunts,* she thought. "There is nothing that's gonna change my opinion of you and Paris and Erica feel the same way. Whatever happened over there no longer matters, okay?"

She swallowed hard. "Okay."

They met the rest of the group in the living room. Erica had a nose split and gauze wrapped around her. The most terrifying night of her life was explained away to her parents as a bad fall. While her and Erica didn't heal as fast as Paris or a demon, her nose would be fixed within the week, which would probably lead to a lot more questions.

"Wonderful," Paris mumbled. "I'm in this house again." Lola couldn't help but agree with the sentiment. The memories from the past few days made it hard to live here at times.

"What's going on?" Erica asked Kate.

"The Council is impressed with you," Kate said.

"Really?" Ken said in disbelief.

"Yes, killing the leader of the largest nest in San Francisco is nothing to take lightly," Kate said, and then she backpedaled. "Well, it was the largest nest."

"What do you mean?" Lola asked.

"We got an update on the Huntresses that raided the motel you told us about. It was mostly deserted, only a few stragglers," she said and grabbed Lola's backpack from the side of the armchair. "They found this though."

Lola took the bag eagerly. Her phone, wallet, keys, and schoolwork were all there. But Ms. Marshall's planner was not. Had it been lost in the fight? It didn't make sense for a demon to grab it in their escape.

"And what about the order for protection?" Paris asked.

Andi sighed. "Based on what you did Thursday, they don't think you need it. They just plan to move your training up to January." That was only a few weeks from now.

"Of course that's what they're doing." Ken sighed.

Paris looked at the aunts in disbelief. "There was a demon in their school, and there could be more, but the Council thinks it's okay to just go on as is?"

Kate nodded. "I know," she said. "Which is why I wanted to ask you to go to school with them."

Paris' eyes widened. "Excuse me?"

"Yes!" Lola exclaimed. Paris going to school with them was something she didn't know she needed until now.

"Paris is going to school with us? As a student?" Ken said.

"No, Paris is not," Paris replied.

"You said it yourself that there could be more demons in the school," Andi said. "It's best if you're there with them."

Andi was right. Paris had been the one to kill the demon. Between the four of them, she was the only one with the strength to fight back.

"Even if I did agree, how long would you have me doing this?"

"Just for the rest of the school year."

"The rest of the school year?" Paris repeated in disbelief.

"I don't see the problem here," Kate said.

"I know it may be confusing, seeing as nobody respects my sleep schedule anyway, but I am nocturnal," Paris explained slowly.

"It's only eight hours of the day."

"Only?" She blinked. The group waited expectantly for her answer and she let out a sigh. "Just when I thought things couldn't get any worse." After getting Paris' official confirmation, her aunts left the group alone.

"I suddenly can't wait for winter break to be over," Ken commented.

"Oh, shut up," Paris said.

"This no protection thing is bullshit," said Lola. The Council didn't think they were capable. They just didn't want to waste resources on them. Lola wondered if the Huntress who died here had anything to do with that. A flash of a hand bursting through a chest ran through her mind, causing her to swallow hard.

"Do you think Brooke was telling the truth?" Erica asked. "About this not being over."

This had been bothering Lola for days. Brooke said there would be someone else after them. There was no reason for her to lie about that.

"Maybe," said Ken. "She knew we weren't going to hand ourselves over. I don't think she was just trying to scare us."

Even after all this, they had no idea why they were targets in the first place. Lola recalled her time in the cell. The demon had mentioned something being bright, but what did that mean?

Paris put her hand up. "Let's make that next month's problem, okay?" she said. "Like me, having to wear your ugly ass uniforms is now a problem for next month."

"Wow," Ken said. "You know Clearwater's uniforms are blue and orange? You got lucky."

"Those poor poor kids." Paris shook her head.

Lola let herself take in Paris' words. Next month's problem. That sounded good to her.

When her friends were gone, Lola found her way back up to her room.

She scratched out the verse she had written. It was bad. Just like everything else she had written in the last four months.

The bass felt steady and comfortable even though she had never played it before.

Her hands moved on their own, strumming a familiar melody. Her dad wasn't a musician, but he knew a few cords here and there. When Lola first told him she wanted to play, this melody was the first thing he taught her.

She hummed along to the tune now. If she closed her eyes, it was almost like she was back home, singing with him until dinner was ready.

There was a knock on her door and Kate entered. "Hi," she said. "What are you playing?"

"I'm just messing around," she said. "Is that it?"

Kate carried a mug in her hands, no doubt filled with the elixir she had brewed this morning. Her aunt nodded passing along the cup.

Lola stared at it nervously. She needed to take it. After all the magick she had used the other day, there was no telling the consequences that would come from her curse. The elixir would nullify those effects, but her father's warning and admittance against them still ate away at her.

But this wasn't about her dad and it wasn't about her either. It was about her friends and how she needed to be strong for them. And being strong meant using this cursed blood of hers for something good. She would need to make peace with the fact that everyday she'd be doing something her dad never wanted. But perhaps she had found the one thing more important than that.

Lola looked Kate in the eye as she raised the cup to her lips. She downed the liquid, swallowing down her fears and her father's disappointment.

SUNDAY

Sunday stepped out of the taxi and immediately concluded that San Francisco needed to be set on fire. Unfortunately for her, a disease called stupidity had quickly spread throughout her nest, keeping the city intact so far.

It was an ugly night. Gray storm clouds cast overhead while her boots made splashes from the downpour earlier that evening. There was a sudden crack of thunder and Sunday felt it was safe to assume her hair was going to get wet. As people began to scatter, walking among them proved to be more difficult than she thought. Happy tingles, which were more like electric shocks at the moment, assaulted her body as she moved through the crowd.

It was hard not to pause and stare longingly at all the souls she was missing out on. She didn't even want to think about all the missed opportunities she had seen on the way here. A drunk girl arguing with a bouncer, a woman with an unimpressive bob demanding a refund from a vendor. Hell, there was even a denied marriage proposal that left the would-be mother-in-law rather furious. So many chances to stir up discourse, gone.

She pushed forward despite it all. She wasn't here for souls. She was here for retribution.

Sunday finally came across the alley right between the townhouse and the carryout. The pavement was stained black from the rain. She wasn't sure if it was the alley's natural scent or if damp trash was infinitely worse than regular trash.

At the very end of the alley were the few competent demons Sunday knew. The ones that were still alive anyway, she thought. She had saved as many as she could before the raid had taken place. But the few that stayed behind, that called her a liar and a poacher, now paid the ultimate price.

The three greeted her with respectful nods when she reached them.

"This is the right symbol?" she asked, directing them to the brick wall on their left. In white chalk a symbol was drawn. Encased in a circle was a pentagram inside a star.

"Yes, ma'am," Dante said, showing her the sketch they had been instructed to follow. Sunday couldn't help it, her heart skipped in delight at being called 'ma'am'. She opened up the brown paper bag she had been clutching at her side. Inside were individual Ziplock bags containing a shard of broken ceramic and three daggers. All stained silver with Nightwalker blood.

Carefully, she removed the items from the bags and placed them on the altar below the symbol. Pictures of their subjects sat on display, being threatened by the flickering candles in front of them.

They would need to do this before the rain ruined the ritual.

"So, what's next?" Ethan asked. Sunday stayed silent, unsure herself. She waited patiently for the presence in her mind that had now become a familiar part of her. After a moment it showed up. *Ah, there he is.*

"Just join hands," she said, following the voice's instructions. "He'll take it from here."

END OF BOOK ONE

Authors Note

Thank you so much for reading *Tear in Reality!* I hope you enjoyed it. Reviews mean the world to authors, so consider leaving one on Amazon or Goodreads and earn my eternal gratitude.

Lola, Erica, Ken, and Paris will continue their journey in Book Two, **Dark Devices,** coming soon!

Acknowledgements

This book is truly a labor of love for me. I've spent the majority of my life so far, thinking about these characters, growing with them. And now that I'm finally able to share them, its been such a surreal feeling.

First, I want to say thank you to Jen. You were the first person to see anything of this book, back when it was just a collection of scenes in a Steno Pad. You enabled this, and ever since, I've decided to make it everyone else's problem.

Next, I want to thank Leilani for your everlasting support for this story and my writing. Printing out the first hundred pages of this book on the schools printer was very unnecessary, but thanks for doing it cause now I have tangible proof of how much I've grown as a writer (seriously I can't believe we showed this to people). Also gonna take this opportunity to expose you as a Ken hater when he's literally done nothing wrong in his life!

Thank you, Connor for keeping me sane throughout this entire process and reminding me to be kind to myself. Forever grateful that I know you and that you'll never be rid of hearing me complain. Perhaps once I finally scrape together enough change for an audiobook you'll finally read this thing.

Thank you to Moonpress Design for the beautiful new cover. You really brought my vision to life and were amazing to work with. Thank you to Kay (@kmortonedits) for polishing this bad boy and getting it ready for publication.

I also want to thank my family for nurturing my love for writing and allowing me to pursue it despite how unpractical and weird everything I do is.

Big thank you to my writing families, VS and Spiciest Black Writers (we are in fact the spiciest around), for cheering me on throughout this entire process and offering me such amazing support and feedback.

Finally, I want to thank you lovely reader, for taking a chance on this weird little story, buckle up, it gets weirder from here.

About the Author

Scarlett Hathaway is an urban fantasy author and lover of all things spooky and weird. From comics to screenplays, she's been writing for as long as she's been able to hold a pencil. When Scarlett isn't obsessively plotting 7 books at a time, she can be found watching Sabrina the Teenage Witch reruns with her black cat in Washington D.C.

You can find more of Scarlett at scarletthathaway.com

instagram.com/sbscarlett222

tiktok.com/@sbscarlett222

goodreads.com/sbscarlett